PRAISE FOR

"A truly spooky story set in the Somerset Levels, which had me on the edge of my seat."

"*In the Moors* has a ... shocking twist at the ... journeying that have ...

—Ronald

"A real page-turner, *In the Moors* cost me several hours of sleep because it was so un-put-downable! An engaging heroine, a landscape at once so real and so menacing, and an intriguing mystery had me enthralled into the wee hours!"

—Mara Freeman, author of *Kindling the Celtic Spirit*

UNRAVELED
VISIONS

NINA MILTON

UNRAVELED
VISIONS

A SHAMAN MYSTERY

MIDNIGHT INK
WOODBURY, MINNESOTA

FIRST EDITION
First Printing, 2014

Book format by Donna Burch-Brown
Cover design by Ellen Lawson
Cover photograph by David Mendolia
Editing by Nicole Nugent

Midnight Ink, an imprint of Llewellyn Worldwide Ltd.

This is a work of fiction. Names, characters, places, and incidents are either the product of the author's imagination or are used fictitiously, and any resemblance to actual persons living or dead, business establishments, events, or locales is entirely coincidental.

Library of Congress Cataloging-in-Publication Data
Milton, Nina.
  Unraveled visions / by Nina Milton. — First edition.
    pages cm. — (A Shaman mystery ; #2)
  ISBN 978-0-7387-4005-8
  1. Shamans—Fiction. 2. Mystery fiction. I. Title.
  PS3613.I59198U57 2014
  813'.6—dc23
                        2014015725

Midnight Ink
Llewellyn Worldwide Ltd.
2143 Wooddale Drive
Woodbury, MN 55125-2989
www.midnightinkbooks.com

Printed in the United States of America

For my chicks, Becki and Joe

ACKNOWLEDGMENTS

I would like to thank Lisa Moylett for her tireless energy and brilliant understanding of what makes a good book great.

PROLOGUE

THE RETRIEVAL WAS UNCEREMONIOUS and without dignity. The woman's body was winched from Dunball Wharf at 5:13 p.m., dripping with sluice slime. The hip bones shone white against the sun, and there were fish swimming in her belly.

It had been the hottest day that summer. The mountainous heaps of sand at the Dunball Wharf Aggregate Works had dried out so completely that a choking dust rose from them. The waters below had heated until their reek oozed into the nostrils. No one wanted to move fast and sounds were muffled, as if the late-afternoon sun had thickened the air.

The two detectives had arrived as the body was trundling on a gurney over to a white tent, where the pathologist waited like an adjudicator at some macabre contest. The woman was found stripped of any clothing and the technician had thrown a green sheet over her poor mutilated and rotting body for that short journey. But the gurney jerked as its wheels stuck to the walkway, which was so burning hot it was melting the policemen's thick soles, and the woman's head slid to the edge, her heavy locks falling free, as if she'd just unpinned them. Despite the river weed and silt, her hair was still glorious; as black as a nighttime lake, not tampered by bleach or dye.

Detective Sergeant Gary Abbott had stepped forward, his hand outstretched, and touched the woman's hair, crying out like a distressed relative. "Take care with her, for God's sake!"

I know this, because Detective Inspector Reynard Buckley told me so, months later, in hisses and whispers directed at the black winter sky, his big, knuckled hands hiding most of his face. It hadn't been the drip of sloughing skin that distressed him. It had been his sergeant's reaction.

On the way to the wharf, Gary Abbott had been his usual cocky self. He'd put on the flashers and put down his foot, taking every obstruction as a personal challenge. "Body got trapped in the Dunball Clyce," he'd joked. "Ve-ery nasty, that Dunball Clyce... whatever the fuck it is." Of course Abbott knew it was the sluice at the Dunball Wharf, where the King's Sedgemoor Drain fed into the River Parrett; every Bridgwaterian did. It was just the sort of quip Abbott would make, trying to distance himself from any emotion on the job, which is why Rey had been puzzled by his reaction at the site.

And then, apparently, on first examination at the scene, the pathologist had stated that because the body had undergone prolonged scavenger predation, bacterial action, and abrasion, it was impossible to estimate the date or time of death or even say if she had been dead before entering the water, which was the one thing the detectives really wanted to know. But she had said—and this was why I was able to recall every word Rey whispered—that fresh-water specimens sometimes displayed abdominal protrusions; sections of gut that had burst through the skin, speeding aquatic decomposition. It reminded me of how unwanted spirit energy can intrude into a person's ethereal body, demonstrating its existence as strange, projecting emanations, which a skilled shaman can sometimes observe.

Rey hadn't quizzed Abbott until the body had left the site.

"What was all that about?"

"Nothing."

"C'mon, Gary. Were you IDing her?"

"Really, no. She just reminded me … was all."

Abbott moved away. They had been planning to interview the boy who'd found her, a seventeen year-old lad who worked on the dredgers. He'd spotted bits of white tissue in among the silt sucked from the river bed. At first, apparently, he had thought it was a large, dead fish, but then an entire piece of intestine arrived and he had fallen to his knees on the deck and vomited. Abbott had strode off to get his story, but Rey told me that he'd never believed Abbott had meant "nothing." He had meant, "wait until I've checked it out."

Rey Buckley understood that line of thinking. Sometimes he'd let a hunch brew for a while in the same way. I understood too; you have to stay patient, but alert, until something drops down into the fermentation. Then, suddenly, it all makes perfect sense. If Abbott needed time to brew his thoughts, that was fine.

Trouble was, Abbott never did let on. Not in his lifetime.

ONE

GUY FAWKES NIGHT

BRIDGWATER CARNIVAL. MARDI GRAS late into the black winter night. Take your lover, or the kids. I'm off lovers, for the moment, and you tend to need one of those if you want kids. So I took my long-term friend Debs.

I guess if Debs and I met now, for instance at this carnival, we might never become friends. But I met her when we both lived in a children's home called the Willows. We helped each other through that weird and wicked time, and we are each other's only good memory of being a kid in local authority care. Sometimes what friends shared back then is more important than what they share right now.

We don't meet up often, and when we do, we don't sit about moaning about our bad start in life. We go out and get wasted.

Debs was trying to see over the heads of the pavement crowd. Her heels gave her a promising start, but there were just too many people crushed against the barriers. "We won't see a thing back here. We stayed too long in the Duke."

"Ye-ah. Because it's freezing out here."

Debs hailed me with her Heineken. "Drink the bugger up, Sabbie! Better than thermal knickers!" Frankly, she looked pinched with cold to me. She'd had a bit of enhancement in the bosom area and, well, it cost, so gotta show it off, right? I put my arm round her. "Don't worry about getting to the front. All the good stuff is up in the sky."

Debs is a nail technician. Tonight her nails were black with silver stars. Her hair was bright blond and her lippy was pink, whereas my leanings are more dusky maiden. I wear my skirts long and my nails short. Like Debs, I have my own little business—quite similar in a lot of ways. Debs makes people's hands beautiful; I try to restore their inner parts to health.

I am a therapeutic shaman, a job I love to my soul. I walk with spirits and elementals to find a person's past troubles and future purpose, help them make sense of the world. But even a shaman is allowed a night off, and here we were, at getting on for midnight, slightly wobbly because white wine and lager are a bad mix.

The carnival had finished an hour ago and most families had taken their little ones home as the last carnival float evaporated into the distance. Only the die-hards stayed for the giant squibs, getting more bombed out as the clock ticked on, hoods up against the early-November wind scuttling along Bridgwater High Street, sitting with their backs against the barriers that ran along the pavement's edge or in the glow of shop doorways, waiting for the squibbers. In Bridgwater, in sleepy Somerset, we don't have fancy fireworks on carnival night. No rockets or fountains or waterfalls in six different colours. Just squibs; fast, gigantic, noisy, and smelly.

5

"They're here." I pointed a gloved finger. "The squibbers."

Debs pushed against shoulders to get a glimpse. Her face fell. The squibbers were mostly older men in hard hats and yellow jackets. If Debs had been thinking of chatting them up after they'd finished with the fireworks, she was rapidly changing her mind.

"It's a great honour," I yelled into Debs's ear. "Holding one of those giant squibs."

"Looks like a bleeding dodgy one to me."

"You have to be born in Bridgwater or be on the carnival committee or something. You know Abby, from my birthday? Her mum held one last year."

Debs shook her head, unable to remember my party, let alone any of the party-goers, apart from the bloke who'd spent the evening with his tongue down her throat. Doubt if she remembered him, either. "You might do it, then?"

"No ..." She hadn't been listening. "I wasn't even brought up round here, was I? To be fair, Debs, we weren't what you might call 'brought up' at all."

The squibbers were forming a line in the middle of the road, their faces set like a platoon about to depart. The crowd surged forward, thronging in, tight as a tube ride. From between the heads in front, I could see the fireworks mounted on their wooden holders, coshes the squibbers would raise firmly in both fists.

A line of fire was being set. It ran down the centre of the road like a fuse on its way to a pile of dynamite, burning bright in the darkness, the start of an ancient ritual.

"All I'm saying is they're dead proud of squibbing in Bridgwater."

Six hundred years back, a local man had been at the thick of the Gunpowder Plot to blow the Houses of Parliament—and the king—sky high. Bridgwaterians hadn't like that one bit. Hidden behind the glitter of fairy lights, the boom of music, and the party in the streets was a celebration of a seventeenth-century execution; hanging, drawing, and quartering. Earlier on, the first float in the carnival procession had been a tableau of Guy Fawkes, a broken man on his knees in front of his interrogators, resplendent in their doublets, big boots, and natty lace collars. There was glee on their faces; they might not have brought their stretching rack and knee-crushers onto the float, but it wouldn't be long before they'd be applying them.

At a shout, the double line of squibbers dipped their coshes into the running fire and, as quick as they could, lifted them high above their heads, ready for the first explosions.

Something bashed against my shoulder. A bloke, pushing through the High Street crowds. I could only see his back, but I knew him at once. I knew him from his gait, his build, the sheen of his waxed-down hair. It was Gary Abbott from Bridgwater Police Station, after some felon. He was sprinting now, not even stopping when he knocked against a child. He was running away from the action, the only person indifferent to the squibs. He swerved off the High Street into a narrow space between shops, the lane that led to St. Mary's Church.

Detective Sergeant Abbott ... not exactly a Facebook friend. I don't forget people who are hateful to me, and Abbott was full of acid hate. I could still taste it at the back of my throat.

"Debs?" She didn't hear me. Cracks of noise, each squib fizzing skyward and exploding into a million stars that rained down on us in a storm of light. The squibs roared and pounded and blazed and the crowds screamed and yelled. Debs was yelling too, her beer can raised in salute.

Abbott had left the child sprawling. The sight sobered me. I went over, crouching to help the little boy to his feet. He was determined not to cry, spinning off to cling to the trouser leg of his dad, buried careless into the crowd.

A shadow gleamed on the pavement. An Apple iPhone. Not the child's, I knew that. I weighed it in my hand. People don't leave a name on their mobile; there was nothing to identify it. I slid it into my coat packet and went over to where the boy clutched at his father's trouser leg. I tapped the man on the shoulder.

"Excuse me, have you lost..."

Crack! Whoosh! Fizz! My words were lost in noise and light. The world was spinning. Irritation pinched the man's face. I'd interrupted him in the process of filming the squibs... on his phone.

"Sorry—nothing." I winked at the little boy and turned, bumping straight into Debs.

"Sabbie! You're missing it all!"

"A man I know. Abbott. Gary Abbott."

"Oh, it has to be a *man*."

"No, a copper... running..."

The black wing of Abbott's open coat had flapped like a bat. If an iPhone had swung from his pocket, he wouldn't have noticed. He was too busy knocking down kids on his way to police glory.

I can never help snooping after people, even though it gets me into trouble every bloody time. I sprinted after Abbott. Okay—I wasn't up to sprinting. It might have been more... stumbling. Seeing Abbott hadn't sobered me as much as I'd hoped.

I reached the bottom of St. Mary's Lane. It was narrow and shadowed. The church loomed at the top, spot-lit in amber and white, the illuminated masonry glowing like a phantom. There was no sign of Abbott in his batwing coat.

St. Mary's had been open earlier for carnival goers, offering coffee and cakes, but now its massive doors would be bolted, the square empty, apart from the odd drunk or the odd pair of lovers. I could hardly believe that Abbott had a sweetheart, or that he'd meet her in that deserted place if he did. No, he was after someone, a pickpocket or pusher he'd seen in the crowd.

Fizz! The sky sparkled. Stars tumbled. My eyes were half-blinded. *Crack! Bang!* People shimmied around me as if everyone was dancing. I caught my ankle on a chained-up cycle at the bottom of the lane and pitched forward.

"Hey, Sabbie!" Debs clutched at my arm. "You okay?"

"Gerroff," I squealed back. "I'm not pissed yet!"

The world was suddenly filled with silence and my voice sounded loud within it. The squibbing was over, just minutes after it had begun. The town sank into midnight shadows. The crowd's roars sank to mutterings. The air smelt of gunpowder.

"That was cool," said Debs. "Pyrotechnics. Loud. Hey," she added, and her finger pointed along the lane. "Who is that?"

A figure had emerged from the dark recesses of the lane. A woman advanced towards us. Her dress—no, her *gown*—brushed the ground and was layered with frills as red as her lips. She had been watching us; her eyes were on us and she held out her hands, the fingers moving as if she were playing an invisible harp.

"Bet she was on a float," I said in a low voice to Debs.

The long procession of lorries had rolled their glittering tableaux through the town for almost an hour earlier that night. I had a vague memory of a spinning gypsy scene on one float; swirling frilled dresses, guitars, a glowing fire in a forest clearing, dancing to something that sounded Greek.

"I am Kizzy," said the gypsy figure. Her voice was as cracked and croaked as one of my hens. Over her head she'd draped a fringed shawl, pinned with a brooch of tiny glass jewels. Her face was sallow in the dim light, her eyes black with kohl. She'd come so close to where we stood that I could smell her market perfume and the beer on her breath. "For little silver I see future."

My mind was mussed-up with men in black, bangs and explosions, hanging and drawing. I couldn't work out what she meant, but Debs knew straight away.

"You do fortunes." Debs was already rifling through her bag. "Can you do me?"

I butted in. "Debs. I've just told you your fortune."

We'd had a girlie day, waiting for the carnival to begin. I'd read the Tarot for Debs and she'd done my nails in fair exchange. Underneath my woolly gloves I sported a French manicure that would last no longer than the next workout in my vegetable plot.

"Yeah," said Debs. "But this one's called Gypsy Kizzy. C'mon, Sabbie, it'll be fun."

"You should never have two tellings on one day. You must wait to see what the first fortune brings." I looked again at the woman. "You're not a proper fortuneteller if you don't know that … are you Kizzy?"

"I seven daughter of gypsy mother. She seven daughter. I haf second sight." The skin on her face was plump and soft. Her eyes were clear. She was trying to keep the ancient gypsy act up, but her voice was rising, losing its grizzled tones as she forgot to play her part. She was younger than me—no more than a teenager—all dressed up for the carnival. She'd transformed herself into someone who might have lived in a gypsy caravan and thought she'd have some fun with the punters, full with drink and full of the loud night and the costume and the spinning dance she'd done on the gypsy float.

"See, I do that for a living too." I wanted to explain to Kizzy how it was my job to walk in the spirit world, to gain advice at a deeper level and bring it back to the material plane for my clients. But my brain was hurtling towards shut-down and I couldn't find the words. Not in the right order, at least. The bottle of white wine I'd had in the pub felt acidic in my stomach; it made me long to sit down somewhere feathery and warm. I fumbled with the zip on the bag slung over my shoulder and dug my fingers in. "I'm a profesh ... I tell fortunes. So we'll pass on the divi—the divination, thank you."

I thrust a rectangle of card at her.

SABBIE DARE
Shamanic Healing,
Reiki, Reflexology, Aromatherapy
& Tarot Readings

Kizzy managed to read my card while not taking the pierce of her gaze from my eyes. Perhaps she didn't read the card at all. "You haf second sight? You see future? You seven daughter of seven daughter!"

"Uh, nope, I don't think so."

"You might be," said Debs. "You don't know anything about your mum or dad, do you?" She waved a couple of tenners at the girl. "Go on, Kizzy. Do my friend. Then we'll be even."

I glowered at Debs. "If I wanted my fortune told, I'd do it myself."

But Gypsy Kizzy had already snatched Debs's money, folding the notes around my business card. With a single finger and thumb, she stashed the little pack between her breasts. I'd never seen anyone outside a black-and-white movie do that before, and I was so busy gawping I hardly noticed when she caught up my right hand, rolling back my glove and running a finger over my skin. This is an old trick. Stroking the palm relaxes the client.

She took her time, peering at my lines under the dim light from the High Street. "You belong to different place than this." She did not look up. "You came from over much water."

I groaned in my head. I was about to meet a tall man, travel widely, and have three children.

"I see good fortune," said Kizzy, stretching my palm as if it was a crumpled cushion. "Money come."

"Spot on!" yelled Debs.

Okay, I *had* come into some money lately, but a lot of good it had done my finances. I'd ended up with a Saturday job as well as my proper one.

"And boys-friend," said Kizzy. "New man in life."

"She's promising you sex!" Debs squealed. "About time!"

"You forgot. I've sworn to stay off men forever."

"Important man," said Kizzy, still intent upon the hieroglyphics of my hand. "Big honour is him. Everyone love. Smell good, look good."

"Wow!"

Kizzy impaled Debs with her gaze. "Look good but no *be* good. No. No."

"That sounds like Ivan," said Debs. "Don't you think, Sabbie?"

I mentally cursed Debs for giving Kizzy all the information she needed to make her dodgy predictions. Telling fortunes at the squibbing was probably a dare. Getting it right had to be beginner's luck.

I tugged at my hand. I didn't want to hear any more. "Okay, thanks, Kizzy. You've made your twenty quid, and we've got to go."

She held on to me. I found I was staring directly into her eyes, those sharp black pupils. They weren't full of giggles and dares. They spoke of darkness. Of distrust and distress.

"Are you all right, Kizzy?"

"Me?" She stuck out her chin. "I good."

"You don't look good. You should go home now."

She flung my hand at me. "Warning to you. Be warned. Not good boys-friend lead to danger. Lead to death!" Her scarf had fallen, revealing a waterfall of dark hair. She flicked it with an exaggerated shoulder gesture.

I backed away, out into the lighted street and the quiet bustle of crowds making their way home.

Debs skittered after me in her Stella McCartney boots and snatched at my elbow. "Hey! I didn't get my money's worth."

I barked a laugh. "It was my life she was picking over."

"You didn't like it because she was so spot-on."

"What rubbish." Was the girl a Roma? Did she have second sight? Her black eyes and exotic accent suggested it.

I looked over my shoulder. She hadn't moved, but shadows had fallen over her as she called out to me, "I see true!"

"Go home, Kizzy," I called.

Gypsy Kizzy hadn't finished. She had to have the last word. Her voice thickened into sadness. "I am sorry. There is danger. It starts with death."

———

She thinks about death. How sweet it would be, arriving like a crow, a crow with a rasping caw and with wings so wide she could hide in their shadows. She prays that the crow of death will come soon.

When she wakes the next morning, there is pain. Then she remembers the night; the sudden desire to run, the struggle as she is overcome.

She is shivering with pain. When she moves, even to bend her knees, pain rises as a bitter chill inside her core and tightens like a jacket belted across her chest. As if there are buckles that cannot be loosened. Every time she takes a breath, she feels the buckles burn into her ribs. If she moves an arm, the pain lacerates like a hunting knife.

Her father treasured his knife. Two bevelled edges, both kept sharp. It could slice equally through blades of grass or sinew and bone. Its handle was glowing walnut decorated with symbols burnt into the wood. There were brass finger rings he kept polished. It didn't fold like her brothers' blades; once it had possessed a leather sheath, but Tatta kept it wrapped in old flannel. Stolen beauty is worth more to the keeper, he told her, smiling. His teeth were yellow, huge, magnificent.

Her eyes open as she remembers Tatta's smile, and she is returned to pain and cold. The cold comes from inside her, like the pain. She risks moving her arm to wrap herself against the cold and the hunting knife slices through, sinew and bone.

She is the stolen one now. Worth more to the keeper.

TWO

I'D NOTICED THE NEWCOMERS as soon as they moved into my road.

The house had been empty, the To LET sign sliding sideways onto the patchy front lawn, until a couple—newly wedded was the rumour—took the property on. I got all excited, because up until then, I'd been the youngest resident in the street. I thought we might at least chat over the front gate about things that were relevant to the twenty-first century. But the bloke set off early for work every weekday in a metallic blue Fiat Punto, not getting back till late. His hair was cut short at the back and he wore shiny shoes, except on weekends, when he shinned up a ladder, transforming the grey rendered walls with creamy paint. I tried saying hi as I passed him by, and a grunted reply would float down, but not much else. He looked twenty-four going on forty, while his wife looked twenty-four going on fourteen. Maybe she *was* fourteen; she certainly didn't go out to work.

Neither of them stopped to chat with anyone. The neighbours were beginning to gossip. They never needed much scandal to chew the fat. They were saying the couple had something to hide. Once or twice a week the girl would zip past my house on the way to the local shops bundled into a wraparound Aran coat, mittens, scarf, and bobble hat, adding an umbrella if it was pouring with rain. I would have asked her in, but she always scuttled by so quickly I never even had time to raise my hand in greeting.

I got to thinking, the way she hunched her shoulders inside that coat, she looked like a dog who'd escaped from a kicking.

And now, at barely gone nine on a Saturday morning, she was standing in my kitchen, holding an empty egg box, looking fuzzy around the edges. Maybe it was all that wool, but the carnival had finished only hours back and alcohol units were still roving round my bloodstream looking for someone to bite.

"I heard that you sold eggs." She took a step towards me. "How much is half a dozen? I wanted to bake a soufflé."

The thought of soufflé made me swallow over a throat that tasted of innards.

"We live up that way," she said, pointing through the wall. "Me and Andy. Andrea and Andrew, but it's an awful mouthful when you say them together, so I've shortened mine to Drea. It's what my little sister used to call me 'cause she couldn't get the whole name out."

I was shocked to hear so many words teem from her mouth, especially as I had said nothing since she'd knocked on the door apart from "come in." I'd tried, but there was some sort of packing between my tongue and the speech part of my brain, similar to the stuff they put in attics. I did some sterling muscle work on my mouth and managed a smile. "Sorry. Carnival hangover."

"Oh, right. Me and Andy talked about going. Was it good?"

"Er, yeah. Same as ever … sorry … I haven't got enough eggs to let you have any today." The truth was that the thought of opening the nesting box made me heave.

"Okay," said Drea, as if she'd already dismissed the idea of a soufflé. She looked round, taking in the decor. "I like the way you've got things."

"Do you? Really?"

I've lived in many places, but this was … the motherland. I'd worked hard to get it nice, both the oversized garden and the under-sized house, and every speck of dust was mine.

"Nothing like the one we've got. The kitchen and dining room are poky."

"It looks more spacious than it is." I poured water from the tap into a pint glass and downed the lot, hoping to fight off the loft insulation. "This is my entire living space. Kitchen-cum-diner-cum-lounge. I eat in here, surf the web, sink a bottle of wine, you name it."

"What about the living room? At the front?" She waited until I'd put down the empty glass then continued. "What d'you use that for?"

"That's my therapy area. I use it for healing work."

Naturally, she already knew. I have a laminated poster in my front window to help clients find my house. Sometimes, people ring the bell on impulse. I need the extra work I get in that way; it's why I put all my contact details on the back of my cards.

She flashed a beaming smile that was total playacting. "I guess I'm curious."

She didn't fool me for one moment. It wasn't my eggs she was after. I ran myself another pint of water.

"Would you like to take a look?"

The therapy room was the heart and hub of my working life—a boxy room containing two mismatched wicker chairs, a homemade desk draped with muslin, and a pile of floor cushions.

I breathed in the atmosphere. The air smelled of burnt herbs. I went over and pulled the cord so that a cold November sun could slant through the binds and the muslin drapes. Below the window was my altar. It held my working tools, my pottery otter, and a tiny image of Persephone, goddess of the otherworld, along with a few small crystals.

Drea shuffled in behind me as if the room might snap at her. She went straight over to where my various certificates hung in cheap frames. "Oh," she said. "You've got a degree."

"That does seem to surprise people." I busied myself lighting some candles. "Don't know why. Everyone has a BA nowadays."

"True."

"Did you go to uni?

"What? Yes. Exeter. My parents live in Launceston, so it felt just far enough away—I could still get back at weekends." She grimaced. "But I didn't finish. Didn't get my degree."

"That's a shame."

"I don't care. I've got Andy now. I'm an old-fashioned girl, I suppose."

"Nothing wrong with that." I though of my garden with its carrots and chickens. I laughed and it felt good, as if I'd been holding onto my breath. I went over and sat at the desk in the hope she might do the same, but she continued to stare at my certificates.

"You're a Reiki Master?"

"Yes. Are you interested in that?"

"I don't even know what it is."

"It's a gentle form of therapy that balances the chakras. You simply lie still for an hour."

"I don't believe all that Eastern stuff."

"You don't have to. Reiki actually comes from Japan, but it's very accepted in the West. It channels a natural healing energy, and people feel a benefit whether or not they believe in a vital life force."

"Do you?"

"Do I what?"

"Believe in a life force?"

"Isn't it everywhere you look?"

"Yes!" Drea was suddenly animated. "Of course, that's so true!"

Finally she propelled herself across the room and sat on the other wicker chair, crossing her ankles like a girl at a fifties dance.

I waited until she was settled before I spoke again. "Actually, I practice Shamanic Reiki. I combine healing from the spirit world with the channelling of the energy."

I was trying to get a feel for Drea, but the only thing that was coming from her was a sensation of chill. She was hiding everything under layers of Aran wool. She hadn't even taken off her scarf. It was as if she was knitted into the garments. She jiggled her bag. "An hour, did you say?"

I nodded, not quite looking back at her.

"Only, I've never done anything like this before."

"That's true of lots of my clients."

"Okay. Could I have one now?"

"What, right now?"

After two pints of water, the throb in my head had faded, and I couldn't afford the financial luxury of turning down work, especially as Drea was already holding out the correct fee in ten-pound notes. Maybe she was a spur-of-the-moment person. I could identify with that. I suspected if I forced her to make an appointment, she wouldn't keep it.

"Okay. If you don't feel comfortable at any time, though, that's fine. If you say stop, I'll stop. If you want to leave, I'll return your money."

Drea gave a stiff nod. She swayed on the chair, as if about to faint. There was sweat on her upper lip.

"Why don't you take off your coat?"

She tightened it around her. "I'm fine like this." But she pulled off the hat and stuffed it into a big patch pocket. Her hair picked up the electricity and flew as if shocked at the sudden exposure. It was baby-fine and the colour of cork matting, cut into a neat bob. She took off her mittens and smoothed her hair into place.

"Let me explain what happens. I will pass my hands over you. The healing energy moves through me from outside."

Drea spoke very quietly. "If it's from outside you, then it's God's power."

I wasn't going to argue—God and Goddess, each had their place. "Reiki restores equilibrium and well-being. If you've got any sort of problem with your general health you want to tell me about, I can work in that particular area."

I passed her the questionnaire I get new clients to fill in. If nothing else, it makes me look a tad more professional.

"I'm as fit as a fiddle," said Drea, working through the checklist with quick flicks of the pen.

She looked as wan as an Elgin Marble to me. "Um, what about... d'you have any emotional difficulties?"

"No."

"Relationship problems?"

"Absolutely not."

She came back fast as a rapper, but she was not adept at fibbing. The lie was in every particle and wave of her answer.

"So there is nothing particular you want me to work on ... nothing that concerns you at the moment?"

Drea's cheeks darkened. Not so much a blush as a blue tinge.

"You don't have to tell me what's bothering you. If you like, you could write it down. That way, it would be unspoken, but sort of 'in the air' as I work."

I heard a tiny gasp, a sucking of breath. "Could I?"

"Of course."

I handed her a scrap of paper and a pen. She had pale, tapered fingers with a single ring; a plain wedding band. She cut her nails straight across, not painting or even filing them. I could see the whiteness of the half-moons delineated against the gentle pink of each nail. I still had my pristine French polish and for once I felt more dressed up than a client.

I moved away as she buried her head into the writing. I shunted some floor cushions together and gestured that she should make herself comfortable on them. She folded the paper into a tiny square and slid it under the cushions, then tested them with her hand as if not trusting their contents. Finally she sank down with a little hiss of relief. I draped a thick fleece over her and put on a CD of soothing sounds.

"I'm going to prepare myself." Already, my voice had dropped a tone and my eyes were beginning to shift perspective. "I'll be a moment or two. Just relax."

I went up my stairs and had a long pee and a good wash of my face and hands. I drank another mug of water in the kitchen, leaning against the worktop. I was waiting for Drea to appear at the door and tell me she'd changed her mind. When that didn't happen, I wondered if she'd already scarpered. I stole into the therapy room. She hadn't moved. Her eyes were closed, and she didn't respond when the door clicked shut. She was almost in a trance already.

———

Shamanism and Reiki are linked on an intuitive level. They have a synergy—separately, they work well, but combined, I find they work more than twice as well. When I place my hands over a Reiki client, I allow myself to drift into a light trance state, so that I can sense their seven chakras—energy centres. However, I don't often see them as they're depicted in illustrations: blazing rainbow colours that move through the spectrum; they come to me a variety of ways, showing a person's inner story.

I moved my hands lightly above Drea to see if any chakra spun faster or slower than it should. At the base of her spine, Drea's root chakra was a rich, thrumming note, as if someone was playing a red bassoon. It felt healthy enough. Her heart chakra felt fine too, its green glow like the light that shines through hazel leaves in the summer. Below it, the chakra at the solar plexus was a little sluggish. Drea was probably not a confident person. Maybe she had problems relating to others. Okay, I had already observed some of this from watching her life from afar, but the chakras were reinforcing my guesses.

The sensation around her lower abdomen was dry and shifting, like sand dunes held together with nothing more than marram grass, how when you walk over the top of them your feet go from under you and you're sucked into the sand. Her sacral chakra had lost all its energy. It was curled up on itself, as if it didn't want anything more to do with life.

This chakra holds the key to sexuality. The Sanskrit word is *Sva-dhisthana*, meaning sweetness... pleasure.

I thought about the clipped nails and the thick Aran and the mouse-like scuttle to the shops. Where was the pleasure in Drea's life? Was she using knitting and soufflés to prevent facing unspoken difficulties?

I rested my hands on her shoulders to initiate the contact. She sniffed a breath through her nose but didn't fully wake. I began my steady work, taking myself deeper into a dance of the senses.

After an hour I whispered to her. "Okay. Take your time."

Drea gave a feminine little snort and began to stretch.

"How d'you feel?"

She breathed deeply in through her nose. "It did relax me, I must admit."

"Good. You should sleep well tonight."

"Your hands were very hot." She was still under the influence, her voice slurred.

"That is the channelled energy. I'm confident you'll feel the benefit. The treatment might take away that edgy feeling."

She stretched again and began to sit up. "I'm not edgy."

"Perhaps I got the wrong idea. I—"

"I'm not an edgy person at all."

"Your systems are basically sound." I hoped to start with some good news. "Your throat chakra is a little closed, but I find that in a lot of people who have quiet voices. The chakras above that—the indigo centre in your brow and the violet centre at your crown—are well open, spinning extremely fast. I think you may be quite a spiritual person."

"Every living soul has that capacity." Drea looked at me directly, a gentle strength in her eyes.

"The sacral chakra felt a little unbalanced." I placed my hand over the base of my own belly. "It's related to water and emotions and, for want of a better phrase, women's problems." I stopped, wondering why I was being so coy. Why I hadn't mention the *s* word? Was it because Drea shrank away from me as I spoke, her face puckered?

"I don't have problems."

"Great! I'm sorry if—"

"You don't know what you're talking about. It's bunkum, all this chakra rubbish. I don't believe in any of it."

"No." I caught her gaze. "That's evident, Drea. But in Eastern philosophy, chakras are part of the nonmaterial form of your body; the first place ill health or emotional trauma shows up. I felt a worrying strain within your sacral chakra. You don't have to take any notice of what I felt, but that doesn't alter the fact."

"I don't have problems at all. I've never been as happy as I am now."

"Your root chakra showed that. It's showing me how secure you feel."

She smiled properly, and for a couple of seconds, her face lost its pointed, dour look. "It's our first house together, Andy and me. He—" She broke off.

"He what?"

"We've put the past behind us. That's all."

I gave her a tiny, suspicious glance. It was almost as if Drea had come here today to prove something to herself. That the past was behind her. Or that the therapies I offered were "bunkum."

Drea got up from her floor cushion, her thin legs as uncoordinated as a newborn foal. "No, that was nice. Well worth the money. I already feel like I've had an extra night's sleep."

"Don't forget, the Reiki was only the first half of the therapy. You've paid for a shamanic interpretation. As soon as I've got an hour, I'll journey for you."

"Do what?"

"I'll enter your spirit world. What I see is a sort of landscape. It should give us a picture of what your chakras were telling us."

"That sounds horrid." Drea busied herself, pulling on her mittens. "Like you're going to poke around inside me."

I tried to smile. "It shouldn't be horrid. It clarifies things and paints a picture of where you are."

"Well..."

Most people can't wait to hear about themselves, and I didn't think Drea was any different. "I'll write everything down for you. I might be able to suggest some meditations or yoga postures. I'll pop my report round, seeing you're just up the street."

"No, don't do that." For the first time, she touched me. I looked into her face and saw alarm.

"It's no trouble—"

"I'll pick it up. Maybe come round when you've got some spare eggs?"

We moved from the therapy room into my hall. She tucked wisps of hair under her hat, gearing herself up for sub-Arctic conditions as she waited for me to open the door.

"Dreadful about the shooting, isn't it?" she said.

"What shooting?"

"It was on the breakfast news." Her eyes widened as she spoke. "Someone killed a policeman."

"Not local I hope?"

"Sounds like it. They found his body in town last night. It made me go cold when I heard. We moved here because Bridgwater is

25

supposed to be a nice, peaceful place, and almost straightaway there was that body they found in the summer."

"The girl that drowned in the Dunball Wharf?"

"Yes. Only she didn't, did she? She was thrown in there, they said. It spooked me. And now someone's been killed on the night of the carnival."

I saw the sky ablaze with squibs, heard the roar of the crowd, the crack of the fireworks, the flapping, bat-black coat.

I closed the door behind Drea and went straight into the kitchen. I booted up my laptop and searched the West Country news site I follow on Twitter.

CID officer shot during Carnival was the most recent tweet. They weren't giving a name yet, describing the dead man as … *a member of the Avon and Somerset CID.* Gary Abbott was a detective sergeant in the CID. I looked up, remembering him. When I'd known him, he'd been a detective constable, and I doubted that he'd suddenly changed for the better with his promotion. It couldn't be Abbott; only the good die young.

I went through to the link to find out that Drea had been listening more closely than she'd suggested. A body had been discovered early this morning at the back end of the shopping precinct, where the stores had their delivery bays and rubbish bins.

I scratched my hairline. Not the churchyard. I tried to recall the explosive darkness of last night. What had I seen? A man obscured by shooting fire and raining sparks. A knee-length coat flapping in the night wind. I'd been sure then that Abbott was the wearer. I'd lost him in the firework excitement. Or had he dropped to the ground, the noise of a gun masked by gunpowder? If I had walked up the lane, would I have seen him being dragged away? Would I have been shot in the crossfire?

I thought about coppers, the risks they took. Someone had wanted a detective dead. Although I might have joked in the past that I'd've preferred a deceased Gary Abbott, I would never have meant it. The thought of him shot and dumped among garbage filled me with trepidation, and the sickness in my stomach confirmed it.

I shrugged. "Could be anyone."

THREE

"Any chance of a cup of tea?"

I bounced up from my bar stool. Debs stood on the other side of the working top, her makeup back in place, the spikes of her dip-dyed hair looking jaunty, and her sparkly bag on wheels zipped up ready for the trip back to Bristol. I'd half forgotten, after Drea and the news about last night, that she'd been sleeping in my spare bedroom.

"Debs! Remember the bloke last night at the carnival? The copper I saw running?"

"Sort of..."

"Someone was shot last night. I think it could be him."

"Blimey," said Debs, shaking her head as if she had something irritating an ear. "He's not ... he's not that detective you had a thing with, is he?"

"No. Not him. That was Rey. Only we never 'had a thing.'" My knees gave way for a second—until the dead man had been named, it could be any detective. "Please don't even think that it might be Rey."

Detective Inspector Reynard Buckley. Rey to his mates. He'd been given promotion after the successful closure of the Wetland Murders case. Abbott had got a leg-up too. After it was all over, Rey had begun popping in to see me on his way to work. He'd listened to me moan on about Gary Abbot, and I'd managed to get Rey to admit that Abbott did annoy him; he thumbed through classic military vehicle mags in the car and banged on about the rules of things like Australian football until after closing time. And it worried him that after a night's drinking, Rey and a couple of other cops would have to help Gary out into the night and check he'd got home to his partner. Back then, I was still seething at the way Gary Abbott had treated me, and Rey's stories confirmed it: Abbott was a smug, spiteful, cynical slime ball with a hatred of anything he couldn't understand. But in truth, I knew Rey was secretly fond of the guy. He'd worked alongside him through a nasty investigation, after all.

By the time they'd found that unnamed girl at the Dunball Wharf, Rey's morning visits had all but stopped, and I'd been glad, because nothing had moved on. He'd come into the kitchen, eat a boiled egg if the hens were laying, drink a coffee, then bomb off to work, like I was some sort of café. He'd never suggested a date. He'd never kissed me.

Since then, the only thing that had kept me going through the long, lonely nights was his continually changing photo on the social network sites.

"I'm going to put the kettle on and make us some toast," said Debs, taking charge. "You look dreadful."

"I'm trying to piece last night together, Debs. Because they ask you to phone, don't they, if you have any information? Even if it turns out to be nothing. And I might've been the last person to see Abbott alive."

"You might not have seen him at all!"

"I saw a man running. He was so focused he didn't even realize he'd knocked over a little boy. I picked him up. He'd fallen onto a mobile phone. Not his dad's . . ." I trailed off. "I stuck it in my pocket. Goddess, Debs, it could be Abbott's phone."

I put my hands over my eyes. I felt suddenly sick; sapped by the Reiki treatment and lack of nourishment and too much booze and the thought that there was a crucial piece of criminal evidence stashed in my coat pocket. I slid off the stool and went over to the sofa, where I'd thrown my coat and bag when I'd got back last night.

"You don't know it was Abbott's phone for sure," said Debs, from the sink. "Could have been anyone's. And if it was a cop's, I bet it's locked and passworded against theft."

"He didn't stop when he knocked the boy over. He ran up the lane to St. Mary's and . . . disappeared."

"That gypsy might have seen something."

"She must have seen Abbott pass her in the lane."

"What was it she said about your future?"

"Dunno. It was probably all bunk—" I slammed my teeth together. This morning, Drea had dismissed my belief of Reiki, calling it bunkum. Last night, I had dismissed they gypsy's forecast in almost the same terms. But surely the gypsy costume had been a carnival game?

For the first time I clearly recalled Kizzy's soft hands and Debs's delighted squeal . . . *she's promising you sex!*

"She said something very odd, Debs, when you think about it. Something about danger leading to death."

"Well, it did, for this copper, didn't it? So she got that right."

I rested my coat back down on the sofa and started to search my bag. "I can't find the phone." I tipped the contents of my bag out onto the sofa. "I did have it, Debs. I can remember at least some of last night. Maybe I dropped it too."

Debs came over and did the same fruitless search. She stood erect. "Jeans pocket?"

"I was wearing my green skirt, wasn't I? No pockets."

"Then don't you see? We gave that gypsy twenty quid to tell a fortune and she took the money *and* the phone. She had us twice over."

"I'm certain she didn't have the second sight."

"No," Debs agreed. "But I'm certain that she was a thief."

———

Bridgwater Police Station rose before me—mean, hard, ready and willing to enforce the law. Above my head, rows of square-set windows. At ground level, solid brickwork and shutters. They can see you coming, but you can't see them. It was months since I'd been in the front office, but apart from the posters on the walls, it hadn't changed.

I waited in line to be seen by the duty officer and wondered if I'd get the chance to clap eyes on a certain detective inspector. He probably wouldn't be here, or be the one to take a statement.

"Can I help you miss?"

"Yes, ah …" I brought my striped Doc Ms up to the counter. The police constable behind it was looking through me, her entire face deadpan. She was so smart, so polished and ironed, while I looked so … *alternative*. "I'm not sure. That is—I'm not sure if I can be of any help, but I think I might have seen something last night."

"You think you witnessed something?"

"Yes. That is—I have no idea. It depends."

"Depends on what?" The door behind me swung open and another member of the public came in. Some chap who'd lost his wallet or something. Illogically, I lowered my voice and leaned close to the glass partition. The PC swayed back. She didn't like the breach of security. "It depends on who died yesterday. I mean, who was shot."

"I'm sorry, miss, but you're not making much sense."

"Was it Detective Sergeant Abbott?"

I saw a flicker pass across her face, a wavering muscle that was under control in seconds.

"I wondered if he was missing an iPhone, the dead officer."

She paused for a single heart beat before speaking. "If you could take a seat, miss."

"What?"

"Please, wait over there." She picked up the phone and spoke into it, too quietly for me to hear. I leaned against a wall. The man was with the duty officer now. I got so caught up with the story he was telling—how a dog had shot across the road in the dark last night, how he wasn't able to stop, how there hadn't been a name on the collar—that I didn't see the detective until he was standing over me.

"I should've guessed," said Reynard Buckley.

I jumped. "Guessed what?"

"If there was every another nasty case, you'd turn out to be part of it."

He didn't give me chance to respond, even to ask what the hell he meant. I simply followed him through corridors and up stairs until he stopped to open a door.

We went in and sat opposite each other at a table. I'd given statements to the police before, long, involved sessions where the questions were lined with suspicion. But surely this would be quick, easy. After a few moments of silence I raised my shoulders in a Gallic shrug. "It's probably nothing at all." Rey didn't reply. He drummed his fingers.

"Look," I said, "I'm—"

"Can you wait for the interview to formally begin?" said Rey.

I slammed my mouth tight.

By the time a uniformed officer turned up, the recording equipment had been switched on, and the interview begun, I'd lost my nerve. I had no idea what to say.

Abbott had taken against me the last time I'd brushed shoulders with the police. He'd had a way of closing his eyes that was more uncomfortable than an outright stare. He'd sworn at me, with intent, hoping to throw me off balance. If Abbott had been conducting this interview, the fact that I'd lost a vital piece of evidence would have been all he'd need to mock and taunt me. And from the vibes coming from Rey, he was tempted to try the same game. Anyway, it wasn't a vital piece of evidence, was it? It had been dropped before Abbott had died, while he was pursuing...his killer? I blanched at the thought. At least they now knew why it was missing; they could call up the logs from the phone company if they were interested, couldn't they?

"I feel a bit of a fool," I said. "But I only put the phone in my pocket so that I could ask the father of the little boy if he'd lost one without him seeing it." I hoped that made me sound logical...or at least more sober than I'd actually been. "Then there was this girl from a float, all dressed up as a gypsy, pretending to tell fortunes. I have no proof that she took it, but someone did."

They stared back at me, reaffirming the "bit of a fool" part without having to say a word.

"I haven't been a lot of help," I finished.

"On the contrary," said the constable, emotionally numb to any atmosphere that was pulsing red round Rey and me, "this will be very useful. Police deaths are always taken with extreme seriousness."

"Extreme seriousness," echoed Rey. "Your friend, Deborah Hitchens. We'll be having a word with her. She should have come with you."

"I know," I said, looking away. "It was Debs who pushed me into having my palm read."

"I thought you were a shaman. Why would you want your palm read?"

"We were only mucking about."

"There seems to have been a lot of mucking about."

"It was the *carnival*, Rey. People go to have fun—if you recognise that phrase."

"How much had you both had to drink?"

"Oh! Well, what with the pubs open late, we were probably quite … ankled."

Rey passed a hand over his number-three crew cut. He hadn't allowed it to grow by a single millimetre since our last meeting. "I'll see you out."

His words were formal and toneless. My innards felt as if they were dropping through my body, part by part. *Don't get affected by this*, I told myself, not knowing if I meant the knowledge that Abbott was dead or that Rey wasn't pleased to see me.

He watched in silence as I got signed out. I took the chance to try to defend myself.

"To be fair, Rey, most people had been drinking, not just us."

He didn't reply. I made it to the door without my knees giving way, but the door had become obscenely heavy, as if locked against absconders.

Suddenly, Rey was beside me, his hand tucked round my elbow. "Fancy a quick coffee?" he asked. "I'm gasping for a fag."

"Don't want to remind you of established legislation, but you can't smoke in cafés."

"No worries. Follow me."

He shrugged himself into a combat jacket and I tagged after him as we went down Northgate and up a side road, where a street vendor was doing a roaring trade in snacks from his van, mainly, I fancied, to on-duty cops. Rey fished in his pocket and paid for two paper cups filled with dubious brown liquid.

There were no tables, so we perched on the flat low wall to one side of the van. Rey balanced his cup on the stonework and fished out his cigarettes. "Want one?"

"You know I don't smoke." I didn't drink coffee, either, but I kept that to myself. "I gave up ten years ago, for the good of my health."

"You gave *up* ten years ago. For Pete's sake, how old were you when you began?"

"Eleven," I said, grinning. "I was a hard-knock kid. Mind you, when I went to live with Gloria, I had to hide the packs and suck mints, but that made it more fun. Do you remember Gloria?"

"Your foster mum? Of course I do." He shielded his cigarette and lit it with a cheap lighter.

"Look, I'm sorry … you know … that your friend was shot."

"He was a good copper," said Rey. "But not good at sharing."

I let that sink in. "Was Gary on duty at the carnival?"

"He was doing the same as everyone else, I imagine. Having a good time."

I put my hand to my mouth. "He was with his family? How awful for them."

"He'd got a girl, she's got a kid. They'll likely be all over the telly, so no harm in telling you. Yeah, in a way, I suppose he was a family man. Not like me."

I was thrown into a flurry of thoughts. Was Rey hinting that hooking up was out of the question? Or that he was still free and looking? He watched me flounder around.

"He loved his promotion. Took over my well-worn shoes with a vengeance. Worked his hunches, did Gary. But nah. He wasn't on duty last night."

"He was running. Like he was chasing someone."

"Yeah. Well, 'off duty' isn't the same as 'not working.' Cops are always at work." Rey blew smoke away from me and changed his tack, as if he didn't want to show where his deeper thoughts might be taking him. "They're still talking about you, at the station."

"What? Why?"

"You did the impossible, on the Wetlands case. You're a mystery, and you know how cops like a mystery."

I snorted. "Cops don't usually replace truth with invention. I didn't do anything mysterious, not in the end. I stumbled into the scene of the crime was all."

"Even so, you deserved your reward, Sabbie. What you were eligible for, I mean. The money the *Mercury* put up."

I looked down at my brim-full coffee. The reward for finding a child killer. I hadn't been thinking of a reward as I'd faced a murderer with cruel madness in their eyes, and it had come as a surprise when I'd received the cheque.

"What did you do with the money in the end? Don't tell me, let me guess." He raised his eyes to the clouds, in mock deliberation. "A herd of milking goats?"

"Idiot," I said, but little sparklers were going off inside me. Rey had retained quite a lot about me. Maybe he'd been thinking about me, like I'd been thinking about him. "It was a hefty sum. I couldn't see how I even deserved it, but my foster dad talked me into spending it wisely. Funny, isn't it, for a couple of seconds, you're thousands of pounds richer and in a blink you're as poor as a Kentucky fried mouse."

"What? You've spent it already?"

"I bought my house. Well, put down a deposit and took out a mortgage I can't afford."

"Your house," said Rey. "You bought your house?"

"Yes." I laughed. "I didn't think the landlord would've let it go, but the market was kind to me. He'd purchased it as an ex-council property and he couldn't wait to get it off his hands."

"You never struck me as the venture capital sort," said Rey.

"I've never had any capital, that's why." I smiled to myself. The house wasn't "capital," anyway, not to me. It was a tiny bit of land where I could be myself. I had planted a sapling, in celebration, and I intended to sit under my black poplar tree when it was twenty years old and able to shade me from the noon sun. "The repayments are crippling. I'm having to sell my car because I can't afford to run it. At least, I *would* sell it, if I had a willing buyer. And I've taken a Saturday job. Like I'm a school kid. Can you believe that?"

"I don't believe it," said Rey. "You seemed to work all hours anyway."

"Behind the bar at the Curate's Egg. I'm quite enjoying it."

"Doesn't that put a damper on your social life?"

"It's a pub, bean brain. I'm there this evening, if you want proof."

"Love to, but Sabbie, we'll be working into the night." His hand slapped my upper arm, as if I was his mate. "Thank you for coming in. The public's support on this one is crucial; every tiny scrap of evidence. Whoever did this will feel the full weight of the law, and that's a crushing blow, believe me. Gary was my colleague and my friend and some bastard has just shot him through the head. I need to make an arrest soon."

"Through the head? This was a someone who knew how to use a weapon?"

He didn't reply. He was pursing his lips as if he realized he'd allowed classified information to seep past them.

"Do you have any idea who shot him?"

"Not a clue. But that's how we usually start. No clues." He grinned. "And then someone like you comes along and starts the ball rolling."

"Not much of a ball."

"Don't knock it. There'll be coppers crawling round St. Mary's before the hour's out and I'll be one of them."

"I saw you on the telly," I said, more to keep him from leaving than anything else. "When you found that woman."

"Yep, fifteen seconds of fame due to a Jane Doe. Hope it was my best side."

"You sound like every hard-nose cop! It's an unsolved death so it's okay to forget her because she wasn't ID'd. You never hear about it on the news anymore."

"Might be a dead donkey to the press, but murder cases are always active until they're solved. You can quote me on that."

"It's sad. That the people who loved you don't even know you're gone."

"Maybe no one loved her." He crushed half his cigarette into the wall and swallowed the last of his coffee. I surreptitiously tipped mine over the back of the wall and handed him the empty cup. He walked over to the bin and threw them in. He'd be gone so soon.

I stood up as he came back. "You never pop round anymore."

"To be honest, I was starting to feel guilty. Like I was using you as a greasy spoon stop on the way to work."

"Impudent wretch." I gave him a playful slap on his hand, aware it might be the last time I touched him.

"I didn't mean ..."

"Honestly, sometimes I'm overrun with eggs."

"Yeah. I recall." Our breath was white in the cold air, and we were standing so close it mingled. It was hard to believe that we'd never kissed.

"You seeing anyone?" he asked, rushing over the question as if he didn't want me to hear it.

"To be honest, since Ivan ... I've been wary ..." I broke off, out of breath.

"Don't let one bad experience put you off."

"I'm not desperate to have a man in my life."

"Oh, come on. I can't believe there isn't someone out there who's perfect for you."

A laugh gibbered out of me. "Sound advice, I'll bear it in mind."

Rey squeezed my arm in a goodbye gesture. "See you, then."

"See you." I tried not to make it a question. The glowing, sparkling sensations that had erupted inside me as we'd talked were distorting into hard lumps in my stomach. I watched him go, re-establishing in my mind the shape of his body, the way he walked.

"See you," I repeated, whispering the words like a wish.

FOUR

THAT WENT WELL. MONTHS without seeing Rey, and in the space of one murky, undrunk coffee I'd called him a) an idiot, b) a bean brain, and c) an impudent wretch. To reinforce my position, I'd also told him I didn't need a man. However hard I tried to re-imagine the conversation, it still ended up with Rey suggesting I find someone else ... i.e., *not him.*

Anyhow, I didn't need a man. I would never want a man in my life just for the sake of having one. It would have to be someone I was unable to live without. Sadly for me, Rey was growing into just that person. It had been a slow but steady process. It had started when I opened the door to him one day and found him ... interesting.

My hands shook as I unchained Hermes. Hermes was my fancy new mode of transport. He got me round Bridgwater traffic for far less dosh than my Mini, but being a butch yellow mountain bike, he didn't do it with quite the same level of weather protection. I'd called him Hermes in the hope that he'd give my feet wings.

I swung onto the saddle and swore all the way home—*bugger-bugger-bugger*—a swirl of *buggers*—which is a great approach to cycling if you plan to end up under some wheels.

By the time I'd let myself into the house and poured a glass of water, I was convinced. I would do well to avoid Rey. He had archaic attitudes and overassertive body language, and had proved himself capable of using others indiscriminately (e.g., me). It would be better if I never saw him again.

I strayed into my therapy room. I didn't have clients booked for the day—any further clients, that was—and I didn't need to leave for work at the Curate's Egg until around six. I should finish what I'd started with Drea. I took a quick shower and changed into my long black dress. The transformation was almost instant; from gibbering love-sick fool to shaman.

In the therapy room, I used my rattle—stiff calfskin filled with dried beans—to alert myself to the subtle energies Drea had left behind, then settled on the floor cushions. I draped a scarf over my eyes. I was aiming for a light trance state. To enter the otherworld, I have to let go—the more I think about it, the more I struggle, the harder it becomes to leave the outer world and reach my spirit portal. It's a bit like weeing. You've got to let it … flow.

The constant beat of the bodhran, a Celtic hand drum, thudded from the CD into my body. A single note rose above the beat; the skin of the drum, vibrating as it was struck. The singing note filled my head. My mind relaxed. I saw the rushing brook where Trendle lived. It grew in my mind until it took full shape; the distant hills, the flower meadows, the river bank, sun-dappled. Heather tickled the soles of my feet. Such a deep purple with such a rich scent, my head buzzed from it. No, not my head. The bees buzzed from it, moving with intent from one nectar-laden bud to the next. *Bzzzzzz...*

Trendle splashed up from some deep otterly place. "Greetings Sabbie."

"Hi, Trendle."

I lay on my stomach and reached down into the stream. My palm fitted over the soft, damp crown of Trendle's head. His spiky whiskers twitched. He smelt of river fish. In fact, I thought I spotted a droop of tail fin in the corner of his mouth.

I've known my animal guide for over four years. He started by appearing in my dreams, then in the real world, or the apparent world, as my shaman teacher, Wolfsbane, likes to call it. I saw *Tarka the Otter* lying on top a pile of books in a charity shop and had to buy it. I saw a stuffed otter at the nursing home where I worked. And before I knew it I had otter postcards, soft toys, and ornaments all round my bedroom at Gloria's house. By then I was studying the arts and skills of the shaman with Wolfsbane and was working with my otter in the otherworld.

Trendle is so cute and playful I sometimes have to remind myself that he's actually a higher being than me, presenting himself as a river otter so that I can see and understand him. I would not venture into the otherworld without Trendle, because it can be a dangerous place. Enter unwisely and you can return confused by misinformation or befuddled by wicked dreams. The otherworld can turn you to madness, there's no question, I've seen it happen. Shamans need to be stable, grounded people or they can end up hanging by the neck from their own banisters. That's why I love my veggie garden. It keeps my feet literally on the earth.

"What is your desire?"

My desire. The first rule of the otherworld; know why you're entering.

"I am here to journey for Drea. Except … she only half agreed. Didn't she? I had the feeling she wasn't keen on the whole process, but my instincts … my instincts …" I took a breath. "Will I even be able to enter her otherworld?"

Trendle scrabbled close to my ear. "How Drea's world feels, and what we find there, will tell us whether she wants us in it."

My stomach screwed into a ball of trepidation. However happy she insisted she was, I didn't think Drea's spirit world would be nice to visit. "Which path?"

"This one."

Trendle extended his scratchy forepaws, closing my eyes. I felt the temperature change; cool on my cheeks and arms. I opened my eyes.

I was in an ice temple. The whiteness forced me to squint. Every wall glittered. The vaulted ceiling, high as an abbey, gleamed with sheer, wet gloss. Icicles hung down like slender stalactites. A single drip from the end of one landed on my forehead, making me jump with a shot of freezing pain. I looked down. My bare feet were standing on solid ice. Its bitterness struck my soles.

"This is a cold-blooded place." I gazed round, seeking out something that might be a gift for Drea; a single symbol that I could offer her. There was nothing but the sheen of frozen white. "Trendle? Is it this something to do with winter, or thaw? Is that what I offer Drea?"

Trendle didn't reply. He was too busy showing off, skating across the ice, his legs splayed, trying out figures of eight while I shivered. If I wanted to get out of here, I'd have to look for answers myself.

On the far side of the ice room was a ledge that ran the length of the wall. A girl lay curled on her side away from me, a single knitted blanket over her. Even in this otherworld, I couldn't help thinking that was a dangerous thing to do, to lie along a block of ice.

"Drea?"

She didn't move. The cold had put her into a sort of suspended animation. I skidded over the ice floor. Something blocked my way. It was a serpent. It had come from nowhere, taking shape in front of me, rearing up until it balanced on a final coil of tail. There was so much of it that its head touched the ice ceiling. Seconds later it had curved its body down towards me. Our eyes locked gaze.

The snake was as thick as my waist and the colour of green slime, with darker and lighter blotches down its scales. Its bulbous head was a dangerous yellow and from its mouth a tongue flicked, black and forked into two sharp points, millimetres from my face. Every fibre inside me screamed. I had entered a dreadful place and this was a dreadful being. Trendle had skated off on some wild otter adventure, leaving me to work out if the snake was here to give us answers.

"Are you Drea's power animal?"

"I am Anaconda."

"Are you not a long way away from the warmth of your natural home?"

"Time and place can change. Home may change."

I didn't want to forget a single word of what Anaconda was saying; I was sure it had meanings only Drea would understand. "Do homes change for the better?" I asked.

"Duty and purpose can change."

"What is your duty and purpose?"

"First, do no harm. Next, protect my kin. Last, keep my secret."

"What is your secret?"

45

Anaconda didn't like this. He clearly felt I'd been presumptive to ask. I saw malevolence flicker in the small eyes. I heard the girl give a trembling sigh, as if even her breath shivered with cold. I tried to dodge past Anaconda, but he intercepted my move and I collided with him. His scales felt dry on my bare arms. My feet slid from under me and I fell on the ice, hard as concrete but much colder. It burned through my dress.

His tongue flicked. His head lunged at me. The razor-sharp points of his tongue plunged into my belly. I heard my throat scream in the world of my therapy room. My hands covered my stomach. There was no blood. This was a spirit wound from a serpent without a poisonous bite. Anacondas, I remembered, crushed their prey. I tried to slide away from him, wriggling like a snake does, struggling to gain a grip, but I was shivering so much my hands and feet refused to cooperate. I could hardly feel my body now. The bite wasn't poisonous, but it had sent me spiralling into hypothermia.

A spray of white ice chips swirled up as Trendle shot past me. Foam flew from his mouth. "Be gone. Be gone!"

His little body didn't come above the coil of the snake's tail, but his protective fury altered the balance of things. Anaconda reared and attacked. Trendle was ready. He spat and hissed and sprang, his body stretching into a wired pole, his jaws wide and full of sharpness. His fish-tearing teeth dug into the snake's neck. Blood oozed and stained the ice. Anaconda was so massive, I thought he would fling Trendle away and attack again. But my otter's bite provoked an explosion of change. In the blink of an eye, the ice temple dissolved.

I found myself in a new, though no less treacherous, place. Dark water thundered past, inches away. I was standing on the edge of a river, hanging for dear life onto the trunk of a tree, the rush of river water only a slip of my foot below me.

The roar of the river was intertwined with a woman's voice. She sang a high song that seemed to have no words and no tune and a rhythm that changed as only a river can—one moment soft and clear and slow, then next brisk and sparkling. I had heard that song once before, and it had filled me with a yearning that had saved my life.

Standing under a bare winter tree on the river path was a spirit presence; a woman in a shimmering grey cloak who only came to me when I needed desperate help.

"Lady of the River ..." My teeth chattered as I spoke.

"Yes." I saw her majestic face. There was an element of sadness and loss behind her eyes, or maybe in the furrows of her brow. "I am a water spirit, a dissolution of foam and form. I am the river that divides. The treacherous one. The violent one."

"I never know—"

"You are confused, are you not?" I'd been going to say I never knew if I could trust her, but she stopped my words before they left me. Her lips were the colour of poisoned apples and they moved as if she was whispering a spell. "Past and future, clients and quandaries ... they're easily confused."

Sometimes people want their shaman to change their past, not their future. Drea had told me that the past was unimportant to her, and yet I was sure the past had a lot to do with her problems.

The Lady's voice broke into my thoughts. "Can you help your client face her past, Sabbie? Even the most skilful shaman cannot give advice over issues they refuse to explore themselves. It is true that the paths can be snarled, but that is part of the Tides of the World of Spirit."

Tides of the World of Spirit? I'd never heard the phrase. My shamanic teacher, Wolfsbane, had certainly never used it, and he did love his high-flown archaisms.

"You sang to me when I was ill. When I was unconscious and lost from the world. You brought me back; you and Bren Howell between you."

She bowed her head. "That was then. Now, you are enduring again."

"I remember something you told me once. That I was a survivor."

"Indeed, but you should not linger here. Return to the solid world, Sabbie. Heal yourself."

So much was happening in the one journey. I had to sort it out in my mind. Was the ice temple Drea's spirit world? Why had the snake attacked me? And who was this river goddess that returned each time I was desperate for help? My mind was filled images and I tried to slow them down. I looked round for Trendle, but he was probably still battling the serpent.

As he'd sprung at Anaconda, I had caught a micro-second's glimpse of the girl. She had rolled onto her back, her arms over her face, her body revealed—a sudden vivid image of her rounded stomach, like a fairy hill on a flat landscape.

Everything slotted into place. I'd felt some disturbance at the sacral chakra when I was giving Drea Reiki. I'd thought it might be some sort of upset or disorder. But now I was sure; Drea was pregnant, or hoping to be.

———

I was numbed with cold as I roused from the journey, and too exhausted to think. I sat cross-legged on the floor cushions, the fleece pulled round my shoulders as I scribbled down my journey notes. There was a tingling at the base of my stomach. The psychic attack had followed me into this world. Anaconda had aimed at the place I'd felt Drea's disturbance ... the sacral chakra.

I went over to where I kept my aromatherapy oils. I pulled up my black dress and rubbed a drop of lavender into the invisible wound. The box containing my chakra crystals lay close by. I chose a smooth piece of carnelian, a deep and beautiful blood orange, and lay down on the cushions again, placing it over the little spot of lavender. I pulled both fleeces over my bone-cold body and closed my eyes, trying to visualize healing.

I lay half-dazed. It took all my efforts not to fall asleep. I tried to think through the events of the shamanic journey, but it was hopeless; I was too exhausted for thinking. A roaring sound took over my head. It might have been rushing water, or the hiss of snakes, or the shifting of glaciers.

Or the song I'd first heard when, eight years ago, I had been unconscious and in hospital. I finally understood that the Lady of the River had known me long before she'd made herself known to me.

I polished the carnelian and placed it in its box. I put the lavender oil away in darkness. I shifted the floor cushions into a pile at the side of the room.

Something fluttered from a cushion and floated to the ground. The scrap of paper Drea had written her question on lay like a moth resting before dark, still folded over and over.

A shaman must search out the hidden inside people. They see around corners, understand subtle energies. By being curious, questioning, they can bring back amazing answers. But me ... sometimes I'm too inquisitive for a shaman's good. *Nosey* is the word. There's no helping it.

It wasn't my place, as her therapist, to pry into anything Drea had not given me permission to know, but my whole being was burning up with curiosity. Anyhow, permission is a subjective term. If she'd not wanted me to know, surely she would have stuffed the paper into her bag.

I lifted it between finger and thumb and opened it as if it were ancient parchment. Drea had printed three words:

AM I SAFE

My mouth refused to shut. *I've never been as happy as I am now,* she'd insisted, but in my mind I saw the half-frozen girl on her shelf of ice, captive of her snake totem, pregnant with child.

This journey would be too distressing to relate in length to Drea. It was possible that she didn't even know yet that she was pregnant, presuming my guess was right. It was a guess, after all—the swollen belly could be symbolic of an unborn event, or even some localized ailment. Usually, in a journey, I'm offered a tangible gift for a client; a symbol or icon from an otherworld being, some words of comfort or illumination, or something ethereal, like a shower of sparkles. This was no more than the hint of a gift, and I had to find a way that would allow her to accept what I'd been shown without scaring her.

I staggered upstairs and pulled on jeans, socks, and a warm sweater. I splashed and dried my face, staring into the bathroom mirror. I looked mangled. I went down into the kitchen, made myself a hot mug of crushed lemon balm leaves with honey. I cut thick slices of yesterday's bread and topped them with banana.

I ate my scratch tea while my laptop booted up. I swilled my cup and plate and wrote a carefully worded letter for Drea. I asked if she had an affinity with snakes or serpents. I suggested she embrace the colour orange, the vibratory colour of the sacral chakra ... orange scarves, for instance. I thought she might like to look for a carnelian of her own, perhaps as a piece of jewellery. Normally I'd recommend the appropriate essential oils, but as it was possible she might be pregnant, I suggested she treated herself to a bag of oranges or mandarins, instead. I suggested a single, elementary yoga position for her to practice. I chewed my pen. How could I describe my gift without describing the journey in all its ice-cold detail? *I think you might be pregnant* felt brusque to rudeness. In the end, I wrote ... *In the journey I seemed to see something or someone unborn, a happiness not far from fulfilment.* I had a duplicate CD that featured mood music alongside the sounds of a running stream and chirping birds, and I slipped that into the envelope along with the letter. I grabbed a jacket. I needed to get this to her while the Reiki was fresh in her mind.

———

It was already dark when I left the house. I noticed someone standing at the bonnet of my car. I hadn't driven Mini Ha Ha for several weeks. She'd stayed by the kerb, a FOR SALE sign in her front and back windows. Up till now, no one had fancied a test drive, but it finally looked as if I had a bite.

I strode through my front gate. "It's a good price for a 1970s Mini Cooper," I began. "Classic paintwork in fair nick, racing strips still intact—" I trailed off. The chap gawping at my car was Drea's other half. "Oh, hi. Andy Comer, isn't it? I'm Sabbie—Sabbie Dare."

He'd been smiling patiently as I'd gone through my spiel. "Ah, this belongs to you, does it? I did wonder. I've driven past it every night for weeks and I just had to walk back down and have a gander. Mini's are inimitable, aren't they?"

"Yeah. 'Specially if they've still got their badge, 'cause people tend to nick them."

"I'm not really in the market for a new car, I'm afraid."

"Heck no. You've already got a great little vehicle for driving round town."

He nodded. "I need it for getting to Taunton every day. I work in that insurance office on Stonegallows with the big glass frontage?"

"Looks like you're settling in." It seemed weird that I'd managed to chat with both my new neighbours on the same day. "I've actually got something for Drea. I was just about to pop it up to her." I pushed the envelope at him.

"What's this?" he asked, turning it round in his hands.

"It's …" I stopped. Client confidentiality is important to me, and just because they were married didn't mean that I should be spouting off to Andy. "It's … just a CD I said I'd bring round."

And then, like a pop-up on a screen, I remembered her words. *No, don't do that. I'll pick it up …*

To my horror, Andy was peeling open the seal of the envelope.

"Hey," I said. "It's not for you!" He hardly seemed to hear. He shook the letter free of folds. "Has Drea told you about this morning?" I was suddenly sure she had not. "It won't make sense to you."

He glanced up from his reading. "It makes perfect sense." He'd gone from chatty neighbour to cautious sceptic. The vibes coming off him suggested he was wavering between a natural tendency to politeness and an erupting anger. "It makes perfect sense because I've already seen the poster you have in your window." He held the letter between a finger and thumb, as if it was impregnated with contagion. "I guess it's a free country, after all."

"Sorry?"

"I'm not asking you to stop whatever it is you do, but all this isn't something Drea and I choose to be involved in."

"All Drea had was a Reiki treatment. And yeah; that doesn't give you the right to read her mail."

"Whatever. Fact remains, I don't want Drea mixed up with that sort of thing." His voice shook as he reined his emotions in.

I tried to calm my own. "Reiki is harmless! It can bring amazing clarity to problems."

"Well, luckily, we don't have problems."

Before I could stop it, my stupid mouth snapped open. "Seems like Drea's got a problem—you."

Andy's face began to pink up. "I don't want to row about this. I'm just telling you now that Drea won't be coming to your house again."

"You mean you'd stop Drea if she wanted to work with me? I'm sorry, but I can't—"

"Drea is fragile in a lot of ways."

"I'm aware of that."

"She would agree, if she was here. She'd want me to say this to you."

"Andy, for that to be true, she'll have to tell me herself. Of her own volition."

"You don't understand. She doesn't always listen to me, or even to her more sensible self. She's easily led."

"Didn't you mention *free country* a minute ago? It's been a couple of hundred years since wives were supposed to obey their husbands."

His face went from pink to purple. My screensaver couldn't have done it quicker. He was controlling his fury, but it was taking all his strength. His voice became a snake-hiss. "Believe me, I am well aware of that." He seemed to make a decision. A second later, I discovered what it was. He tore at my letter, ripping it into strips, then squares. They flew from his fingers. He dropped the envelope and trod on it. I heard the CD crack.

My voice deserted me. All I could do was stare at the little squares of paper as they skittered along the damp pavement.

"Stay away from us." He brought his face close. "It's *codswallop*. Don't you think people can't see that? And it's *dangerous* codswallop. I am never letting evil back in our lives."

I managed a smile, to show him he'd failed to knock me off my rockers. "I'm sorry you feel that way, but, really, you can't speak for another person, not even one you live with. I won't believe that's right."

Andy turned and strode up the street towards his newly painted house. I didn't bother to watch him go. I collected the CD and as many bits of ripped paper as I could, then I went in and threw myself onto the sofa.

Today had been a three-peak challenge: Police interview. Malevolent spirit snake. Raging husband.

I checked myself. No. Four peaks. I'd also screwed up with a nonboyfriend.

FIVE

FULL MOON

My therapy business has always balanced on the pointed end of the financial skewer. People forget to turn up then expect to make another appointment. People don't turn up at all; sudden nerves or a change of plan. In the run-up to Christmas, numbers were dropping drastically. No one could afford to take care of their spiritual health at all.

When I was paying rent on this place, the slow periods weren't such a disaster. If there wasn't enough in the bank, I'd stop meeting friends for a drink and eat last year's freezer food, or even sting Philip for a loan because he knew I'd pay it back. But since I'd got the mortgage, I didn't feel I could ask Philip for money; he'd been my biggest influence on how I should spend my sudden windfall.

None of my friends advised me to buy my house. They told me to travel the world—all except Debs, who wanted to take me to London and spend, spend, spend. A holiday was tempting. I had been no farther than the caravan Gloria and Philip keep at Brean since moving in to Harold Street. But I'm trying to build a clientele, so I didn't want to be gone too long. In the end, I went away with Marianne, a former client. She's from Holland and she showed me the bewitching towns and the wide flat vistas, rich with tulip fields. We met up with some pagans we'd been messaging on the web.

I came home and saw the man from the building society, who kindly organized things so that my monthly outgoings shot up. Shortly after that, I took the job at the Curate's Egg. Working there nudges my balance from debit to credit.

Anyone who drank at the Egg already knew that Kev, the landlord, was tearing his hair out over staffing—a feat nigh impossible, as he lost most of it years ago. Even on Saturdays he ran the show with the dubious help of a single barman called Nige, who resembled a member of the Doors and had the speed of a battery-operated milk float. One night, after me and my friends had been waving our tenners for about an hour, I slid behind the bar and took my mates' orders. Then I had to serve everybody else, of course, because the rest of the punters weren't in on the joke. As it turned out, Kev hadn't even known it *was* a joke, and I've been working there on Saturdays ever since.

Kev provided a taxi for his late staff. Nige always got dropped off first, so it was getting on for the witching hour when I climbed out of the minicab on this particular Sunday morning. I was knackered but stone-cold sober. The cab pulled away and Harold Street became silent and still. I glanced up it, towards Drea's house.

Exactly two weeks ago, I had given Drea a Reiki treatment, and Andy had crushed my CD and transformed my letter into confetti. I suspected that Andy would have been happy to paint the words *Evil Whore* in red across my front door, but in fact, I hadn't seen either of them since that day. I hadn't even spotted Drea on her way to the shops.

A fortnight had passed since the carnival too. Bridgwater was still in shock over Gary Abbott's death. When a copper is killed in such a small, law-abiding town, it's an extraordinary event. The local papers and websites were applying every angle they could to keep the story going. But all they could do was add to the bonfires of gossip and guesswork, because the police were keeping anything they'd discovered too close to their chests for it to get into newsprint.

The funeral had been massive. I'd wanted to go, to pay my belated respects to a man I'd loathed in life but found I could forgive in death. I had stood across the road in the crowds, hidden from view as Rey and five colleagues had shouldered the coffin into St. Mary's Church, followed by Abbott's girlfriend, draped in black and gripping the hand of a little boy. The massive crowd was entirely silent until the hearse finally drove away to the crematorium.

Bridgwater felt less safe without Abbott on duty. Sardonic and intolerant though he might at times have been, I also knew he'd been a good cop. I locked my doors with more care and had started to glance behind when I cycled after dark. And now, hurrying down my side path at quarter to twelve on a bitter mid-November Saturday night, I felt suddenly watchful and uneasy.

Inside the open porch, something moved.

I stopped in my tracks. In the dark, my house looked fragile—ready to be picked open and laid to waste. They were always warning you not to confront burglars on your own. I had once confronted a murderer on my own, and I never want to repeat that experience. Robotically, my hands went to my head, to the curls that were now just ten centimetres long. A flash of fear shot through me. I hadn't meant to move. I'd meant to stay stock still until I had a plan. Now I'd lost the element of surprise and I still didn't have a plan.

"Hey." It came out all croaky with an unsteady waver at the end. "Hey!" That was better. I stepped off my path into the night shadows in the hope the intruder would hurtle past me, through the gate, and down the road.

A low *burr* of sound came out of the porch, but nothing rushed by. I crept closer. There was some sort of bundle in the corner. It stirred like an animal, but it was too big, even for a dog. I grabbed my bag and held it in front of me as protection, which on later reflection made it seem more like an offering.

Something white floated out from the darkness of the bundle. A pale hand. "Sorree … sorreee …" A form uncurled and stood. A slight frame, a narrow face veiled by a fringed shawl.

"Would you like to explain what you're doing?"

"Sorree," she said again. "I fall … sleep."

"In my porch?"

"I … you … Sabbie Dare?" She had a strong, uncertain accent that reminded me of something.

"How d'you know …"

"My name is Brouviche." I could see how slight she was, both shorter and skinnier than me. She still held out her hand. In the palm lay something I recognised instantly—one of my business cards.

"You were waiting for me?"

"Please." She pulled off the head scarf. Her hair gleamed like jet. She flicked the hair out of her eyes. An image flashed into my mind. Carnival night. The wind along the street. The smell of cordite in the air. The dark, narrow lane. A gypsy dressing in frills of red.

There is danger. It starts with death.

The death of Abbott.

"You were at the squibbing. You're Kizzy."

I'd given her my card, and she'd found my house. When had she got here? It could have been any time since I left early this evening. Underneath the wrappings her face was as pale as hoar frost.

"You'd better come in." I unlocked the door. Every client I invite in begins as a stranger, and some of them are very odd indeed. I didn't feel threatened by this young Romani.

The heating was off in the house, but it was warmer than outside. I put on the lights and filled the kettle. The girl hooched up against the arm of the sofa, her fingers knotted together, her brown eyes trained on my movements. "I am not Kizzy," she said. "Kizzy is my sister. I am Mirela Brouviche."

"Oh, gosh!" I could see now. Her eyes had less command than the fortuneteller's and she looked younger, hardly old enough to be out at night. I pulled a stool from under the breakfast bar and sat on it, facing her across the coffee table. "So, why were you in my porch?"

"Is sister."

"Gypsy Kizzy?"

"Is gone."

"Gone?" I echoed.

She gave an abrupt nod. "One morning, I wake. Kizzy not in bed. Not in house. Not in work. No place. And clothe gone too."

The kettle clicked off. I made some tea because I wasn't sure how she'd take her coffee—maybe thick and black in tiny cups? She didn't look up to explaining and I wasn't up to asking.

"I count. One week. Two week. I ask, where can she be? No one know." Mirela took fast little sips of her tea, like a bird at a fountain.

"She's been missing for two weeks? But that's when I saw her, two weeks ago. I saw her at the carnival."

"Two weeks, yes. I count each day. Think: today, Kizzy will be back." She paused to sip her tea, wrapping thin fingers round the mug to warm them. They seemed to me to be the fingers of a child; hardly longer or fatter than my niece Kerri's fingers. "When we first come here, Kizzy say, 'don' worry, Mirela, I look after you.' Then she say, 'don' worry, Mirela, I be back soon.' But no back. I am stuck! Alone." She put down her tea, mostly because she'd begun to weep, quite silently, the tears oozing and trickling. She wiped her wet eyes with a scrap of greying paper that might originally have been wrapped around a plastic knife and fork.

"How long have you been here?"

"Two month. It not like was promised."

"What were you promised?"

"Good wage. Happy. But, no wage, no happy." She pushed the tissue up the sleeve of her matted woollen cardigan.

"You don't think your sister went home, do you?"

"No. Not home for Kizzy. She like it here. She say it better—Bulgarian gypsy not spat on here."

"Even so," I said, thinking that gypsies were unwelcome everywhere. "Your family must miss you both."

She gave a wet sniff. "Itso miss me."

"Itso?"

"My boy."

"Your boyfriend?" I said, a bit cautious. "How old is Itso, Mirela?"

"He one year on me. Seventeen. We want join hands and marry. But Itso … no bride price for Tatta. So I go to bride market."

"What's a bride market?" I said. "Is it like a show where you can choose your wedding dress, the cake, all that?"

"No!" Mirela laughed, once. "Girl on show, not cake. Gypsy girl love it … talk, talk, all time before, buy makeup; can't wait. Wear

60

best clothe. Dance. Nice day out, see many men. Hopeful men," she added, with a touch of humour. "Make thousands *levs* if wealthy man. For family of girl."

"Did you have to go to the bride market?"

"Yes. At Horse Easter in Zagora. Kizzy been before, but no good offer. Wait for best offer."

"Would your family have forced Kizzy into a marriage?" I asked, recalling her sharp, confident movements when she read my palm. I didn't think she'd agree to anything she didn't want to do.

"Kizzy did meet man at Bride Fair. Stanislaus. He not Roma. Bulgarian-British. He say, 'come England, work. Wage good. Four euro hour.'"

"Sounds like this Stanislaus deserves a whipping."

"You have this punishment?"

I laughed. "We do have a minimum wage, and four euros is well below it. You should tell someone official about all this."

"Yes. We saw man. We tell story. But him ask so many questions. Too many. He like stray dog; lick your hand then bite your hand." Mirela crawled even farther into the corner of the sofa. For a second, I sensed the energy field around her body. It was shrunken, dank, and sliced thin, like canned mushrooms. I could understand why someone official, even if they wanted to help, would seem overwhelming; frightening.

"What did this person say they would do for you?"

"Nothing. Useless. Kizzy say if we go back to him, we lose job. Get thrown out work, get thrown out country."

"Are you here without visas?" I asked, not wanting to use the phrase *illegal immigrant.*

"We are EU in Bulgaria now," she said, shifting a little. "But gypsy hard to get passport."

"No wonder your wages are so low. They're getting away with murder."

"Kizzy say we move on. Go find better thing to do. More money. She say find save and go back head high. She say, 'Mirela, take little risk.' I don't like. She say, 'Mirela, you so *uncool.*'"

"Uncool?"

"Like I will never dip my toe."

"In case the water's too cold?"

"In case the water poison."

I was piecing her story together as best I could. "So, Kizzy asked you to leave with her, but you wouldn't, so ... so she went without you."

"Many days go by. No Kizzy. No phone call, no nothing. She in trouble. I know it. Know!"

"You think she's in some sort of danger?"

"In my blood, yes, but this strangely. Kizzy like ... *e balwal* ... she go where she want, no asking."

"*Balwal?*"

"The wind, yes."

The skin of her face was drawn tight and looked sallow under my dim lighting. I didn't think Kizzy was the one in trouble. She had run off and left her little sister behind in a strange and unforgiving country. In comparison to Mirela, Kizzy *was* the wind, following her own wild course.

I knew I should persuade her to speak to the police or seek some sort of official help. Surely she wouldn't be blamed by the authorities for the mess she was in.

I thought about Rey. To be honest, I never needed much excuse to think about Rey. Could I take this to him? Despite my promise of

boiled eggs, he hadn't popped in for breakfast since I'd gone to confess that I had lost Gary Abbott's iPhone.

"Sabbie?"

I was caught up with these thoughts, and it took me a moment
to realize more silent tears were rolling down Mirela's cheeks. "I
have no luck, to find my sister. You try, for me. You have second
sight. Kizzy told me so."

"But it was her who told me my fortune, not the other way
round."

"You are shaman." She looked at me directly, holding my gaze
with her black eyes.

"I don't work like a Romani might. I would travel into the otherworld and find gifts or advice that might point us in the right direction."

"Yes. That is good."

She seemed so sure that it was me she wanted help from. Instead
of going to the police, or back to the person who had helped them
before, she'd chosen a British shaman. I guessed it was what her
culture would have done, if they'd needed such help.

I searched my memory cells for anything I'd learnt about Bulgarian shamanism. I had done a little round-the-world project,
while I'd been studying with Wolfsbane. I was sure Bulgaria was
rich in ancient culture, but the only thing I could bring to mind
was that Orpheus had come from that region. And all I knew about
him was that he was Greek god of music and had gone into the
underworld to fetch home the wife he loved—not your average
sort of bloke, then.

Mirela stuffed a hand into the brown felt bag she'd brought with
her. It was worn thin and stained with puddle splashes. A seam was
bursting open, the contents bulging through. She must have carried

it across the continent of Europe, packed with false hope. She pulled out a mix of tens and twenties, some ripped, some just dog-eared, all of them crushed into her palm. "Please, Sabbie. Do something now. I can pay."

I pushed the money back at her. But her urgency helped me to decide. She was right. Now was the time. I glanced through the kitchen windows. It was a foul night. I could hear the November wind shaking final leaves from the trees. Mirela was no more than a kid and a stranger in this country, and she'd lost the only person who cared about her. I'd been in that situation ... something like that situation ... so many times.

"I guess you could stop over." Hopefully, she was used to mess, dust, and a sunken mattress because that's all my spare room offered. I was already trying to remember where Debs had left the hot water bottle.

She smiled. She had the same sharp teeth as her sister—not quite as straight or polished as the teeth of Bridgwater girls, but arranged in a sexy smile that might bite through the heart of any man. "Thank you, Sabbie Dare."

———

In the therapy room, I lit only the central candle. It hid the clutter that I'd pushed to the corners of the walls. I'd done a couple of massages and a Reiki before I'd left for the Curate's Egg and I hadn't been in here since.

"Would you like to help me prepare the room," I asked, "or do you want to watch?"

Mirela took a step forward as if volunteering. "I help."

"Good. That's good." I passed her a broom of birch twigs.

She laughed. "I clean up?"

"You clean away the bad spirits."

Dust flew up as she swept the laminate with vigour. I'd forgotten to tell her the act only needed to be symbolic. Under her breath I heard her mutter in her own language.

I arranged the floor cushions, then took my wand of yew and drew a circle with it, reaching out with my arm from the centre of the space. I lit the incense in its shell dish and lifted it on the palm of my hand. The aroma was a blend of the herbs from my garden with added resin of frankincense and some dried juniper berries. The smoke traced the shape of the protective circle. I followed this with sprinkles of water from Glastonbury's red spring and spoke the ritual words.

"*With fire in air I consecrate this circle. With water from earth I consecrate this moment. With all my will I declare this is sacred space in sacred time.*"

"What you say?" asked Mirela, her voice low.

"That we have created a place and time for our work tonight," I said. "What did you say as you were sweeping?"

"Eh …" She frowned, trying to bring the words into English as best she could. "Go out! Out! Go away, badness of Beng, bad luck of Bibxt, bad spirit of Mulo. Not welcome here."

My eyebrows shot up. "Mirela, that's fantastic—perfect. You're a Romani, all right. So, now we've got rid of the bad spirits, we can request the presence of good ones. Do you have a good spirit we could invite?"

She nodded. "Devla is our god."

I stood at each aspect of the circle; north, east, south and west, to call in their elementals, totem animals, and sacred winds. Then I moved to the centre, where Mirela stood, still holding the besom.

"And I call to Devla, god of the Roma, to be here at this time, to guide my spirit journey and offer inspiration."

Once Mirela was lying on the floor cushions inside the circle, I covered her with a fleece then took her wrist and loosely attached it to mine with a silken cord plaited in white, brown, and green. This cord would guide me towards her otherworld. One hand out of action, I got down on my own cushions and covered myself as best I could.

I pulled a dark scarf over my eyes. If I was lucky, I'd move close to that twilight zone between reverie and almost-sleep where you suddenly recall nothing of the outside world. From there, the otherworld was a blink away. But I tipped a little too far, and in moments I was deep asleep and dreaming.

———

An owl flew in front of the moon. It was all stealth, silent in the soft breath of the night. I was standing beside a rock face that rose above my head, above the trees, until it seemed to touch the moon. The owl disappeared behind the rock's peak and I noticed there was a slit at its base, wide enough for my body to slip through. I couldn't resist. I pushed through into a deep and narrow cave. A little moonlight illuminated the floor and I took cautious steps forward. The cave greyed into blackness. I could see nothing at all. The point of a stalactite scraped against my head. I put my hand to the wound and realized that my head was shaved as it had been nine months ago, forcibly and down to the flesh. I shuffled a few more metres before I noticed the gentle light that flickered in the far distance. Deep inside the cave was a man, carrying a candle cupped in his palm. I could make out that his hair was dark and dreadlocked, but his skin shone in the candlelight like pearl. I thought he'd just got out of bed, because he seemed to be wearing nothing but the sheet he'd pulled off it and a pair of loose leather sandals.

He did not acknowledge me but kept walking towards me. After a moment or two, I saw a second figure loom out of the darkness. It was a woman. Her face was warm honey in the back-glow of the candle flame.

The man spoke. His voice was low, but the tones echoed around the cavern. "I can't look back."

"No," whispered the woman.

"I must not look back," the man repeated, but his eyes were distracted and shifting. He told her he must not look back because he longed to do so. He longed to look at the woman with all of his heart.

They passed me, moving towards the gashed mouth of the cave.

"I must not look back," he said again, and my tongue dried with the knowledge that he hungered to look back.

Don't look back, I thought, *please, please*, but his whole body was jerking now, his head twitching, as if the temptation to turn had become irresistible.

"Don't look back!" I hadn't meant to call aloud. I had interrupted his resolve. He looked back. His eyes fell on the woman, the beautiful, slender creature with her deep brown hair coiled on top of her head like a sleeping snake.

"DON'T LOOK BACK!"

———

I woke with a shout and a snort, my tongue half in my throat, my eyes gritty. The candle was guttering. I might have been asleep for about half an hour. Beside me, Mirela had curled onto her side on the floor cushions and was even more deeply asleep than I'd been, breathing slow and regular.

I unpicked the silk from my wrist but left it tied to hers. In the kitchen, I wrote down my dream, although I didn't think it signified anything at all. It was the product of my most recent thoughts before I'd slept … Orpheus and his wife. Eurydice—that was her name, I remembered now.

Mirela hadn't moved a muscle. It seemed stupid to wake her and send her to a cold dampish room, so I threw the second fleece over her, snuffed the candle, and left her there.

I was halfway up the stairs when my callous, suspicious underbelly sounded an alarm. I slipped back down and carried my mobile and laptop up to bed with me.

SIX

EVEN A MINUSCULE CHINK of light coming through the curtains is enough to wake me at dawn nowadays. It must be something to do with growing up. I groaned and pulled the duvet over my head. Five minutes later, my mobile chirped a wake-up call. It was Sunday, and my diary was crammed with therapy appointments. It was Sunday; I'd had my late shift at the Egg and got home to find Mirela.

My eyes opened with a ping. Would she still be downstairs or would she be gone?

Mirela was curled on the floor cushions. Under the fleece, her body was as spare as a stripped twig. It looked as if she hadn't moved since I last saw her. She was a teenager, so naturally she could sleep for England.

Or in this case, Bulgaria.

She thought I had second sight. That was the trust between us. But it had been *her* sister who told *my* fortune, and, even taking her intent with a massive pinch of salt, she'd got a lot of things right.

She'd spoken of a fortune, which I'd already won and lost, and warned me off no-good boyfriends, of which I'd had my fill.

She'd forecast death. A man had raced past her on his way to his death. She'd forecast danger; I'd seen fear in her eyes. And now she was missing.

———

In the chicken coop were five eggs, two as big as a child's fist. Ginger and Melissa didn't lay all that often now, but when they did, their eggs were as full as bombs. I thought Mirela deserved an eggie breakfast before I sent her on her way. I took her in a mint tea and shook her gently.

She moaned low and sweet. "Mmm?"

"Mirela, hi there."

"Oh!"

I could see that she'd forgotten where she'd slept for a moment, but she sat up like a child and sipped the hot tea. "What you see?"

"See?"

"Last night. With …" She demonstrated the way I'd tied us together. "You have gift to tell where my sister is?"

"No." I shook my head. "I have nothing for you."

"Oh."

"Unless the legend of Orpheus in the underworld means anything."

"Who?"

I hadn't held out much hope. Her people were Roma. Orpheus was nothing to do with them. It had just been a dream. "I will try again, Mirela. In a day or two. Do you have anything of your sister's I could use? To help me find her otherworld?"

She reached for her shoulder bag and brought out a zipped, plastic makeup case, stained with lipstick smears. From this she pulled a piece of shiny card. At first I thought it was a large postage stamp, but when she handed it to me I could see that it was a reproduction of an icon—the Virgin Mary in summer blue with a golden halo. I turned it over. On the back was a scribble of biro in Cyrillic script.

"This is Kizzy's?"

"She carry it from home."

"She is a Christian?"

"Of course. We all are."

"I stupidly imagined ... after last night ... when you summoned your god ..."

"Believe God, Devla, Madonna, and spirits of dead. Satan and bad spirits too."

"Right, the full works!" I squeezed her arm. "We should apply the same principle. Your sister has to be somewhere. To be honest, some real-world searching wouldn't be a bad thing."

"Where I look?" She paused. "Where *you* look?"

Yep, there it was, that sinking feeling as my stomach hit my knees. I'd offered her a bed. I'd offered to work shamanically to find her sister. And now it looked like I was offering some practical help. "We should really report your sister missing officially. But let's start by going back to the person in authority you both went to see. Who is he?"

"Quigg."

"What?"

"Mr. Quigg. Agency for Change."

"Is that one of those charities that help displaced persons?"

She shrugged. "Him no help."

"He might be waiting for you to go back to him. He must deal with disappearances all the time. He could be a lot of help, Mirela."

Her lip trembled. "I had lovely dream."

"Last night?"

"About Itso. He was in big fight."

"Oh, no," I cried. "That was a nightmare!"

She laughed. "Good dream. Itso win. True dream; big fists, good punch—one! two! Itso tall, fast. Good at winning." She raised a fist in a jab. "Him bare knuck since four, five."

"What …" I tried to be cautious. "You mean your boyfriend's been fighting since he was little?"

"'Course. All gypsy men must fight. Itso show his brother now he almost three. Learn moves. Fast on foots. Fist hard. Go-go for little-boy contests."

My head was throbbing with the images she painted. "That cannot be so. I don't believe it."

"What if honour is threat?" Mirela pointed out. "What if other family steal horse? What do then?" Her face was taut with pride. "Itso fight when Kalaygia family steal his tatta's horse. But that family coward. They sneak off. Disappear. With six horse."

"This was your dream?"

"No! This is the true! Why Itso no money."

"Do Romanies have money, then?" It felt an uneducated question, but Mirela didn't seem to mind.

"Much money to metal and horse."

"So … you came to Britain in the hope of making enough money…"

"Buy one, two, many horse. For Itso pay Mama and Tatta bride price. Then, I go home."

"Yes. You're too young to be here on your own … exploited." I felt my eyes narrow. Her skin was baby soft and her eyes were clear as jet dropped into milk. "How old did you say you were, Mirela?"

She grinned at me. "I old enough to marry. Old enough to work."

"Old enough to know your own mind," I admitted, thinking aloud.

"Yeah. I am no leave without Kizzy. You will tell where she is."

"Mirela … I can't *promise* to be of help."

"You already help. Good friend."

I sighed, hoping she didn't hear. "Would you like an egg for breakfast?"

Mirela was a charming combination of femme fatal, innocent child, and hoary old gypsy. She ate both double-yolkers, giggling when I called the bread slices "soldiers."

"Exactly when did Kizzy leave?" I asked. "Can you remember?"

"Yes, easy. November six."

I took this in. I'd met Kizzy late on Friday night, bonfire night, November the fifth.

"All start with carnival," said Mirela, hardly noticing my shock. "We get up on lorry; wave to people, do little dance over and over. Mr. Papa make us."

It was hard to make sense of it all. "Your father?"

She sort of giggled. "No. Papa Bulgaria?"

"Right! Got you! The takeaway shop on the Quantock round-about. Are they the people you work for?"

"Yes. Good Bulgarian cooking." It sounded like she'd been drilled into saying this, but I had to admit, I'd eaten Papa Bulgaria food and their veggie options were nice.

"So that was the float with the gypsy dancers."

"It was Kizzy's idea. To do the dancing."

"And dress up?"

"Yes. She is always good ideas, my sister. Always say she wants to make better life, more money."

I knew what she meant. There were people—Debs was among them—who could not stay still in their lives.

"She wake me up late. Say we should both go." Mirela gave one of her careless shrugs. "She say I will easy make bride price money for sake of Itso. But I say, 'what you mean? Where go?' And she shake her head. Say, 'you know, Mirela. You know.'"

"Did you know?" I asked, caught up in the tale.

"No. If I know, I would go find her. And she just start pack case right then and puff! She's gone. Like that." Mirela clapped her hands, once, loudly. Suddenly, I wanted to find Kizzy badly. I was longing to give her a good slapping down.

Before Mirela left for her shift, she wrote out her address and telephone number. Then she kissed me on both my cheeks, shouldered her bag, and followed my directions to the bus stop into town. I promised I would contact her as soon as I had any sort of news.

———

By six p.m. I was in profit, knackered, and ravenous. A dangerous combination. Images of instant food laden with bad carbs and dripping with trans fats floated before me. My health-food options were the wilted veg in my storehouse and garden. Or, I could order a veggie takeaway from Papa Bulgaria. I'd bought food from Papa before, but as the shop was the other side of town, I'd had it delivered by scooter. This time I thought I might struggle there and back on Hermes. I was curious to take a look at where Mirela worked.

She'd be behind the counter, and although I didn't have anything further for her yet, it would be good to check she was okay.

I'd done a lot of thinking since Mirela had left my house this morning. Or to be more specific, I'd been thinking of one thing. Me, Debs, and Gypsy Kizzy might have been standing a few metres from where a shooting had taken place. But when Debs and I had returned to the High Street, Kizzy hadn't followed us. So it was possible that she'd gone the other way... up the lane into St. Mary's Square. She might have seen something. She might have seen something, *and been seen by someone.* Perhaps all of that had unnerved her so much she'd scarpered that very night. And stupidly, I hadn't asked Mirela if Kizzy had mentioned this when she'd woken her up after the carnival.

I was beginning to have second thoughts about what a lowdown bitch of a sister Kizzy was. Maybe she really did have to disappear fast.

A noise—loud and sharp as a gun retort—burst inside my ears. I let out a shriek that shot through the stratosphere and went hurtling into space. Outside the kitchen window a dark shadow moved.

"Sabbie?"

"Dennon Davidson! You horror!" It was my foster brother, tapping the glass with his car keys. I let him in.

"You getting jumpy, sis." Dennon shrugged past me and rummaged in the fridge. "Not again. No Coke!"

"I've got fizzy water and organic cordials. I make my own up, now." Dennon groaned. "Hey, but I was just about to go out and get some food. D'you fancy that?"

"Why not. It'll do to celebrate with, for now."

"Celebrate?"

"I got a promotion."

I did a double-take. Dennon worked for the frozen-food chain Iceland. He was one of the boys that stacked your order into the delivery van. His major responsibility was not getting the bags mixed up, and he couldn't always be relied on to do that. "Sorry? What did you say? You caused a commotion?"

"Show respect. I said I've been promoted to manager."

"*What?*"

"Yeah. God's truth. I'm a trainee."

"Trainee ..."

He took a breath. "Trainee deputy under-floor manager."

We looked at each other then burst out laughing. "Let me get this straight. You're going to train to manage an under-floor."

"Don't forget the deputy bit."

"Yeah. Wear your star with pride, Den. I bet Mum's sur— pleased."

"She is. She sent me down here. She wanted me to give you these photos." He passed over an A4 buff envelope. "Mostly Charlene's kids ... that sort of thing. Sorry."

"No, just what I need. You were right, my nerves are raw."

"Food first," said Den, jangling his car keys. "Let's roll, sis."

———

Papa Bulgaria takeaway shop provided seating for waiting customers, benches along the inside of the windows that fronted the road. They were barely visible under the bums of hungry punters. There was a queue at the counter too. Mirela, in a white cotton overall and a little white cap with red and green stripes, was serving along-side a guy with hair that glistened under a thick coat of gel. He was glaring at his customers, a couple who simply could not make up their minds.

I'd left Dennon to find a parking space, but I had his order and I knew what I wanted. I got into the queue, trying to catch Mirela's eye, but when it was finally my turn, it was the guy who was free to serve.

"Yes?" He spoke through the cocktail stick he held between his fine, white teeth.

"I'd like moussaka and chips and the banista with salad, please."

He scribbled the order onto a pad. "What else? Colas?"

"Uh, yes, better give me two."

He slammed my order through a spike on the serving hatch and yelled at one of the kitchen staff in a language that sounded gloriously exotic. He ripped a raffle ticket out of a book and slid it over the counter at me. Number 59. His nails looked manicured and his body moved with purposeful agility. He had that shape some girls salivate over . . . tight butt, narrow hips and wide, pumped-up shoulders. He knew it though; I could see it in the way he looked me over. When he finally shared a smile, it was the sort that robbed you of every stitch of clothing.

"Hey, d'you think I could have a quick chat with Mirela?"

"You can see she's working."

"I know, but . . . just couple of seconds, please?"

He swept his heavy fringe from his brow, displaying an irritated edge of impatience. Clearly his mother had never taught him to say please or thank you. Or even okay. But after a few seconds working his cocktail stick with his tongue, he took over for her and let her move to one side.

"Thought I'd come and see where you earn four euros an hour," I joked. But I kept my voice down. Her body language was telling me that the slick-gelled guy made her nervous. "I was wondering though, if Kizzy had said anything about what had happened at the carnival after you went home."

Mirela didn't have to think. "She tell 'bout you; seven daughter of seven daughter."

"I never said I was that," I exploded. "She's the one who's a seventh daughter."

Mirela made a face. "Not true. We are the only two girl childs of my mother. But to say seven and seven like that, it is ..."

"Tradition?"

"Tradition," said Mirela, adding it to her English lexicon. "She gave me twenty pounds. Inside money your card."

"So ... she knew she was planning to leave. She even thought she wouldn't need the spare cash."

"She said fireworks had been good. She look ..." Mirela circled her hand, unable to find the word.

"Scared?"

"Like fireworks still in eyes."

"Okay ..."

"Mirela!"

The queue had grown since we'd started talking. "Coming, Stan."

I snatched at her hand. "What's that guy's name? Did you say Stan?"

"Yes. I told you. Stanislaus. That is him."

So it was Papa Bulgaria who hunted the bride market for new and innocent employees. Of course, it was not surprising that they'd want Bulgarian staff, but why Romani? Was it because they would accept the lowest pay?

I wandered away from the counter, clutching my ticket. There was still no space on the window seat. Most customers were gawping at the telly tuned to the Discovery Channel that was hinged onto the wall, or down at the floor, deep in empty-bellied thought. Among them, I spotted an Aran bobble hat and matching mittens.

"Drea!"

She glanced up. Her face told me that she'd been hoping I wouldn't see her.

"Oh. Hi."

"Look," I said, stepping as close as possible to her, bending a little. "I owe you an apology."

"No. No you don't. It's me. I should never have come to you."

"But you did. You followed your instincts, nothing wrong with that."

"I should never have come."

"Number forty-seven!" yelled Stanislaus. The man sitting next to Drea got up and took his order away. I slid onto a cushion that swirled with sequins. "You been okay, Drea?"

"Yeah, fine."

"I still have a copy of the shamanic notes I made after your Reiki." I looked at her for a moment. "You did know, did you, that Andy…"

"Yes, of course. I'm sorry if Andy upset you."

"Drea, he almost scared me."

"He's just… trying to protect me."

"Listen, Drea, I went out with a man like that, not long ago. They *say* they love you, but that isn't the point, is it? It's how a person shows love that counts. Some men think that getting angry…violent…"

She pulled a raffle ticket from her patch pocket and examined it. Number 48—her passport out of this place and away from me. She folded the ticket into two, into four, as she'd folded the paper under the cushion. *Am I safe.* I laid a soft hand on her arm. "In the journey…I thought you were having a baby."

"What?" She didn't even attempt to lower her voice. "How could you do that?"

"Sorry? I…"

"How could you…*know that?*" She was gritting her teeth—almost grinding them. "That is impossible."

I'd taken quite a risk talking about this private issue, one that originally I had been planning to explain gently, not blurt out. But meeting her here seemed like more than chance. "I need to explain this properly. Go through my report with you."

She had lost all her colour. I could almost see through her. She spoke in a sharp whisper. "You have heard the voice of the devil. That is what this is. The devil speaking inside you. And I won't listen."

"Number forty-eight," yelled Stanislaus. He dangled the carrier bag from one outstretched finger but looked at me. He'd enjoyed the promise of a cat-fight and was sorry to see it terminated.

Drea rose from the bench and fisted the carrier. Her face seemed swollen and shiny, as if she was crying inside. A few strides later, she was through the door and stepping into a car. The driver's face was obscured, but I knew who it was. As they pulled away, I saw Dennon's ancient Vauxhall reverse into the space.

As soon as my food was ready, I snatched the bags and headed out, calling to Mirela as I reached the door. "I'll be in touch, sweetie!" I wanted Stan to know that she had friends in this town. But when I glanced his way, the Bulgarian simply flicked his oiled hair from his eyes and winked at me.

———

"Aw, look at this!"

An hour later, and we'd finished the food and were chatting on my sofa. Dennon was leaning back, his baggy jeans sticking straight out under the coffee table so that his Nikes showed from the other side. His fingers were flicking—both hands—which meant he was in sore need of a smoke. I was curled next to him with my stockinged feet tucked under me, cooing at the photos Mum had sent over. "Kerri in her ballet leotard!"

"That was her grade one exam last month."

"I'm in this one. Rudi on his sixth birthday. Look at that chocolaty mouth."

"Yep," said Dennon. "You always was a messy eater."

"Shurrup." I poked him with an elbow. The photos made my head feel as light as a gas balloon. At Rudi's age, what I can remember of it, I was mute with terror most of the time. There are no chocolatey pictures of me on birthdays, and I never had a pretty pink leotard or ballet pumps, either. By the time I was six, my mother was dead and I was faced with the first of a series of foster homes. Inside my head, I was terrified as a baby rabbit, but I fought being little and lost with miniature fists and teeth and the toe caps of shabby sneakers. At some point I stopped moving around people's homes and ended up stuck in the Willows.

"What's this?" Among the pictures I'd found a plastic wallet. The paper inside had the yellow look of parchment. Visible through the clear plastic was my name ... SABRINA ISOBEL DARE. I flicked at the snap and slid my fingers in. The document came fluttering out. I looked up at Dennon. "It's my birth certificate."

"So? You must've seen your own birth certificate before."

"Not like this. I've got one of those mini ones. This is …" I put the empty food cartons on the floor and spread the sheet over the coffee table "This is everything."

"Mum prob'ly found it in one of her big clear-outs."

"No, Dennon. It's a pristine copy." I looked up. "Those pics were just a ploy. She sent you over because she didn't want to be here the first time I saw this."

"What, you mean she went out and got it?"

"She's always trying to convince me I should trace both sides of my family. But what family? You all's my family. I don't want any other."

"'Course you don't, man. Sniff round in the past and bad bits are gonna show up."

I laughed. I hadn't yet had my thirteenth birthday when I went to live with the Davidsons. Dennon was eighteen months my senior, although *senior* was not the word for the things we got up to. "We're both reformed characters now," I reminded him.

"Yeah, sad, innit?" Dennon gave me a nefarious grin. "Remember those first solo rides? Seventy along the M32?"

"Up to ninety, once you had your provisional license."

We'd both been well proficient in so many things—driving, smoking, drinking, hitting on the opposite sex—long before we were legally entitled. Other indulgences were never going to be legal at any age. Gloria and Philip threatened to chuck us both out each time we got into trouble, but, thank the goddess, they never carried out their threats.

"Best to put the past behind you and move on," I said. My words seemed to echo Drea's. What has she said? *We've put the past behind us.*

I touched the document with the pulp of my fingertips. PLACE OF BIRTH: SOUTHMEAD HOSPITAL, BRISTOL. MOTHER: IS-ABEL TREVINA DARE. ADDRESS: THE HATCHINGS, ZOTHER-ZOY, SOMERSET. FATHER: LUCKY LUC RAMEAUX. ADDRESS: ST PAULS, BRISTOL. OCCUPATION: CAR DEALER.

I stared at the form, entranced. I had never seen my father's name before this. My mother had always lived alone … hadn't she?

"When I was at the Willows," I began, "I had to do this scrap-book, you know?"

"Yeah?"

"The social workers made me stick photos in, that sort of thing. I hated it." I couldn't remember why I hated it, but I could taste the emotion. It made my heart race. "*The Hatchings* reminds me of my hens. But I bet it was a kid's home like the Willows. After all, my mum was still a kid when she had me." I shuddered.

"Your dad sounds wicked."

"*Wicked*?"

Dennon raised his eyes in despair. "Wicked name. And car dealer? Yeah, *dealer*, all right, but St. Pauls ain't 'xactly renown for its Audi showrooms, is it?"

"Do you think he's French?"

"What?" Dennon laughed. "Look at you, man. If your mum was white, like you're always saying, your dad's gotta be black."

"I know that."

"Don't think you do. You're in denial, sister."

"You're talking rubbish. I know who I am. I'm a shaman."

"Yeah … a black shaman." He reached over and tugged at a lock of my hair. "You grew your hair down to your bum and that made it nice an' *straight*, like you a white girl wiv a tan. But not anymore, sis. Now you got a Afro like me."

"I was scalped, Dennon. Not my fault that I now I resemble a labradoodle."

But deep down I knew that Dennon—so proud of being second generation Afro-Caribbean—was a smidgeon right. Until I'd met the Davidsons, I'd been brought up by my pale, blue-eyed mother and by white middle-class social workers. I understood the theories of identity. That didn't mean I had to like them.

"His name's French."

"His address ain't."

"Don't you think it's weird that my mother came from round here?" I thought we'd always lived in Bristol. Sordid rooms and council flats, so damp I could still feel how my nose was constantly sore and red with running. But Izzie Dare had come from Somerset and here I was, settled in a Somerset town. Had my unknown roots pulled at me?

"D'you think I should look into things?"

"Nah," said Dennon. "Lotta bovver, innit?"

———

Inside the room, down in the pit of her narrow bed, there is not much light. He keeps the curtains closed, heavy and thick, and she's glad. She doesn't want light. The sun burns her eyes when it seeps through the curtain edge. It is sleep she craves, spiralling down into it. The pain passes over the threshold of her dreams, but it's filtered, tangible, something she can get away from. Sometimes it's her boots that hurt, the white ones that always pinched her toes. In the dream she can kick them off and dance, high on the grassy hill, looking down over the city, the skyscrapers, and the snake of roads.

Uncle Plamen's clarinet winds like a snake through the dance. The tune wiggles the girls' bums under their fringed shawls. She is showing her sister the moves of the dance, the way to hold her arms. The sun is strong on their bare skin, it catches the strands of copper woven in their long hair.

But it doesn't last. Pain snakes into the dream. Pain becomes the winding howl of the clarinet, and she is crying out until she wakes herself.

"Stop playing! Stop playing!"

He is standing by her bed. He smiles. He's brought broth for her. She shakes her head. She could not manage a mouthful.

"I'm not getting better," she says.

"You need to rest. Rest is healing."

She closes her eyes. In her mind she's back on the hill, a fringed scarf around her hips.

"I need my sister."

She is so afraid of dying without seeing her again.

SEVEN

Pulling on my heavy black dress always makes me keen to journey. This morning was quiet—who wants to see a shaman first thing on a Monday?—and my thoughts were still with Mirela. Kizzy's icon waited for me on my desk. It didn't lie flat because it had been folded and unfolded so many times. I lifted it into the palm of my hand. There was no immediate message, but it felt heavy with its own story. The Virgin Mary smiled out at me. It's my belief that she is, in fact, a very ancient goddess. Virgins and mothers have always been treasured. I like the theory that in ancient times women were revered, respected, and worshiped, and that the first deities were earth mothers who birthed the earth, or, like the goddess Gaia, *were* the earth.

So this Christian symbol spoke to me, telling me that I should treat it with respect. I fetched my scarf and tied it like a bandana across my forehead, the fringe of soft fabric covering my eyes so that, once cross-legged on a cushion, I could focus only on the icon resting on my lap. I viewed the picture through the fuzziness of fringe for several minutes then began to chant.

Come to me, Ancient Mother
Hear my singing
Hear my song.
Come to me, Ancient Mother
Aid my crossing
Help me cross.
Come to me, Ancient Mother
Through fire, air, and water
And the earth that is your own.
Come to me, Ancient Mother
Hear my singing …

The chant was on my tongue, in my throat, then my heart, solar plexus, loins. I was all chant. The journey could begin.

———

A forest path. Trunks of tall evergreens were all around me. Their needled branches were black in the darkness—it was a starless night. Trendle rested against my feet. He looked up at me like a faithful pooch, but I'd learnt the hard way that it was best to take his spirit world advice.

"Hi, Trendle."

"Good morrow, Sabbie."

"Which way shall I go?"

"You wish to visit the world of the Romani? Follow the path through the trees."

But as I walked, the forest thickened and the path disappeared. We pushed our way through dense ground cover. I could no longer see Trendle. I dipped down into the weeds and bracken and lifted him onto my shoulder. He lay there like a debutante's stole, silent but alert. His fur had the damp smell of rotting weeds. I could feel him breathe.

"Wherever are we heading?"

"This way," said Trendle, enigmatic as always.

The firs were as tall and straight as masts—I suppose once felled that's exactly what they'd become—and the smell of their resin made my nostrils tingle. It was hard to gauge the time of night, but there was a very slight lightening towards the east, and I could sense dew popping on my skin like invisible rain. It was moving towards dawn.

A howl ripped through the dank air. Wolves, not far off. Trendle was heavy on my shoulder as I picked my way forward. I wore no shoes, just my black dress, but the forest floor was soft with bracken and damp pine needles. The wolf howled again. His cry moved up my spine like an insect. I whispered to Trendle, "He sounds hungry."

"He sounds greedy."

I kept moving between the trunks, a curving, zigzag path with no way markers. After what seemed a long time my ears picked out a distant sound, high and plaintive, that was not the cry of a wolf. On the air I smelled wood smoke.

"There's music. A fire. Are we close to people?"

I followed the notes of a high lament. Suddenly I was in a clearing. A man stood tall, his outline black against the flames of a fire. He held a violin under his chin, drawing the bow across it with a passion. As my eyes adjusted, I realized he was not alone. Several women were dancing to his accompaniment. Their arms were high above their heads as they clapped and shrieked. They spun and skipped, the hems of their long dresses swirling dangerously close to the fire, encouraging sparks to fly out and spiral skywards. They had fixed flowers of the forest into their hair and as they whirled the petals floated away, taken by the currents of the night breeze. The fiddler did not dance, but stood with straddled legs, his back and knees bending in time to music, his head nodding as if an entire orchestra followed his lead. His tune filled me with longing. One woman turned to me and beckoned.

Come and dance!

I could not have resisted, even without an invitation. The music the man created from strings and bow enchanted my feet. In real life I can just about manage a few salsa steps, but in this trance I could move like a diva. The other women stepped back, creating a circle around me as I pirouetted and leaped. I could hear myself laughing with almost ecstatic joy.

I thought the dance would never end. I didn't want it to. I could've danced forever without an aching muscle or losing my breath. But the music came to a violent halt. The fiddler let his violin drop to his side. The women become motionless. All eyes were trained on the edge of the clearing. The gypsies backed away. They became shadows, leaving me to face a wolf.

This was a spirit wolf, I was sure. Grey hair lay thick on his frame; his eyes glowed with yellow light. The pace of his feet was steady and confident. His teeth shone in the firelight, his mouth drawn back into a snarl.

I mouthed to Trendle, "It cannot do me harm."

"Beware. If a wolf comes in friendship, it will offer you inner strength and the deepest kind of wisdom. But if it comes as your enemy…"

"What?"

"It will bring you down by the neck."

"Your otter is right, of course," said the wolf, as it came up to me. "I will grant you nothing but the right of terror."

"I am here to find Kizzy Brouviche, for good or ill."

The wolf grinned as I spoke, as if I'd said something that amused it. "You will listen to me, Sabbie Dare. You will be shown directions. Follow, and you will discover."

"Where will I find these directions?"

"There are many that will appear to you." His tongue lolled from his muzzle and saliva drooled and pooled on the ground. "The place of blame. The place of absolution. The dark place. The place of no escape. You will find little in some, and confusion in others. In some you may be rewarded. Do not expect satisfaction from any answer."

It was hard to process this. "Are all these to appear to me in journeys?"

"You must search the apparent world. But your spirits are there to guide you."

"Do I know these places? Or do I have to seek them out? Should I look in the obvious places first?"

"That is shrewd. Now you show me your gums, as we wolves say."

A single gypsy woman moved from the grey edges of my vision, dancing slow steps. The wolf gave her a disregarding glance and began snuffling in the undergrowth.

The woman raised her voice in song, such a high voice that it sounded like a child's.

Come to me, Ancient Mother
Hear my singing
Hear my song,
Come to me, Ancient Mother …

When I looked back, the wolf had retrieved a stick and was trotting towards me with it in its mouth. It was panting with that curled grin that dogs have when they're really enjoying themselves. The wolf dropped the stick at my feet. I picked it up, avoiding the drool that covered the middle. I raised it above my head, meaning to throw it for the wolf, but it leaped the length of its own body, its hind legs leaving the ground, and snapped it out of my hand. It laid the stick, with stony patience, on the ground again.

"Is this your gift, Wolf?"

It did not reply. It loped to the edge of the clearing and sat with its muzzle pointing to the clouds. It let an eerie howl float into the night. Then its hind legs kicked out and it was gone.

The howl stayed with me for a long time, lifting every hair on my scalp.

———

Mirela lived not far from the town centre. Her street was lined with rows of tall houses blackened from long-standing grime. I braked and Hermes came to a stop outside the number she'd given me. I chained my bike to the garden railings and climbed the three stone steps to her door. There was no bell, so I banged hard.

A lanky guy opened the door. When he spoke, his accent gave him away as Bulgarian.

"I'm after Mirela Brouviche."

"Yeah. Upstairs. I show." He slid his arm through mine, as if we were about to be announced at a ball, and tugged me up the spindle-bannistered stairway. He loomed over me, being one tread in front and taller to begin with.

"Don't worry." I shook him off. "I'll find her."

"You too pretty to be left alone." He had a "nothing to lose" grin wrapped round his face. "Look—that door there." He knocked on it using a sort of coded tattoo.

Some long seconds went by before I heard Mirela's voice, muffled and monosyllabic.

My escort said something in Bulgarian. Almost instantly, Mirela came into view, but her face dropped when she saw me.

"Hi," I began. "Sorry to barge in when you're at home, but—"

"Home?" Her brow knotted. "This not home." She faded into a room that smelt of musty washing. I followed, slamming the door on lanky lad. Three would definitely be a crowd.

It was only a little room. There was a double bed, a sink near the window, a chest of drawers littered with dirty crocks and a chair hung with discarded underwear.

She stood in front of me, the spark I'd seen in her eyes as she'd spoken at the door completely faded.

"You thought I might be Kizzy, didn't you?"

"That bugger Petar make me fool."

"So you've heard nothing?"

She gave a dismal shake of her head. I wrapped my arms round her and hugged for a long time.

"This is a rundown on the shamanic journey I've done for you." I pulled out my report and laid it on the bed. I'd used a lot of what I laughingly called "illustrations" in the report; pen and ink sketches of the forest, the gypsies, the wolf, and his gift and directions.

She stared at it. "What it say?"

I read the report out to her, word for word, then passed her the paper. "The stick the wolf left is a spirit gift I'd like you to offer you shamanically."

"Okay." Mirela put out her hand.

I smiled. "You would need to lie down, on your bed, and I'd blow it into you."

With no further comment, Mirela climbed on the bed, lying on her back, her hands clasped on her stomach.

I spent a moment visualizing the stick, replete with dog-drool and mud. I described the gift aloud, in a quiet tone. Then I cupped my hands over Mirela's heart chakra and blew with a huff of air, sending the image into her.

"Does such an image mean anything to you?" I asked. Mirela didn't respond, and I spoke more plainly. "Would a stick say something? Or throwing a stick for a dog? Anything like that?"

Mirela had closed her eyes. "Where is my Kizzy?" she whispered.

I straightened up. I had meant to ask her if she knew anything about any of the four places the wolf had spoken of, but I was already overloaded and confused by his instructions and I didn't want to pass that on to Mirela. "To be honest, I think it's time for action. I was hoping that we could go and see Mr. Quigg together."

"Quigg! Rubbish!" Mirela wrinkled her nose. "I don' trust. Kizzy don' trust."

"Don't worry. I'll be your advocate—help you ask the right questions and get some proper answers. That's why I got here in good time, so we could do it before you start your shift." I tried another smile. "How d'you feel about that?"

Mirela stuffed my report into her brown felt bag. "Okay. Let's go."

———

The Agency for Change was situated a walk away from the centre of town, close to the canal and above the Polska Café. This was a lovely little joint serving Polish food from nine in the morning to nine at night. I'd been there once, with an old boyfriend, in the evening when the candles were lit on the square wooden tables and soft twenties jazz played from behind the counter. In the day it tended to service the immediate area along the canal—a tyre replacement garage, a legal firm, and a slightly amateur recording studio—as well as the Bridgwater Poles who liked to pick up their community gossip from the café.

Mirela led me up some outer stairs and through a bottle-glass door into the agency's office. A receptionist just out of babyhood was taking phone calls that were giving her a succession of nervous breakdowns.

"Excuse me," I said, eventually. "We were after Mr. Quigg. We don't have an appointment, but it's urgent. Any chance of seeing him?"

"Oh, he's on his coffee break." Her left hand was tangled into the tong-straightened locks of her tight ponytail. She didn't leave off playing with the strands even when she had to take a message. She simply slammed on the speakerphone before searching for her mislaid pen. I was getting an excellent idea of the sort of problems they dealt with here. "You could try the café."

"Won't he mind?"

The girl didn't reply. Mirela tugged at me. She understood what I hadn't; you took your chances with the Agency for Change.

We followed the savoury scents down to the café. It was warm and buzzed with chatter. A woman with a face severed by premature lines was serving two office girls frothy coffees. Otherwise the café was filled with blokes. Some had the oil of car maintenance under their fingernails, or guitars slung over the backs of their chairs, but there were several dependable-looking fiftyish guys in suits and I thought Mr. Quigg could be any of these. We went up to the counter.

"What can I get you?" said the woman. She had a faint Polish accent—something you hear a lot around Bridgwater.

"Nothing," said Mirela. "We are speak to Mr. Quigg." But her eyes had grown huge, like a child at a sweet counter, as she looked at the display of cakes.

"Hang on, we could have something. My shout. D'you fancy a doughnut, Mirela?"

"*Paczki*," said the woman. "Polish doughnuts with strawberry filling, sprinkled with orange peel as well as sugar. Very nice."

"Yum," I agreed. "We'll have two, and one tea and a—"

"Coffee," said Mirela. She wandered off, weaving between tables, while I paid for our order.

"In Poland," the woman behind the counter continued, "we say that if you don't eat a single *paczki*, you will have bad luck all year long. So we all eat them at the carnival on *tlusty czwartek*—Fat Thursday."

"That's so interesting," I said, wondering if every new customer was offered a little Polish food story when they came in. "When is Fat Thursday?"

"The week before Lent begins."

"Great day for stocking up on your consumption of doughnuts," I joked, recalling the way Gloria and Philip always gave up chocolate for Lent (and had expected the three of us kids to lay off it, as well).

Mirela had settled at a table in a far corner of the café, where a man was drinking coffee. He stood to offer me his hand as I made my way over.

"It's Fergus, Fergus Quigg."

"Er ... Sabbie Dare." For a second, I'd forgotten my own name, mostly because Fergus had a gaze that captured you and refused to let you go. His eyes were small but as blue as wild speedwell.

He was not dowdy or middle-aged at all. Hair the colour and texture of wild grasses was caught in a black elastic band, and his face was shadowed by a day-old beard. He wasn't a tall man, but his thigh muscles were defined against his jeans. If he'd been English, his build would have been described as "of yeoman stock," but soon as he spoke I knew he was Irish. He had a gentle, soft-rain accent that managed to hint he could keep his own counsel, under all sorts of duress. I grasped his hand. Warm, it felt, and it applied just enough pressure to make someone feel … mmm … *cared for*. I tried contrasting it with the touch of Rey's hand, which was rougher, as if he didn't sit at a desk all day long—or care for you much, either, despite the handshake.

"Thank you for seeing us at short notice."

"No problem," said Fergus, directing me to an empty chair, his hand lightly across my back. "I'm always delighted to meet anyone with the same interest in the dispossessed as I have."

"Right." I wasn't sure how to respond to that. "I guess you remember Kizzy Brouviche, Mirela's sister?"

"Indeed." He lowered his voice a little. "I recall that the older Miss Brouviche had a strong influence over her sister."

I glanced at Mirela. Her mouth was in a pout and she was staring down at her hands, tight around her bag.

Fergus turned towards her. "When you came last time, I recommended you both leave your employment at Papa Bulgaria. Have you been thinking about that?"

"Huh?" Mirela flashed a panicked look at me.

"That isn't really why we're here," I began, but at that point, our order arrived.

"Thanks, Maria," Fergus said for us.

"You are welcome," said the woman, and topped up his cup with coffee from a jug.

"Mirela spent the night before last at my house," I said. "She hasn't seen or heard from Kizzy since the Bridgwater Carnival."

Fergus nodded for a while. Pale lashes fluttered almost shut over his eyes, as if he liked to think before replying. "You know, that's a constant problem. When you're from another country, you can disappear like morning mist."

"Why would she go away with almost less than a goodbye to her sister?"

"Did she tell you where she was going, Mirela?"

"No," said Mirela, and bit into her *paczki*.

"That's our problem," I pointed out. "Where to start searching."

"Perhaps Kizzy doesn't want to be found," said Fergus. "She had a good dose of spirit in her."

"You deal with this sort of thing a lot?"

He nodded. "We're here as advocates for people who find themselves in the UK without the right papers or much knowledge of how the systems work."

"I'm surprised Bridgwater keeps you busy."

"The Agency for Change is a national charity, at least where it can afford to be. The Bridgwater office covers all of Somerset." Fergus pushed his chair away from the table so that he could cross his legs. "That's from Yeovil right through to the Severn Estuary. And we're always strapped for cash, of course, seeing the government doesn't give us a groat."

"What would you advise Mirela to do?"

"Her first step is to go to the police station and report her sister officially missing."

Mirela screwed up her face. "*Politie?*"

"I promise you, all they'll do is take the details, file and distribute them."

"Not *politie*. Kizzy no like."

Fergus's gaze flickered at me, as if this confirmed everything.

"How much do you know about the takeaway, Papa Bulgaria?" I asked him. "Mirela says that this chap—Stanislaus—went over to Bulgaria and told Mirela and Kizzy they would earn four euros an hour, without explaining how little that is."

"This sort of racket goes on a lot, of course, now the European Union is almost a passportless state. There's an EU quota for the food processing industries, but they wriggle underneath."

"Yes," I said, lowering my voice. "But in the case of Romanies, I don't think they're here under any quota."

Fergus took a sip of his coffee. He seemed to need a lot of deliberation time. "Papa Bulgaria is a complicated set-up. Agency for Change has been investigating it for a while. Looking at back records it's clear the firm can easily obtain passports in Bulgaria. The workers seem to think this is magic; they'll agree to anything after that. When they came to see me, I could only recommend to the Misses Brouviche that they got out immediately."

"It seems to be a matter of honour, working with people from back home. Hoping for what you've been promised."

"It all looks legit, from the outside, at least. But from the very start, the workers owe large amounts of money. They pay by installment for their passport and journey here, which costs a lot less than they imagine. I've been trying to nail down the illegalities for months. Jesus, it's not my job, but I enjoy prizing information out of these low-lifes, showing them up for what they are. There's an element of satisfaction in it. So I have done a little digging on Mr. Papazov."

I gawped. "Is that really his name?"

"Yes. He's lived in Somerset for a number of years. He's got two shops, one here and one in Finchbury. He also owns residential property. You'd guess where Papazov scores there."

"Does he use it for the workers' accommodation?"

"He does," said Fergus, tapping a finger on the tabletop. "And charges whatever he likes for rent. When the first pay cheque arrives, it's almost in negative equity. They can't live on their docked wage packets, so they're offered loans to top them up—at exorbitant interest rates."

I let my jaw drop. "It's a complete scam!"

"It's reprehensible."

"Why aren't the police interested?"

"Oh, they are. Papazov has a nasty reputation. But he also has friends. He's generous to the right people. And these things are hard to prove."

"So his workers put up with it."

"They don't know the country, they don't know their rights. As far as I can see, most of the previous workers wandered off in the end; no doubt they dissolve into the underbellies of big cities."

I nodded. I'd been wondering if Kizzy had gone to Bristol, or even London. This seemed to confirm it. But Mirela was staying loyal to the firm. She wasn't buying into anything that involved authority. I turned to her. "Why are you so dead against going to the police? Has Mr. Papazov told you you'll get into trouble?"

Mirela looked up from her coffee cup. Her face had taken on a pinched looked. I realized that this was what she feared; people talking about her, over her head, in a language she was still coming to grips with. Had she chosen a shaman in the hope I was off the grid and would do things without involving authority? Two years ago, she'd've been right. But now, with a mortgage in my name, I was getting towards respectable-citizen status. Maybe I should be as worried about that as she was. "I can see Fergus wants to help you," I said. "We can both help in different ways."

"Ah, light is dawning," said Fergus. "You're some kind of investigator. You're not a journalist?"

"I couldn't write for toffee."

"Right, so, a journalist then." He caught my eye. "I'm teasing. But I blame the press for a lot of my client's problems. The tabloids especially are not kind to outsiders. I'd like to ban the sweeping statements they're prone to make, all of them inflammatory. They lack the empathy to know that we are all outsiders … of one kind or another."

"I check that box," I agreed. I slid my business card over the table.

He glanced at it, then at me. "Shaman? That's surprising."

"There aren't many in Bridgwater. I pretty much have a monopoly."

He flicked a smile at me. "I'm surprised you haven't found Kizzy Brouviche already. Don't you just … er … spin round and round then fall down, or something?" He'd managed to trap my gaze again. His massive lashes swept up and down like geisha fans. "Ah, what I would give to watch you spin and fall!"

If he thought I wouldn't be able to cope with a mild bit of flirting, he was wrong. "I always take practical steps before I start to spin. Otherwise the spirit world would be inundated with requests, wouldn't it? They'd have to form queues or issue tickets or something, then where would a shaman be?"

"So, spinning aside, what have you come up with?"

I glanced Mirela, but she was zoned out of the conversation. She had polished off her *paczki* and was looking at my report, her finger moving in turn to each little sketch. "We need a bit of grounded help. Where would you start asking around?"

"If Kizzy is using her real name, and I can't see why she shouldn't, she may have booked into a hostel somewhere."

I'd only met Kizzy once, but my image of her was clear; the last of the squibs raining down as she approached us in the lane wearing a centimetre of makeup and bright-red ruffles. I didn't think she was really in the business of fortunetelling; she'd just seized the opportunity to make some extra cash. I lowered my voice. "I can't help thinking that she's been enticed onto the game."

"I'm sad to say a lot of these girls do end up in the sex industry. From the outside, the money seems good."

"She wouldn't get a lot of ... trade ... in Bridgwater."

"Ah, it's not that bright and shiny. And Taunton isn't far away. There are dance clubs and massage parlours that hide behind a very thin veneer of decorum. Besides, she could be anywhere."

"Do you think she's gone off properly? London, say."

"I can't tell you. How could I?"

"Couldn't you check?"

"I can contact hostels across the country legitimately, but the sex industry is an unwholesome place of work. They don't like questions asked."

"I saw Kizzy at the carnival. I'm worried because it's where the policeman was shot."

"Really? The detective that died? Jesus and Mary. But surely she isn't involved with that?"

I glanced down at my plate. I hadn't even started on my doughnut. I didn't want Fergus to see me with sugar and orange peel all
round my mouth. I took a discreet sip of tea. "I suppose you meet
people from all over the world."

"I do, at times."

"If someone was black but had a French surname, where might
they come from?"

"Oh," said Fergus, rubbing at his blond stubble. "Algeria, or the
Congo? Then there's Morocco ... Chad ... the list is extensive." I
nodded at him, pretending to be less interested than I was. "Senegal,
of course. Africa springs to mind first, but on the other side of the
Atlantic, there's quite a few French-speaking Caribbean countries.
Does that help?"

"Helped confuse me, I think!"

"You don't look the sort to be easily confused."

He took another sip of coffee and put the cup on its saucer. I
fancied Fergus was also a sort—the sort that trifled with every female who crossed his path. It might have been fun to bat chat-up
lines for longer, but Mirela had stuffed my report back in her bag
and was already on her feet.

"We go, I think," she said.

"Thank you, both of you, for coming in. I'll be certain to put my
ear to the ground." He was so good at making a person feel they
were important to him. He fingered my business card. "I'll be in
touch."

Suddenly, she was the chirpy, buoyant Mirela again. She slid her
arm into mine and yanked me away from my *paczki*. She was the
height and weight of an Italian greyhound but with the same super-
strength. We were waltzing away from the table before I could draw
breath. "See you soon, Mr. Quigg!" she called from across the café.

She dropped her voice and hissed to me as I was shoved along. "I have idea. Yes. Great idea. Come quick, I tell."

––––––

"Mirela," I began, as soon as we were in the street. "That was a bit rude. Mr. Quigg hadn't really finished speaking." I didn't bother mentioning the fact I hadn't finished eating; the doughnut would only have given me face spots and a zip problem.

"Quigg! He open mouth, go yak ... yak ... but nothing come out. What he say that any good?"

"He is going to check the hostels. Surely that's a start?" I didn't want to admit that so far, both Brouviche sisters were uncomfortably living up to the Roma stereotypes. Neither seemed to have any respect for Fergus's authority at all.

"This much important than Quigg." Mirela pulled my report from her bag and pointed to the picture of the wolf. "Tell me 'gain about places?"

"In my journey, I was told to look in the place of blame, the place of no escape, the place of absolution, and the dark place. But I don't have any idea where any of these might be. Why, do you?"

"Yes, 'course! Place of blame is Mr. Papa's shop." She had a clear, bright look in her eyes.

"Mirela, that is the one place Kizzy is not."

"But for sure, is place of blame."

I nodded, remembering what Fergus had just described.

"Wolf told you. Look in place of blame."

"I'm sure I can imagine."

"Only worker imagine."

"Yeah, but ..."

"You find out! When you get job!"

I dawned on me finally that when Mirela said something, she usually meant it literally.

Fergus was the only person investigating the Papa Bulgaria scam, how it was run on cheap, almost slave labour. Because the police couldn't act—possibly they couldn't be bothered to act—without sufficient evidence.

"You want me to work at Papa Bulgaria?"

"*Da!*"

Bridgwater is a place where a dark skin tone stands out like a monk's habit in a karate club, so at Papa's shop I might appear to be something I was not; desperate, far from home, penniless. An interview for a job would be a good way to meet the owner of Papa Bulgaria and find out what people really got paid. After all, I didn't have to take the job, did I?

"Mirela," I asked, "have you ever met Mr. Papazov?"

"He come one time a week. Wednesday, do numbers."

"Would I see him if I applied for a job?"

She nodded. "This is good. This ver' good, Sabbie. This is real investigate."

"Right," I said. "You get me an interview with Mr. Papa, and in the meantime, we go to the police and report Kizzy missing. Is that a deal?"

"Okay," said Mirela. And she grinned like a teenager who had just got all her own way.

———

Mirela and I parted company when we reached Wemdon Road, her to go to work and me to fetch Hermes from the railings outside her lodgings. But when I got back, my bike was nowhere to be seen. I stupidly walked up and back down the entire street, unsure which house railings I'd chained it to. But when I looked closer, I spotted my bike chain, tossed into the narrow strip of front garden. The links had been sliced through with a bolt cutter. I stood with them in my hand, gawping. Then I walked up the path and hammered on the front door.

Petar the lanky lad opened it. When he saw me, his face transformed into what he considered to be his charm offensive. Offensive it certainly felt. I raised the chain so that it was between our eyes. "Know anything about this?"

"No, nothing," he said, sealing his guilt.

"I'm going to report the theft to the police and name you as number-one suspect, using this as my evidence."

He curled his fist around the chain, so that our hands brushed together. The contact made me shudder and I pulled away, but as I did so, he yanked, and the chain shot through my fingers, scratching and burning as it went. He hurled the chain into the house; it skidded across the ancient linoleum and curled itself around a chair leg.

"Good luck," he said. And slammed the door.

I went on knocking for over ten minutes, but no one came. By then, my hands were sore and shaking with fury. I'd forgotten: the Greek god Hermes was a tricksy little bugger when he wanted to be. He had winged sandals so that he could lift off and disappear whenever he chose.

EIGHT

"I can't believe it," said Marianne. "You plan to get a job serving in a takeaway?"

It was early on Tuesday evening and we were sitting at the patio table in my garden. It was cloudless and bitterly cold, but that meant we had a fabulous view of the full moon—an ancient silver coin hanging above us.

The moon had risen almost immediately after the sun had set, and Marianne had come round straight from work. We were drinking in moon-glow.

Marianne was an executive for a public relationship company. In her working life she dealt with flow charts and Venn diagrams ... whatever they were. She was from Holland, where everything's contained within dikes and ditches, and I knew she liked to have her life tightly controlled. She was as willowy and preened as the storks you see on Dutch roofs, and we'd been shamanic buddies for over a year now. She usually came round for the full moon so we could bathe under it—last summer, if we were positive no one could see, we skinny-dipped in the moonbeams. This evening though, skinny-dipping was not on the cards. We were bundled into layers of coats and scarves with added duvets.

I had explained my journey in the wolf forest to Marianne. She knew I would not give her Mirela's name, but we always managed to chew over cases without IDing my clients. Then I'd told her about Fergus Quigg and Mr. Papazov, and the interview arranged with him tomorrow at lunchtime.

"Guardians love to nudge people into things," I hazarded.

"Why would they nudge you into taking a dead-end job?"

"I don't have to take it," I said. "The interview is ... research. The spirit wolf might have been talking of Papa's shop when he told me to look in the place of blame. It was the first thing in my client's mind, at least. No harm in snooping around."

"But the takeaway wouldn't want their staff to leave," Marianne pointed out.

"Okay, but someone who works there might have information about her, perhaps without realizing it. Anyway, they're running a massive scam that involves conning innocent people. I'm as keen as Fergus to find out what's going on at Papa Bulgaria."

Marianne gave me one of her Dutch looks. "Perhaps you are keen on Fergus too?"

I tried not to grin. "He's charming ... actually he's quite a flirt, but we have a professional relationship. And *anyway*," I said, scowling at Marianne because she had started to chuckle, "it's more to do with cash flow."

"Cash flow?"

"Yeah. Cash is flowing out of my account and not even trickling back in."

"It's probably a seasonal dip."

"I'm a householder, Marianne, I can't afford dips."

"You are mad. They'll pay you nothing. You would better spend your time finding clients for what you are good at—your therapy work."

"Okay." There was no point in arguing. For a start, she was right. I gazed up at the moon and tried to take my mind off Mirela. "It would be nice to meet like this for the seasonal festivals. You know, celebrate the wheel of the year."

"Ah," said Marianne. "I've seen that in my own country, rituals for the solstices. The next one would be the Winter Solstice."

"Yule is more meaningful to us than Christmas, wouldn't you say?"

"I'd like that. I have some friends who are Wiccan, you know."

"No," I said, my ears pricked. "I didn't know that."

"Avalon and Teddy. They were the priest and priestess of a coven near Glastonbury. But it imploded."

I laughed. Marianne's English is impeccable, so I had to assume she didn't mean exploded. I had an inappropriate but enjoyable image of black pointy hats and broomsticks all melding into a black cauldron. "There's Garth and Stella too," I said. "The couple I met last spring. The parents of the little boy who was snatched?"

Marianne winced. "I remember."

I nodded in recognition of the memories. Garth and Stella had spent almost two weeks not knowing if their son was alive or dead, but the experience brought them back together spiritually, and I thought they might be interested in celebrating Yule.

"That is six persons. A good number for a small ritual."

"Sounds great."

We lapsed into silence. The moon glowed down on us, transforming the garden to silver. After a while, Marianne said, "We should make a wish. You first."

We often made a wish or a challenge to ourselves, when there was a full moon. I threw off my wraps and stood up. I could feel the sheen of moon-glow. I sucked in a deep breath of it and focused on the pure, round beauty of the winter moon.

"I need to be shown," I began. What did I need to be shown? "O moon goddess—grant me insight! Am I taking the right route with my new client? Are my decisions the best decisions for her? For me? Where is the place of blame? Is it Papa Bulgaria? What might I find there?" I picked up the bowl that stood on the table. We'd filled it with red spring water from Glastonbury, so that the moonbeams would saturate it and make it even more powerful. Its icy bitterness slid into my stomach. I felt I had swallowed my answer, and all I had to do was wait for it to materialize. I passed the bowl to Marianne.

"I would ask one thing of the goddess," she said. She was staring into the bowl, scrying the water. "To grant, in this season of gathering darkness, safe passage to Geoff's father, that he may leave this Earth with ease and peace."

I knew that Geoff was Marianne's partner. He was an IT consultant and a really nice guy. She hadn't told me that his father was dying. No doubt she would when she was ready. Silently, we picked up the wrappings we'd tossed aside and went into the kitchen, leaving the bowl of water to lap up the moonlight.

I sliced a new-baked loaf and unwrapped some cheese. We needed to bring ourselves down from the moon and onto *terra firma*. Marianne uncorked the wine she'd brought. I put on some Celtic music because we were in the mood for pipe and bodhran.

We sat on the sofa balancing our plates on our knees and I was lifting the first mouthful to my lips when the doorbell chimed.

"Damn."

"People always call when you least want or expect," said Marianne.

"Yeah, why can't they come round just as you've finished cleaning the house instead?"

The bloke in my porch was tall, with very white skin, as though he rarely saw the sun. Even his scalp was white; I could see it glow through a ruler-straight parting in black hair that was bottle-dyed to hide the grey. His moustache was tidily trimmed and as black as the hair above it. He was in a tidy black suit. A thin tie was restrained against his shirt by a fat enamel tie pin. He carried a black case.

Cold caller, I thought. I'd brought my glass of wine to the door, in readiness to shoo an unwelcome visitor away.

"Good evening."

I sipped my wine, taking the path of least commitment.

"Isn't it a beautiful world God has given us?"

I grinned at him, in the mood to shock. "Or the goddess."

He pressed his lips together, displeased, and the moustache jerked like a salute. "God's great love is free for everyone. We are walking from door to door, so that people in this town can have the chance to learn more about that."

"I'm afraid none of this is of interest to me."

"You are not interested in God's love?"

I wasn't going to answer his trick questions. The man shook a flyer at me. "We are requesting that you take time out to peruse this short leaflet and join us in our mission to live our lives to the glory of the Lord."

I kept my hands behind my back. "Is this like the Mormons, something like that?"

"We're a smaller group who invite you to worship and pray with us on Friday evenings. We love and follow the Lord and fight the devil."

Devil. That word didn't often enter my world, but I hadn't forgotten Andy Comer's hiss ... *you have heard the voice of the devil* ... as he ripped up my letter to Drea, and that hiss reminded me of the journey I'd taken for her, the way the snake had reared and attacked me. In an odd kind of way, this man in his shiny suit reminded me of Anaconda.

"I'm sorry. I'm not interested." I tried closing the door, but he got himself bodily inside the frame. He might profess not to be a salesman, but he certainly knew the techniques.

"Young people like you need a faith in their lives."

I stepped back in sheer amazement. He stepped into the gap. He was almost in my hall and for the first time I felt a little worried.

"I would like you to go away now," I said.

"I can see it in your eyes that you need the love of Jesus. Poor child, you're moving through life without a direction." He lifted his chin and his voice seemed to follow. "Taking in wine and pleasure instead of God's goodness. I ask the Lord to offer you repentance so that you can find the way—so your life can be enriched and your soul saved!"

"I'm not lost. I believe in the ancient gods."

He frowned. Telling people with missionary zeal that I'm a pagan is usually sufficient to put them off—send them howling down the path—and I was hoping that this guy was ready to take the hint. I wasn't in the mood for a theological debate with a stranger.

"God's love is for everyone. So many young people—"

"Not this young person. Try elsewhere." I started to push the door against his shiny leather shoe. "Down the road. There's some young people in need of … whatever it was …"

His moustache looked satisfied with the promise of further pickings. He began to move back over the doorstep. "Which number would that be?"

"I dunno," I said, in desperation. "Try the newly painted house."

Finally, I was able to get the door tight shut. But through the spy-hole I could see that he hadn't budged from my porch. We were standing on opposite sides of a closed door. Maybe he was thinking that if he hung around I'd open up again.

A few seconds ticked by. Then my letterbox flap opened, making a wild snapping sound. I jumped. A sort of yelp came out of me. The flyer he'd been hawking fluttered onto the doormat.

"Horrid," said Marianne, coming into the hallway. I nearly fell on her neck, she looked so in charge and together in her tribal print top and slim leg black jeans. "I heard it all." She picked up the cream-coloured flyer.

CORE
Children of the Revelation Enlightenment
The Time of the Second Coming is at Hand
The Rev Eric Atkinson and his congregation implore you
to listen to the message of
The LORD of the REVELATION
We meet to worship, pray, and praise God each Friday
Seven p.m. at Charter Hall, Bridgwater.
The children of the lord will be saved first.

"CORE... never heard of them," said Marianne.

"Never want to again." I tossed the flyer into the recycling and we returned to our little feast and our plans for the Winter Solstice, but I couldn't quite shift the memory of this Eric Atkinson person, leaning in too close to me, trying to make out who I was. I'd felt his power ooze from him like mustard gas... arrogant, even vengeful, the sort of guy who sought out vulnerable people because he knew they made the best converts... he'd as good as told me so... young people who are lost. I was sorry I'd mentioned Drea's house. I'd been too keen to get him away from my own front door to think about what might happen at theirs. His oozing presence had robbed me of my wits. But it would be okay. Andy would be at home. Andy would bulldoze him off the porch step. He'd bulldozed me, quick enough.

———

Daybreak Wednesday. It was half-seven and icy cold in the garden. The hens fell over their skinny little legs to get into the run as I put down their hopper of pellets. All except Florence, who was busy making eyes at Kaiser the cockerel. Despite his youth, he was already lording it over the females. I swear Florence was wiggling her tail feathers at him. "You tart!" I chucked some extra feed her way.

I'd never clapped eyes on a hen until I went to live with Gloria's family. The first thing that Dennon had said to me as I rolled my suitcase up the front step of the Davidsons' terraced house was, "Hope you like getting up early on Sundays."

"What?" I'd replied. Come to think of it, that was almost all I ever did say, back then, apart from the longer version, *wha'ever*. I was coming up thirteen and as angrily inarticulate as it was possible to be.

"Sundays. Crap. All day."

"What?"

"Church at nine in the morning. Yeah, and she *makes* you go. Then it's *the walk*."

"*What?*"

"That's Dad's department, the walking."

"What, back from the church?"

"You'd be lucky. It's all over the friggin' fields."

"What fields?"

He'd sniffed. "You'll see."

"I bloody won't see. I don't get pushed around."

But the first time Philip made me get in the car with Dennon, Gloria, Charlene, and a pair of boots, all I actually said was, "*Wha'ever*."

It wasn't just fields. We had walked through woods and pine forests, along tow paths, around lakes, up little hills, farther up bigger hills, and sometimes along ridgeways. But we always stopped for a picnic or a pub meal if it was wet and often took in something nice to see ... a ruined castle or a craft centre or something. I liked the petting farms best, got quite into the ugly goats and dippy sheep, but I definitely fell in love with hens. They're feathered like queens and feel as soft as duvets when you pick them up.

When I moved into Harold Street and started tilling the soil (as Philip puts it), it seemed natural to get some. I chose ex-battery hens, the sort without feathers and a lifetime of "stuff" that no analyst could attempt to heal. I named them all after aromatherapy oils, in case it helped. Someone gave me a not-so-sweet-smelling cockerel—Cocky Bastard—ready and willing for chicken nooky morning, noon, and evening, but not one chick was born of his seed, as ex-bats don't get broody.

Then one night, a fox got in. A fox, hen-keepers tell me, will always eventually get in, whatever you do. I was left with three hens, which became nine when a farmer called Sandy gave me some chicks. One of those sadly died from a mysterious chicken illness and another turned out to be a very cocky male... definitely a Kaiser. I called the new girls after pop singers. Don't know if that was irony, because I'm never sure what that is. So now I have six hens to talk to: Florence, Emili, Jessie, Rihanna, and the final two of the old-timers Melissa and Ginger.

"What am I going to do about Drea?" I asked the hens. Seeing her in Papa Bulgaria on Sunday evening, and stupidly sending the mustard-gas preacher up to her house, had started me thinking again. The journey I took for her still made me shiver. I thought about her reaction to what I'd said in Papa Bulgaria. She must think I was even weirder than before. But if she could read the letter I'd put so much thought into, I was sure she'd understand.

There were a ton of things needing doing in the garden on a dry early winter's day like this one if I was going to eat next year, most urgently, spreading the pile of horse manure I'd got free from a riding stable. When it had arrived in old horse food bags, I'd piled it into a steaming heap. But now it was dry and crumbly and ready for the veg beds. I pulled on some gardening gloves and got to grips with it.

Once my muck had been spread, I took a shower and printed out a copy of Drea's letter. Over my breakfast egg, I read it through. It looked innocuous to me; Andy couldn't have read it properly before tearing it into pieces and demanding I never speak to his wife again. But every weekday Andy was at work in his insurance office.

I placed six of my eggs in a box and shrugged myself into my coat.

The gate squeaked as I walked up Drea's side path. She opened the door before I could knock and stared at me without speaking—without even altering her expression. She examined me as if I was a rather unloved pet who had gone missing and returned smelling of the sewers. I wasn't sure if she was going to kick me off the path or offer a saucer of milk.

"I've brought you some eggs," I began, thrusting them forwards.

She took them without complaint—without acknowledge-ment—hugging the box to her solar plexus. It was the first time I'd seen her without her outdoor garments, but I wasn't surprised that she was wrapped warmly in a hip-length cardi over a high-necked shirt of mauve brushed cotton and a flared tartan skirt.

"I don't mean to quarrel with you, Drea, or persuade you of any-thing. Or pry into your business, but—"

"Don't mean to pry?" Her tone was mocking, but it quavered.

"I do realize that you might not want to see the results of my shamanic journey, but it is part of my Reiki treatment. I've brought over a letter explaining some of what I saw in your otherworld. When we talked the other night … I didn't make much sense … "

"It's not that I don't believe you want to help." She looked pre-ternaturally cold, as if haunted. Her ice temple spirit world was not far away. "You can't help. You *can't*."

"I guess that's true. But I do feel that … that you need help, Drea."

"Please—don't—interfere. You don't know about me. You don't know anything."

I leaned away. A swift kick from her lace-up house shoes seemed in the offing. "It's your husband, isn't? You're terrified of him. I do understand."

"How did you..." Her eyes widened. "You talked to him. And you knew... about the baby." Her cold hand slid round my wrist. "It's bad, seeing things, *knowing* things. It's a sin."

"I don't see into the future as such Drea, but on a shamanic journey, time disappears all together. I get sensations, images, symbols. Read my letter and you'll see."

She was biting her lower lip. "I thought I was safe here. It's a nice place, isn't it, Bridgwater?"

"Oh great," I said, hoping sarcasm wasn't creeping into my voice. Nightlife: pathetic. Shops: limited. Other facilities: they closed the swimming pool and keep promising to replace it. Then I thought about the atmosphere in town, and the solidarity of the carnival, how local people work to make it a winner every year. "Yeah," I said. "You're right. It's a nice place."

"I'd be sad to go. I don't want to go."

"I saw a snake," I said. "He talked about changing homes—moving on."

"A snake? There was a snake?"

I swallowed. "The snake told me that duty and purpose can change."

"But the snake has a creeping mind." Her voice had turned to steel. "The most accursed animal of the field."

There was a silence. My mouth opened and closed, but no sound came out. It felt as if I'd tumbled into a puzzle maze and had no idea of the exit. I made a decision to stuff the letter into my pocket, but in that second she snatched it out of my hand.

"Drea," I began. The door closed with a judder.

At least she hadn't kicked me down the path like a mangy cat.

NINE

At one in the afternoon, Papa Bulgaria had a row of hungry people on the embroidered cushions and Mirela was caught up with a queue of customers. I raised my hand in salute, but she hardly had the time to wave back. We'd agreed to meet after she'd finished work, anyhow.

Stanislaus was leaning against the counter with an order sheet in his hand, making himself heard above the TV. "Excuse me," I said, but he ignored me so I tapped him on one clearly defined shoulder blade. He turned his head, flicking his hair as he did so. "I'm here to see Mr. Papazov."

"Oh, you," he said. He lifted a hinged flap and I passed into the business side of the room. "Sabbie *Daar*."

"Yes."

"The friend of the Brouviches."

"That's right."

He pointed to a door to one side of the shop. "Up the stairs. Knock on door of the office. Mr. Papazov is waiting for you."

He managed to make it sound as if I was dreadfully late. I guess I was a couple of minutes overdue, but I became less and less keen with the entire idea each step I took up the grimy staircase. At the top, I knocked on the door as instructed and waited until I heard a grunt.

Behind a heavy desk, squeezed into one of those faux Victorian swivel chairs, was a thickset man with looming eyebrows and a jowl that would not have looked out of place on a bull mastiff. On the desk before him were a laptop, a pile of ledgers, an extremely fancy cordless phone, and a small crystal wine glass filled with a liquid the colour of mouthwash. Behind him, on the top of a filling cabinet next to a grimy window, was an old-fashioned cassette player, covered with fluff and smears of food. Music flowed from it, the sort of tune that makes you want to twirl until your skirts fly out in a circle—if you've got skirts to twirl, that is. I guessed that somewhere there was a cupboard of these cassettes from the old days that no one had thought to replace with something more digital.

"The music is good," I said.

"Why do you want job here?" growled Mr. Papazov. His accent wasn't as pushed into the background as Stan's, but nevertheless, this was a businessman who might chat to someone from the County Council with ease. He clicked shut the slim lid of the laptop and glared at me. His eyes were faded brown but penetrating.

By trying to peer into me, he'd offered a glimpse of the internal Papa. I felt faintly sick. I'd brought to mind Fergus Quigg's words... *Papazov has a nasty reputation.* I tried to lick my lips, but my tongue was too dry to do the job.

"Er ... Kizzy and Mirela. They told me there are good jobs here."

Papazov seemed to swallow this whole. Maybe he actually believed that his staff were content, or maybe he was just good at closing down his reactions. "So, you need a job bad?"

"Yeah," I lied, playing the part. "Just part-time though." It seemed
like a contradiction, but he didn't query it.

"You ever done work like this?"

"I've got pub experience."

"There are two daily shifts. Eleven a.m. to five, and four p.m. to
ten. The roster is worked out by Stanislaus."

"I wouldn't want to do more than three shifts a week. Earlier in
the week, rather than later." I gave myself a mental poke. I wasn't
planning to work here at all. Just snoop around.

"Many of my staff do double shifts for more money."

I nodded. I bet they did. With all their earnings stolen away from
them, Mr. Papazov's workforce became a company of slaves.

"Where d'you live, now? You want better accommodation?"

"No, I'm okay for housing, thank you."

"You live local? You know the area?"

"Yes, well, I've lived here a few years."

"Serve or scoot?"

"What?"

"Locals can earn more by delivering."

"Right. How much more?"

"We like hard workers. Harder work, more pay. Can you ride
scoot?"

"What? Oh . . . ride a scooter." My cheeks lost their warmth. My
past relationship with two-wheeled vehicles was chequered to say
the least. "I've owned a Honda bike."

"You've got UK licence?"

I scrabbled in my bag, pushing the contents round … purse, gloves, picture of all the Davidsons outside the caravan, half a bag of imperial mints. When I finally flapped my licence in front of him, he hardly glanced at it.

"I'll give you a very nice scoot for delivering," he growled. "Ver' cheap second-hand cost—six hundred and fifty all in."

"You're telling me I pay for this scooter?"

"It is yours to keep. Keep and drive when you like. There's no markings on scoot, just the helmet. We give you the helmet," Papazov added, as if he was Santa.

"And … is there paperwork? To say I keep the scoot—er— scooter?"

A scooter was a tempting proposition, cheaper to drive than my Mini, and infinitely better than my stolen bicycle. I thought about the morality of getting deliberately caught up in Mr. Papazov's grimy game for at least half a second. He was ripping off his employees and I didn't see anything very wrong in ripping him off as well.

"Of course, paperwork." Papazov's voice grated along in a low gear, sounding faintly and disconcertingly Russian.

"What's the arrangement? How much of my wage will you take out to pay for the scooter?"

"You'll need to ask my son. He deals with wages."

"Your son?"

"Stanislaus."

I followed him down the bare painted stairs.

Mr. Papazov opened the door to the kitchen with one shoulder. The smell was overpowering as spices burst and meats seared. The gleam from the surfaces made me blink. The room was fully tiled from ceiling to floor in white and lit with fluorescent strips. The worktops were equipped with a large sink and several gas burners, and there was a long stainless-steel island in the centre filled with chopping boards and sharp knives.

"It's very clean," I said.

"You think Bulgarian kitchen would be dirty?"

"No, no, of course I didn't—"

"You think we are *all* gypsies here?"

"You mean Roma?"

"Roma? *Tsiganski*. Gypsies. Like your friends." To my horror, he tossed his head away from me and spat on the gleaming tiles. "Dirty, lazy beggars."

It took me a second or two to realize he was using the words in their literal sense. "Mirela and Kizzy don't beg."

"Ha!" He flashed a glance at me. "You do not understand them at all. You are not their friends. They *have* no friends." He raised his voice. " Jimmy! Clear this up!"

A young boy in a white apron and little white cap skidded past with a J-Cloth and a spray gun of cleaner and bent over the gob of spit.

Papazov strode over to the far side of the kitchen, where a deliverer was sorting through the takeaways in their white, green, and red cardboard boxes. "Max! Take Highgate order first." He snatched a cardboard box from the delivery guy's hands and pointed him to another pile. "Soup and mix salad; be fast to keep hot. Petar! Careful not to break."

At a pair of sinks under the window, the lanky lad from Mirela's lodgings was aproned up over a t-shirt with damp sleeve hems. Bubbles floated from the water in the sink. Petar was the washer-up in this establishment. I grinned. The lowest of the low.

Stanislaus came into the kitchen behind us holding a bundle of orders. I saw him half glower at his father and thought that Mr. Papazov probably didn't work here very often, but when he did, he threw his weight around without knowing what was going on.

Papazov turned to Stan. "You want that I hire this one?"

"Yeah, cool." Stanislaus grinned at me. "Come over here, I'll show you ropes."

I was still watching the young cook mop up the spit. The elder Mr. Papazov had snatched his apron strings and hauled him upright almost before he'd finished the job. "Jimmy," he said, yanking him over to where a chopping board sat on a working top. "This batch. This pork for the Kavarma. How you cut this? It is completely wrong."

"But," said Jimmy. "I didn't do it." His Somerset accent seemed to blur the words, but then I realized he was shaking with fear. He was skinny, even for his age, half the girth of the middle-aged Papazov.

The older man brought back his arm. I could see the boy knew, long seconds before the fist struck his jaw, that he would be hit. He didn't duck or step away. He took the punishment. This wasn't the first time.

"Who prepare this meat?"

The boy flinched at the words, as if they held more pain than had the blow. "Me. I'll do it again."

"Good."

I stood motionless, gripping my bag much tighter than it needed. My heart beat was filling my entire chest cavity.

"Good boy, Jimmy." He ruffled the boy's hair with plump fingers bound tight with gold rings.

Suddenly Stanislaus was beside me. He flicked at his fringe and a shock of blue shot through the hair like the flit of a butterfly. He spoke in fast Bulgarian to his father and Papazov replied, his voice the sound of beach pebbles moving under the force of the tide.

"Okay, Sabbie *Daar*," said Stan. "I'll show you the scoots. Trial ride." He put a hand on my shoulder. It felt like he wanted to run it over my breast.

"I don't think I'll bother showing you my driving skills," I said. "I've got eyes in my head. The staff get hit. Why would I want to be hit?"

"No one would hit a nice girl like you." Stan's customary cocktail stick bobbed up and down. "But if workers are lazy, yeah, they need to know. They take the blame, of course."

Jimmy *had* taken the blame; I was sure he hadn't cut that meat.

"I haven't been told my wage," I demanded. "What's the pay rate? Is it in my contract? How much would I actually take home at the end of the month?"

His pace slowed. "You ask a lot of questions."

"Mirela told me she got paid well and it was nice here."

Stan gave a deep sigh as if I represented all the trials in his life. "You earn eight pounds an hour as well as keeping the vehicle. The scooter payment is ten percent of its value per month. It's tax-and-insured ready to drive and in ten months, you own it outright."

I pointed to a Yamaha parked right under the shelter. It had to be at least 900cc and its black and brushed gold paintwork shone. "I'll have that one," I joked.

"That one is not for the staff." Clearly, Stan could not take a joke.

"Is it yours, Stan?"

"No. It's parked, that's all. This one will be yours."

Stan was ushering me towards a rather yellowy white scooter that needed a good wash. I could guess that the market price for this old beast was nearer five hundred pounds. A thought came to me as I looked it over. "Is this the scooter Kizzy drove?"

"Why?" said Stan. "You sentimental over things like that?"

"I … I just wondered if she took her scooter with her." Although, looking at the lightweight frame, it would have taken her weeks to get to Bristol, let alone London.

"She's not ready for the roads of Bridgwater. She serves in the shop."

"D'you know where she's gone?"

"Don't know, don't care. I don't like the gypsies any more than my dad."

"Why do you employ them then, Stan?"

"Why d'you think?"

"Because they're cheap?"

"Hard work pays here," he said, echoing her father. "That's all you need to remember."

"Would you give Kizzy her job back if she wanted it?"

"Why should I? She upped and left us short. If she breezed in now, I'd sack her on the spot."

Suddenly I was even more determined to find out what the staff here really knew about Kizzy. I stuck a leg over the seat of the scooter. "Let's get on with this."

———

I met Mirela at half-seven outside the police station. It was raining hard, with a fast wind, the sort of weather that makes you feel a lot wetter than you actually are and a lot colder than you'd like to be. Mirela must have waited for a while, her face was so wet from rain it looked like she'd been crying. Maybe she had. Distress was rising from her in waves. I gave her a hug and felt her shoulders tremble.

"You okay about this?"

She nodded. Reporting Kizzy as a missing person had been a condition I'd given her; I could see she'd become determined, even though she looked terrified of entering a police station. She was very different than her sister. I doubted that Kizzy would have searched so hard for Mirela if the tables had been turned.

A clerk filled in a standard Missing Person's form. He asked for Kizzy's details plus a lot more about the sisters' status in the UK. It was plain that he didn't give a toss and reinforced this by telling us the police would not make an effort to find an adult who had announced she was going away before disappearing.

"Is Detective Inspector Rey Buckley on duty?"

"I've no idea, miss. Why d'you ask?"

"I think I mentioned Kizzy Brouviche to him. When he interviewed me about Gary Abbott's death."

The words *Gary Abbott's death* fired up his responses. He left immediately and within half a minute, he'd returned with Rey.

Rey managed a smile, but it didn't reach his eyes. Usually they glittered with a greenish tint, but this evening they were a dull brown. The stubble around his chin was transforming into a beard. I didn't think Rey would look good with a beard.

"This is Mirela Brouviche," I began. "She's the sister of the Roma."

He hadn't taken us anywhere private. We were standing in the reception area. At gone eight p.m. it was quiet. Most of the staff had already left for the day, and Rey's posture was reminding me that had been his plan too.

"What Roma?"

"The one that nicked Abbott's phone."

Mirela's eyes flashed. When the occasion called for it, she could be as hot-blooded a gypsy as her sister. "Brouviches do not steal!"

"She might have needed to, Mirela. She might have needed the money … to make a journey, or pay for glamour photos."

"She give to me money."

That was true; Kizzy had left the twenty pounds she'd made from Debs with her sister. Perhaps she really had believed that soon she would be loaded.

"Miss Brouviche," said Rey, "I'd like to interview you about your sister's disappearance. Would you agree to that?"

I knew that what Rey really meant was *your sister's proximity to the death of my colleague,* but Mirela's eyes widened with possibilities; someone was finally taking her case seriously. She scurried after Rey and I found myself once again sitting in the public area under a wall of wanted posters.

I spent my half-hour's wait worrying about what I planned to do next. The wolf had given me four cryptic places to look. *You will find little in some, and confusion in others,* he'd said. *In some you may be rewarded. Do not expect satisfaction from any answer.*

Even so, I'd already nailed one; the Papa Bulgaria takeaway shop was indeed full of blame. All the time I had been there—proving I could ride a scooter, learning the order system, poring over a map of the vast delivery area—an iciness had grown inside me. It had started as a maggot of misgiving eating at the wall of my stomach. Mr. Papazov was not in the running for smooth-talker of the year, and Stan was a sleazy sliver off the same chopping board, but it was more than that. The grease and dust and whirling music in Papa's office's had burrowed into me, until I only had half a mind on what Stan was saying. I'd nodded at intervals as it all floated above me, while in my head the music whirred round and round until I was back with the dancers in the forest, listening to the wolf. *The apparent world is where you must search.*

Now I intended to look for the dark place. I was running with the idea that Kizzy might think she'd make more money selling her body than selling bolyarska. Fergus's suggestion that she might have gone to a city seemed less likely now that I knew she didn't have a scooter. I fancied that there were plenty of dark places hidden in the towns of Somerset. *It's not that bright and shiny,* Fergus has said.

"Sabbie?" Mirela was tapping at my arm.

I jumped at her touch. Rey stood at a little distance. His face was almost grey. Disappointment and frustration was like a smell in the air. Mirela had been no help to Rey; he'd been no help to her.

I struggled up from the bench, unable to take my eyes from his. I could feel my heart's rhythm, but it was not racing; it had slowed to a dull *thud-thud*, as if it knew there was no hope for anything. Not for Kizzy or her sister. Not for Rey Buckley or me.

"We go, now," said Mirela. "They are pigs here too." She gestured behind her, a hand movement that might have been rude, but luckily was indecipherable to the British police force.

For several long seconds, I tried to sort out the golfing umbrella I'd brought. I was struggling at least as much with my thoughts as I was with the brolly. All I had to do was look up and say, *I've got loads of breakfast eggs at the moment* and throw him a smile of camaraderie. All he had to do was call my name.

"Sabbie," he said.

The umbrella was slowly sliding from my fingers. I hardly noticed that Mirela had caught it as it fell.

He was close now. No part of our clothing or skin touched, but if either of us had moved, that would change—everything would change. I was as rigid as a fossil; I wouldn't have been able to touch him even if I'd needed to.

"Sabbie, you're not getting caught up again, are you?"

"What?"

"You always have to do it, don't you? Meddle in the work of the professionals?"

I could feel my cheeks, then my neck and my ears, warm until they were pulsating. "Yeah, I recall," I said. "You think I'm a damn dumb civvy."

Rey had the grace to look discomfited. I turned on my heel. I was still boiling and only half-heard the last thing he said as I flung myself towards the exit.

"There's someone out there with a gun, Sabbie. Someone out there with a knife. Please take care."

TEN

MIRELA WAS WAITING ON the steps of the station, the umbrella already up. I let the door swing shut behind me. What had Rey meant? A gun and a knife? None of the reports on Abbott's murder had mentioned a knife. I thought about the death of the girl in the Dunball Wharf. Was he talking about that? Did he think that killer was still out there? I shook the thoughts out of my head and slid my arm through Mirela's lean one.

"We can do without them. We'll go about our own enquires. It's what the wolf said to me. *The apparent world is where you must search.*"

"Where?"

"The sort of places Kizzy could make money fast in Bridgwater. Dark places."

Mirela's sallow skin flushed to rose red. "You think she walk streets."

"No, but…" I took a breath. "We should at least eliminate the possibility. You know," I added, realizing that she might not, "massage parlours."

"Massage?" Mirela's forehead wrinkled, but she wasn't that innocent. "Where men pay for sex?"

I could see she hated the idea. Maybe there was a better move than this, but at the moment, my mind was a blank. The police were indifferent and Fergus had said he could only check legitimate hostels. That left me and Mirela to do the dirty work.

"We'll kick ourselves if we don't try."

"Kick?"

"What I've been thinking is that Kizzy might be trying to get some money together quickly, enough to get you both back home."

We reached Mini Ha Ha. Earlier, I'd pulled off her FOR SALE signs, convincing myself it was important to let her have the occasional run. We strapped ourselves in and drove out of the centre of town.

Bridgwater has a few sleazy areas, but none of them are downright scary. Even so, I didn't fancy catching a bus to where we were headed. We parked up in a long street at the marshy end of town and sheltered in a shop doorway while I grappled with the umbrella again. The shop was closed and emptied, but it had once sold carpets; several books of samples were strewn on the dust-ridden floor the other side of the window.

"I don't want to force you into this," I said. "It's just a hunch. Or elimination, if that makes sense."

Mirela was squaring her shoulders to the task. "The dark place." She'd really taken the shamanic journey seriously.

"Once we've covered everything the wolf suggested, I can return to the otherworld and search there again."

"We do it."

The heavy rain clouds seemed to reinforce the street's decline. The street lamps reflected their dull glow into orange puddles too numerous to avoid. Apart from a betting office and a shabby-fronted pub called the Dogs Bollox, the massage parlour was the only going concern. I'd driven past it a couple of times when I was out, not giving it a thought. I certainly had never thought I'd walk through the door.

The words BELINDA'S BUNNIES had been sign-painted on the window, surrounded by stencils of perfume bottles and oil amphora, and the declaration that, *Massage is good for the soul. You can choose the masseuse of your dreams for a gentle, discreet, and very relaxing experience. Half an Hour £20.*

"Twenty pounds?" I said, louder than I meant. "That's less than I charge."

Mirela gave me a look. "It is to get them in door."

"Oh. Like a down payment." I could see that Mirela might teach me a lot.

We were both shivering. The wind was whipping through the denim of my jeans, but it wasn't just that. The idea of going over the threshold gave me black dots in front of my eyes.

Mirela shoved open the door and we went into the foyer. It looked grimy, but the low light coming from bulbs covered by pink shades hid most of the dust. The smell of artificial flowers hit me, instantly setting up one of those drilling headaches. In the dim light I could see Mirela was glancing about with sharp eyes, as if Kizzy might open the one door that led to the hinterland of the shop and walk up to us at any second.

Someone who could paint a fair representation of a fluffy bunny had covered the far wall with artwork. The rabbits wore bow ties and top hats and were peeking over their shoulders so that you could see their big white tails.

A book case stood on one wall, littered with photos of the girls on offer propped up in the sort of frames I use for my therapy certificates. Toy rabbits featured in these pictures; they were often the only thing that was keeping the masseuses from catching a dreadful cold.

I couldn't help staring. The girls in the photos were tanned, toned, and as slender as bamboo sticks, but their breasts were like blown-up beach balls. Debs had thought she'd done okay with her enhancement—it had sure cost her enough—but honestly, she'd been robbed of silicon.

"Yes?"

Tucked into a corner of the foyer, a woman sat behind a Perspex security window. There were two holes in it; one to talk through, and, at counter level, a little arched mouse hole right in front of her. The woman was unlikely to be used for a future photoshoot; she was well over forty and had decided that Pan Stik was the answer to her wrinkle problems. Possibly to the extent of never washing off the previous layer. Her hair fell in stiff waves to her shoulders. It was that kind of blond that shines green in the wrong light … and this was the wrong light, especially when she bobbed her head forward to get a better look at us through the Perspex.

"You come asking for jobs?"

I hesitated. How were we going to play this? Tell the truth from the start or string a line? We hadn't even discussed it.

The woman got fed up of waiting for us to make up our minds. "Only I'll tell you now, your boobs ain't right. They'll need improvement. And you"—she pointed at me—"will 'ave to shed at least ten pounds."

"We don't want job," Mirela snapped.

"Are you Belinda?" I asked, hoping I sounded polite.

"As much as anybody."

"Right. Well, look, we're only here in case you can help us."

"I can't help you unless you get enhancement and lose ten pounds."

"Thanks for the advice. But we're ..." I didn't think this woman, whatever her name turned out to be, would be any more interested in missing persons than the police. "We're looking for this girl's sister. She went off and we wondered, has she come for a job here?"

"She the same boob measurement as her?"

"Er ..."

"Is that all you care 'bout? Fucking tit size?" I'd never heard Mirela swear before and it foolishly shocked me. I put a hand on her arm, but she shook it off as if dislodging a fly. She strode over the carpet tiles, almost tripping on the one that had come loose. She put both palms on the counter. "You know girl like me? Tall more? Bit old? Call Kizzy?"

"No. I don't know Kizzy. Wouldn't employ her if I did. I don't like aggression, see. Wouldn't employ her, not if she's like you. Now get out my shop."

A silence fell, into which came the click of the street door. A man in a puffy anorak and the sort of slip-on shoes that show too much sock walked in.

"Evening, Roy," said "Belinda."

Roy's eyes rested on us. They were the watery blue shade that developed as you lost your twenty/twenty vision. His hair was a grizzled pewter colour made up of black with too many white strands. He was breathing fast, as if he'd run down the street rather than be spotted coming into Belinda's Bunnies. "They new?"

"No," said Belinda. "Loretta's free, if you'd like her."

"I'll have this one." Roy put out a hand and touched Mirela's chin with his index finger.

"She don't work here, Roy. You want to pay me, or what?"

"Oh, yeah." He brushed close past Mirela and stuffed a handful of notes through the mouse hole. He hadn't noticed the way Mirela had frozen at his touch; as though his finger on her chin and the brush of his anorak on her arm had turned her into rock salt.

I took her hand and yanked her towards the door, which was still swinging on its hinges. I pulled it sharply closed behind us.

The story of this street was the same with each shop we passed as we fled. Adverts on the backs of postcards, mainly phone numbers and a woman's name, littered the vacant windows. I ground to a halt. The rain was coming down hard now. I handed Mirela the umbrella.

"Put it up, okay?"

I went over to a window and began scanning the cards. I wondered what Kizzy might have written, if she'd put a card in this window. Or if she'd found someone who might write a card for her, and for other girls. I looked up, water falling in my eyes, and stared at the windows over the shop fronts. The upper stories were being used. People lived or worked in the rooms. But Bridgwater was not going to give up its secrets easily, not to two girls who looked shit scared because, frankly, they were.

I wheeled round from the shop window when I heard Mirela's cry. Roy had come up the street after us. He was already standing so close to Mirela I could see no air between them. He had her chin again, this time between his thumb and forefinger. Inside Belinda's Bunnies he'd seemed weedy and insignificant, but he was head and shoulders taller than Mirela as she shrank away from him, and he was using his wiry strength to back her into the next shop doorway.

"Nice," he said. "Nice."

At first I didn't understand what he'd said. His breathing was still short, as if he had a lung disease. I could believe his breath smelt stale in Mirela's nostrils. And his speech was slurred. Perhaps he liked to take a few drinks at the Dogs Bollox before a trip to Belinda's.

"Nice," he said again, and I heard him plain. The word chilled my body.

"Stop it," I said. I don't think either of them heard me. "STOP IT!"

Roy turned slightly, allowing me to see that he'd pushed up Mirela's raincoat. His hand was halfway down the front of her jeans.

"Look," he said his tone reasonable. "Piss off, will you?"

I couldn't think what to do. A zillion ideas were fuddling my brain, but they were all stupid—dial 999 on my phone, go back to Belinda for help, attack Roy with my bare hands. While I was thinking about them, Mirela took advantage of Roy's sudden lack of concentration. A scream came out of her. "One! two!" She grasped my umbrella with both her fists and brought it down over his head.

It actually missed his head and rammed into his shoulder. The action, rather than any pain or hurt, stunned him.

"Go for it," I cried, like the street cat I was at heart.

I thought Mirela would run. I was ready to take off down the street. But she didn't budge. She altered her grip on the umbrella and rammed the point into his chest. He keeled over, not quite going down. While he was trying to regain his balance, she struck again. This time a sound came out of him, like he was exhaling the last breath he had, and he stumbled past me.

Mirela followed, the umbrella gripped by its stem like a javelin. I snatched at her, recalling how proud she'd been of her boyfriend's bare-knuckle prowess. Looked like Romani girls were pretty good at fighting too. Roy was already staggering towards the safety of Belinda's.

"You were amazing," I said. "I thought you were going to do that guy in!" I put my arm around her. Her figure slumped as the anger oozed out, leaving only sorrow. "Come on, Mirela. Let me take you home."

My legs felt shaky as I controlled the clutch and gas pedal. "I didn't think doing that would be dangerous," I said. "I was wrong. It was scary. And we didn't find anything out anyway."

I shuddered with the damp chill of the night and turned up the heating.

Mirela muttered something. "Kizzy had to go."

"What?"

"When she woke me, night of carnival. She said . . ."

"What?" I urged.

"She said it would mean great riches."

I was silent. I couldn't process this, and I didn't think Mirela could help me. Had Kizzy meant what she'd said? Did she actually believe it? Or was it one of those made-up romances, like being the seventh daughter of a seventh daughter?

"She'd been excited," I said, remembering what Mirela had told me about fireworks in her eyes.

"Okay, yes. But was frightened too."

I felt my throat constrict. "Did she tell you that?"

"She not need to." Mirela began to sob. "These places for massage are ver' bad."

Sometimes, you had to string what Mirela said in her limited English into a more coherent translation. "Are you saying Kizzy might be doing something like this? Or not?"

"Gypsy girl should keep pure for her marriage day."

"Really?"

"Yes. Olden time … tradition. Gypsy girl to stay pure, or no husband."

I tried not to look surprised. Each time I was with Mirela, I learnt something new about the Romani. Even so, I fancied Kizzy was not so pure. Maybe away from parents and culture, she had thrown off the Romani traditions.

I pulled up outside Mirela's house. "Do you ever ring your Mama and Tatta? Or your boyfriend?"

"I too ashamed." She looked at me with dark, wet eyes. "I already in place of blame, am I not?"

———

"Don't you want this job?" snapped Stanislaus.

It was quarter past eleven the following morning. I had been wandering the back streets near Papa Bulgaria, searching for the staff entrance, for the last half-hour and had finally presented myself for my first day as a takeaway deliverer, something I hadn't imaged actually doing, even when I was signing their rubbish contract. But clients were not gracing me with their presence—or their cash—and Christmas was nagging on the horizon, filled with present buying and the need to get back to Bristol. Even if they took a chunk out of my wages for the hire-purchase of the scooter, at least I'd have something cheap to get around on.

"Did you bring a street map?"

I pulled an A–Z of Bridgwater out of my bag and waved it at Stan. The phone started up and he dashed to take the order, yelling behind him, "Go and get your helmet. Double quick."

"Helmet?" I mouthed at him. I tried to remember that bit of my so-called orientation. The layout of Papa Bulgaria was simple; the original shop consisted of the room upstairs where I'd had my interview, with front-of-house directly below. The kitchen was a large extension. I was in the lobby behind it that and led out into the yard where the scooters stood under cover. The changing room and loo was off the lobby. I pushed the door. Inside was the boy Mr. Papazov had bullied. He was in the act of sticking his legs into his white chef's trousers.

"Oh," I yelped. "Sorry!"

"Don't worry about it. Unisex changing room." He gave me a grin. "First day?"

"Yeah. Sabbie. Hi. No idea what I'm doing. Almost got the sack already."

"Everyone gets the sack every day in here. I'm Jimmy, by the way."

"You're from Bridgwater, aren't you?" I took in his pale face, a rash of spots over the forehead and chin. His West Country burr was pleasantly high; it hadn't yet dipped to the lower octave range of older inhabitants.

"North Petherton, but yeah. Born, bred, and buttered in these parts."

"Whatever makes you want to work for this outfit?"

"Same as you, I suppose."

I strongly doubted that. I thought something up quick. "Sort of ... want to gain a trade then move on?"

"Got it in one. Went through the catering diploma at college but that don't mean squat unless you've got experience. These were the first lot to offer me something."

"Great." I nodded like a back window dog. He must be gaining proficiency in taking blows, at least. "So … what are you here? Sort of sous chef?"

"Mostly it's just me. Stan cooks when he's got enough serving staff, but we're thin on the ground at the moment." He dropped his voice a little. "Mr. Papazov doesn't do much actual work. Better at breathing down necks if the truth be told."

And breaking them, I thought.

"You've been here a while, then?"

"Yeah, too long."

"Did you know Kizzy Brouviche?"

"Of course. Her sister still works here, but Kizzy's moved on."

"Where d'you think she moved on to?"

"She didn't say. Didn't think to tell *me*, at least."

"You didn't get to know her well, then?"

Jimmy's face darkened, as if a cloud had come over it. His spots seemed to glow as his skin blushed. He finished getting his kit on and squeezed past me, disappearing into the kitchen seconds before Mirela rushed into the little room. There were pink spots on her cheeks and her eyes were wet with the cold air outside. "Name of Virgin! Too much sleepy. Stan will kill." She threw off her coat and zipped herself into an overall. She lifted the locally famous Papa scooter helmet off a peg and passed it to me. It was painted with three thick bands of colour. "Flag of our country," she said. "White, green, red."

I dragged on one of the ubiquitous yellow jackets that hung next to the helmets and followed her out into the kitchen. Mirela veered towards Jimmy, who was chopping onions sharp and swift. I saw her touch his cheek with a slender finger.

"You cry that things?" She pointed to the onions. Her voice was lower, a little gruffer than normal, and Jimmy's heart was practically struggling out through his ribs. His legs buckled as he bounced away from the chopping board. Above the half-raised zip of Mirela's overall a line of flesh frothed from a red bra. I couldn't quite reconcile her flirting with her earlier talk of retaining purity.

I slid over to Petar, gearing myself up for warfare.

"I'd like my bike back," I said, feebly adding, "please."

Petar lifted his shoulders like they were cleavers. "I don't know you. I never see you."

"The yellow mountain bike you nicked from me? The one I chained to your front garden railings? The one you used a bolt cutter to steal?"

His eyelids slid over his eyes. The action was languid, unconcerned. "I don't like you. Go away."

But it was Petar that moved away, slowly, as if he always moved as little as possible. I stared after him, unable to think of a back-up plan.

"First orders," yelled Stan. "Have you got that soup on yet, mate?"

"Yes, chef," Jimmy yelled back. It was more of a squeak. He was trembling twice over, from pressure and from passion.

Stan was grinning at me. "Okay, Sabbie *Daar*. Let's see how well you know the roads. Two out-of-town orders, both for good, regular customers." He made a swipe at his hair. "And one is a big deal, ten portions, so don't get them muddled. Check the addresses on your map now and get going soon as the food is ready."

I strapped on the crash helmet and wondered how long I'd cope with looking like an over-patriotic representation of the flag of Bulgaria, a country I'd known nothing about a week ago. But I was learning fast. In fact, I was beginning to think this might be quite an interesting job.

ELEVEN

Pop-popping along at the top restriction of thirty miles an hour, I finally reached the village of Westonzoyland, the location of my first order. I pulled up outside a low-built detached house with pink rendering. I didn't even have to ring the bell. There was a chap on the drive, waxing a very new Toyota Land Cruiser. It was hard to tell which bits he'd waxed and which he hadn't; it was inky black from nose to tail. He hailed me, putting down his buffer. "Ah, lunch."

"Mr. Grace? I have your snezhanka salad and patatnik plus bean soup?" I'd been looking forward to saying that the whole journey.

"Thank you." He had mousy hair which was greying at the temples. As he smiled, crows' feet either side his brown eyes smiled too. "Except it's Dr. Grace."

"Oh, sorry." I checked my order form. "There's nine pounds sixty-eight to pay."

"Come in a sec." He pulled the door wide and disappeared into the house. I stood in the thick pile of the hall carpet and looked around. There was a cello on a stand in the corner of the hall and a mountain landscape in oils on a pale wall.

While I waited, I took a look at the next address—a house called the Hatchings in the nearby village of Zotheroy. Something about that address made my spine buzz, even though I knew I'd never been there. Why did it feel familiar? The name on the order—Mitchell—meant nothing to me.

Finally, Dr. Grace returned with the exact money. "Don't think I've seen you before," he said. "New to Papazov's?"

"Yes, I am."

"Enjoying the challenge?"

"Actually, you're my very first order."

"Gracious!" he laughed. "Glad I had the right money!"

"Yeah, thanks, it does make things easier. I don't suppose you can tell me the best way to Zotheroy, could you? There seemed to be a choice of back roads."

He came out with me and stood by my scooter. "Go back to the main road and keep going until you get to the crossroads with the A361. You'll see a narrow unmarked road that comes off there. Head along it towards King's Sedgemoor Drain. The village is signposted at the next junction."

"Thanks. I'm glad you know the surrounds!" I said, without meaning to, but his cultured voice suggested he was not a West Country local.

"Oh, I've been here a while. And you?"

"Couple of years. I'm from Bristol originally."

"What on earth dragged you down to soggy Somerset?"

I made a face. "Er … boys and business."

"Hope both have been a success."

"Not as such. I'm bad at relationships and I wouldn't be working for Papa if I was good at business, would I?"

We both laughed. "Well," said Dr. Grace, "you should find the next call fine so long as you pick up that first turnoff."

"Thanks."

It felt like a friendly start to the deliveries and I waved behind me as I sped off ... *sped* being a maximum acceleration of nought to thirty miles per hour in not even sixty seconds.

Thanks to Dr. Grace's advice, I was soon on the road to Zotheroy, keeping my eye open for the Hatchings. As I did so, that buzzy feeling I'd had earlier began to fall into place. Dennon's cute grin flashed into my mind ... the birth certificate lying on the coffee table. The Hatchings in Zotheroy. My mother's address before I was born. Crazy. I couldn't wait to take a look.

I spotted the house sign and negotiated a windy, gravelled lane that ended in a herringboned driveway. A massive turning circle was landscaped with a sculptural array of shrubs and bushes. The red brick house loomed up, its white-framed windows set geometrically square and its chimneys standing high and proud. This was some place of origin.

A woman came out of the house while I was pulling the paper sacks of foil containers from the top box. "This is all very late. We have guests and we were expecting to eat almost fifteen minutes ago."

"I'm sorry. Uh, you're quite hard to find."

She peered. "New, are you?"

"Yes, just started." I made a fuss of the order form. "Can I confirm that your name is Mitchell?"

"Mrs. Mitchell, that's correct. I paid by card, of course."

"Can I help you in with this? There's too much for one to carry." Truthfully, I was longing for a glimpse of the interior, even if the place and people had changed over the years.

"If you would." She marched along the driveway, actually carrying nothing. I followed behind Mrs. Mitchell, holding the carriers low in case the handles broke from the weight of two courses for ten people. I tried to keep her in sight as she passed the pillared front door—obviously I was destined for the tradesperson's entrance—and turned a corner.

When Gloria and Philip took us on our Sunday walks, they always promised we'd have the picnic when we reached the top of whatever hill they'd chosen to torture us with. We'd toil up, watching the summit get closer as Dennon larked about and Charlene threw sticks for the dog. I'd be thinking, *not far now, not far now,* but when we reached the top there would always be another hill tucked behind it, and as the grownups urged us on, realization would dawn; farther and farther horizons would loom as our stomachs growled, long before we'd actually reach the top.

Well, the Hatchings was like that. We walked past rows and rows of windows and turned another corner. I shook my head in disbelief. These were *wings.* My mother couldn't have lived here unless she'd been a maid with a bed in the attic. Then, with a rush of relief, it came to me. It was all an error. This place had nothing to do with me at all. My mother probably came from one of the little workers' cottages I'd seen in the village.

Finally, we reached the kitchen and I made a pretence of helping her unload the food. "This is a fine old house," I said. "Does it have much history?"

"It's late Jacobean," said Mrs. Mitchell. "My mother opens it up occasionally, if you're interested."

I took her in. She was not as tall as I'd first thought. She just looked tall, stood tall. Her hair was ash blond, highlighted cleverly to prevent it looking coloured, but seeing a hairdresser every week can leave hair lifeless and hers did not shine; there was no gloss to it. Rather, it had the shimmer of gossamer. She'd backcombed it into a French pleat that stood high on her head, adding to the illusion of being able to look down over vast cities without climbing hills or towers. I wanted to place her in her fifties, but it could be her attitude that was middle-aged. Her face was a little puffy under the eyes, but mascara and lippy were doing a good job of detracting attention from that fact, while too much sun bed was achieving the reverse.

"Your mother?"

"My mother, yes." She finally turned back to me. "Lady Savile-Dare."

"Dare?" I echoed, unable to think further than this single word.

"Savile-Dare. We have costumed tours in the summer. And a candlelight concert in December." She pulled open an inner door and called, "Lettice! Lettice!"

A girl of twelve or so appeared in the doorway. She was wearing jodhpurs and had a smear of mud on her nose.

"Good lord, Lettice," said Mrs. Mitchell. "You look appalling. Why haven't you bathed? I was hoping you'd help me with lunch." She shook her head, dismissive of all the stresses of her life. "Well, anyway, can you fetch a leaflet for this girl? Then run and *get changed.*"

"I can help you with it," I said, "seeing I was so late. I—I didn't know I was coming here. Not till I looked at the map."

Stupid words were falling from my mouth without bidding, but she didn't respond. She wasn't even listening, which was just as well. I fished a dog-eared business card out of my jeans pocket and laid it on the scrubbed kitchen table, but Mrs. Mitchell was not going to examine the card of a hawker who had gained unauthorized admission. Impossibly, she rose in height. Her mouth was drawing inwards, as if she was thinking of sipping a margarita. "That won't be necessary, thank you. And it does look as if my daughter was unable to put her hand on the events leaflets, so that will be all, if you don't mind."

I stood my ground, the keen wind of my breath in my ears. "You can warm up the soup in a microwave quite quickly," I said, mostly because I wanted to be the last person to speak. Then I slipped out through the back door and refreshed my memory on how to find my scooter.

———

It was cold work, delivering takeaway in late November. I felt shivery to the bone by the time I got home. It was quarter past five and already very dark. Despite being allowed some soup and salad at lunch time, I had a Grand Canyon emptiness in my stomach and there wasn't much in the fridge, apart from half a carton of milk, already on the turn. I went into the back yard with a flashlight, tucked the hens up for the night and rummaged around the storage shed. This might once have been a coal house, but it's a lovely cool place to overwinter veggies. There were some old potatoes in a sack and a big tub filled with sand where the carrots were buried. Last summer, a long string of onions hung against the wall; there were only five left. I cut a small one down. Four. I grabbed a spade and tramped down the garden to where the leeks grew.

I washed and chopped my leek, onion, carrot, and spud, and fried them up in a pan, adding some dried thyme, salt, and black pepper. As soon as the veggies looked soft, I threw in a cup of water. I waited until it was bubbling, checked the flame was low and poured myself a glass of wine I couldn't afford but badly needed.

I was still trying to get my head round the Hatchings. Was it a massive, stupid coincidence? When I'd seen the address on the birth certificate, I'd assumed it was a children's home, not a stately residence. Lady Savile-Dare. What a name. "Sod you," I said under my breath. I wasn't sure who I was talking to, but the shimmering presence of the River Lady came into my mind. *Even the most skillful shaman cannot give advice over issues they refuse to explore themselves.* I wouldn't put it past the spirit world to bring Mirela to my door solely so I'd take that job and find the Savile-Dares. The spirit world can get very involved once you start with it.

Like before. It was eight years ago that I'd had my motorbike accident. I'd bashed my head and fallen into a deep coma, where I'd met the spirit form of a Cunning Man: Bren Howell. Later, I met him in the flesh. He and his wife Rhiannon had been the first step on my path to discovering the inner worlds, and the three of us agreed that my bike accident had helped me understand that.

Life is full of strange turns of chance that shape the things we know and do. If Gloria hadn't sent me the birth certificate, I wouldn't have bothered following Mrs. Mitchell into the kitchen of the Hatchings. And if I hadn't seen Gary Abbott chasing through the squibbing crowds, I'd've never met Kizzy.

I longed to unload this to someone. The sort of someone that you can talk to by rolling over in bed when you wake up. The someone who asks how was your day, honey, when you get home at night. But that bloke didn't exist in my life at the moment. I loved my work and my little garden, and the hens helped some, but I did miss living with other people. Sometimes, I longed to hear chatter from downstairs when I woke. It would almost be a joy to queue up outside the bathroom or hurl insults at a social worker one more time. Or roll over and find someone snoring into the other pillow.

I'd sworn I would never investigate my birth certificate, yet within weeks I was in the kitchen of my mother's old house. At least, it was possible the Hatchings was my mother's old house, and that the people in it were my relations.

Once I've met someone, I can recall their features, their name, and most of what they've told me. I have to be careful not to get cross with people who are less good at that stuff—who haven't clocked my name (*my* name!) on third introduction—and I'm surprised when people confess they can't remember back to before they were five or six. I wonder what has happened to the memories they should be having. So many first things happen early on; first time on Santa's knee, first day at nursery, first ice cream.

I can summon all that to mind, if I wish, but I prefer not to. It's like a casket I keep firmly shut. The memories are hidden away, as if they'd been folded in tissue against fading.

Quite a few of my very early memories are good ones, and I have evolved a theory that even then I knew I should store the nice stuff up carefully and discard the bad.

There were times when my mother was up to being a good mum. They can't have been frequent, but obviously they were numerous enough to keep our heads below the parapet of the Social Services' gun-sights, for no one tried to take me away from a woman who was mostly out of her head. But when life smiled on Izzie Dare, she'd assume we'd behave like sisters. She'd scream at me, *We are not staying in!* (as if it had been my decision to do so), zip up my pink anorak, and we'd be riding a bus, with her whispering, *What shall we do when we get into town, Sabrina?*

What we mostly did, I fancy, was sit in a coffee house or window shop our way around the department stores, but we were doing it together. We were *out*, that was the thing. I can remember ploughing through a knickerbocker glory with a long spoon, swooning over the sweet coolness, and watching the laser displays on pub walls as I fell to sleep on her lap. After I'd started school, she'd have little hesitation in pulling me out of class, setting a trend that continued until my last hour as a pupil. On hot summer days, we'd bus it to the seaside—Weston-super-Mare, I presume—somewhere anyway with a pier full of slot machines that would take up all my two-p pieces while Izzie at first made faces with the best of the men, then disappeared behind the rides with them. I never searched for her—not while I still had money for candy floss or trying to winch up a squashy teddy from the pile of cheap watches.

Shortly before she left me, she took me to the first Bonfire Night I can recall. I am very clear about this memory. I know I was in Miss Goodwin's class, as I went up from Reception to Year One five months before my mother died, so it *had* to be that November the fifth. I clung to her as we watched the fireworks rain down because, although my head was filled with starry wonders, I was terrified that the explosions could hurt her. I don't think I ever worried that things might hurt me. It was in my heart from the first that my mother was the vulnerable one.

The past binds us all up; it's never finished with. By the time I got back to checking my soup, I'd had a good rifle through my casket of early memories, without once recalling the disapproving features of a younger Mrs. Mitchell. I had "aunties" galore, but none of them was her.

The soup looked good, but too thick. I threw in the half pint of milk and gave the lot a go with my soup whizzer. I stayed beside it, watching it slowly bubble up again.

No photo was passed down to me. No locket around the neck of the dead woman containing a whisper of a heritage. That sort of thing only happened in Victorian novels and, as I'd never read one, there was no possibility that it might be happening to me.

———

I was washing up my bowl and glass when my phone rang. I snatched at it. I could not afford to miss calls from prospective clients. "Sabbie Dare."

"Oh," said a high voice. "Sorry... I've got your card. Sabbie Dare, Shamanic Therapist?"

"Right." The girl sounded so young this could be a prank call. "Can I help you?"

"Oh, sorry. I'm Laetitia Mitchell."

For a moment I was thrown. This didn't sound like the Mrs. Mitchell I spoke to at the Hatchings.

"Lettice to my friends. I hate my real name."

I couldn't help a chuckle. "I'm the same. I hate my real name as well." I was trying to be chatty, put her at her ease now I knew who she was, but she came back very quickly.

"Sabrina? That's your name?"

"Yes..."

"Ma chucked your card in the bin."

"Not in need of a shaman, then."

"You didn't leave it for that reason, though, did you? You're a relation or something, aren't you?"

"I'm honestly not sure, Lettice."

"Ma thought you were a gold digger."

"I'm not after anything. I was delivering your lunch."

"Truly? Only … she doesn't know I'm calling you."

"Then it's not a great idea that we talk. It makes things look even more of a conspiracy, when actually they're the exact opposite. Serendipity."

"What's that?"

"Things that just happen."

"Like fate?"

"Sort of."

I told her about my birth certificate, how I'd refused to cast eyes on its details until they'd been thrust under my nose. "All I know is that I'm the daughter of a woman called Isabel Trevina Dare."

"That's my aunt's full name," said Laetitia, in a whisper. "I think you're my cousin."

"What?"

"My mother has a sister she never talks about."

I was unable to reply. The thoughts whirling in my head had dried my tongue.

"I want to meet you. I really do."

"Look, Lettice … it's important not to have secrets with people you don't even know—me for instance."

"Oh my god, Ma's coming," hissed the girl. "Gotta go." The line went dead.

I put the mobile down with care, as if it might bite me—or worse, ring again. So when the door bell went moments later, I leaped off the floor.

Andy Comer was standing in the darkness of my porch. He didn't speak. His shoulders were spasming with anger. Something gleamed white in his hand. It was my letter to Drea, screwed into a ball. Clearly he hadn't appreciated its arrival in his house.

"You," he said. There was whisky on his breath. "You ... told her to go."

"That's not your business."

His shoulders came up around the tops of his ears as he leaned in on me. "Whose business is it, if not mine?"

"Drea's." I wished my voice sounded stronger, but a thin squeak was all I could manage.

"She's left. Gone back!" He smoothed the crumpled sheet and appeared to read some of it. "She was gone when I got home."

"Good," I said. "You didn't deserve her. Think I can't guess what is wrong with that girl?"

"No!" He was shouting. "You couldn't guess. And she would never tell you."

"She didn't have to."

"What have you done?" His voice dropped, as he reined himself in. He was good at that. Usually controlled ... in public, at least. "You don't know what you've done."

He raised his hands. He seemed to grow, under the streetlamp. I was winged into Drea's journey; the snake looming over me. I was sure I'd done the right thing in giving Drea that letter, and secretly, I was pleased with the result. I didn't need to listen to this drunken man's ramblings.

"Well, screw you," I said.

I slammed the door.

TWELVE

Saturday night, and the Curate's Egg was jam-packed and throbbing with sound. There was always live music, although Kev, the manager, was not fussy about auditioning, so the quality varied from finger-tapping to ear-clapping. He's a people person, is Kev—good with the punters—but probably tone deaf and definitely can't spell. When I'd first started working here, I'd sneaked around all the blackboards... *Happy Ower! Live Music Tonite! Reel Ale buy the Glass*... taking a bar cloth to the offending words. There wasn't much I learnt at school (let me rephrase that—there wasn't much I learnt in the classroom), but I seem to naturally be able to add up and spell. Quite useful skills for bar work, along with a steady hand and a steely eye.

Tonight we'd been threatened with a jazz band, but as they got going I could see—well, hear, I suppose—that they were closer to R&B than jazz, which was more up my street. I'm a survivor of Brit Pop and trance, but luckily for my job at the Egg, I enjoy the decades before I was born.

This band was loud and energetic with a lot of oldies that were making people get up and dance, even though the Egg doesn't possess a dance floor. Every seat and standing place was taken and the floor was already wet with beer. The Egg had been a pub long enough to have started out with straw on its floor, and sometimes I'm of the mind that we should put the straw back down, but Kev is perversely proud of the way he pulls the weekend punters. He doesn't do food—you're lucky if you can choose your flavour of crisps—and the downing rate is so high that by time the band's on its second session, there are more cases of alcohol poisoning behind the doors than at an unsuccessful AA meeting. Not everyone is sheets to the wind, though; people do come here to catch up with the local music scene and there's always a few aficionados crunched into corners, their entire bodies pulsing with the beat. There was one tonight, sitting so close to the band his ears were endangered, a half-finished pint before him and his head low over the table, scribbling into a notebook.

I looked again. It was Fergus.

I wove towards him, collecting glasses as I went. "Hi!"

"Hi," he said, closing the notebook. "So this is where you work."

He had shaved. I spotted the vestige of a dimple at the centre of his smooth chin.

"Don't think I've seen you here before," I said.

"Ah, but that's because you didn't know me before."

"Fair enough. What you writing about?" I pointed to the notebook. "Not checking out the pub's employment record are you?"

"Pardon me?"

"I know, I know. The band's belting it out above safety levels."

"I could hang around until they've done their gig."

"Okay."

I introduced him to a couple of the regulars to get him chatting. I'd been joking about the secretive writing, but Kev would throw him out if he thought he was making notes about the temperature of the beer. I kept glancing over at Fergus, wondering where I stood with him. I'd expected him to come and lean on the bar, so we could chat some more, but he stayed where he was, talking mostly to the band's little following, until after they'd dismantled their gear, at which point he helped them carry it out.

Bit by bit, the punters strayed into the cold night. It wasn't the sort of place where they beat each other to a pulp or barfed in neighbouring doorways, but I was happy to see them depart.

I was giving the bar a final wipe when Fergus walked over to me.

"What did you think of the band?" I asked.

"Okay. Not my entire cup of tea, if I were honest."

"What's your cup of tea, then?"

"Folk and roots. I like to taste and try from around the world."

"I heard some Bulgarian music this week. At least I assumed it was Bulgarian."

"I love Balkan folk. It's very east/west."

"Oh, right," I said, nodding like I knew what he meant.

"And a wide variety of instruments: bagpipes, woodwind, fiddle..."

"You know a lot about all this."

"Music is my dream, so it is."

"Your...dream?"

He nodded. "I love my job. Agency for Change. Of course I do. It's important. Essential, I believe. But it isn't what..." He trailed off.

"What you love?"

"Absolutely. Passion. You should have one in your life, wouldn't that be so, Sabbie?"

His notebook was still in his hand. It had parchmentlike, hand-cut pages and on the cover was a design in Celtic knotwork; an intricate weave of spirals within circles, all interlaced and unbroken. It was the sort of book you buy as a gift at an ethnic market stall. I wondered if someone had bought this for him to write in.

"Is that what your notebook's for?" I asked. "To record your thoughts about the music you hear?"

"Not at all." He lifted it in reverence and slid it into an inner jacket pocket. "This is my dream. To write the songs that others love to hear."

"You write songs?"

"I'd sing them, if anyone would employ me to do so."

"You could ask Kev."

"Be careful. You haven't heard my songs, yet."

"Oh, he'd take anyone." My hand shot to my mouth at my gaff, but Fergus laughed; perhaps too long and too loud, but it was a rich, Irish laugh and it made me giggle too.

"Thanks for the recommendation. It deserves recompense, indeed. Shall I write a song for you? A love song, perhaps. 'Shaman Girl,' or some such. How does that sound to you?"

It sounded like Fergus was in high flirt mode. I could feel my skin warming up under his slanted smiles. Without even meaning to, I tapped his arm. If I'd had a fan to hand, I'd've slapped it closed and used that. "You are outrageous!"

"That I am. An outrageously dreadful fellow. So, Sabbie, what are you planning for later?"

"I usually go home and flop into bed." The double meaning dawned and I rushed on. "There's a taxi waiting for me. What about you?"

"I promised to show up to a friend's party."

"Sounds fun."

"Would you care to take a look with me?"

"Yeah, why not? Just give me about ten seconds to tart myself up to party standards, okay?"

"Ten seconds is surely all a girl like you needs to make herself look beautiful."

Wow. I dashed into the back loo and started pulling my bag apart—deodorant, hairbrush, lippy. Odd compliments he offered, but nice nonetheless. Fergus was from Ireland after all, so his chat-up lines were going to sound quaint and lyrical but full of guile too. I liked that. I decided Fergus would be refreshing to get to know.

And Rey had given strict instructions on that subject: find someone new.

———

"Fergus! You're here at last! And you brought tottie!"

As we'd walked along the empty streets of Bridgwater, it had belatedly occurred to me I might have got the wrong end of the stick. By *party*, did Fergus mean half a dozen Irishmen sitting round with Jamesons in their hands, talking about the good old days when knee-capping was the national sport?

Luckily, the guy at the door was young, in possession of a slopping pint, and yelling to make himself heard above the thud of nineties garage music. I wasn't going to let his sexism fly over my head, though.

"You got my name wrong," I said, as we unwound ourselves from our outdoor wear. "It's Sabbie, not Tottie."

"Oops. I spend my day grappling with the inequalities of our immigration system, and sometimes I need to break out. Juke. Short

for Justin." He offered his hand and I shook it. "Cath is about somewhere," he added in Fergus's direction.

"I work with Cath and Juke," Fergus explained.

"Agency for Change?"

"Yep," said Juke. "*Agency* as in *agenda*. Wouldn't you say, Fergus?"

"Guess so."

I passed Juke the bottle of Blossom Hill that we'd prized off Kev
and we waded into the kitchen over the legs of a bunch of people
propped on either side of the hallway. Steam rose from them and
mingled with a Ms. Dynamite beat.

The kitchen was crammed. Getting to the drinks end of it proved
a matter of putting your head down and going in. Fergus spoke into
my ear. "I hope this is your sort of thing." I grinned at him and he
grabbed my hand and charged into the throng.

Armed with Buds, we stepped our way back to the living room,
where the rugs had literally been taken up; I could see one rolled
and leaning against a wall like it was waiting for a partner. Twenty or
more people were dancing on the laminate, crammed into the space
left by pushing the sofas back to the walls.

"You want to ..." said Fergus.

We shuffled into the crowd and began to gyrate. Well, Fergus
gyrated, whooping and waving his arms in that male "I can dance"
way, while I did little pointy movements with my feet.

We swayed in and out of each other's close-up zone as the beat
notched itself to a climax, sometimes almost touching, sometimes
apart. But the next track brought the pace down. Fergus put a hand
on my arm—a light touch that I could ignore if I pleased. I moved
in and he slid his arm around me. Turned out we were on the same
eye level. I'm five-five in the trainers I always wear at the Egg. Fergus
couldn't have been much more than five-six or -seven. I liked that,

the way I could look directly across at him. His breath had a yeasty scent and he had one of those mouths ... not too full, not too thin, not too wet, not too dry ... Lips that might make a girl yearn to lean in to test their fit.

"You've never said if our ale is as good as the ol' Guinness," I teased.

"Ah, now that would be telling. I don't drink the black stuff over here. I like to sample all things English."

I lifted my chin and my cheek brushed against his. I'd warmed up with the dancing, but Fergus's skin still felt chilled.

"You're cold," I whispered.

"Jesus, I don't mean to be," said Fergus. "I just come across like that sometimes."

He kissed me, and our lips really did fit, like the way a peach can be halved, then perfectly slotted together again.

He was going to do me so much good, was Fergus Quigg.

Finally, a sofa became free and Fergus grabbed it. He turned to me as if he meant real business now we'd claimed our snogging space.

The kisses tasted good, but there was a wheel, spinning inside my brain, that kept up a nagging chant: *You've never tried a Reynard kiss. How d'you know how his compare?*

Shut up! I kept responding. *Just shut up. Rey* told *me to do this.* He thought I was a damn dumb civvy. He'd be delighted to know I'd found a respectable boyfriend.

I surfaced from the kissing without an answer, but I had a sudden desire to shift my body away and let my thoughts catch up with my actions—something a girl should always do. I had to work out if I wanted Fergus for himself, or as a substitute Rey.

Fergus straightened too, and our knees touched. A million embryo thoughts burst into my brain. *Is that touch anything like the electric charge that sparks between Rey and me? Am I breathless? Is my heart aflutter? In any case, how long can a girl go without sex?*

"Have you seen anything more of Mirela?"

I half jumped. I'd forgotten Mirela in the passion of our embraces. I gave Fergus a quizzical look at his change of subject. "Yeah, of course."

"It's great you're keeping an eye on her."

I recalled our adventure at the massage parlour. I didn't plan to tell Fergus about that; he'd think I was a shaman's rattle away from unhinged. "She's so vulnerable on her own. I will personally strangle Kizzy, when she turns up eventually."

"Turning up isn't necessarily on the cards, Sabbie."

He was right; wherever Kizzy was, she didn't seem keen to get in touch. But on the edge of my peripheral vision, I couldn't rid myself of the images that had been on the telly in the summer. The girl, drowned and dripping, pulled from the water only a few miles away from where we were now sitting. And to this day, no one knew the name of that victim or who had killed her, or even how she had died.

"Could Kizzy be dead, Fergus?"

He was silent for long seconds. "She could be anything, I guess."

"I mean, why else would she walk away from her teenaged sister?"

"She didn't strike me as someone who'd think too deeply about that. Get an offer, take it while you can."

I could see that this had been his conclusion from the start. Perhaps Mirela also knew this, harsh though it was. Her sister had called her "uncool"... *like I will never dip my toe...*

"Did you manage to check the hostels?"

"I drew a blank, I'm afraid."

He came back with his answer so quickly, I gave him a slow look. "Drew a blank as in 'no point in bothering'?"

"Truth is, I can't see Kizzy in a hostel with one shower between twenty women. Can you?"

I shook my head. I was beginning to despair of finding Mirela's sister. My journey to the gypsy fire had been less than forthcoming, our investigations into darkest Bridgwater had been a complete failure, the police were not interested, and it was becoming transparent that Fergus Quigg wasn't going to come up with any trumps, either.

"I meet a lot of people like the Brouviches, of course," said Fergus. "They've had all kinds of appalling experience. Finding one concerned, impartial friend, like Mirela has with you, is nigh on impossible for them."

"The great British public aren't renowned for their love of outsiders."

"You're right," said Fergus. "What you've offered this girl is pretty rare. Most people are not out-and-out xenophobes, but they don't realize how frightened or how guilty outsiders like Mirela feel. In work, we can offer them amity and even absolution, but that's not as genuine as finding a proper friendship."

I pounced on his words. "Is that what you do, Fergus? At the Agency for Change? Offer absolution?"

I'd been intent on finding the places that sounded threatening; dark and blameful. Perhaps I could tick *the place of absolution* off my search list.

Fergus was still talking. "Romani are regularly removed from their homes all over the EU. It's a silent ethnic cleansing that's ignored, even condoned."

"Why are people so cruel to strangers?"

"It's family, isn't it Sabbie? I'm from a big Irish family and I can tell you, day-to-day, we used to hate each other's guts. But as soon as one of us was threatened from outside, we'd stick up for each other to the death. We were family."

"Yeah, *family*, okay …"

He held up his hand, and that was just as well because my knowledge of family was a little scrubby. "From families come clans, and clans form into tribes. And from tribes grow countries … states. It doesn't even seem to matter how similar you look. The Irish don't look much different from the English, for instance, but they underwent centuries of hatred." He stopped short. "Ah, forgive me; I'm in lecture mode. I like to play devil's advocate. But then the devil takes me by the toe and pinches."

"I guess you've kissed the Blarney Stone." Stuck his tongue right down its throat, if you asked me.

"Jesus, I'd never do that. The locals pee all over it. It's just for the tourists." He paused and gave me a quick smile, enough to make something behind my rib cage go *chirp*. "At least, *that* sort of kissing the Blarney. There is another, indeed."

"And that is?"

"I'd need to know you far better before I disclose that to you."

Whoa, I thought. *Is he inviting me to bed?* At that moment, it felt like a sideswipe from off the field of play.

I was perplexed by the man—the atmosphere kept changing— long sofa kisses had become a professional discussion and then snapped into what felt like a tacky proposition. Perhaps with his strict working philosophy, he struggled to leave his sense of duty behind when he was off duty, and only managed it by wandering into minefields.

"So," I said, trying to trace our conversation safely back across the minefield, past blarney and devils, "you look after … what? People from the EU?"

"Among other things."

"Such as?"

"I support people who are applying for asylum."

"Helping them stay put in this country?"

"When we can. We try to work in sympathy with the immigration authorities."

"In sympathy? How can you do that and look after the interests of people like Mirela?"

"To be honest, the agency sort of straddles the divide between the protest groups and the law. When we take a case on, we're not looking to blame anyone on either side. We want to listen and help."

"That sounds like a line from a website."

I was becoming a bit tetchy—I definitely preferred Fergus in amorous mode. He stood up, brushing down his jeans, as if he had picked up on the tone of my voice.

"Fancy another beer?"

"Okay. Although I'd better go easy. I've got clients tomorrow."

While he was struggling towards the kitchen, I took in my surrounds. The party was getting raucous. The music had turned sultry and couples were practically having vertical sex on the dance floor. Scented whiffs of wacky baccy drifted around. I had thought Fergus a little too diligent for my taste when I'd met him, but I'd only seen a thin layer of the man in the Polska Café. He was beginning to round out.

"What're you doing here on your lovely own? Not deserted you, has he?" Juke flopped onto the sofa beside me.

"He's gone to get drinks."

"He'll be lucky." Juke was wearing bleached jeans and a dark suit jacket with an artificial daffodil on the lapel, the sort you get when you put money into a charity box. He had a two-inch beard that looked incredibly soft and so well spread out I could almost count the hairs in it. The beard was golden brown, contrasting with the darker hair that swept horizontally across his forehead. In between the two shone Juke's face, his round cheeks almost red after a night of partying. He had a nice smile, though.

"Are you running out of booze?"

"Perish the thought. But getting to it is now a route more perilous than a sponsored charity trek to Machu Picchu."

I smiled, to tell him I got the joke, then shifted across the cushions because he'd laid his hand on the sofa between us, as if getting it in position for his next move. I hadn't yet forgiven him for calling me *tottie*.

"D'you work with Fergus? Or alongside him?"

"Yeah, you got it. The three of us run the branch together." Juke crossed his arms over his chest, as if he was practicing for being a Christmas angel. He massaged both his shoulders at the same time. "Fergus says you're a shaman."

"That's right."

"Fascinating."

I gave him a discouraging smile. "It's not *fascinating*; it's how I live my life."

"I've always wanted to meet one. A shaman, that is. But I was kind of visualising some spaced-out old guy sitting cross-legged under a cactus teaching people to fly."

"Sorry to disappoint."

"Oh, you don't disappoint," said Juke. "I'd love to know more about the whole thing. I've read several books."

I bit back my first reply—*that'll make you an expert then*—but it was hard to take Juke seriously. I'd already slotted him into the post-student bracket of insensitive and butterfly-minded. "I don't think a party is the best place to talk about this."

"Right! I should come to you then, learn how to do it?"

"Why not, if you've got the time—several years—and the commitment—hours every week." I tried to keep my voice from dropping to below zero Celsius. I was praying for Fergus to hurry up with the drinks.

Juke's hand stopped massaging his shoulder and made the quantum leap to my knee. I caught his gaze and held it as I gently removed his hand and patted it down on his own knee. I'd tried not to embarrass him, but Juke took a long pull of lager to recover from the snub. He drank from a fancy pewter tankard with a handle in the shape of a key. That was sweet; he was drinking from a twenty-first birthday present. He was a babe, and he should be careful not to hit on older women.

I spotted Fergus holding bottles above his head like cats whose necks he'd wrung. I jumped up from the sofa and drove through the throbbing mass of dancers until we met.

"Look, Fergus, I hadn't realized the time."

He handed me a Bud and glanced at his watch. "Indeed so, it is late."

"I have to be up at the crack of dawn to feed the hens and prep my therapy room."

"You look the very sort. Early to bed and early to rise." He gave me a smile that made my heart warm towards him.

"I'm sorry, Fergus."

"Understood. Will you stay for one more dance, maybe?"

The music had changed. Something sweet by Bruno Mars was making me want to sway. I wound an arm round his neck and burrowed into the hollow of his left shoulder, where his t-shirt felt soft and his aftershave smelt nice.

His hand rested warm on my ribs, the fingers tickling, as if trying to resist the temptation to crawl towards my breast. A mix of emotions swilled inside me. He'd been hoping I'd go home with him. And why shouldn't I? Fergus Quigg was fit and fanciable, but he was also a coworker in the search for a missing girl. I decided I had made the right move telling him I'd be sleeping alone in my own bed tonight. It would be best if our wires didn't get too crossed.

———

She's sleeping when he comes, a deep sleep, full of dream. She's on Tatta's horse, the brindled mare, and she's flying; racing the ridge of the high hills, clutching the unbrushed mane in both fists. The warmth of the mare's coat is against her legs. She can smell its ripeness. The pain that runs like iron bars through her has diminished to an ache the dream explains away as a stitch. She's laughing into the wind when daylight floods into the room. She wakes, a bit at a time.

"Here," he says. "If you want, you can write to your sister."

She pulls herself up and leans into the writing pad he's rested on the duvet. Pain rips like a bullet. He lays a ballpoint on the pad. "Write in English."

She shakes her head. "She won't understand."

She can hear his impatience. "Tell her this. That she should come here and visit."

"Here? Where is here?"

"Tell her we'll pick her up and bring her to see you."

She nods. She starts to write. She's a slow writer. She hisses through her teeth. She's panting with the effort to even hold the pen. She bites her lip to hold things in place until she's done. She bites so hard, blood drips onto the bedding. Onto the paper. He wipes it off with a tissue.

"Good," he says. He smiles his not-smile. He helps her to lie back. He closes the curtains.

Her breath is very thin now, as if she's galloped for miles.

But he's destroyed her dream, and another will be a long time returning.

THIRTEEN

IT WAS SOME YEARS since I'd had proper paid employment; I'd forgotten how your free time whizzes by. Already, I was halfway through Tuesday's shift for Papa Bulgaria and I felt a lot more confident, both on the roads of Bridgwater and round the shop. I was almost enjoying it; it was okay to be one of the guys again, sharing moans and jokes with workmates. I was learning the tricks of the trade too. For instance, Stan could only *guess* the time it took to do each batch of deliveries. I was popping back to Harold Street to throw the hens some corn and even do a few chores.

As I drove through the heavy rain, I found myself passing the Agency for Change. I wasn't sure if seeing Fergus was a great idea. In my books, it was polite to contact someone you'd spent the night necking, at least to text—HEY! GREAT KISSER!—but I hadn't heard from Fergus at all since the party. On the other hand, I hadn't got in touch with him, either, but I had thought about him a lot. After a couple of dances and my final beer, Fergus had called me a cab. He didn't have a car, he'd told me, but neither of us were in state to drive anyway. He waved as I got into my taxi, and I was hoping that we could reestablish our original relationship—two people both wanting the best for Kizzy and Mirela. With that in mind, I decided to pop into his office for a professional-based chat.

It was the same ponytailed girl on the Agency for Change reception desk. "Mr. Quigg's doing some calls. He won't be back in the office this afternoon, I'm afraid." She looked bored, dull, and undernourished, but frankly, not a bit afraid.

I was on my way back to my scooter when I thought of the Polska Café. It was half past one; Fergus might be having his lunch. I pulled at the heavy door and went in, scanning the room, especially the corner Fergus occupied last time. He wasn't there.

I refocused my gaze towards the café's interior. The back of a head. Close-cropped brown hair. Wide shoulders packed into a combat jacket. DI Rey Buckley was sitting at a small table near a window, talking to a woman. She was younger than he, and she had the sort of hair I'd been so proud of only months ago. So long you could sit on it. Only hers was glossier than I'd ever got mine, even with de-frizz shampoo and straighteners. I peered closer without actually moving. I didn't think I'd ever be able to move again, for I could see even from my position in the doorway that her hand was resting on the edge of the table. And Rey's was resting on top of it.

Rey had loved my long, dark hair. Hadn't he? And then it had gone; shaved off and replaced with a tangle of slow-growing corkscrews. His morning visits trailed off. I wasn't the same Sabbie as when we'd met.

No wonder he'd told me to find someone new.

———

When I finally arrived back at Papa Bulgaria, I was still catching my breath … catching my dignity. I glowered with doom and damp.

Stan pounced on me. "You've been gone ages. What were you doing? Rowing a boat?" For Stan, that was quite a witty comment, but I bit back a retort. I peeled off my helmet and scratched at my head. "Don't play with your hair!" Stan yelped. "Hygiene!"

"Oh, give me a break."

He seemed to take this literally. "Okay. Half hour maximum, while the next orders heat."

I took him at his word and wandered over to Jimmy. "What's spare? Seeing his lordship's said I can take my lunch break."

Jimmy passed me a foil container. "Cancelled order. Veggie moussaka. Enjoy."

"Cheers, Jimmy," I said.

I went into the changing room and put my feet up on the bench so I was leaning against the wall. Wet coats dripped on me, but I was grateful I was able to think for five minutes. I pulled the cardboard top off the moussaka and dug the plastic fork in.

Max wandered into the changing room and sat on the other bench, his knees splayed. He had soup in a mug and a dry pitta and looked at my portion with some envy.

I smiled. "Hi."

"Hi there."

I'd been trying to gently prize information out of Papa's staff about Kizzy and her sudden going-away. I'd discovered that Mirela, Kizzy, and Petar hadn't been the only Romani to work for Papa Bulgaria; there had been many others in the past. It occurred to me that I should go and find out about the Papa Bulgaria shop in Finchbury, where I might meet other Roma workers. But I was nervous of doing this. I didn't want Mr. Papazov to realize what a nosey parker I was.

Although Max was a member of the Papazov clan, he was turning out to be a laugh on the quiet, and I decided it was time to quiz him.

"How well did you know Kizzy, Max?"

"I didn't mix with them." He gave me a sheepish look. "I'm sure you think Bulgarians stereotype these gypsies, but honestly, they do live up to expectations."

"I'm no better," I confessed. "I met Kizzy at the squibbing, still all dressed up. It struck me she was in the business of picking up men. But Mirela swears Roma girls stay chaste."

Max shrugged agreement. "I've heard that. Tinkers and horse thieves, but they consider prostitution as bad as slavery."

I tried not to groan aloud, remembering Mirela's umbrella fight outside Belinda's Bunnies. All because I hadn't got my facts straight.

"No one seems to care that Kizzy's been missing since that night."

"I didn't say she was pure as the driven snow. She was a looker. She was a tease. She'd sell herself, but she'd have to stay in charge. Pole dancing, say. Or maybe tacky porn movies, that sort of thing."

Max rested his pitta on his knee and steadily sipped at the soup, suggesting this conversation had gone as far as it was going. I polished off the rest of my own lunch in silence.

I slung the empty foil container and the plastic fork in the bin and glanced at the time. If I didn't get back to work in five or so minutes, Stan would come yelling for me. I went into the staff loo for a pee and a splash of the face at the miniature sink.

Then I sat back down on the loo for a moment because I felt suddenly out of sorts. The morning whelmed up on me; seeing Rey like that with the dark-haired woman. My breath came fast for no reason. I could feel drops of sweat on my forehead. My eyes opened wide with the realization this wasn't a passing moment. Patches of darkness were taking over my vision. I was about to faint and I was, like some old lady, locked in the loo.

————

Miss Dare.

She is trouble, that one.

My vision was filled with the snake I'd encountered in the ice temple. Anaconda. The bile-green scales went on and on, stretching into a murky distance. Its head twisted and its beady eyes took me in. We stared at each other. I saw the evil tongue flicker and the sensation of its bite came back to me. The snake slithered round my waist, squeezing the air out of my lungs.

I tried to struggle, pushing with both arms against Anaconda's dry scales. He didn't like that. He reared up, as he had in the ice temple, and directed his aim. The forked tongue pierced the skin of my arm at its tenderest point.

Miss Dare…

My eyes squeezed shut with the pain. I felt a cry warble over my dry throat. When I looked again, the snake had gone.

Miss Dare… Sabbie.

Someone was tapping the back of my hand. "Sabbie?"

I was still leaving the dream state, only half aware I was in the changing room at Papa. A man in a light suit with a crisp, blue-striped shirt was leaning over me.

"Did I faint?"

"You've been out for some little while."

I recognised the voice, but it took a second or two longer to understand that I knew the man. It was the doctor who'd been my first lunch delivery.

"Dr. Grace!"

"The staff here summoned me because you collapsed."

I was slumped on a plastic chair. Stan was hovering like a footman. Dr. Grace bent down, and I saw his black doctor's bag on the floor by the chair.

"I have given you something to help relieve your symptoms."

I struggled to sit up. "I felt very odd. In the loo. After the moussaka."

"It wasn't the moussaka," said Stan. "Dr. Grace has eliminated that. We don't get bugs here."

"I have examined you," said the doctor. "I can't find an underlying cause. I think it might have been pressure of work? Would you say that might be the problem?"

I'd put my hands over my face. "I've made an absolute fool of myself."

"Not at all." The doctor gave his smile that crinkled the lines around his eyes. "Don't be in too much of a hurry to move. Take your time."

"Yeah," said Stan, his voice dry as martini. "Keep your feet up for a few more ... seconds."

"I think it would be good if this young lady was allowed to go home. She should rest."

Stan blanched at the doctor's suggestion. "You are joking me."

"No, Stanislaus, I am not."

"We're so bleeding short of staff we'd have to close the shop."

"I'm sure you'll manage. You asked for my advice ..."

"Yeah, okay, but all she had was a little fainting fit."

"My *medical* advice." The doctor clipped his black bag shut. "Sabbie, there's a plaster over a puncture wound on your arm where I gave a little tonic to revive you. You can remove it at bedtime." He lifted my wrist between his thumb and fingers, a final check on my pulse. He shifted his shirt cuff to read the second hand of his watch and I spotted the faded ink of a tattoo; a brown line resembling wood disappeared behind the sleeve. The idea that this practised physician had once been a free-spirited youth made me smile.

"You go home," he said. "Take it easy for the rest of the day."

"Why not?" said Stan. "Take it easy. But don't take it you'll get paid."

I crawled home. I didn't feel ill, precisely, but I did feel world-weary. Fainting like that only confirmed it; seeing Rey with his new girl had taken all the wind out of my sails. I craved sweet foods that would fill the dreadful ache inside me. I eyed up my new toy and licked my lips. The shiny chrome and bottle-thick glass liquidizer sat next to my bread machine, and they probably exchanged stories about previous owners when I wasn't listening—the breadmaker had come from a boot sale, and I got the liquidizer for a snip on eBay. I whizzed up a speckled banana, a wrinkled kiwi fruit, some yoghurt, honey, and a fistful of oats, throwing in some ice chunks. The smoothie glugged into a pint glass. I took a big gulp and the chilled flavour hit the roof of my mouth like a charged battery. I swung my feet onto the sofa and zapped on the TV just in time to watch a mindless programme about antiques.

I rolled up my sleeve and peeled off the little round plaster Dr. Grace had put over the injection site. The puncture wound was already gone; a bruise no bigger than the top of my finger the only evidence I had ever needed a doctor. I vaguely wondered about the tonic he'd administered. I should have asked him what it was, but I'd been too fuzzy-headed.

The image I'd seen came back to me. Anaconda had been as determined as ever to do me harm. I often re-enter previous journeys when I dream, and they sometimes twist into something more sinister. I needed some insight into what my dream of Anaconda had meant.

Or maybe all I needed was objectivity. My mind had registered a snake's crushing squeeze round my waist. In the apparent world, Stan had to manhandle me out of the toilet onto the chair. And the moment Anaconda had pounced with his forked tongue was clearly the scratch of the hypodermic.

Not a vision at all, and nothing to do with Drea Comer.

———

I'd drifted into a halfway sleep when the door bell chimed. I swayed through the hall, still too dozy to consider the important question of who might be at the door.

It was Andy Comer. "Please can I have a word?"

He sounded like half his vocal chords had been removed. He looked worse than he had on Thursday night—pale, nauseated, weightless—as if the intervening weekend had drained him like a vampire. I opened the door and he took a couple of steps through then stopped. He brought his hands from his coat pockets and interlinked the fingers. "I don't know what I want to say."

I primed a wisecrack—*that makes a change*—but the look in his eyes, a deep, troubled brown, shut me up.

I steered him into the kitchen and made him sit on the sofa.

"I'm sorry," he said. "I've interrupted you." He was staring at my glass as if the contents might have been some concoction of magic mushroom and mind-bending cactus.

"Banana smoothie," I informed him, downing the rest and putting the glass in the sink. "Can you tell me what you want?"

He shifted on his seat. "I took my temper out on you and I need to apologise."

"Oh," I said.

"I have to set the matter straight, I suppose."

Goddess, I thought. *He wants to confess, and he wants me as his confessor.* I tried to think back to my counselling certificate. What did one do with men who finally admit they have poor temper control? All I could think was, *don't tell him he'll ever get her back.*

"I met Drea at Exeter University," he began. "She was a quiet girl, serious—studious, actually. For a start, she didn't get wasted every night in the campus bar. She didn't seem to have many friends at all, and when I got chatting while we were waiting for a lecture to start, well, at first I couldn't see why that was, because she was nice; friendly, kind, it seemed. Interested in me as a person."

It was the sort of thing a girl would say about a boy's chat-up line, rather than the other way round. "She left uni, didn't she. Before finishing?"

"Yes. You see, by then, there was no hope. She'd been love-bombed."

"Love-bombed?"

"You've never heard of the term?"

"Uh—" I found I had to cough before I could reply. "No."

"It's a horrible thing. It's like targeting … grooming, almost. I mean, you have to see it from Drea's point of view. You're lonely. You're away from home. All around you are kids having fun—they got to know each other so quickly. But you're shy, you have trouble making friends. And you had a good upbringing. Church every Sunday for Drea. She was already entrenched in …" He stopped and looked up at me sharply. "God's love. Can't be anything wrong with that, can there?"

I shook my head. It creaked on my neck.

"It's a sidewinder approach. All smiles. Extremely nice, interested in you."

I frowned. "Who is all smiles?"

"For Drea, it was Martin. Martin Ayto. For me … it was Drea."

"What?"

"Drea love-bombed me. Because once you are love-bombed, you need to love-bomb others. They love-bombed her—she love-bombed me. Knowing she did it for a higher authority gave her the confidence, you see, stopped her shyness getting in the way."

There was something I wasn't getting. "Who is this Martin Ayto?"

"No one. He left quite soon. Got out, sensible blighter."

"Left what? Got out of what?"

He looked down at his hands, still linked like the rafters of a church roof. The knuckles were white. "The Children of the Revelation Enlightenment."

I had to stop and think. The words struck a chord—the clunking chime of my letter box, the single sheet of paper wafting on the hallway breeze, slowly sinking onto the mat. I took a moment or two to bring the name up from its lost place. A feeling of chill spread in me. "Eric Atkinson?" I asked.

"Don't play it all innocent," he said. "You sent him over. It was deliberate."

The chilled feeling paralysed me. I couldn't move, speak. Finally, I managed to go over to the store cupboard and pull out the recycling box. I sifted through. A creamy coloured flyer. As I extracted it from between dead envelopes and old newspapers, the smell of mustard gas came to my mind, like malice, spreading, paralysing.

I tried not to show how upset I was as I passed it to him. "Is this what you mean?"

"Yes. Children of the Revelation Enlightenment. CORE. We were both part of it. It took us a long time to extract ourselves. Once you've committed..."

"Once you've been love-bombed?"

"Yes. One you're in, it is almost impossible to get your head round leaving. You believe the only way to save your mortal soul is to stay. And they wrap tentacles around you. Especially Drea. Eric had his eye on her from the start. Every so often he marries another one, you see—"

"Marries? *Another one*?"

"Yes. CORE is faintly associated with Mormonism. CORE doesn't allow bigamy for every man, just the leaders. Eric is in charge of the southwest UK division. He can have as many wives as he likes."

"Are you saying Drea is married to this man?"

"She's been his wife for four years." Andy's face was like thunder. "She still wears his ring. She bore his child."

I put my hand to my mouth. No wonder Drea thought I'd been so clever and insightful. I'd been warning her about Andy. She thought I knew about her real husband. I'd told her I'd seen a baby. She thought I knew what I was talking about. I sat heavily on the edge of the coffee table. I recalled the little scrap of paper she'd written on, when I'd given her the Reiki treatment. *AM I SAFE?*

"She's gone back to him." The words thudded out of me like lead pellets.

"Yes. No. Back to her faith. Back to her son. Back to Devon."

"Devon? But he's here in Bridgwater."

Andy snatched the flyer off me. "What's going on? He's based on the south coast."

"They're expanding?" I hazarded. "The love-bombing is successful?" Then I thought again. "Or maybe he was looking for you."

"Not me. Drea. His God-given wife."

Andy didn't raise his head, but I knew what he was thinking: I had showed Eric right to their door.

———

I was a few minutes behind for my last shift at Papa this week. Okay... I was twenty minutes late. Stan was bouncing on the spot, his face shiny with heat even though the oven had only just fired up. He was screaming at Jimmy to get on with the salad. The boy was cutting through a white cabbage with a knife so sharp, there was blood on his fingers. Stan yelled orders at Max and Petar then turned to me.

"Late! Late again! Late as bloody usual, you useless *Tsiganski*-lover!"

"What's got your wand in a knot?" I snapped back.

"Mirela's not here."

"What?"

"She phoned to say she's not coming in."

"Did she say why?"

"No." Stan thought about this for a moment. "Maybe I didn't ask. I get pissed with these gypsies. I've had to bow and scrape to my cousin Vittoria to get her to cover." He gestured to where a streaky blonde was examining her nails.

"Is she ill?"

"No. She's a bloody lazy *tsiganski*."

I couldn't help snapping back. "All you think about is your profit margin. Kizzy's been missing over three weeks. She could be dead for all we know. Show some sympathy for her sister."

"Kizzy isn't 'missing.' People go on holiday for longer. Don't worry your pretty head. Gypsies are streetwise."

"Yeah," Jimmy called from his chopping board. "And street walkers, if you ask me."

"I've heard that Roma girls will not go on the game unless they're forced."

Stan's cocktail stick bobbed as he grinned. "You heard wrong."

"Those sisters were in your care."

"Yeah, *my* care," said Stan. He started moving towards me, gesturing with his hands. It felt like anger, but he didn't look angry. His voice quavered and he looked miserable and overworked. "Perhaps I should blame you for my loss of staff. Everything was fine here, until you showed up. Mirela was keen to get on with the job she's paid to do."

"You pay Mirela shit wages, Stan. And Kizzy might be in danger!"

"Nobody's in danger, except you. You're in danger of losing your job."

I got out my mobile and called Mirela. The ringing tone went on and on. It was a communal number, a telephone in the hall. Was she too ill to get to the phone, or had she gone altogether? I started getting ready for first orders, pulling containers from the cupboard above Vittoria's head. I threw her a "hi," which she perfunctorily re-turned.

"Have you met the Brouviche sisters?"

Vittoria shook her head. "Stan says Kizzy was trouble from the start. She didn't even offer notice. Just took off."

"And now Mirela has too?"

Vittoria shrugged and went back to her nails.

"Okay, first order!" yelled Stan, his arm above his head. I snatched the details off him. I was keen to be out on the road.

———

The door to Mirela's house was unlocked, so I let myself in. I stood on the greasy linoleum of the hallway. Was Hermes tucked away in the back yard? Was it worth having a poke about? I shrugged and went upstairs. Hermes would be long gone from this house.

I tapped gently on Mirela's door. There was no reply for long, nerve-racking seconds, but then I heard a faint voice.

"*Tak*?"

"It's Sabbie, Mirela. Can I come in?"

"If you want. Door not locked."

Mirela was in bed but fully clothed. Celebrity magazines were strewn across the old bedspread and at the bottom was a plate with a sandwich curling on it, one bite missing.

"You okay?" I could see she'd been crying. "You're not all right, are you?"

She shook her head. The curtain of hair swung against her cheek, lank and unbrushed.

"Are you sick?"

"No. Yes. No." She lifted a corner of sheet and wiped at her face. "What is time? Are you delivering?"

"I had to come and see if you were okay."

"I okay, Sabbie. Tomor', I go back work."

"Duvet day, we call it." Although as I plonked my bum on the edge of her bed, I could see that they didn't supply duvets in this pit of a lodgings.

I fancied Mirela was too exhausted to bother talking to me, but there was something I really wanted to ask her. I'd been thinking a lot about how Andy Comer had described CORE; the way Atkinson used his love-bombing techniques on susceptible people. The mustard gas man was attracted to young girls ... he had as good as told me so at my door.

"Mirela, have you ever met a man called Eric Atkinson?" She gave me a dull stare. "Or Kizzy? Did she ever mention something called CORE? It's to do with following a faith. With the Bible."

She shook her head. I believed her. Already I could see what a blind alley this was. Kizzy had talked about "great riches." I'd thought the words felt archaic, something Atkinson would spout. But in my heart, I knew Kizzy had not been talking about her place in heaven. Besides, she would see right through someone like Atkinson.

"I have letter." Mirela was looking at me steadily. "Kizzy. She send me letter."

"A letter? That's wonderful. But why only send a letter? Why can't she ring you? Why can't she come home?"

"She is resting." Instantly, I could tell Mirela regretted telling me this.

"What, like an actor?"

It wasn't much of a joke, and Mirela didn't get it anyway. "She tired from all work at Papa Bulgaria."

"Aren't we all." I made a face to show solidarity. "Would it be possible for me to see the letter?"

Mirela gave a gypsy shake of the head that tilted her chin upwards. "It not for you, Sabbie."

"No. Of course not. I'm sorry." I put my hand over Mirela's. "I wish you would tell me everything, Mirela. Because if I was honest, I don't think you have, have you?"

Mirela took a long time to answer. I held my breath as I waited. She turned her palm upwards and gave my hand a squeeze. "People whisper. The boys whisper. Max, Petar."

"What do they whisper," I asked, whispering myself.

"Papa ... sometimes, they carry ... not food ..."

"They ask the deliverers to carry something else?"

"No—not scoot. I not know. Not much. Maybe nothing."

"What's Papazov up to? Is it drugs, Mirela? Was Kizzy involved?"

She didn't respond. Without thinking about it, I asked, "Is this anything to do with the murdered policeman?"

"No! No, nothing!" She shrugged. "How I know? I don't know 'bout that."

"Do all the boys whisper? Jimmy as well?" I was thinking I might get more out of Jimmy if I approached him about this.

"Him! Jimmy useless. Max laugh at him. Kizzy laugh. She say all men in this stink country useless. Jimmy, he can't fight. He can't get money. What good that sort man?" She climbed out of the bed and padded over to where a black canvas suitcase lay open on a chair, half-filled with clothes. "Itso my sort man."

"Are you going somewhere, Mirela?"

"Itso book me ticket home."

"That's a great idea." But it made me worry. Mirela would never desert her sister. Unless Kizzy had said something in her letter. Had she instructed her sister to leave Britain? Mirela would do as she was told. But why would Kizzy tell her to go home? Because she was as afraid for her little sister as I was? Or because she was enjoying her new life and didn't want Mirela to bother her?

"Mirela, please let me see the letter." Surely Kizzy had explained where she was. I stared into the case, where I fancied the letter would be buried.

Mirela didn't reply directly. "I want Itso so bad, I call him, at last. He agree. I go home. We plan gypsy wedding." Her mouth stretched into a proper smile of joy. I felt a real urgency. Mirela should go back; the sooner the better.

"Do you have to get to London for your flight?"

"No. Two flights. Bristol to Brussels. Brussels to Sofia. Long day. Be at Bristol six morning Wednesday next. Ticket at airport. Itso meet me Sofia late in night."

"How will you get to the airport?"

She shrugged. "I hitch or something."

"I'll take you." I hardly stopped to think.

"Take?"

"I'll drive you to the airport."

"Why?"

Because, I was thinking, it would teach me some humility as a shaman. Mirela was no more than a child and I'd done nothing good for her since she fell into my life. I wouldn't have slept anyway, thinking of her hitching through the night to Bristol. One missing Brouviche was quite enough.

"I think it's great that you're going home, Mirela. There are dangerous worlds in Britain for people with no family or ties, and I'm frightened that Kizzy might have fallen into one. That's why I'll take you to Bristol. I want you to get there safely."

"Safe?" Her voice was husky with emotion. "What is *safe*? Where is *safe*?"

"Anyhow, it'd be easy for me. I'm not using my car a lot at the moment; it could do with an hour's run."

"Thank you." Mirela wrapped her arms around me. She smelt of exotic oils—juniper, neroli. Against my shoulder, I could feel the pulsing of sobs. Her cheeks were wet on my neck. "Thank you," she whispered, "thank you, Mother Mary."

The words made my heart heavy and full of dread.

FOURTEEN

Why did I keep seeing snakes?

An enamel tie pin, no bigger than my thumbnail. Eric Atkinson had worn a pin on his tie that night at my door. I hadn't clocked it properly then, but now I was staring hard at the tiny details; a worm-like creature wound round the pin's head, with a wide red mouth, chocked with teeth.

The wearer of the pin was a chap my own age, a "greeter." He had his name on the lapel of his cheapish suit: Lee. He'd approached me as I'd walked through the doors of Charter Hall, a community space in the middle of Bridgwater that coped with everything from political rallies to pantos. Tonight it was the venue of CORE—Children of the Revelation Enlightenment. Andy Comer was parked down the nearest side road, while I was part of the crowd trickling into the meeting. I'd come hoping I'd find Drea, but on first glance around, she was nowhere to be seen.

"Can I take your coat?" said Lee.

I hugged it to me, still chilled from the weather in the streets. "Is that a snake?" I asked, pointing to the pin.

Lee girded himself up. "We call it the serpent of old, who is the devil. The snake was there at the start, in the Garden of Eden. It's the form the devil assumes when he is up to evil work." He began to chant, "*Those who take heed of that old serpent, Satan, will be dealt with. They will be stripped and sent to the place of no escape until their sin has been confessed and forgiven.*" His eyes blazed. My spine crept.

"Well remembered."

"Book of Revelation. I know the whole text."

"But it leaves an image with me that's quite terrible. Like the Spanish Inquisition or something. A place of no escape where you're made to confess."

"That is the message of the book. Better to be saved now than wait upon the Lord's wrath."

He was drawing me towards a serving counter neatly arranged with cups and saucers. A middle-aged woman with bony elbows stood behind it, holding an enormous teapot and trying to smile.

"Your coat?" asked Lee. "I can put it in the cloakroom? I need your full name for the ticket."

I told him, thinking, what the heck, and he floated away from me. I sipped my tea, letting my gaze roam, hoping for a glance of Drea. There were quite a lot of "greeters" and, to my surprise, a fair amount of punters milling round. Conversations floated over my head. It seemed that half of Bridgwater was searching for something to give meaning to their lives. I got chatting to a girl whose boyfriend had dumped her.

"I just want to know the reason happiness keeps passing me by," she said.

"Yeah, we all want to know that." I laughed, but she didn't follow my lead. "I'm not sure Eric Atkinson will fill in the right details."

She looked quite shocked. "You have to give it a chance. Why bother coming if you're not going to give it a chance?"

I was sure my true reasons for being here would shock her even more. Andy had taken a lot of persuading that I should do this alone, but he was finally won over by the argument that Eric wouldn't recognise me. I certainly hoped he wouldn't. I was wearing a smart jacket and a slender businesslike skirt, and I'd slicked back my wayward hair with mousse. I felt like an old bag, but the important thing was not to look like the pagan wino he'd met on his search for Drea.

Just after eight, the heavy front doors were closed with a thud. The greeters ushered us all into the theatre area. People drifted towards the rows of seating as if they were about to watch a full stage performance. I sat on the edge of a row and on the edge of my seat.

Hanging at the back of the stage were two banners. They looked homemade but intricately crafted. The one on the left was a deep electric blue, appliquéd with pretty felt flowers right around the edge. At the centre was a white lamb and a yellow crown.

The Lamb Slain For Us Made King

The words formed a rainbow of letters tumbling down one side. It was sweet; innocent, appealing, unlike the other banner. This had a background of bottle green. Its border was an elongated circle of barbed wire embroidered in grey. Inside was the same spiralling serpent I'd seen on the tie pin. It roared flames that licked purple lettering above and below.

By His Stripes ... Are We Healed

I shuddered. It wasn't barbed wire, it was thorns.

The lights dimmed and Eric strode onto the stage. He looked a heck of a lot smarter in his suit than I did in mine. He'd been designed by Italians from his tie to his leather-soled shoes. Why would he want to look so well-off compared to these ordinary West Country folk? I suppose it was something to do with identity, not to mention envy. I'd researched this sort of thing—inspirational speakers—during my degree, but, typical for me (typical for the student population in general, I guess), I could remember almost none of it.

The people in the front rows applauded heartily when Eric appeared. I checked the backs of their heads. I had the feeling these were his cronies—members of CORE. But there was no one there who resembled Drea.

The applause died. Eric held no notes and used no microphone. I could sense his presence from ten rows back; I was sure everyone could. Eric, even standing silent waiting for attention from his audience, had charisma in skip-loads. Then he began.

"The Lord rides on a swift cloud. He spreads his canopy over his throne, so to examine our failings. A day will come which will be the day of vengeance for the Lord in which sins are examined." He raised his face as he spoke, the palms of his hands lifted in unison. The words were clear and precise, the voice exulted. Tumults of images flowed from his lips. It was hard not to believe he was reading from a cue card. I glanced over my shoulder to check there wasn't one. I saw Lee standing in front the exit door, feet astride, arms across his chest. Some of the other greeters had the same stance.

I glanced again. Yes, the menacing feeling I'd had the first time hadn't gone away. They reminded me of bodyguards. But they weren't there to keep the general public from mobbing Eric (although I was sure they would soon step into action if that occurred). They were there to stop people leaving before Eric had finished spinning his words into silken thread.

For several minutes I couldn't think of anything else. As Eric's spiel moved fluidly from the sadness in people's lives to the state of the Western world today, I got up, trying not to let my chair seat bang, and wriggled out of my row.

Lee intercepted me.

"Please stay and listen. There is so much of importance Eric hasn't covered yet."

"I need the loo."

"Can you not wait until the talk is over?"

"Too much tea," I said, hopping about. "I've had surgery you see, on my—"

"Okay, I will show you the way."

I grinned to myself. Lee wasn't any different than any other bloke. Serpent or no serpent, the thought of lady's plumbing scared him to death. But I hadn't terrified him enough for him to leave my side. We left Eric listing all the ailments of society, each one caused by a lack of religion, and went back into the entrance lobby. When we reached the loos, Lee planted his feet firmly. It was clear he was going to stay outside until I'd finished.

I locked the door behind me and leaned against the back of it. I'd been hoping for a poke around. I could kick myself. I'd lived in Bridgwater for four years and had never been inside Charter Hall before. I'd've had a head start if I'd known the layout of the building. I pulled a flush and washed my hands, long and slow, then put on the electric hand dryer. Making the right noises would keep Lee happy. Meanwhile I was trying to work out where Drea was. My hands were super dry before it occurred to me that Drea might not be here at all.

Finally, I emerged.

"It's a shame you've missed so much. But Eric will talk to everyone after; you can ask anything you like."

Hmm, I thought. *Doubt if he's going to answer* my *burning question.*

"Actually, I think I might go. I wasn't really enjoying it."

I watched him take this in. "Why not try another five minutes?"

"No, I don't think so." Lee opened the door to the theatre. On stage, Eric was still striding about. Even so, I had the feeling that he had seen my antics and was watching me. "Can you get my coat, please?" My spine crawled so badly I wanted to run into the freezing streets, coat or no coat.

Lee made a little bow. "And your name was ... "

"Sabbie Dare."

He disappeared down some stairs.

On stage, Eric was mesmerising most of his audience. No one was fidgeting, playing with their mobiles, or coughing into their hands. He'd finally got on to the subject of the Book of Revelation, and I couldn't help becoming interested in what he was saying, seeing I knew little on the subject.

"We are so easily taken in by the Lord of Darkness." He paused for effect and scanned the auditorium. I slipped into the shadows. "Satan moves around this world doing harm and we put it down to bad luck, our own mistakes, other people's weakness, or we blame it on the government. But the Bible says ... *and the great dragon was cast out, that old serpent, called the Devil, and Satan, which deceiveth the whole world: he was cast out into the earth, and his angels were cast out with him* ... He whispers in the minds of people ... in your mind, telling you that evil-doing will get you all you have ever desired."

He pointed one finger towards us. "I know you are looking for miracles. Every time you buy a lottery ticket, yes? The Bible states clearly that God can perform miracles. But, my friends, beware. The devil can perform them too. God help the person that cannot tell the difference!"

Eric had unbuttoned his jacket; when he strode the length of the stage, it flew behind him. "The Bible tells us to put on the whole armour of God. Here in CORE—Children of the Revelation Enlightenment—we show you how to achieve that." His voice reached a crescendo. "For we wrestle not against flesh and blood, but against principalities, against powers, against the rulers of the darkness of this world, against spiritual wickedness in high places."

I'd almost forgotten that Lee had not returned with my coat. I peered down the corridor. It was empty and silent. He was nowhere to be seen.

Then I heard the giggle.

I held my breath. I know human ears don't really prick up, but I was sure mine took on elfin points. A toddler's silly laugh; I'd heard similar so many times in my sister Charlene's house.

What would a child be doing here?

I took a couple of steps along the corridor. My dress shoes were a tad big. They clipped against the floor like an overactive set of castanets. I glanced down the stairs, fearful that Lee would hear me. Where *was* Lee? There must be a lot of coats in that cloakroom. I pulled down my mouth. Clever ploy. In this weather, no one was going to leave without their outer garments—once they've been spirited away, you were stuck. I suddenly felt safer. Lee wouldn't be back in a long while.

The door to the reception room, where we'd been served tea, was closed tight. I turned the handle. Two women were washing teacups at the sink behind the counter, their backs to me. They didn't hear the click of the door. But the little boy saw me immediately. He was scooting on a small red three-wheeler, making motorbike noises. I grinned at him, a big wide smile. He let out another of his irresistible chuckles. He had typical two-year-old rosy cheeks and a white-blond fringe over dark eyes. He skidded to a halt and stuck a chubby finger in my direction.

Even then, the two women didn't turn. The older of them was the bony-elbowed lady who had served me my tea. She was chatting with all the energy of someone who knew she was right. The younger woman dipped her head over her work, wiping a saucer with care. Her fine, pale bob fell into her eyes. I could see the resemblance between mother and son.

"Drea," I said.

She swung round, staring at me, not moving, except to relax her hold on the saucer so that it slid to the floor. It bounced once and fell evenly into two pieces.

The other woman was not so tongue-tied. "I'm sorry. This area is out of bounds to the general public. Health and safety."

"I'm not general public. I'm here on health and safety grounds."

Her eyes narrowed. "Oh yes? Let me see your authority."

"Mental health," I said. "Drea's mental health and safety."

I watched the woman's cheeks suck in as if she'd applied a vacuum pump to her lips. The fine red lines below her eyes were tinged with purple. "Come here, Zachariah," she ordered, and the child's face screwed with caution. He skittered over to his mother, who had sunk to the floor to retrieve the broken china.

"I want a private word with Drea," I said.

The woman took a moment to work out her next best move. Finally she strode towards the door, turning as she reached it.

"Stay there and don't enter into *any* discussion," she ordered. For a moment, I thought she meant me, but she was talking to Drea. Bossing her so easily.

When the door had slammed behind her, I hunkered down so I could look into Drea's eyes. "Andy sent me," I said, simply.

"Go away."

"You don't have to listen to that woman. You can make your own decisions on who to talk to."

"You don't know me at all."

"That's true. I had no idea what you were going through."

She bopped up and threw the saucer in the bin. "Go away."

"Drea, I wanted to say ... I think you've had to be very brave."

That made her turn to me. I saw confusion on her face. I'd known all along that there was no point in me grabbing her arm and dragging her.

"I cannot imagine how tough it must've been to leave your little boy." He ran past me and I reached out, not quite touching the top of his silky head. "Then choosing again ... leaving the man you love."

"There are higher loves."

"Okay. But I've seen Andy. I know how deep his love goes. How he's grieving for you—"

"I'm not leaving."

"Remember the notes I gave you? What the snake said? Duty and purpose can change?"

"The snake's words are poison. Do not take heed of that old serpent, Satan."

"Don't you look around and regret your decision?"

"No."

"You have to stay with your son, then?"

"I have to stay with my God."

"Drea, I can't see how a merciful God would want you—"

The door burst open at this point. Eric Atkinson filled the doorway. The bony-elbowed bitch hovered behind him.

"You are to leave this place directly."

"Funny, I thought you were keen to welcome people in." My heart was hammering and I was sure it would show in my voice. "You said anyone could repent of their sins."

"Not you." His fist closed round my arm. His mustard-gas breath filled my nostrils. "You are the serpent's child."

My knees buckled, but he held me so secure I couldn't fall. All I could see was Anaconda; his malevolent eyes and a black tongue with two sharp points. Anaconda could crush you if he wanted. That was how I felt, breath lost from crushed lungs.

"See her off the premises," he said to Bony Elbows.

"I need my coat. You took my coat."

His lips stretched into the closest he could get to a smile. "It seems to have been mislaid."

"I'm not leaving without my coat!" I was shouting even without meaning to. It was as if the coat was a talisman that would ensure no harm came to me.

"I'll get her coat," said Drea in a mucousy whisper that told me she was close to tears.

Eric propelled me out of the room, pushing me along and nodding at me as if in agreement with something, whispering into my ear as if we were intimate friends.

"Don't think I don't know about you. My wife has told me how you enticed her into your sordid world. You, missy, are courting Satan with what you do."

In the auditorium, I could see the greeters had lined up along the stage, each sitting at a little card table from the storage area. They were taking names and other details from queues of punters who were patiently waiting to climb the set of steps that led onto the stage. There hardly seemed a person who wasn't in the queue, and although I presumed that most wouldn't follow up their sudden conversion to CORE, they certainly weren't witnessing my exit.

Eric pushed me bodily into the street. It wasn't quite up to O.K. Corral standards—I didn't roll down the steps and into the dust as the saloon doors swung shut—but my coat did come sailing after me, landing on the wet pavement.

The last thing I saw was Drea's face. Her eyes were red and puffy, but not wet.

I wasn't surprised. I didn't think crying would be allowed in CORE.

———

By nine fifteen, every punter had left Charter Hall, and, in ones and twos, the greeters started to make their merry way. Some of them hugged on the steps before turning in various directions; one couple went off arm-in-arm. Another bleak ten minutes passed before there was any sign of Drea.

I was crouched at the back of a shop doorway opposite, keeping a careful watch on the steps I'd recently rolled down like a drunk.

It was icily cold. My feet had complained for a long time, but now they'd given up in disgust and gone numb. No wonder I'd been insistent about my coat, although it had been sheer bloody-mindedness at the time—I *had* to let Eric know I wasn't easily beaten. But now I was shivering inside it, a gentle juddering movement that was

199

probably the only thing keeping hypothermia at bay. Andy was still down the side road with the heater on while I slowly turned into a cryogenic block.

The heavy doors opened and the final COREs came out; Drea pushing her son in a buggy, followed by a young female greeter and Bony Elbows, who was in charge of carrying the little plastic bike. The three women stood together, waiting for Atkinson to douse the lights and lock up. Involuntarily, I leaned forward. Atkinson was holding a second child, a baby of about nine months, which the younger woman took in her arms. A chilling realization came over me. All these women were married to him. This was his harem.

They set off along the street by foot, keeping together, talking in low voices. Atkinson turned round quite deliberately and stared back along the road. I flattened myself against the shop door.

He hadn't forgotten me, and he hadn't underestimated me. My plan had been to forewarn Andy when Eric came out, but I would have to wait until they were almost at the corner before I'd be able to make it back to him. Not that we'd properly discussed what we would do then, apart from follow Atkinson's car to see where they went. I'd known from the start that Andy hoped I'd be exiting with Drea and her little boy.

I hadn't got through to her. Her eyes had stayed dull and unresponsive as we'd talked. Perhaps Atkinson was slipping her some kind of drug to make her docile? But watching her walk alongside him, nodding to anything he chose to say, I changed my mind. This was straightforward brainwashing. She was still loved-bombed.

Through the plate glass of the shop front, I saw a dark flash, fast-moving. Someone sprinting, head down for speed, then head up, arms raised, calling.

"Drea! DREA!"

It was Andy. He had seen them pass and could bear to wait no longer. He'd clearly made an executive decision.

"Drea! Wait!"

Atkinson stopped the procession of women and children. He turned, legs slightly astride, to face his rival.

"Are you coming back to us, Andrew Comer?" he asked, smooth and cool.

Andy spoke. The group was twenty or so metres from me, and although I could catch Atkinson's raised tones clearly, I didn't hear what Andy said. But I saw him stretch out his arm. Drea turned away. Alone of the group, she paced fast down the street, the buggy rumbling over the paving stones.

"Leave or stay," said Eric to Andy. "Stay or bother us no further."

Andy didn't respond to that. He stretched up, right onto his toes, as if trying to reach Drea without moving from his spot.

"DREAAAAA!"

She didn't even look back. She was completely trapped in the place of no escape.

———

I threw myself into the Punto's passenger seat. Andy was already revving the engine. He swung away from the kerb. His tyres squealed as we turned onto High Street. The CORE group had disappeared.

I thought back to the first time I'd seen Drea. The things she'd said about her life in Harold Street, as if it was the most wonderful place in the world. I'd thought she was in love ... well she *was* in love with Andy—no doubt—but now I could see that it was more than that. Her new life glowed with bliss, full of light and music, because it was for one night only, like Bridgwater Carnival. She'd pushed

CORE into a tiny corner of her mind, knowing it would be only a matter of time before she was pulled back inside it.

This made me feel temporarily better. In the end, I hadn't been entirely responsible for Drea going back. It had been inevitable.

I'd assumed that Eric and his harem were on their way to some boarding house or rented accommodation, but as we took the roundabout, I saw them turn into the Market Street car park.

"I'll keep my lights on main beam," said Andy. I understood. You can't recognise a car so well through its headlights.

We watched as they all piled into dark-blue, seven-seat Discovery. It seemed a gargantuan vehicle, even for a harem, but then, I don't suppose there is any point in trying to save the planet if the end of the world is nigh. The beastie vehicle nosed out. We trickled along, some metres behind. A couple of times they accelerated so easily that the poor little Punto almost lost them, but thanks to Bridgwater's wonderful array of traffic lights, we caught them each time.

"Have they spotted us?" I asked.

"No idea," said Andy.

By the time they hit the Taunton Road, they were cruising, blatantly breaking the speed limit. As they headed for the southbound M5, Andy gave up the chase and turned back.

"At least you've seen her," I soothed. "At least you know she's physically okay."

"They must be coming up once a week," he said, as if he hadn't heard.

"But is it coincidence that Eric found Drea?" I asked. "Or have they been looking for her, town by town, mission hall by mission hall?"

Everyone was searching for someone. In our search for Drea, I was reminded of Mirela's search for her sister. Had I isolated another of the spirit wolf's places? CORE was without doubt a place of no escape. Drea's prison.

The wolf had been clear from the start that he'd offer bogus and genuine clues, and that I might find "no satisfaction" from some, but there *was* satisfaction in ticking another place off my list, even if it didn't get me any further forward with my quest to find Kizzy.

FIFTEEN

"Hey, Sabbie!"

I jumped. Treacle-coloured liquid and ivory foam were churning over the sides of a pint beer glass. Half an hour into my Saturday night shift, orders were flying across the bar at the Curate's Egg, but I'd been so deep in thought that I'd forgotten about the slow draw of the Guinness tap. Nige flicked it shut, surreptitiously wiped the glass, and placed it on the bar. He gave me a wink. "Grin if you had sex last night."

It was one of his lines—he never understood why female punters didn't fall for them.

"Sorry, Nige, mind not on my job."

It was usually Nige who lived deep in his own little world, but tonight I couldn't get my mind off CORE and the Comers.

Andy Comer had rung my bell at half-eight this morning, the Punto ticking over in the street outside. He'd looked as if he hadn't slept. "I'm about to drive down to Exeter."

"That's where CORE is based?"

"Yeah. They own a huge place, an old house on the outskirts of the city. Do you fancy the trip?"

"I'm working, I'm afraid. Therapies all day and barmaiding this evening."

"Sorry, it was daft of me to ask at such short notice." Andy had looked embarrassed, as if wanting someone to hold his hand made him a wuss. But I had been chuffed; after a dreadful start, we'd become friends-in-arms.

"Take care," I'd warned him. "Eric Atkinson flung me down the town hall steps, and I'm innocent compared to you. You're the man who stole his bride."

The more the serpent's image seared into my mind, the more I began to wonder about my journey for Drea. I'd been completely wrong about Andy. I'd assumed he was the serpent in Drea's life. I hadn't followed a simple rule of shamanic visions: they never quite tell it like it is. They slant things, leave things out, mix things up. This is mostly, I believe, because the otherworld works outside any rules of the apparent world. It's a multidimensional place where space and time are elastic and there is no morality—it is as shifting as quicksand and as slippy as quicksilver. Symbols and ciphers are how it operates, and the shaman has to be a code-cracker as well as a healer. But the Curate's Egg was not the place to contemplate such things. I gave myself a shake, passed over the dripping pint of Guinness, and took the punter's money.

"Go on," said Nige, as I counted out the change. He flicked a thumb at a dark spot near the band. "I can see you've gone all lovey-dovey on me. Have ten minutes with him before the band starts up."

"What are you going on about, Nige?"

"Your boyfriend."

I looked up and saw Fergus, tucked into his favourite place, the end of the bench that ran along the far wall. It was generally free because once the band got going the decibel range became suitable only for those operators of heavy machinery who had brought appropriate ear protection.

I was kind of surprised he was here. I'd been too caught up with seeing Rey in the Polska Café to think further about Fergus. An entire week had passed since we'd gone to his workmate's party, and he hadn't contacted me at all since then—not as a date or as a professional. I poured a pint and carried it over to him. He was dressed in a dark brown jacket, a light brown sweatshirt, and beige corduroys. The clothes matched his skin and hair tones, making him look like a sepia photo, something from a past era, and the "life is earnest" expression he always wore on his face affirmed that.

"Hi," I trilled, as I reached him. "Nice to see you again." I put down a frothing jar of Wild Cossack. "On the house."

"Ah, kind. You were busy serving when I got here. Otherwise ..."

"Actually, I've some news about Mirela I should share." I slid towards him along the bench. "She says she's had a letter from her sister."

"Indeed."

"She wouldn't let me see it, Fergus."

Fergus took a long slug of the Cossack and placed it precisely on the beer mat. "The two of them are so different. You know, when they came to see me, Mirela brought sweets—something she'd carried with her. It was like Turkish Delight. Bulgarian Delight, I suppose. She reminds me of that—sugar-dusted jelly."

"Yes," I said. "Sweet. Innocent. Unprotected."

"Kizzy wasn't sweet. Not innocent. Raw with sexuality. She made eyes at me, I can tell you." He gave a clipped laugh. "Difficult to resist."

"Would you speak to Mirela about the letter?"

"What? You mean find out what's in it?"

"I don't honestly know if there really is one, but I thought, seeing as she respects you…"

"Does she? I'm not so sure. I have no influence over her, Sabbie."

Mirela's words about Fergus were in my head … *ask, ask, ask, but no do*. "Maybe if you could offer some practical help to her, things might change."

"I can't start helping her until she starts trusting me. Neither of the Brouviches showed that much respect, if I was honest."

"What about the Bulgarian Delight?"

"Ah, but you see, Sabbie, that was just a sort of tradition when you meet new people."

"I didn't get any."

"She probably ran out."

I sighed, trying it keep it silent. Fergus's reaction was perfectly proper. Her letter was her own affair and neither of us had the right to pry. "Mirela's got a ticket back to Bulgaria," I told him. "I was wondering if Kizzy's letter told her to go home."

"You're the shaman," said Fergus. "If that's what you're seeing…"

"It's just a gut feeling. One thing I am sure of: Mirela will be home soon. I'm driving her to her flight."

"Jesus, that's a great relief to us all." He gave me a glance. "It's good of you to take her, Sabbie. When is she leaving?"

"Wednesday, a morning flight to Brussels."

He nodded and concentrated on his pint again, behaving very casually. His body language was telling me he didn't like rejection. By the end of the party, he'd picked up the message … *you're nice, Fergus, but not for me*… and his natural response was to back away.

Weirdly, his sudden coolness made me want his attention, made me want him to fancy me again. I tried one of Mirela's sizzling looks that transformed young boys to jelly, but without checking in a mirror I couldn't tell my success. I might've looked more irksome than irresistible.

I tried chatting about nothing, to loosen the atmosphere between us. I asked him how he got to the pub, as he didn't have a car. He said he could walk from his flat, one of the spanking-new builds near the old river dock. I discovered he was twenty-seven, ten months younger than me. Not that it mattered a jot. All that mattered was how at the party he'd wanted to feast his eyes on me, while tonight, he hadn't touched even my arm; his hand covered the ornate design on his notebook as if that was far more important.

"What're your plans for tomorrow?" I asked.

"Not sure about that yet, Sabbie. What about you?"

"I'm off for a walk. You know, hiking boots, the lot."

"Going with someone?"

"My foster family. Long-standing shared hobby. I reckon we've covered every mile of West Country in our time."

I could feel him warming up. His smile returned. Fergus was circumspect with his smile, almost using it as a weapon at times. I'd noticed that when I'd watch him talk to Mirela.

"Didn't realize you were once in the care system."

"Yeah. A survivor, is how we usually put it."

"You're a constant surprise, Sabbie." His hand strayed towards my arm, which was bare from the elbow down and purposefully resting on the table between us. He stroked my skin with the back of his index finger.

An eardrum-trembling squeak interrupted us. Although to-night's band was mostly acoustic, they had the usual standing circle of wired monolithic speakers that were struggling with feedback.

Fergus leaned in really close and spoke into my ear. "The Charcoal Burners. I was hoping to have a word with them before they start."

"About your songs?"

"That's right. Just to show them what I'm doing. Might not come to anything."

When he'd started to stroke my arm, he'd left his notebook lying on the table and I reached over for it. I gave him a playful grin.

"You mean that band will see what's inside here before I do?"

Fergus almost leapt out of his seat. He snatched the notebook from me. His smile had been snatched away too, and I could see he was having to resist hiding the book behind his back. For no good reason, my heart had started to pound.

I slid along the bench, keeping my gaze on him. "You'd better grab the fiddle player, then, while he's doing nothing."

Hot and cold, I thought, as I got back to work. *Likes to keep you guessing.* I wasn't sure if I wanted to join in the game.

I went behind the bar, ready to serve the next customer.

Rey was standing there, a tenner in his hand.

"What can I get you, officer?"

Rey looked all around him, as if he knew I was secreting a man somewhere. "For your information, CID aren't keen on being referred to as officers."

"Got you, *officer*." I wanted to be ruder than I managed. I wanted to ask him what the hell he was doing here, why he wasn't with his new girl. Then it washed over me: the realization that he was only here to ask me something he needed to know.

"A Tennent's for me and whatever you're having."

"Okay, thanks ... I'll have vodka and tonic, if that's all right."

I served several rounds of customers while Rey swallowed at the pint I'd pulled him. Out of the corner of my eye, I watched his Adam's apple bob. I fancied he'd lost weight in the last nine months. Rey was a free spirit and the pressure of promotion had probably hit him hard. He'd no longer be able to follow his gut-felt leads and his own slightly dodgy style of detection. Instead he'd have to guide a team through the minefields of modern policing.

"Look ... er ..." he said, as I paused for a moment at the till. "I thought I ought to ... well ..."

"What?" It hadn't occurred to me—before this second in time, anyway—that he might have spotted me exiting the Polska Café like a cat escaping from a firework.

"I didn't mean to sound ... er ... rude ... when you brought the Roma girl to the station."

I gawped. He'd come here to apologise. I couldn't bear the thought. "Don't worry about it," I said, fast. "You have to do your job. I might have been a bit rude back."

He nodded. Maybe he was grateful I'd pulled him out of the mire; more probably he would think it his due. "I don't suppose the sister has turned up, has she? I wasn't sure if Mirela Brouviche was clear that we'd want to be informed if she did."

I shook my head, my lips clamped shut. I ought to tell him about the letter and Mirela's flight plans, but I held off.

"Every connection to a police killing ... every link is important. All we've got at the moment is a gypsy in the lane where an eyewitness report places Abbott as last seen."

"I told you that," I said, stating the obvious.

"Yep, and it's getting towards the top of the priority list."

"Do you think Kizzy might have been caught up with the shooting of Abbott?"

"No arrests. No leads worth speaking of. No fucking idea, if the truth was known."

"She's written to her sister," I said, knowing I should have told him this long ago.

"Saying what?"

"No idea. But Mirela's packed the letter into a suitcase and plans to go back home."

"I asked her to contact me if she heard anything." He stared at the bar while he thought. "I know you want her treated gently. I'll send one of my female colleagues in, first thing Monday morning."

I felt a sense of relief. After letting Abbott's iPhone slip out of my hands, I was pleased I could offer even this tiny lead. I had an image of Kizzy coming out of the night shadows. She'd been there when Abbott had rushed past her. His body had not been found near St. Mary's church, but I was betting the police thought he'd died there. Had Kizzy fallen into a gunman's hands?

No. Because she went back to her room. She'd told Mirela about my so-called second sight.

My stomach twisted into a knot as I thought how I almost went up the lane in pursuit of Abbott. I could have been shot down too. But Kizzy stopped me.

"Abbott was a good cop, but not what you'd call the world's greatest note-taker," Rey continued, hardly noticing I'd gone somewhere else entirely. "According to his girlfriend, they'd gone to the carnival for an evening out. But one thing is clear: the person who put the bullet in didn't believe he was there to watch the floats. I've

211

been steadily befriending his girlfriend. Trying to find the answer to why he sent her and her little kid home and stayed behind."

Something jogged in my brain. "I saw you," I said. "Talking in the Polska Café. Was that his girlfriend?"

"Kate? Must have been. She doesn't know much. At least, if she does, she's holding it tight." He took another hard pull of his pint. "She's shocked, grieving, scared. Or it's the language difficulty, perhaps."

"She's not British?"

"She came from Poland. Her chap left her, with this kid on her hands. Abbott stepped into the breach."

"Very noble."

"Yeah? Well she's certainly cut-up about his death. I'm sure she'd spill the beans if there were any."

"There's a lot of Polish in Bridgwater," I said. "Makes me wonder about the Bulgarians."

"Yes. The Brouviches."

"And the others. The long-term ones. Like Papa Bulgaria."

"You know about Papa Bulgaria?"

I snorted a laugh. "I *work* for Papa Bulgaria."

"You're crazy. Whyever would you do that?"

"Would you believe it's the money? Or the nice shiny scooter I get to ride?" I waited for a retort; he waited for the full picture. I dropped my voice and leaned over the bar. I was fizzing, deep inside, from the understanding that the girl in the café was Abbott's girlfriend. I even risked doing the barmaid thing with my cleavage (such as it is) and smiling with a glint on my teeth like in a toothpaste ad. I glanced in Fergus's direction. It wouldn't do him any harm to know there was competition (such as it was). But his head was back in his notebook, pen scribbling furiously.

"Okay. Mirela told me about a massive employment scam going on there."

"Sabbie, please don't turn gumshoe again. It's common knowledge that the Papazovs didn't get where they are today by selling nice soup."

"You don't want to hear about anything I find out, then?"

"Employment law is outside my remit, thank the lord. Tell the uniforms."

"I thought I might get word of Kizzy from the other workers, but they're not very forthcoming. I've been wondering about a micro tape recorder. Don't suppose you keep that sort of stuff at the office?"

"Sorry, we're clean out of surveillance equipment at the moment."

"Pity. We'll just have to use a dead-letter box drop, then."

"Just remind me that you're joking, Sabbie. Papazov is a sleazy character. Not the sort you'd want to cross. I don't want you waking up to a nasty surprise one morning."

"The head of my favourite horse lying beside me?"

"Your own head lying beside you."

"I wish I didn't have to work for Papa, but to be honest, even a pittance is welcome money at the moment, what with Christmas coming and everything."

"Yep. I'll certainly be expecting my usual gold cufflinks."

"You'll be lucky to get a card. I'm going to celebrate Yule instead. The Winter Solstice. Cheaper and better."

"How're you fitting your therapy work in with delivering fast food?"

"It's so sluggish there's no problem at all."

"Thought about a leaflet drop?"

"Shamanism doesn't work like that. It's best if people are pulled to me. Word of mouth, deliberately searching the small ads, that sort of thing."

"What about the aromatherapy side of it? Surprised you're not handing out flyers with every Papa Bulgaria meal."

"Rey—that's a really good idea!"

"Glad to be of help." Rey emptied his glass and looked ready to depart. I was ambushed by an urge to grab the front of his marl grey sweatshirt and hang on. I searched around for a topic that might hold him here a while longer.

"Have you heard of CORE, Rey?"

He put the glass hard on the surface of the bar and examined me. "What?"

"Children of the Revelation Enlightenment. It's a religious sect."

"Going to join, are you?"

"Definitely not. Their leaders marry lots of young girls … I mean bigamy and that. Well, rape, in my view."

"Oh, please, Sabbie, don't give me any more sidelines to investigate."

"I'm not joking, Rey. This chap is crazy scary!" My raised voice floated across the pub. The music had stopped while the band rifled through their notes and lubricated their dry throats. In the corner pew, Fergus lifted his head and stared at me. "They are all so spooky. Not quite in the real world, if you know what I mean."

Rey laughed. "And you are?"

"Okay. I can see you're not interested."

"You know him by name?"

"Eric Atkinson. He came to my door. He was searching for someone who had run out on the sect. One of his wives. And now she's gone back. She was too indoctrinated to resist."

214

"CORE, you say?"

"They meet at Charter Hall on Friday nights."

"You'll need to give me more than that," said Rey.

"Oh! Right, well, he comes from Exeter. This girl's partner has gone down there today to see if he can find her. I did wonder if Kizzy had got lost inside the cult, but really, she isn't that sort."

"So. Can I assume you've already poked your nose in? Probably in a manner that put everyone's back up?" I couldn't think of a reply to this, but Rey didn't need one. "You don't seem to be able to help yourself," he went on in a blithe tone. "You need a bodyguard. Or a police escort, or something." He pulled out his wallet, and flipped a little white card onto the bar top. There was his name, followed by his title, and a mobile number.

"D'you hand these out to the criminal classes, so they can ring you for cosy chats?"

"Certainly don't. But I want you to have a number you can get through to quickly."

"Why?"

"Because you tend to get yourself into situations that need a direct response armed unit, that's why."

"I ring and you come running?"

I watched him suppress a smile. "Keep it on your person."

I turned the card over. He'd scribbled his address in pencil. "Wow," I exclaimed. "You live close to ..." I trailed off. I'd been about to say *close to Fergus*, but probably that wasn't wise. "Close to the police station."

"Not close enough, at times." He gazed into his empty beer mug in a profound way for a moment. "Well, I'll be off."

I searched my scrambled brain for something more to keep him there, but in the pause Kev tapped my arm and quipped, "Work here, do you?" and I was instantly involved in a complicated round of drinks. By the time I looked up, Rey had gone. And when I looked over into Fergus's corner, he'd disappeared too. Neither of them had bothered to say goodbye. I felt as adrift as a leaf in a drain.

SIXTEEN

DARK MOON

It was a blustery day, typical early December, but that hadn't put my foster father off. After lunch in the Davidsons' caravan—Gloria's famous egg, tomato, and potato pie, a slice of which melted in your mouth, exploding with sweetness and salt and filling you up to bursting—we'd marched out on the customary Sunday walk. We'd ended up at the edge of Brean Down, a fat finger of land sticking out into the Bristol Channel. I'd chased Kerri and Rudi and their father over the little tumps that stick out of the rough landscape, playing rough-and-tumble to warm ourselves up. The wind was high and bitter, blowing in from the grey sea. Philip was pouring hot tea from a flask for the adults, except Dennon, who had brought his own Coke.

"I've done some research online, since I came here last," I said, settling down on the car rug. "Those tumps are a Bronze Age barrow. And there was a Roman temple here, too, after that."

"I believe it was used in the Second World War." Philip hugged his tea. "It's certainly an elemental place."

He was right. The sea was vast, looking out towards Wales, and the land was so wild I was sure I could feel ancient whisperings from thousands of years before us. Although on reflection that might be Rudi having me on.

"How's trade in the therapy business?" asked Dennon, stretching out his boots.

"Wow, is this Dennon Davidson, under-the-floor-deputy-sheriff speaking? Have you transformed into a business person or something?" My phone chirped me a message as I was speaking and I shot Dennon a look. He had a habit of sending lewd jokes. "Is that you?"

"Nope."

I extracted my phone. It was hard to read the screen in the wind and cold, and I stared at the message a moment or two too long, puzzlement emanating from me like body odour. Dennon snatched the phone and read aloud.

"CAN WE POSS MEET? SAY @ STARBKS STREET WEDS? LV LETTICE XX. Ugh? Where's Starbks Street and why do they love lettuce?"

"I have no idea," I said, hoping he'd believe me, but Gloria smelt scandal on the wind and was reading over her son's shoulder. "Is it Starbuck's *in* Street?"

"It's a bloke," said Dennon, grinning. "Someone well into salad. Naughty."

"If you must know, her name is Laetitia."

"Of course," said Philip. "Laetitia. I had a great-aunt on my mother's side by that name. We all called her Lettice."

My foster dad has never lost his Jamaican lilt, even though he hadn't lived there since he was a small boy. Whenever they returned from a Caribbean holiday, his accent was stronger for a couple of weeks. The dark power of the vowels always made me grin with delight. Although it was Gloria's idea to let me start visiting their house while I was at the Willow's children's home, it was Philip who had said, "We'd be glad to have you stay with us for a while if you want, Sabrina."

Naturally, my response was, "Wha'ever. An' it's *SABBIE!*" But I have never forgotten his words. They formed my future.

Loving someone because you can see some tiny, almost extinguished spark in them can't be an easy thing to do, especially when no one is demanding it of you. But the Davidsons had always done that for me. For a while, I dreamed of getting rich (reaching the top of the charts was my fave scenario) and showering them with presents. But I don't think they mind that I never managed that.

"Who is Laetitia? Is she a client?"

"Nooo," I said, brushing my palm over the grass.

"What?" said Dennon. "Come on, sis, I can always tell when you're lying. Your teeth go on edge. Like this." He barred his strong teeth at me and growled.

"You *put* me on edge. And how can I be lying? I haven't said anything."

"That's not right, for a start," said Gloria. "It's usually impossible to shut you up."

I stared up at the sky. It was almost black with unspilt rain. Very soon I reckoned it would come down in torrents and we would be sprinting back to the caravan. "None of this will do me any good," I began. "And it's all your fault, Mum."

"*Mine?*"

"You know how I believe magic works. You deliberately sent me my birth certificate. That was all that was needed."

Her eyes widened into popping mode. "You've done some investigating?"

I could see that I might as well tell them. It would mean explaining about Papa Bulgaria, and that would mean explaining that I was strapped for cash. Not that they hadn't guessed already—Gloria definitely suspected something, she kept leaving pre-cooked dishes in my fridge and twenties under the bananas in the fruit bowl. The entire story was filling my throat, clambering to spill out, word upon word.

"It sort of starts with the Bridgwater Carnival," I said.

———

I drove home for a short-notice aromatherapy massage, getting back just before four and immediately prepping my therapy room for a client called Shona who hated to book ahead, because, *when I'm stressed out, I'm stressed out—I don't get advance notice.* I wasn't going to complain, having confessed to my entire foster family that I was running two part-time jobs to pay the mortgage. (I didn't realize until I checked my balance a couple of days later that Philip had transferred five hundred pounds into my account when he'd got home. Crafty. If he'd tried to push a cheque on me, I would've ripped it up, but it had dropped into such a big red pit, there was no money to return.)

After Shona had paid and left, utterly de-stressed-out (her words), I bit the bullet and rang Lettice.

"Sabbie." She was hissing close into the phone, and I guessed she was at home.

"Hi, Lettice, thanks for your text. You okay?"

"Er … yes. Fine." She raised her voice and began speaking in a normal tone. "Hey, want to meet in Costa's on Wednesday or what? Wait, I'll get my diary."

I heard her pant up some stairs and I guessed she was heading towards her bedroom where her mother wouldn't eavesdrop on the call.

"Lettice," I began. "I'm going to have to decline your invitation."

"Oh, okay, I was thinking that Street's out the way for you, but we could meet in Bridgwater? It's a school coach stop."

"Laetitia," I said, trying to sound like her mother, "before you go on, it's not the distance. It's the ground rules."

"Sorry?"

"We both know that your parents would not be happy if we met."

"They'd be fine, honestly."

"Why are you hiding in your bedroom, then?"

"Oh," Lettice wailed, "I just wanted to get to know my cousin!" She dropped her voice as if we were already conspirators. "My first cousin, I mean, like, both my first cousin and the first cousin I've ever *had.*"

"I'm sure you have lots of friends—"

"'Course I do. The girls in my year are heaps of wicked fun. But that is not the same as *family.* Grandma always says that, and it's true. All I want to do is meet."

"Not behind your parents' back, Lettice. And I don't think they would agree to this, do you?"

"Don't see why," said Lettice. She'd started off all in charge of things, but now I could hear her sulky-kid side rising to the surface. "It would be cool to have a chat."

"What about?"

"I dunno. Like, whatever you talk to cousins about … sort of, what we have in common. You know, like one of those 'me' things on Facebook."

"No," I said, feeling wearily grown up. "I don't know."

"Oh, like, 'what books are under your bed,' or, 'if you were an animal, which one would it be.' That sort of thing."

"Right," I said, adding a chuckle.

"For example, I'd be a dolphin. They're highly intelligent and I've already done snuba."

"What is snuba?"

"It's like a combination of snorkelling—which is naff; I always get nostrils full of salt water—and scuba. You're actually attached to the boat. It is the coolest thing. We did it in Hawaii."

I had to pick my words carefully, or I might end up hurting her and I really didn't want to do that. "You see, that's the problem. I've never snubed, or whatever. These things just reinforce how different our worlds are."

"That's not important."

"No, of course it isn't, not at all, but …"

"So what animal would you be?"

"Look, what I'm trying to explain is—"

"Go on. Just think. For a moment. What would you be?"

"An elephant," I said, letting out a tortured sigh.

"Oh my god! Why?"

"Because they love their babies and mourn for their dead."

"See? I love that. We're cousins, through and through."

"Maybe, but unfortunately your mother thinks of me as someone who delivers takeaway."

"I don't care! I don't care what she thinks—"

"But I do. It's important not to have secrets."

"Okay!" She'd almost reached shrieking pitch, but brought her voice under control. "Okay, I'll tell them. I'll get their permission to meet you. Yeah, why don't we both meet you? Me and Ma? In Bridgwater? There's got to be a Starbucks in the town, hasn't there?"

"There is a Costa's, but Lettice—"

"Please, Sabbie. I don't want an epic fail on this one. I'll talk to my parents, promise. Me and Ma'll meet you there after school one day. Good plan, right?"

"We'll see. See how it goes."

"Cool," said Lettice. "Sick cool. Be in touch, cuz!"

She rang off. I stared at my phone. How did that just happen? Phrases like "little finger" and "wound right round" sprang into my mind. *This*, I thought, *is why I'm not mature enough to have kids of my own.*

The call had left me feeling empty and exhausted.

I turned on the telly and while it was blurting out early Sunday evening stuff, I made a quick pizza by cutting the thick bottom off a stale loaf and spreading it with tomato puree, fried garlic, tomato and onions, some ripped basil leaves, and slices of mozzarella, then sticking it under a slow grill. I actually prefer this to the expensive take-out version, which I couldn't afford anyway.

I had to start asking some serious questions about my working life. It was crazy to squeeze the therapy business between three Papa shifts and Saturday evenings at the Egg. I sipped my herbal tea and thought about what Rey had said. If I did a flyer drop as I scooted around Bridgwater, and fitted any new clients in wherever I could, I'd build up my bank balance a bit before saying bye-bye to Papa. Not for one second did my conscience worry me about delivering leaflets on Papa Bulgaria time. I might even use the backs of their flyers to create my own little advert.

The TV ground towards the evening news. Pictures of a desolate coastline were appearing on the screen, with the looming menace of a nuclear power station. I looked up, interested. This was Bridgwater Bay. It was no more than ten miles north from where I lived. And a few hours ago, if the weather had been clearer, I'd've been able to see Hinkley Point from where I'd been sitting on Brean Down promontory.

"Police are confirming as suspicious the death of a female whose body has been found near Hinkley Point," a newsreader almost shouted, over the urgent beat of the signature tune.

I scrabbled for the remote and turned up the sound.

Figures of police strode in and out of a white tent that stood stark against a black sea. A policeman was being interviewed, but it wasn't Rey. It was his boss, Detective Superintendent Anthony Horton, a rugged-faced man whose mouth didn't seem to move as he spoke, as if out of sight somewhere there was a ventriloquist, operating this dummy in a suit with wide lapels and a slightly skeewiff tie.

Maybe he hoped the dummy would take any flak coming his way. He certainly didn't let any details slip out. "This is a young woman who has, without a shadow of a doubt, been brutally attacked. We have not yet identified her, but we are at present treating this as murder."

A reporter thrust a mike closer to his face. "Is there a connection between this body and the one found in the summer?"

"That case is still ongoing." Horton's eyes narrowed. "We will of course be considering all avenues of investigation."

I'd been searching for a girl and now a girl had been found. I prayed to the earth mother that this poor creature found in the sea was not Kizzy.

But I knew. A deep misery spread through me. I thought about death. How it came down on someone as animated as Kizzy. How another person, with vile intent, had taken that animation and watched it ooze away. There were no tears, but my eyes burnt as I stared at the TV screen.

My immediate thought was Mirela. Would she already know? There was no TV in her room. I snatched at my mobile. I could at least try the phone in the communal hall before the police came knocking at her door.

It rang and rang. It always rang and rang. I looked up at the screen, where Super Horton was asking the public to come forward if they had any relevant information that might help with enquiries.

That was me.

I keyed the contact number into my phone while it was still running along the bottom of the TV screen. I felt feverish—all hot and cold at once—my fingers trembled as I pressed the buttons and waited for the line to clear.

"I think I may have relevant information about the girl you've found at Hinkley Point," I began. "I think I know who it is."

———

I was desperate for further news. The woman on the help line was happy to take my details and my information, but she could offer nothing in return ... cause of death, time of death, identifying features ... Those were things Rey, his boss, and his team would be pondering over right this moment.

Had Mirela seen or heard the news? Had she also rung the police? They might be ringing her; she was the nearest kin of a missing girl, someone I'd just named as a possible ID for the body they'd found.

I scooted over to her house and thumped on the door. After several minutes, Petar opened it. His hair was mussed and there were crackly bits of sleepy in his eyes. He'd been having a Sunday siesta.

"I need to see Mirela."

He glared at me. "She not here."

"Is she at work?"

"No. She came back from work after early shift. Headache. Stan say she's for chop if she take one more sickie." He lifted his hand like a blade and drew it across his neck.

"If she's got a headache, why has she gone out?"

"No idea."

"Let me in, will you? I want to check for myself."

"You don't believe me, Sabbie *Daar*?"

"Don't *you* start calling me that." I took a leaf out of Eric Atkinson's book and shouldered my way past him. I was tensed, ready for the grip of his arm or a return shove from his sharper shoulder. But he stood where he was and watched me climb the stairs. "She is out. Why you not believe me?"

I was at Mirela's door before I realized it could be locked. If she had any sense, she'd lock it every time she left the premises. But the handle turned and the door slid inwards.

Petar had told the truth, for once in his life. Mirela was not at home. A sneaky thought arrived unbidden in my head. This might be my chance to read the letter from Kizzy. In fact, once the body had been identified, it would surely belong to the police investigation. All I wanted was a quick peek before it got handed over to forensics. That thought made me wary of touching it. I pulled my biker's gloves back on. The first place to look was obviously her canvas suitcase. I took a step towards the chair it had lain on, and stopped dead. The suitcase was not there. I dipped down to check under the bed. There was nothing but fluff. I opened the cheap plastic doors of the wardrobe. My heart lurched. Above my head, hangers dangled freely. Mirela had finished her packing.

I began pulling open the drawers to the small bedside dresser, my gloves slipping on the tiny handles. They weren't empty, but half-filled with the dross that people leave behind when they move on. I took the chair, climbed on it, and checked the top of the wardrobe. There was no letter lying there, either.

If she's gone, she'll have taken the letter.

I tried to piece together what was happening. Mirela seemed sure she'd booked a flight for early this coming Wednesday. Had she been fibbing because she wanted to be left alone to do her own travelling? The ticket was at the airport, apparently, so I'd never seen it. Had she changed her plans because she'd worked out that Kizzy might be the body at Hinkley Point? The news was very fresh; she might not have heard it at all.

I sat down on the edge of the bed. It gave way under me, like cheap mattresses do. Mirela hadn't made her bed before she'd left, but I could hardly blame her for that. My hand played with the crumpled heap of bedding before I lifted blankets and sheet to the foot of the bed. One sock, faded pink. I imagined Mirela looking for it when she came to put on the pair and blinked away a thin film of tears.

A hammering sounded along the hollow hallway downstairs. I leapt off the bed, aware that I was an uninvited guest in this room... in this house. I stood in the doorway, listening to the muffled exchange below.

"We'd like to speak to Mirela Brouviche."

My body went into standstill. That was Rey's voice.

"She not here." Petar was back on doorman duty.

I looked at the bed and thought about the forgotten sock.

In two strides, I was tossing the pillows aside. They were thin foam, stained with hair grease and the sweat of many sleepers. Trapped beneath the fitted sheet was the outline of something rectangular. An envelope.

"She *is* out!" I heard Petar call. There were police boots on the stairs. Without thinking further, I pulled the sheet free, stuffed the envelope into my pocket, and ran from the room.

I met Rey as he took the turn in the staircase. I was standing at the top of them, looking down on the spikes of his hair and the pale scalp showing beneath. He paused as he saw me then came up the rest of the stairs two at a time, a uniformed female officer following on and Petar, the opportunist, keeping a certain distance behind her.

"What are you doing here, Sabbie?"

"I came to see Mirela."

"I've been waiting for you to contact me."

"I didn't know that." I was trying to stop shaking—or at least prevent Rey from seeing that I was shaking. "I phoned the help line. I told them all I knew."

"And then you came here."

"I thought Mirela might need a friend." I tried glaring at him. "To support her when the police came storming in."

He gestured to the officer, who was waiting by his side, as if primed for instruction. "This is Sally. She's here as support officer for victims' families and loved ones. She's here to support Mirela." I watched his lids close over reddish eyes. "Not that you can't support her too, of course."

"She isn't here, Rey."

"Okay. We can wait. Unless you have an idea where we might find her."

"I think she's done a runner."

"You don't mean that," said Rey. "It's the criminal who does the runner."

"Which is her room?" Sally spoke for the first time, but she directed her question at Petar.

He pointed to the open door. "That one. But she's out."

"She's gone," I said.

Rey gave Sally a look. "Take them downstairs. Get the story. I'll be with you soon." He walked into Mirela's room and closed the door behind him silently.

He hadn't really looked at me at all.

SEVENTEEN

AT TWENTY PAST EIGHT the following morning, I scooted over to the Agency of Change. I had an appointment at the police station at nine a.m. I'd been charged with the duty of identifying the body in the absence of Mirela. Before that, I needed to see Fergus. He probably knew the bad news: that Mirela had gone and Kizzy had been found. That Kizzy was dead. But I had a task for him.

I parked and went into the Polska Café, where Fergus had said he'd meet me before starting work upstairs. There he was, in his dark corner, a latte in front of him. I didn't think my stomach would keep breakfast down so I bypassed the woman behind the counter, who I could recall Fergus called Maria. "Hi," I said, taking the seat opposite him. I'd not gone into details in my text, and now I wasn't sure how to start.

"How are you?" he asked.

"Not good, Fergus. Have you seen the news?"

"The local news?"

"All the news." I'd been hoping he'd've put two and two together. "They found a body. By the power station."

"Hinkley Point?"

"Yes. Fergus—I think it's Kizzy."

He blinked, as if only half awake. "Jesus and Mary."

"They're asking me to ID the body. But surely, you knew her more officially than me—"

At that moment, Maria, smiling like a babushka, placed a cup of tea in front of me. "On the house," she said.

"That's so kind," I said, but the woman was already heading to the counter.

"It's the way with the Polish, over here," said Fergus. "They feel they've been offered kindness. They offer kindness back."

Fergus tended to simplify things, and sometimes romanticize things too. I took a sip of my tea. "It's so sad. But now I'm scared for Mirela. She's missing, Fergus. I heard about Kizzy on the evening news and I went straight round. So did the police. But she'd taken off. Piecing things together, it looks like she walked out of her accommodation yesterday after getting home from her early shift. She'd packed all her things and left with them."

"She'd heard the news?"

"That's the odd thing. According to her house mate, she was gone before the news broke."

"Do you think she suspected something like this was about to happen?"

I had wondered that, but it had taken Fergus to put it into words. Had Mirela disappeared because she simply *knew?* Did she have second sight after all?

"I'm thinking, Sabbie, that it's possible Mirela always knew Kizzy was dead."

It was a dreadful thought—one I preferred not to dwell on. "She was distraught at Kizzy's disappearance."

"Okay, but what do we know about her after all? Only what she chose to tell us."

I swallowed. "There's a police alert out. Check a news site on your office computer, Fergus. They're scouring the West Country for her."

"Because she has information? Or is at risk?"

For some reason, my heart was thudding. I hated the way his mind was working. I took an A4 envelope from my bag and slid it over the table. "I found this under her pillow. It's from Kizzy. It might be the last thing she wrote."

Fergus turned it over in his hand. "This is an old envelope addressed to you."

"It's inside. Don't touch it without putting on gloves. Sorry to sound so melodramatic, but I shouldn't have it, not really. It's evidence. I'll have to give it to the police."

"Holy mother of Jesus, Sabbie, what're you playing at?" He put the envelope down as if it was wired to give out shocks. "I'm not going to say that the police play fair with immigrants, but at the agency we have a policy of always playing fair with them. I instigated it, when I arrived here. When dealing with people who break rules, we stick to the rules like superglue."

I put my head on one side and tried to look cute. "You think I'm too nosey for my own good, don't you?"

He smiled. It was his first smile since I sat down—I'd been watching for one ... waiting for one. "The word *bloodhound* does come to mind, so it does."

How right he was. I never could keep my wet nose out of things. Sniffing round the staff at Papa ... snooping at Belinda's Bunnies ... trailing a copper at a carnival. And reading what I shouldn't: a folded square of paper under a floor cushion ... a letter under a pillow. I was more curious than a cat, and look what happened there. Why couldn't I keep things simple? Report to the police and hand over anything I thought might be relevant. Let them deal with it. Let them solve things.

"What does it say?" asked Fergus, unable to help himself.

I managed a laugh, but it didn't cheer me up. "I have no idea. It's entirely in Cyrillic script."

I saw Fergus's eyebrows rise up.

"I was hoping you'd know a translator."

"It would take me a while, Sabbie."

"Could you do a photocopy? I'm going to get into serious trouble if I don't hand it in quickly."

Fergus didn't move. He was staring across the table at me, as if he'd had a shift in perspective. Had he thought of me as all law-abiding and incorruptible? Was he reviewing his Sabbie Dare file and updating it?

"One thing really worries me," I said, keeping my face looped into a smile. "The fact Mirela left this letter behind. She emptied her wardrobe and drawers, but she left the letter under her pillows. As if she had to leave so quickly, it slipped her mind. But I'm positive it would not slip her mind. So I'm wondering if she was forced to go."

"You think someone bundled her out of her digs?"

"Petar said he saw her leave on her own. He's a total heel, though, he could be lying."

"Perhaps she wanted to leave it behind," said Fergus.

"Why would she do that? It must be a treasure for her."

"I'm thinking that if there's an address in the letter, Mirela might go there."

"So she'd need the address…"

"You can always note an address down. But if you don't know where you're going … or what you'll find there … you might like to leave something to show someone else the way."

A curl of hope rose inside me. Had she thought ahead? Left a message? We'd only know that when the letter was translated.

But there was a postmark.

Gloria always examined an envelope first, often turning one in her hands when it arrived in the post, asking, *whoever can this be from?* I had taken a tip from her before I'd slid the letter into my bigger envelope last night. I'd examined the frank. It was in faint red ink, and I'd had to switch on my reading lamp to give myself more light. Bit by bit, I'd made out the date of posting—a couple of days before I'd seen Mirela in her room, where she'd told me she was flying home. I noticed that the letter had been sorted and franked in Puriton. That felt strange; the town of Puriton was hardy five miles away. And in the margin of the single piece of paper inside the envelope—which I'd examined for short seconds—was a smudge of brown. I was still wondering about that.

I was staring into vacant space as I thought this through, focusing vaguely on the woman ordering at the counter. She was beautiful, I thought, high cheekbones and hair like a swinging curtain of chestnut brown. She was chatting to Maria, smiling at a comment as she gave her order. She moved on, sitting at a small table.

There was something familiar about the girl. Slowly it registered that I was staring at the woman I'd seen in here with Rey. Abbott's bereaved girlfriend.

"You okay?" asked Fergus, waving a hand in front my face.

I gave myself a shake. "Sorry."

"Why are you staring at Kate? Do you know her?"

"Do *you* know her?"

"She's an old client of Juke's. I've seen her pop into the office. I know her well enough to say hi to."

"Sometimes I think Bridgwater is like a village; everyone has a link to everyone."

"That's so. You could have fun with diagrams, should you please. I link to the Agency, you link to a completely other culture, and we met through the Brouviches."

"Who link to Papa Bulgaria." I gave a hearty sigh.

"You've kept in touch with that lot?" Fergus asked, not quite a question. I'd never bothered to tell him I actually worked for the takeaway, but now I realized I had a fair amount to share which involved them.

"My original plan was to extract information," I said, glossing over the desperate need to earn some extra cash. "And I have spoken to most of the staff now about Kizzy. But I'm getting very mixed messages." I watched Fergus's brow darken. "I'm desperate to get out of there, but they've tied me into that scooter agreement."

If Fergus'd had feathers, he'd've preened them. I could see he was dying to point out that he'd warned me about this, right from the start. I hated his smug look. I eased the conversation back to the essentials.

"I have to be on my way. Any chance of getting a photocopy of the letter for me? Once the police have got it, they won't be keen to let us know what it says."

Fergus took the hint. "I'll do it now, so I will. Stay and finish your tea."

I watched him go, thinking back to the first time I'd sat opposite him at this identical table. He'd seduced me with his intriguing chat-up lines delivered in his gorgeous accent. Then he'd rejected me soon as he realized they hadn't worked first time round. Now he was acting as if things were back at the start and there had been no pursuit, no flirting, no heavy snogging. I turned my tea round and round in my fingers. That was what I'd wanted, wasn't it? To regain a professional relationship with him? But it made me feel cautious of the fellow from Ireland. And the connection with Gary Abbott's girlfriend seemed all the more puzzling because of that.

I got up from my seat and carried my cup over to Kate's table.

"Excuse me? Would you be Kate?"

"Yes, that's right." She gave me a glimmer of a questioning smile, but I felt enough welcome to grab the back of the other chair.

"Is anyone sitting here?"

Her eyes become bleak. "No one."

"I'm sorry to disturb you like this," I said, sitting opposite her. "Only, it was me, who went to the police—Rey Buckley—after the carnival. I saw Gary drop his mobile in the street."

"You knew Gary?"

"Not well. I was … my name's Sabbie Dare. Gary interviewed me a couple of times over the case that gave him his promotion."

"Ah … yes. He was proud, to be sergeant." Her accent was delightful. Within it I pictured vast plains, primeval forests, and rugged peaks.

"I can understand if you don't want to talk about it. It's too shocking."

She nodded, using the movement of the nod to look me up and down. "One moment, he was my life. Then poof!"

"Not in your life."

"No life."

"And no warning."

She shrugged. "Gary didn't believe in warnings. He used to say, 'never warn the bugg—'" She swallowed the word. "Sorry, he did swear sometimes!"

"The element of surprise," I suggested. "Was that what he was good at?"

"I don't know about his work. But he was a surprising guy. Funny, tender, generous. A good father to a boy who was not his own."

I listened without comment. The description hardly resembled the Abbott who had grilled me—who had damn near spat on me—earlier in the year. It reminded me that people present a different face when they're at work.

"I'm so sorry, Kate. You must miss him unbearably."

"I would have liked to say all these things at his funeral," Kate went on, "but..."

"The police element did swamp it."

"I am not good at talking."

"And they can talk at you, can't they?"

"Even his friends in the force. They keep asking... did he say anything that might help? I say; nothing. *Nic nie.* I don't think they believe me."

"But it's the truth?"

She took a while to answer. "You are questioning me now."

I sat back in my chair. "I have no right. You don't even know me. But, you see, I'm caught up. Because I've been less than helpful in the investigation. I found his mobile but it was stolen from me at the carnival, and Rey Buckley hasn't forgiven me. He wants the person who did this so bad. I haven't forgiven myself, come to that. Me and my mate were pissed out of our skulls by time the squibbing started; we were mucking about. I saw Gary run up the lane to St. Mary's church. Maybe the fireworks masked the gun shot. But no one seems to know what he was doing there. He wasn't watching the fireworks. I saw him run. It was like … I knew, Kate, straight away. He was running like a copper."

She smiled, soft and sad. "Good."

"Good?"

"I don't want my Gary to be dead because of something that was bad luck, something he was just in the way of. If he has to die, he would want to die in the saddle."

"In the saddle?" It didn't seem like a phrase Kate would use. "Is that what Gary said?"

"Yes." She glanced up and I followed her gaze. Fergus was pushing open the café door, the letter back in its envelope, and Maria was heading our way with a plated Polish breakfast. I eased myself up.

"Yes," she repeated. "It is what he said before we left for the carnival."

———

Rey strode along the corridors of Musgrove Hospital in Taunton, skidding on his heel as we reached a sign that said MORGUE. I reeled after him.

Sensations bounced off the walls. I was aware of a smell, vague but rotten, like cabbages left to moulder at the bottom of a vegetable patch, and I was sure the temperature was lower than the air outside, as if someone had opened the door to a very large freezer and allowed the cold to seep out.

It was all my imagination, of course. The chiller sections of the morgue were confined to slide in and slide out coffins that took up whole walls of some room somewhere, like giant filing cabinets. Only when you slid out a coffin would your breath show in the room. Yes, the cold and the smell were my imagination.

My heart heaved as I skittered along the polished floor. We were heading, far too quickly, into the depths of the morgue. Any moment now, Rey would stop, go into a filing cabinet room and draw out a coffin on its runners. Then he'd stand judiciously back from the chill and the stench as I bent over the body.

He stopped so quickly I almost ran into him, breathless from the mini-sprint. "I haven't thanked you yet."

"What for?"

"Helping with our enquiries."

"I didn't think members of the public had a choice in the matter." He glanced over his shoulder. "She's behind us in that room."

"Oh." I felt my shoulders tighten, as if preparing to shudder.

"It can shake people up. Even if they're not closely related to the victim. So you must indicate if you feel unwell. There's a bench, see, you can sit down on if you need to."

I turned to look at the corridor wall. "Out here?"

"Yes," said Rey. "Out here. You don't go in."

We'd arrived. I glanced through a plate-glass window. A gurney stood in a small room, shrouded with a green sheet.

I was terrified that Kizzy would be entirely decomposed, that she'd been dead since she wrote the letter. Or was she dying as I sat on the tumps at Brean Down, looking towards Hinkley Point?

"It's procedure. You observe through the glass. I'll enter the room, pull back sufficient sheeting, and wait for your signal."

"I signal to say I recognise the body."

"Or not. Either way, you can nod or raise your hand to indicate you've seen enough."

Rey entered the little room, closing the door behind him. In the long corridor it was the only room with a window, and below the window, at waist height, someone had thoughtfully placed a rail, so that the grieving witnesses had something to clutch in their agony. I considered, in the seconds it took for Rey to reach the shrouded body and unmask it, how lucky I should consider myself. I did not love this person. My world would not be altered if I recognised her.

The sheet was pulled. I was staring through glass at a dead woman. Her eyes were closed and the lids—all of her face and neck—was thick with fluid, puffed as if stuffed with seaweed. Her mouth was stretched into a horrid grin—*rictus* was the word that sprang into my head. Her skin was as pale as fish flesh. I was reminded of funeral parlours; the way the funeral technician drained the dead of their blood and injected some chemical into their veins and arteries in replacement—formaldehyde, I fancied—but no funeral technician had been near this body yet. It as if her lifeblood had oozed from her as she'd been nibbled by marine life.

But her hair—that long, thick black drape I'd seen under the dim lighting in the lane—had been brushed. It didn't shine any longer, but it was unmistakably Kizzy's.

It took me a long time to realize Rey had come right over and was tapping on the other side of the glass. I had given no signal. I had forgotten everything in the world but the sight of Kizzy Brouviche. I gave a single sharp nod, and looked down at my feet. When I next looked up, the blinds had been scrolled shut and Rey was handing me a plastic cup of chilled spring water. He took me by the bend of my elbow and I sat with him on the little bench bracketed to the wall.

"You recognise her?"

I nodded. "What happened to her?"

Rey didn't reply directly. "You are able to confirm that the name of the deceased is Kizzy Brouviche and you'll be willing to sign a statement to that effect?" He was being so formal. Perhaps it was necessary; perhaps he thought it would help. "And that you'll be happy to give us further details on the deceased, anything you know about her, including the last time you saw her alive?"

That jolted me. "You know when I last saw her alive. I told you. She read my palm on the night of the carnival. The same night Gary Abbott died." I pulled Kizzy's letter from my bag and passed it over.

He took the envelope and looked inside. "How did this come to be in your possession? Did you remove this from her apartment yesterday?"

I snorted. "She didn't have an *apartment*. She had a mouldy, wretched room in a house full of underpaid immigrants."

We were sitting so close on the little bench, our knees were millimetres apart, and I was sure electrons were flying across the gap like shooting stars. As if we both realized it at the same time, we shifted our bodies in opposite directions.

"I didn't answer your question."

"I know that. It's my job to spot things like that." His voice had softened. "Perverting the course of justice is a serious crime."

"I haven't really touched it, Rey."

"I worked that out too. Not many people wear their biking gloves indoors."

I shot him a glance of respect, tinged with a low-grade fear. Rey was a DI now; had been for some months. I had never bothered to wonder how he did his job, or if he did it well.

"Can you fill me in," Rey asked, "on your relationship with both the Brouviches?"

I told him the full story, sitting there on the hospital bench. I started with Mirela, her first night at my house. I described my journey to the spirit wolf. Seeing I was in full confessional mood, I even skimmed quickly over the massage parlour incident. I told him about Mirela and Kizzy's connection to Fergus.

"Agency for Change rings a bell," he said, "but I've never heard the name Quigg. Can you give me his details?"

"Sure." *Body—small but perfectly formed. Hair—a great fuzzy mess. Height—if I lean straight across, I can touch those lips with mine. And he had the hots for me, Rey . . . had . . .* "I think he's in touch with someone at Bridgwater station about the legality of what they do at Papa Bulgaria."

"All right, Sabbie." I could sense his despair . . . his disappointment. "We need another official statement. They're getting to be a habit with you."

He took the empty plastic beaker from my grasp and tossed it into a bin, striding away in his policeman's shoes, heel to toe with a straight back. I stepped behind him like a child.

EIGHTEEN

REY DROVE THE BACK way out of Musgrove Hospital, grimly silent. I stared forward, trying to keep my mind off of the sight of Kizzy's rictus grin. As he reached the hospital exit, Rey let out a long sigh.

"How I'd love to have a nice quiet chat with every surgeon in this place."

"But all local victims end up here for autopsy, don't they?"

He shrugged. "This case isn't twenty-four hours old and it's already doing my head in."

"What? Why?"

"We're not used to murder victims in Bridgwater. We've got a law-abiding population of less than thirty-five thousand. One copper and two young female deaths in four months? So far, we don't even know if any of them are linked."

"I've already heard people saying the two girls' deaths could be the same killer."

"It's a theory, yes. They were both dumped in the waters round here." Rey changed gear and changed the subject. "My scalp's tightening, Sabbie."

"What d'you mean?"

"Always happens when someone isn't telling me everything."

"Right. Must be painful then, being a cop. Constant migraine situation." I glanced sideways to see if I'd wound him up sufficiently then went on. "I bumped into Abbott's girlfriend, Kate. We did have a brief chat. She told me Abbott had said a strange thing on the night of the carnival. That if he had to die, he would want to die in the saddle."

Rey only paused for the briefest of seconds. "Coppers are always coming out with things like that. Don't put too much store by it."

"It felt like it had something … some sort of subtext. Can't you feel that? You get hunches. Good hunches."

"You were my only hunch, Sabbie."

"A good hunch, I hope?"

He raised a single eyebrow. I love blokes who can do that. "Not too good, eh?"

"You saying I've got a wicked side?"

He paused, as if weighing things up. "Last time, you almost got killed."

I laughed, trying to sound wicked, but it might not have come off. "I don't think *that's* going to happen again, is it? I mean what are the odds?"

"I'd say about the same as us ever getting out of this bloody traffic queue."

"I noticed there were a lot of roadworks on the way in."

We had been crawling towards a set of temporary traffic lights since we left the hospital grounds. They had turned red for the third time and we were still a long way back.

"Bloody mess." I wasn't sure if he meant Taunton roadworks or his investigations. "Oh, come *on*, for Christ's sake!" Rey had shot forward until he was so close to the car in front they might have exchanged bodily fluids.

"What's the hurry?"

"Need a coffee, is what. You have to be anywhere?"

"Yes. Papa Bulgaria." I saw his teeth bare, like an amused primate. He hit a button on the console. The radio spluttered into life.

"Go ahead, India Five."

"I've got a witness in the car, done a body ID. Can you phone her place of work and tell them she won't be in for the rest of the day? Helping police, et cetera?"

"Rey," I yelped. "Don't do that. They'll think I've got a record or something!"

His grin spread. "Trust me, a record would speed your promotion in that place." He flicked a switch on the console and a whine started up. He edged out and roared along the wrong side of the road, lights flashing and siren screaming, nosing into first place in the queue just as the lights changed to green.

I was remembering the strange little conversation I'd had with Mirela in her room, the day she'd told me about Kizzy's letter. I'd almost forgotten it. I started to explain this to Rey, but it sounded garbled and invented. Perhaps Mirela had invented it. I only half believed her at the time. Something about moving things. In the scooters? That was it.

"Could it be drugs?" I asked. "They seem too tin pot to be mixed up in anything worse."

"Tin pot is how the drugs trade works. It's dependent on little men who are as quiet and dark as shadows, especially the ones that lie in the middle of the chain of command. The commodity is shifted along the line from producer through wholesale into retail."

"You make it sound like … tomatoes."

"Hmm, tomatoes are close in a lot of ways."

Rey was quiet for so long I thought I'd offended him in some way—not a difficult accomplishment. My heart started to pound. Was Rey scaring me, or was it the sight of poor Kizzy's body? Or was it the memory of Mirela, her eyes red, her voice low and trembly as she muttered what seemed like a confession … *they carry … not food …*

Eventually, Rey took pity on me. "Can I trust you to keep your mouth shut?"

"Yes, no problem."

"There's a Bulgarian cartel. They call themselves *Mutri*."

"What's that?"

"It's Bulgarian or something for a mobster. Perhaps the word I should use is *mafioso*."

I thought about that for the whole of two seconds. "The Bulgarians have a mafia? Why am I not surprised."

"Does it ring bells?"

"Yes, of the human trafficking kind. Fergus Quigg thinks that what they're doing is close to it."

"Bulgaria is a member of the EU now. Their citizens can travel and work within it."

"But Romani don't have proper papers. Papazov charges them well over the odds for their EU passports. They're ripped off precisely because they're gypsies."

"The *Mutri* are infiltrating Britain, thanks to cheap flights from Europe. Wherever we look, there are nice, cosy little family firms like Papa starting up quietly all over the place. Lift the embroidered table cloths and underneath there's a lot more to worry about than paying workers less than the minimum wage."

"Sex trade?" I asked, thinking of the varied opinions I'd heard so far.

"Not so much. Too messy, I fancy. Not the nice, clean profit you get from a bit of internal extortion, some cigarette smuggling, that sort of thing. And then there are drugs." In front of us, yet another long line of traffic was seething in its own exhaust fumes. "Holy Nora!" said Rey.

"So let me get this right. No one has any proof that Papa Bulgaria is part of this … cartel … this *Mutri* thing? Or that they have anything to do with the drug trade?"

Rey shrugged. "Six months ago, a team at the station did a joint operation with the drugs squad—stop and search. We certainly covered both the Papa Bulgarias in our area. But legally and cost-wise we had to pull out."

"You never found anything?"

"It's a novel idea, there's no doubt about it—riders topping up their pay packet carrying the odd kilo of crack. But it was thrown out of the pot a long time back."

"Was that what Abbott was investigating, Rey? Would that be a link between him and Kizzy?"

"I think not. There is no investigation now, and he wouldn't have been part of it in the first place."

"Do you think Kizzy knew she was getting into danger? Mirela told me she'd found a way of making money. *Great riches* was the way she apparently put it."

"Can you expand on that?"

"Not really," I said. I was surprised at his sudden interest in my almost off-hand remark. "Would it be important?"

Rey grinned in delight. "Blue-pencilled, sorry."

"Uh?"

"Can't divulge the information. And believe me, if I could, you'd be the last person I'd divulge it to, you gumshoe in training, you. You're always ready to do our job for us when we are perfectly competent at doing it ourselves."

"Not with much success, it seems."

"I don't want you anywhere near this, okay? Avon and Somerset have a shit-hot drugs squad. They can work these things out for themselves. They turned Papa Bulgaria over and there wasn't a whiff of anything."

"But they were suspicious?"

"We follow procedure, Sabbie. A lot of intelligence is coming in from a lot of sources, some of them extremely dodgy. And the reason I told you about the *Mutri* was so that you are forewarned. Don't even bother with notice. Get out of Papa Bulgaria. Do what you're good at doing."

"Actually, I'm going to take your advice, Rey about flyers—"

"Hang on a sec."

I hadn't realized Rey meant this literally. He put on the siren and lights and swung into such an enthusiastic U-bend I hit my head on the passenger door window. "Ow, Rey, whatcha—"

He tore back up the road, forcing vehicles onto the pavement, and turned left between some houses. "Short cut," he said.

I rubbed my temple. "Let's emphasise the *cut* part of that."

"I did warn you." He was heading into the countryside between Taunton and Bridgwater. I guess he knew these lanes like the back of his wonderful hairy hand, but I couldn't resist pointing out the obvious. "Those lights would have changed. This way is bound to be longer."

"Trust me, I'm a policeman."

"Yes, an extremely impatient policeman."

"Not at all. I can wait motionless for hours to catch my prey."

"Really? Like an alligator?"

"I suspect you think I'll take that as an insult, but you'd be mistaken."

"Like the idea of big jaws, huh?"

We passed fields and woodlands, trees flashing by like the flicker rate in a computer game

"When I last knew you, you were concentrating on your therapies and nothing else. Nothing to sully the waters. Now you're stretching yourself in directions I wouldn't've thought you'd want to touch. Barmaid? Fast food delivery? It's not you, Sabbie."

"When you knew me last, I didn't have a mortgage."

"Maybe it was the worst thing you could've done."

He sounded like he was trying to be my big brother. "Well, thanks for the support."

"Mortgages are a risk. And a drain."

"Just because you don't have one."

"Says who?"

"You aren't helping, Rey." I heard my voice break. I swallowed hard, pressing myself into the car seat. He had raised all the doubts I had at night, when I couldn't sleep, the ones I called "my dreads." Questions like, had I done the right thing buying 43 Harold Street? I'd been perfectly happy living in a house I paid rent for. It was this awful obsession the British have. Caroline and Nora and the Howells and even my foster dad who wasn't even born here, all wanted me to own my own home. I'd listened to their elderly wisdom. Deep down I knew the idea of house ownership had pulled at me like a strong tide. For all my life I have never belonged anywhere. My real mother tore me from bug-infested room to bug-infested room. The foster families sent me back. At the children's home, the staff regularly changed. Even living with Gloria had that "holiday" feeling ... like I'd wake up one morning and be back at the Willows.

I was aiming for security, but if I failed to put loads-a-money into the bank's sticky paws every month, they would take everything away from me. I'd swapped a gentle rhythm with a scrap of soil and a simple place to live with the terror of losing everything I'd ever had. I put my cool hand over the stinging place where I'd bumped my head. It seemed to be the last straw. The stupid, stupid tears came in a hot rush. I cupped my hands over my eyes to stop the sign of them.

"Sabbie?"

Rey had pulled up on the grass verge by the side of the road and was looking at me, all concerned.

"I'm okay ..." I took the hanky he handed me. Did he keep a supply of them for weepy interviewees? I dabbed at my eyes and mascara smeared the white cotton. I only put on the mascara because coming to Musgrove with Rey had felt like a little "date."

"Look, I'm sorry. I said the wrong things."

"No, you said the right things, Rey."

"Life." He grinned. "Bugger, eh?"

"I've got your hanky all dirty."

"S'okay," he said, and kissed my cheek.

The silence crackled. I could feel the cool kiss impression. Rey placed the pulp of his thumb over it. I was trying not to breath like a traction engine. My eyes were so wide the dust in the car settled on their surfaces. I was falling towards him, like falling a great height, into a new world. My lids closed over the dust and we were kissing, hard, then soft, long, deep, lung-emptying kisses, brushing and sucking and bruising each other—lips, cheeks, necks, hair. Rey buried his face into my breasts, which were covered by layers of clothes but I could feel them respond through all those layers to the compression of his kiss.

Then we stopped. He pulled back. He didn't speak. He was staring through the windscreen. I was taking him in, all the things I'd yenned for since he stood in my porch that first time: the no-need-to-comb haircut, the steady, inscrutable mouth. And still he didn't speak or look at me. I knew why that was—a kiss is like a spark on a box of fireworks—it can happen to anyone, anywhere, given tindery conditions. But once you speak the words—whichever way they go—the thing is set, given weight, etched on your mind. Not that I was ever going to forget this kiss—whether it was just the first or definitely the last.

"We both did that, Rey."

"Yes, of course. But it was my fault."

He went to turn the key in the ignition, but I rested my hand over his. "No blame. It's what we both wanted ... *want* ... deep down, you know it is."

His lips firmed into a straight line that made it look like he was in sudden pain. "That's the difference between us. I don't do *deep down*, I do arresting felons. You stroke people until they're better and I shove them against car bonnets and slam cuffs on them."

"I don't see a problem—"

"Well I do. It's why I said go off and find yourself someone ... *nice* ... and you did—you found this Quigg chappy."

"Rey, I don't want Fergus."

251

"You're a match on paper. A better match."

I examined his profile, the sheen of his forehead, the way his nose twisted a little to one side. His eyes were full of regret, but no remorse. I couldn't help it. I let my head turn and my gaze fall upon the inviting back seat of the police car. Now that would be something.

"Absolutely not," said Rey.

"See? You can read my mind."

"Once again," said Rey, "you are involved in a murder enquiry. *Two* murder enquiries. You're about to make another statement, and the likelihood of an interrogation has not been ruled out."

"So you think I know something."

"Maybe you know something without knowing it. I'll have to see what equipment we've got stored in the back offices. Thumbscrews, that sort of thing."

He put the car into gear and did zero to fifty in seconds, then he put on the siren and broke the speed limit all the way to Bridgwater.

NINETEEN

"THIS HAS BEEN THE shittiest week in my entire life," I said, slamming the till drawer closed.

It felt like someone was drilling directly through the middle of my forehead where my sensitive third eye was located. Partly this was due to the fast, twangy music tonight's group at the Curate's Egg were playing—bluegrass from the Appalachian Mountains. Banjo, fiddle, guitar, and two singers with quaintly opposing voices. The man's was guttural and slow and the woman's piercingly high. Not a single song seemed to have a happy theme. That suited my mood perfectly.

Each time I closed my eyes, an image of Kizzy's bloated face hung before me. With each image, the rictus grin got wider. I had only met Mirela's sister once, but I found myself mourning for her. Her eyes had flashed with dark spirit; she'd drawn her tapered fingers along the lines of my hand. And now she lay in the morgue, silent and stiff.

All week I'd been accompanied by a dull ache in my belly. It was there to remind me there was something badly wrong, so that if I began to enjoy the small things of life, just for a minute or two—the way Ginger waddled as she ran for food, a new blender recipe—the ache would start up, to jog my memory. Kizzy was dead. Mirela was gone.

The name Kizzy Brouviche had been released to the press, and I constantly wondered if Mirela knew her sister had died. Surely she would get in touch if that was so? I hoped that somehow she'd got back to Bulgaria, but a search of flights by Rey's team hadn't picked anything up. Or if they had, they weren't informing me. Wherever she was, if she was okay, all she needed to do was Google for news. Did Bulgarian Romanies have the Internet? I was betting they did.

I hated Fergus's suggestion that she'd scarpered because she knew Kizzy had died. If that was so, then, all the time we'd been searching for her together, Mirela had been aware of … *something* at least … which I had not.

Papa Bulgaria was in a state of shock over the news. Petar and Max looked shaken, and Vittoria flopped into tears every few minutes, even though she'd never met Kizzy and had previously slagged her off every time I'd mentioned her. Jimmy was no better. He was weeping into his onions for real now.

Stan was dumbfounded at the news. I could see now that he had believed Kizzy could look after herself. The discovery had stymied him. Far from handing in my notice, I found myself agreeing to work extra shifts. He'd been so grateful that I couldn't bring myself to ask if I'd get extra time, or for that matter, when I'd get my pay, which was now worryingly overdue.

First thing on Tuesday morning, panic broke loose. Less than forty-eight hours after Kizzy had been found, Bridgwater Constabulary walked into Papa Bulgaria unannounced, to inform all the male staff that they'd like to take voluntary buccal swabs. I was out delivering, which was just as well; I would have hated to confront Rey at my lowly place of work. But I heard all about it when I returned. Especially from Jimmy, who'd been tensed up for the rest of the day, which meant Stan shouted at him over every silly mistake.

By the end of the shift, Jimmy's face had puckered up until it was almost all zit. I'd tried to soothe him. "Don't be worried. It's just routine."

"What did they find on Kizzy?"

"It has to be DNA, Jimmy. Be positive; that's good. We can't bring Kizzy back, but this might find her killer."

My insides felt pulled all which-ways; the understanding that Kizzy's death had been waiting in the wings, and I had done nothing to prevent it except allow her sister to get into a brolly fight with a pervert and later disappear into oblivion. I was grieving for both of them—for the firecracker that had been Kizzy and for her sugar-dusted sister. What had Fergus said? Bulgarian Delight.

Tucked right down at the bottom of this shitty week was the smell of a man's skin; the taste of lips and tongue; the touch of his hand against my cheek. The kiss I'd shared with Rey. I recalled the way I'd collapsed in the loo last week. Yes, kissing Rey was like that; lost patches of sight and a juddering chest. *I don't do deep down,* Rey had said, but he'd also confessed that he'd told me to find someone else, not because he didn't have feelings for me, but because he was threatened by love and did the craziest things to avoid it.

"Shitty week?" said Nige, slowing his pace (if that was possible) to answer me. "Tell me about it. Bloke problems, right?" He pointed to tonight's t-shirt, which proudly announced, *Blow jobs are like flowers for men.*

"Piss off, Nige," I said, not holding out much hope. Nige thrived on rejection, believing (at least, according to another of his t-shirts) it was a girl's way of saying yes.

———

Fergus turned up just gone nine, while the band was on their break. He hovered at the bar, avoiding getting served (not a difficult task, considering the speed of my colleagues), until I was ready to pull him his pint of Wild Cossack.

"How are you?" he asked.

"It's been a long week, Fergus."

"You can off-load onto me. I'm used to it, so I am."

I wanted to point out that he could have phoned me at anytime between since Monday, when I'd last seen him, to let me "off-load." But as I was trying to work out how to put this diplomatically, he slid a thin buff envelope across the bar. I realized a translation of Kizzy's letter would be inside. It felt like he'd just offered me a list of counter-espionage suspects. Then someone waved a twenty at me and I stuffed the envelope into my back pocket.

"I'll catch up with you at closing, shall I?" said Fergus.

The twenty waved closer. "Miss?"

Fergus turned away, taking his pint to his bench.

As always, I was doing the lion's share of the work. Kev favoured chatting to his favourite punters over helping behind the bar, leaving me to dash around whenever Nige disappeared for what he called "a five-minute puff." Five minutes in Nige's world was half an hour of everyone else's irritation. Finally, I told him it was my turn for a fag.

"But you don't smoke."

"I'm thinking of taking it up to get the breaks."

It was bitter in the yard. The concrete path that led down to the back gate was slippy with newly laid ice. I sat down on a beer barrel to slice the top of the envelope, and the chill of the metal shot through my jeans into my bum. But I forgot the cold as soon as the translation of Kizzy's letter opened in my hands.

My Sweetie Mirela,

It is not as I hoped. At first, it was hard, such pain, but it is better now. I will be okay, dear darling girl, I am just resting. I thought we could both make good from this, but no real riches offered. I had sharp words with him, but it was useless, but he keeps me here, stuck in this place. So do not do the same as me, sister. Do not go with him, if he comes for you, the man with the snake. Get out. Go back home, which is sweeter than Britain ever will be. Find a way. Do it fast. Go and give my love to Mama and the boys. Tell Tatta I am sorry I made his head crazy.

Your Kizzy

I looked up, almost surprised to find I was in the yard behind the Curate's Egg, rather than some painted, horse-drawn caravan. Mirela had told the truth about the letter; Kizzy *had* said she needed to rest. And Fergus had been way off-target; reading her sister's letter would have given Mirela hope that she'd see her again. But what did Kizzy mean … *it was hard, such pain?* I thought about the final words she said to me, the night when squibbing turned to shooting … *there is danger. It starts with death.* Was she fully aware that Abbott had been gunned down as she read our fortune? Or had she returned to the scene of the crime and strayed into the path of the killer?

I read the translation steadily again. When she wrote this at least, she'd been with someone. *I have sharp word with him.* With who? A man, but not a man she feared. Unless the letter was all bravado, for showing fear wouldn't sit neatly with Kizzy. *Do not go with him, if he comes for you, the man with the snake.*

One reassuring thing stood out: Kizzy had implored Mirela to go home. On those instructions, she'd packed and called her boyfriend. Maybe she was already back in Bulgaria. But if so, why did she leave this letter under her pillow?

It would need some pondering. I pocketed the copy and got back to the bar.

Maybe Fergus could help me decipher it.

Finally the band packed up and the bar began to empty out. Fergus shrugged himself into his jacket and came over to where I was wiping the last of the glasses.

"Did you have to ID Kizzy in the end?"

I nodded. "It was the most awful experience I have ever endured."

"I can empathize," said Fergus. "That DI turned up at the agency with a couple of uniformed cops. Spoke to each one of us in turn. They were hoping we'd be able to contact Mirela. But I have no idea where she is."

"Or if she's okay."

"He can dole out a desperate third degree, can that fellow."

"What do you mean?"

"He took a cheek swab from every male at the office. That boiled down to some elderly volunteers, me, and Juke. We could hardly refuse. And then he told me to open all our files for inspection."

"You should let them do it."

"I did let them do it. They'd have used a search warrant if I hadn't."

"Every bloke who knew Kizzy had a swab taken."

"Fair enough. Sort of in the contract. Agency for Change deals in all sorts of difficult issues. At least when *we're* interviewed by the police we're not beaten up if we don't say the right things. At least we're UK citizens; we're not hassled about having papers. At least we don't have wheals and cuts from the machetes, or memories of rapes and house burnings."

"Hope not." It was all a bit heavy for so late in the evening. I thought back to the first time I'd clapped eyes on Mirela, curled like a wild beast into a corner of my porch, the pungent sensation of desolation oozing out of her frail body. "Of course you're right, Fergus. We have a beautiful planet, and it doesn't belong to any one of us. It belongs to itself and we should try to get along while we're on it—care for it. Care for each other."

"Surely. That's my job. To raise awareness and to keep these people as safe as I can." He flashed a sad smile, suggesting he knew he'd failed in that task.

"What did you think of Kizzy's letter, Fergus?"

"We had hoped for an address, hadn't we?"

"Have you any idea what she means by the man with the snake?"

"Is it a code between them?"

"Only..."

"What?" Fergus sat straighter, as if my next words would be the key that unlocked the puzzle.

"It's a shamanic thing. I've been seeing snakes ... meeting snake spirits."

259

"Sounds desperate. But not very concrete, Sabbie, if you don't mind my saying."

"Okay, what about this? Mirela thought there may be underhand couriering going on at Papa. The police let something slip. Did you know there was a Bulgarian mafia?"

"I did, yes."

"Fergus, you could have told me!"

He looked uncomfortable. "I don't know much … if you've been talking to the police, perhaps you know more than me."

"They call themselves *Mutri*. But Re—that is—I learned that they're not much into the sex trade. It's more drugs. Did Mirela ever talk to you about anything like that?"

"She did not. I haven't a clue. It doesn't ring any bells at all." His hand slid into the pocket where he kept his notebook, as if reassuring himself it was still there.

"To be honest, I'm exhausted with thinking about it."

"Indeed so. When you finish tonight … would you be free?"

"Is there another party?"

"No, but I wondered if you might like to come in, for a late coffee. You know where I live. Your taxi must take you past."

I nodded, a good choice of response, seeing I'd been robbed of speech.

"There was something I wanted to show you."

"What?" But I knew. It would be his songs. Maybe he'd sing them to me. "Shaman Girl."

"I'm thinking you'll be too tired," he said.

"I dunno, Fergus."

"We'll leave it to how you feel, then," he said, and turned to leave.

————

"Can you drop me off here?" I asked the taxi driver.

Nige winked at me as I clambered out. "Nice one, Sabbie."

I didn't move from the pavement edge as the taxi pulled away. In front of me was the fresh-painted sign that directed people to the new block of flats where Fergus lived. Should I follow the signpost? Fergus had invited me. He was waiting for me. But in my hand was a printed card—Rey's card. His address was three or so minutes away, across the road and round the corner. He wasn't waiting for me. He hadn't invited me. He might have scribbled his address down for some other reason.

I stood on my spot, the December wind chilling my scalp. The taxi was long gone. The wind blew, whipping at my scarf like a flag. I had to make up my mind.

———

The door had a jarring bell. I jumped at the sound.

No security chain. The door swung open generously.

"Want to come in?"

I thought about it for a whole second then stepped over the threshold.

Rey grinned. Good start.

I stopped short, mostly because there was nowhere much to go. Rey had crammed himself into living quarters so small, I didn't think my hens would be happy with the space.

"Bijou," I remarked.

"Size has never mattered to me."

"People who say that are usually compensating for their lack of it."

"I presume we're talking accommodation here?"

"Yeah, 'course." My glance was forced downward from his face as if there was a string attached to my chin, but I couldn't see very far. Between us was a bottle of San Miguel.

"Would you like a drink?" he said, brandishing it.

"I'd love one. Alcohol never passes my lips when I'm at work."

"Really? Even though you have a taxi home?"

"Yep, really."

"Wait a moment; last weekend I bought you a vodka and tonic."

"I always ask for vodka and tonic if customers want to buy me a drink."

"You only pour the tonic, right?"

"Sorry for the deception."

"I don't have any vodka. No tonic, either."

"That's okay. I can't stand vodka. But it's the best 'not' drink in tonic; no colour, no smell. I'll have beer, that'll be fine."

Rey pulled down his mouth. "This is my last one."

I laughed. He pushed the bottle at me. I took a swig and pushed it back. He lifted his hands—to say, *no, no, keep it*—and my fist, gripping the neck of the bottle, rammed into his stomach. Not hard. But his muscles were.

"Didn't come here to beat you up. Though it's clear I'd have trouble in that direction."

He mopped a drip of beer on my chin. I breathed in air that felt like sherbet in my throat.

"Shut up," he said.

He was right. Talking was overrated.

TWENTY

I woke into broad daylight and my first thought was, *the hens.* The time blinked from an LED on the bedside cabinet. Seven-twenty. The hens could wait. They'd be quite cosy inside the coop.

Rey's head was buried into his pillow. He was silent and still, in that deep sleep you can only get on Sunday mornings. I eased the duvet back so that I could feast on his unconscious face. I felt as tender towards him as I might looking at a sleeping baby. Rushes of wonderment flooded through me. *So this is love*, I thought.

I thought I'd been in love many times. I had been kidding myself. I'd never felt like this before. It was a surrender. There was a marsh-mallow ecstasy inside it, but that was wrapped with fear. I was terri-fied, in a shivery, stomach-wrenching way, for all the unknowns that might obliterate this moment or get in the way of future moments.

I touched Rey's earlobe. He had the sort of earlobes that tucked neatly into the ear. In the centre of it was a healed piercing. He'd look good with a natty little stud. Diamond, maybe. I smiled. I should be careful not to dress my new boyfriend up like a doll. I have girlfriends who shop for their men and kit them out like cat-walk models until the poor guys no longer know themselves. I wouldn't be doing that. Rey was perfect as he was.

I slid my legs over the edge of the bed and pulled on my t-shirt and knickers. Luckily (or maybe it was my internal hope mechanism) I'd worn a fairly new and slinky thong last night. Thus attired, the essential move right that moment was to borrow a toothbrush.

Rey's flat was upstairs in a Victorian semi-detached. Someone had taken the largest bedroom and squashed a living room and kitchen into it as well. I was grateful that the bathroom at least was through a proper door, but that was almost impossible to shut once you were inside. The miniature sink was covered with old soap stains and shaved-off stubble. The shower cubicle was stuffed full of brownish wet towels, some of which might've started out white. The loo was brown, too, at least the bit under the water. I visualized Rey camping out in his office at work, festering there as he pondered the caseload, arriving back at this place once in a while and not bothering to tidy or clean even then.

I had a pee then ran his toothbrush under the hot tap, squeezed on Colgate and brushed my teeth. I was awake now, so I padded through to the little kitchen area. Rey didn't seem to be interested in cleaning here, either, but I wasn't going to do it for him. I put on the kettle and peeked through the cupboards. There was an out-of-date packet of pasta and a massive jar of Marmite, but not much else. In the fridge was fresh milk, ham, and half a loaf of sliced bread. I thought I might bring him some eggs. Everything else—tea, coffee, sugar—was right next to the kettle, preventing any waste of energy.

I made a coffee and a tea and balanced the mugs back to the single bedside cabinet. Not a long walk.

"Hiya."

Rey opened one eye. "Oh."

Under my t-shirt, I felt my heart lurch. "Don't say it like that!"

"No ... sorry. God, I promised myself ..."

"What? What did you promise yourself?"

"We're not ..." He snuffled and shifted up so that his head was resting on the wall behind him. "I'm not going to be good for you." He reached out and snatched my hand, like he needed to touch it.

I wriggled under the duvet, curling my knees under his straightened legs. "You were very good for me last night."

He put his arm round me and pulled me towards his chest. He had a nice chest. The hair on it was longer than the hair on his head. I put my fingers on his skin, walking them towards a nipple.

"I don't do this often," he said.

I restrained myself from saying that I could deduce that from the state of his bedsit. "Because of work?"

"Sort of."

To my surprise, and bit by bit with long, ruminative pauses in between, he started telling me things. "I moved out of my house two years ago. My wife still lives there. It wasn't anybody's fault; we'd both had flings on the side. We haven't started on a divorce yet. I'm not sure why. So at the moment, we both own the house, even though another bloke is living under its roof with her. I pay my half of the mortgage, and half of any major repairs. The idea is that we'll sell it, I suppose, when things get ... finalized."

"But they haven't got finalized," I pointed out.

"I'm trying to forget. Rather than forgive, if you see what I mean. I can't live with the bloody woman. And to be fair, she can't live with me. If we sold the property now we'd both end up with next to nothing, so I get a manky bedsit and Lesley stays on until the time is right."

"I'm glad you told me," I said.

He laughed once. "Do you know, she comes over sometimes. Washes up. Hoovers. Still got a soft spot, I suppose."

I wasn't going to ask if Rey had the same soft spot, and if that was why they were having trouble "finalizing." "The rumour is that it's hard to live with a cop."

"Yep. Now I've made DI, it'd be harder still. Live and breathe the job, so on and so on."

I'd had that feeling last night. We'd had a great time in bed. I'd wanted him so much. Thinking of the things we'd done made me shudder and press my body closer to his warm one. But Rey had been a lot less present than me. Occasionally, something seemed to come into his head that took precedence even over my body, naked and willing though it was.

"It's how it has to be, right?" He shrugged as I spoke, turning away as if he didn't want to face what might be an accusation. "I'm the same with my clients, especially the shamanic ones. I have to believe their world if I'm to help them. It's a sort of immersion; ideas come into your head that start to make sense…"

"And if you follow those trains of thought…" He turned back to me, realization in his face. "We both solve things."

"Need to solve things. Not all of them get solved."

"True." He swallowed a laugh. "Like our August victim, the body we found in Dunball's Wharf. She's back in the papers and on the telly and, despite the entire station keeping mum, things are slowly leaking out."

"That there's a link between her and Kizzy?"

"It's what they're saying."

"What they're saying is that you'd shelved that investigation because there was no one to pester you to get on with solving the crime."

"We don't shelve things, we wait for a breakthrough. Finding the Brouviche girl at Hinkley Point gave us two lucky breaks."

I wrinkled my nose at the word. "What's so lucky about that?"

"We had nothing to go on with the previous victim. She was forensically sterile; out of sight long enough to remove almost all the forensic evidence." He grimaced. "Whoever did this, they panicked, second time around, thinking if they threw this one into the sea, she would never be found. First lucky break: some idiot went walking where they should never have walked and saw her, hanging above the sea, waiting for the tide. If the tide had taken her, she could have turned up anywhere. The link would never have been made. Second lucky break: someone was looking for a missing girl. You called in and that turned the direction of both investigations."

"What are you saying Rey? Same MO? Is it someone with a knife?"

"We didn't have an MO with the Jane Doe."

"Rey... don't call her that. She once had a name. It's so sad that it was lost in her death. Surely, somewhere, there are people searching, grieving." I didn't need to add that if it hadn't been for Mirela's determination, Kizzy might never have been named, either.

"Coppers are best not getting emotional. Our satisfaction is in getting justice for those left behind."

"You have found something..." I had to stop, clear my throat, start again. "Which is why you're asking for buccal swabs. What is it? Skin traces under her nails? Semen?"

He gave a mirthless chuckle. "You've been reading crime fiction again, Sabbie. Bad mistake. But yeah, because you ID'd the victim, we can target hot spots. Where she worked, who she knew. We're simply asking for the full cooperation of the public. We are not accusing anyone."

"I thought you'd be linking her death to Abbott's."

"I'd love to be able to say yes to that. A cop's death is always the primary investigation, and I'm not going to make any apologies for saying so. I've cancelled the rest of my life until I get a result."

"Surely you're getting somewhere ... leads ... clues and things?"

"Whoever shot Gary, they were clever. They chose the squibbing."

"Because of the noise, masking gunfire?"

"Partly. Mostly because half of Bridgwater was milling about that night. Usually, if someone is gunned down in cold blood late at night on the streets, there will be a small number of people who think they saw something a little odd. But that night? No one saw anything. Because they saw far too much. People running, standing still, shouting, fighting even. People all over the place. The perfect cover."

I could smell it like sweat, the thing he wasn't saying. But he was stroking my hair, and I could think of nothing but the sensation. People used to love to stroke it when it fell to my waist, but now I thought of it as mutilated, traumatized; Rey's fingers were healing me, as if I'd erred in the past, but he could forgive. Why did I feel a need to be forgiven? Perhaps it had been with me all my life.

"It's so awful," I said, after a sleepy pause. "How can anyone deliberately kill another human being?"

"Change or status quo," said Rey.

"What?"

"It's my personal 'motivation measure.' I thought it up." He looked chuffed. "Ninety-nine percent of murders only have one of two true motives: change or status quo."

"What about money? Crimes of passion? Suicide bombers?"

"All of those want one of two things. Either they want change—the big win, a new political situation—or they don't want things to change—they kill their lover's spouse, or kill to stop a crime being discovered. See? Ninety-nine percent. Not complicated at all." He paused, picked up his mug and took a long pull. I didn't speak, I knew I'd be interrupting.

"Statistics tell us that we should always look close by. Around the victim's life. Hence our decision to cherry-pick DNA samples. The glory of that method is not those who offer willingly, but those who refuse."

"Has anyone refused?"

Rey stared into the surface of his coffee as if trying to read the future. Then he put the mug back. "Being DI is like being put in a black cloth bag. You can move around okay, but you stumble a lot and you can't see out."

"Sounds like a bad shamanic journey."

"Tell me about it. The back of my neck is dripping from where my DCI is breathing down it. So without being heavy about this, if you come up with anything... shamanic or not... you knew Kizzy, is what I'm thinking."

I was pleased he'd called the dead girl by her first name. "I didn't know her well, Rey. I only met her the once."

"Don't you think that's weird? As a shaman? You met her on the night she disappeared."

"You don't know the half."

Why had I handed her my card? Passing it over had nothing to do with business acumen. But it sent Mirela to me. *It starts with death.* The last thing I'd heard her say.

"How long was she in the water, Rey?"

"What d'you mean?"

"I'm trying to make sense of the weeks Kizzy was missing. The letter she wrote—was she a captive when she wrote it? How long after she wrote did she die?"

"Sorry, Sabbie. That letter is a forensic field day. Can't say a thing." Rey rested his head against my neck, not quite kissing, more nuzzling my skin. "But I can tell you this, because it's now been released to the press, that she had been dead for around forty-eight hours before we found her."

I put my hands over my face to keep the tears from sobbing out of me. "I wouldn't feel so bad about Kizzy, I'm sure of it, if Mirela was here. I'm so worried that she went searching for her. And now I'm worried that somehow she knew her sister was dead."

"I shouldn't be discussing the case with you at all," said Rey. "Nothing. There are guidelines for problems with ..."

I couldn't make out the words. "Problems with what?"

"You and me." As he said the words, he slid a hand under my t-shirt, resting it over my belly button. He had worker's hands, rough at the heel of the palm, but warm and clean. They had a special magic that transformed me into a formless, brain-dead amoeba. "We should not be having conversations like this one. In fact, we should not be having this relationship. We can't be lovers. Do you see that?"

"No. I don't see it." I pushed him away, thrusting handfuls of grubby duvet to separate us, oozing across the bed like a mollusc disturbed in a rock pool. "What happened last night is rapidly becoming an inconvenience isn't it?"

"God, no. No, Sabbie, but—"

He didn't finish. *I'm not going to be good for you. We can't be lovers.*

The tears I'd managed to keep right down inside me boiled and spilled from my eyes. Rey snatched at my arms and held me. "Don't cry, baby, please don't."

"I'm crying for Kizzy. For her and Mirela." I didn't want to believe that he could make me dissolve into tears.

But as the sobs wracked out of me, I wasn't sure whether I was crying for lost sisters or lost lovers.

———

She was nine or so when her father came back that night, wounded. He sat on the bunk with one arm raised over his head, holding himself erect, swaying only slightly, biting his bottom lip against the pain, while she and her mother had worked with water and clean rags to bind the wound. She tried to fetch and carry for her mother, to not drop anything even though her fingers trembled with shock.

He had uttered no more than two words in his sons' direction and they had left immediately, to seek retribution for the family honour. But, as she'd brought water from the fire, she'd felt his eyes on her, as if registering a lack of presence.

"Where is Kizzy?"

"Out. Who knows?" said her mother.

He sucked air between his teeth as she mopped the wound. "She makes my head crazy. She will destroy our honour, even as my sons exact my vengeance."

"Marry her off, and quickly," said Mama, knotting the rag tight around his chest.

Only in stages did Tatta return to normal life. But once he had, she and Kizzy pulled the bare mattress from the bunk and carried it into the sunshine to wash their father's blood from it.

"Tatta wants you married," she'd whispered to her sister as they worked.

"Let them try."

Now she lies in the dark, moving in and out of restless sleep, remembering all the moments of her past, sweet and bitter and bittersweet. She is so restless that she long ago pulled the bottom sheet into a crumpled heap and now she's lying on the bare mattress, where a dark stain, the colour of a cow's hide, has spread.

She puts the flat of her hand over the stain, but even stretched wide her small hand can't cover it.

Blood, she knows, is an impossible stain to wash away.

TWENTY-ONE

LAETITIA WAS SITTING ON a sofa in Costa's, a recently drained espresso and a glass of iced water in front of her. She was copying from a book onto an A4 pad but raised her pen as she spotted me.

On Sunday afternoon, my mobile had chirped a text: MA SAYS OKAY. COSTAS@BWATER, 4PM 2MOR? DO SAY YOU WILL. LV LETTICE XXX.

It was almost exactly one week since my previous text from Lettice. Maybe she put Sunday afternoons aside for important texting tasks. I read it several times, looking for the catch. I was intrigued, I couldn't pretend I wasn't. And if nothing else, all this—this sudden, so-called family—needed explanation. And possibly closure.

C U THERE. It was a reluctant message, not over-friendly. I didn't want her to get her hopes up. I doubted that Mrs. Mitchell and I would ever become buddies. And now I looked around the coffee shop, I realized there was no Mrs. Mitchell. I stood, hovering by the table.

"D'you want a drink?" asked Lettice.

"No thanks, I've only just had one."

"Oh, okay," said Lettice. "Carbon footprint reduction and all that, I suppose."

The truth was, coffee shops like this were outside my price range and I didn't want to start by owing her even for a cup of tea.

"And I can't stay very long, Lettice, because I'm supposed to be delivering for Papa Bulgaria right now."

Her hair was held into a low, mid-blond ponytail and she was still in her school uniform of navy blue jacket and skirt with checkered blue and white shirt and a stripy tie. I was thinking how cute she looked in it—a lot younger than she'd appeared at the Hatchlings—when a cheerful rendition of Beethoven's Fifth broke forth from her mobile. "Oh, just a sec."

Lettice buried herself into a long, frenzied conversation with someone she'd probably left only moments before. I was hoping that Mrs. Mitchell would appear from the loos at any minute (presuming Mrs. Mitchell was human enough to use loos), but she was nowhere to be seen. I couldn't help feeling a teeny bit relieved. I placed my helmet on the table and went to buy a herbal tea, hanging the expense. When I got back, Lettice was still fiddling with a mobile that could probably do everything except her ironing. On reflection, it could probably do her ironing as well. Watching her, I felt all grown-up and sensible.

"Okay, Lettice," I said. "Fill me in. Shouldn't you be here with your mother?"

"No prob. Ma's coming independently from home. And she's not used to parking in Bridgwater, so puhleese don't panic. Ma has awful panics, she hardly lets me out of her sight for a moment as it is." She waited while I settled opposite her then went on. "I think there are particular deeply rooted causes for the way my mother restricts my freedom. That's sort of why I'm here."

"What d'you mean?"

"You see, I'm an only child and Daddy is too. Ma's no better off. She never *never* talks about her older sister. It's like she's ashamed."

"Your mother's sister?"

"Ya. Isabel Dare. Your ma, of course."

"Lettice, I don't know—"

"See, no one will tell me anything, except that she's as different from Ma as chalk is from cheese. That's how Grandma put it, anyway."

"Do you want … that I talk about my mother?"

She furrowed a peachy brow. "Not precisely … it's just … I never had a cousin, and that's what we are."

"Are we? I don't want to upset your family. I've never searched for my relations. It was complete chance I bumped into them." I steadied myself with a too-hot sip of ginger-apple tea. "People can get very distressed when things suddenly change." I looked out into the street. "You're not trying to fool me, are you Lettice? I'm not easily fooled. If your mother's not coming, I will leave."

"It's absolutely imperative you stay until Ma arrives."

"Really? If your mother is ashamed of her sister, she's not going to take to me."

She played with the strap of her homework bag, a big, square leather case. "I saw Ma chuck your card in the kitchen bin. I got it out and wiped it down when she wasn't looking. I knew you were trying to tell her something. But, honestly, there is no point in talking to clamp-mouth. So after Grandma had retired to her room for the night—she goes off about nine—I made her a cocoa, just how she likes it, and took it up to her."

I suppressed a grin. She came across as a blend of devious minx and sweetheart. I could visualize her, standing there in her grandmother's chamber between the whatnot and the washstand, with cocoa in fine china on a solid silver tray, while the old lady, who (sorry—*whom*) I'd never met, was propped in her four-poster, up to the neck in Barbara Cartland lace.

"Grandma was watching *Trial & Retribution* on Sky. She said, 'thank you, glorious child' like she does, so I went over and sat on her bed, and asked her to tell me a story of when Ma was young. She didn't suspect. She started on about when they all lived at the Hatchings and ran amok in the grounds, and I went, 'and Aunt Isabel, too?' and she went, 'yes, she was a dear girl, then' and touched my nose. 'You are like her, Lettice, in that there is a little unlit taper in your heart. Please don't allow it to explode, as she did.' And I went, 'how did she explode, Grandma?' and she went ..." Lettice screwed up her face. "Bloody hell, I've forgotten what it was!"

"What?"

"How Aunty Isabel exploded. It was typical of Grandma." She giggled. "She loves alliteration."

"*Alliteration*?"

"Yes. Ah, I've got it: 'Licentious lefty libber.' That was it."

"Blimey. Do you even know what those things are?"

"Of course. I *am* having an education."

"Did she say anything else about her?" Suddenly, knowing about my mother felt urgent.

"She did mention where she went ..." She fiddled some more with the satchel straps, and when I glanced at her, I saw that the back of her neck, lowered over the bag, had flushed a pretty rose colour.

"Where?"

"I don't want to say."

"Why ever not?"

"It might offend you." There was a pause. "Grandma is like a time warp."

"Tell me, please."

"She said…" Her voice changed, and I guessed she was mimicking her grandmother's clipped 1950s accent. "'Isabel went to live with the blacks. Last jolly straw. Couldn't have her back after that.' She did say where, but I've forgotten. A saint."

"A what?" But I knew immediately. "St. Pauls?"

"That was it." She looked up at me, her face solemn. "I'm really sorry my family are such freakwits, Sabbie."

"It's okay, I'm trying to make sense of all this too. I'm not sure if I want to take it further or bury it again."

"Can't you ask your ma?"

I turned my head slowly. "What d'you mean?"

"Aren't you in touch with her anymore?"

"She died when I was six—that's twenty-two years ago."

"Oh my god! I don't think even Grandma knows that."

"They don't know Izzie is dead? But surely they'd've been informed."

"They *are* good at keeping family secrets. But there's a sort of *tone* oldies use, you know? When people have died? I'm sure Ma doesn't know about *you*. No one's ever told me I had a cousin."

"I can't believe this." I shook my head. "It's crazy."

"I didn't want to stir things up," she said. "I just knew that if I didn't meet you, I'd be thinking all the time, *I've a cousin*, and it would bug me to death."

I smiled. "Actually, you are the first blood relative I have ever met. Apart from Izzie, that is."

"Inconceivable! How come? What happened to your father's people?"

"I never met him. I didn't even know his name until the birth certificate arrived."

She looked at me with understanding beyond her years. "You poor thing. And here's me worrying over not having a cousin, while you—"

"Lettice?"

"Oh, hi, Ma."

Mrs. Mitchell was standing by our table. Her car keys (platinum plated, as far as I could see) were in her hands, and an expression of unconcealed repugnance was plastered all over her face.

"Who is this?"

"Ma," said Lettice in what can only be described as a drawl. "Don't lose your rag."

"What are you doing with my daughter?" Her face focused on me, like a spotlight in an interrogation cell.

"You didn't tell her," I said to Lettice.

"I'm about to, aren't I?" She turned to her mother, almost formally. "This is my cousin, Sabrina Dare. Oh, and Ma—guess what! Aunt Isabel is dead."

Lettice was accomplished in many skills that I'd not been blessed with at her age, but I can't believe that even the twelve-year-old Sabbie could have been more blunt, less compassionate. Mrs. Mitchell didn't expect it, that was for sure. She put both hands to her face, as if masking a collapse was the first thing a sensible person did in public. She stumbled backwards, her shoulder knocking against the plate glass door, moving mechanically through passing shoppers and off the kerb. Both of us jumped to our feet, but Lettice was first out of the door, yanking her mother back onto the pavement.

"Ma! Ma, it's okay. Sorry—sorry—sorry…"

The words brought Mrs. Mitchell to her senses, and the information hit home. Her faced screwed uncontrollably.

I'd expected her to roar at me. But all she could do was sob.

———

Over the top of an Americano, my aunt's eyes branded me; daughter-snatcher, bringer of nightmares, gold-digger, demon risen from the past. Not to mention the source of acute embarrassment in a public place. She took a tiny sip and placed the cup on its saucer with precision as she tried to prevent her hand shaking.

"Where is my sister?"

"Ma," said Lettice. "Ma, you weren't listening."

"I could hardly fail to hear what you said, Lettice. Sometimes, you can be quite *fishwifelike*."

Lettice snorted then rearranged her face. Even she could see this was not the time to giggle.

"It is hard to believe," I said, trying to make things feel reasonable. "At least, take in. And maybe my mother wasn't your sister at all—it's speculation."

"Precisely." Mrs. Mitchell wore her chin high, as if purposely exhibiting the antique cross she wore round her neck. Today she had let her massive hair down, so that the ash blond glittered around her shoulders as if spun by millions of small spiders. She still had that awful tan, but I was beginning to realize it was neither from a bottle nor a machine, but gained on a pool-side sun bed in Biarritz or wherever.

"Look. I don't want to pursue this either. I never did. Coming to your mother's house was a massive coincidence and we can forget it completely and all go home." There was a short silence, which I filled by blabbering on. "I don't want anything from your family."

"But I want something from you." Mrs. Mitchell knew how to make someone feel uncomfortable. Inferior. She was using her eyes as if they were drills.

"Well ... anything."

"I want to know where she is."

"But ..." Then I saw. "Oh. Right. She was cremated. That's all I know."

"My sister ... has no headstone ... no remembrance?"

This seemed to upset her more than anything. I imagined sepulchres and charnel houses of great antiquity deep in woodland somewhere in the grounds of the Hatchings. "I don't understand why you weren't informed. Your mother must have been her next of kin."

"Frankly, we had rather lost touch."

"I can't see how that makes any difference. The authorities ... someone must have made the arrangements."

"Were you there, Sabbie?" asked Lettice. "At the funeral?"

"No." I cupped my palms over my eyes and rubbed at my face. I wasn't sure if I wanted to revive those memories, buried in my mind. But I hadn't forgotten. Not really. "I was the one who found her. I'm not sure about the timescale, but looking back it feels as if it might have been hours ... days ... before I went for help? I think it took me a long time to accept that she wasn't deeply asleep." I glanced up. "She did sometimes sleep all day. I used to get my own food, if there was any. And my school had got used to my absences, so they certainly didn't turn up, but suddenly there was this old lady—she lived downstairs, I think—warbling a scream. I do remember that scream. The police came, and some chap who turned out to be a social worker."

"You were taken into care?" asked Mrs. Mitchell, in a voice that trembled with revulsion.

"Yes. I grew up in care. Because I didn't know I had a family."

"They should have contacted Grandma," said Lettice. "I would've had a cousin. I would've looked up to you."

"No, you wouldn't," I shot back. "I guess I was fifteen or so by the time you were born. I'd walked out of school. I was a right mess."

"But that's because you didn't have us." Lettice turned to her mother. "You would've taken Sabbie in, wouldn't you Ma? Like in *Wuthering Heights?*"

Mrs. Mitchell must have been more familiar with the book than I was, but she didn't respond. She raised her Americano to her lips, took a slow sip, and placed the cup on its giant saucer. "She must be somewhere."

"Her ashes were scattered, I think."

"And who did the scattering?"

"I don't know."

"I think you could have taken a little more interest in your own mother's death."

"She was only six, Ma," said Lettice.

"I've never taken an interest. I hate the woman." That made them sit up. "She abandoned me. Don't you see? She killed herself, more or less."

"Suicide?" whispered Mrs. Mitchell.

"No. Drugs overdose."

My aunt seemed to reel backwards, even though the chair back prevented it. She pressed her knuckles to her lips, like they do in films.

"But they did make me try not to forget. The social workers and that. If you'd like me to find out more about my mother's death for you, Mrs. Mitchell—well, I suppose I could do so."

Maybe that was what this was all about. Finding out might put my past to rest. I was so deep in thought that I didn't notice at first that Lettice was giggling helplessly, despite the icicle stares her mother was giving her.

"What's funny?" I was a bit irked.

"You can't call her Mrs. Mitchell." Lettice shook her head with mirth. "That's not right at all. You'll have to call her Aunt Peers."

Mrs. Peers Mitchell and I locked glances. I'm not sure which of us was more appalled.

———

I left Costa's as soon as I could, using work as my excuse. Lettice wanted to exchange further details, and I'd ended up swapping Facebook friend requests with her.

I scooted back to Papa for my final round of deliveries (and the usual telling off for the time I'd taken over the last round). The kitchen was drenched in its dire atmosphere. Petar ignored me, Jimmy scuttled around like a cockroach, and Max had taken to cracking obscene jokes as a way to cover his deeper feelings. Whenever there weren't customers to serve, Stanislaus let out long streams of what sounded like very offensive Bulgarian.

I was bursting to yell at someone after meeting Mrs. Mitchell (I refused to call her Aunt Peers) and Stan seemed a good choice. I was fed up with his silence on the subject of my pay. I'd started to worry that part of the Papa scam was not paying anyone anything at all.

"I want last month's wages. A cheque with a payslip."

Stan's face hardened down. "New workers are paid twenty-eight days from when they start."

"Play the game, Stan, it'll be Christmas by then."

"You need a loan? My father can arrange one."

"Let me get this right," I said. "You're prepared to lend me money, but not pay me a fair wage. I don't believe you pay anyone a fair wage, actually."

"Each employee's treated like an individual. We're a caring employer."

"Good. In that case, you'll stop your staff moaning about the DNA tests."

Stan gave a curt nod. "The sooner this guy's caught, the better for business. People aren't keen coming out after dark anymore."

"Stan ... you've never had another worker go missing like Kizzy, have you? I mean in the past."

"No. We've never lost a worker before, never." He eyed me carefully. "Unless we sack them."

I thought about Mr. Papazov, sitting upstairs every Wednesday, playing ancient music. He didn't feel rich, but I bet he lived in some massive house, like Grandma Dare, with a pot of money dirtier even than his greasy tape recorder. No doubt his son hoped to inherit, so Stan stayed right under his father's thumb. Behind his cocktail stick, he often looked over-burdened with the state of things, worn down, snappy when the orders got behind and as jittery as a bad acid trip when his father turned up in the shop, like he'd prefer to be inheriting that pot right now, thank you.

I'd become trapped in this shitty world. I was not leaving without my pay, but, even when I finally got it, a hefty deduction would come out for the hire of the bike I'd be leaving behind, which meant, ostensibly, that I was paying to deliver takeaways. In the meantime, the work constantly reminded me about the grim deal the Brouviche sisters had got from their visit to Britain.

I went into the changing room and surrendered to a bombardment of feelings. The back of my eyes burnt and I covered them with my hands. I wanted to cry for my mother, but I couldn't quite do it. I'd invested all my filial energy into hating her and it was uncomfortable to discover she had a story I'd ignored my whole life.

And Rey had not called. I'd left his flat on loving terms. He kissed me a deep goodbye, but more than twenty-four hours had passed and all I'd got was silence. No texts. No emails. No phone call. No flowers by Interflora—well, I'd never been that hopeful. His words rang in my ears. I was terrified that *we can't be lovers* had already turned into *we are not lovers.*

One night of passion. My entire frame yearned for more. My entire soul.

TWENTY-TWO

THAT EVENING I BOOTED up my laptop and connected it to the printer. I played around with designing an A5-sized simple advert. It was time I followed Rey's advice about selling my therapy skills.

Enjoy a Pre-Christmas wind-down with Therapist Sabbie Dare.
Chose from Aromatherapy, Reflexology & Reiki.
Two-for-one offer…have a therapy session and get the next one free.
Ask about a Seasonal Gift Voucher
The most relaxing present you could choose to give.
Healing Shamanic Therapy sessions also available.

Not sensational, but certainly functional. I found an image of holly and placed it at one side.

From my backpack I pulled a fat handful of Papa Bulgaria flyers, which I'd shamelessly filched from the shop counter, glossy A5 paper, each with its garish orange photograph of savoury dishes. Foolishly, they'd left the backs of the flyers plain white. I tidied the pile and fed it into my printer. I'd done thirty or so before my printer ran out of juice. I examined one. Amateurish, but effective. And it was not the least dishonest, honestly. Every time I put one through a letter box, I'd be delivering the Papa flyer at the same time.

I pulled the unused flyers from the printer. On the back of the first one, I wrote a single word in pen at the top: MIRELA. Before I knew it, I'd scribbled bullet points of everything I knew about her. I put the flyer to one side and started another. KIZZY. The flyers were the perfect size for noting down salient points and this focused my mind. I documented brief accounts of everyone connected with the Brouviche sisters.

I took four more flyers and spread them, white side up, over the coffee table. I wanted to make some sense of the spirit wolf's insistence on directions, the places he'd told me to look. Was it all mist and mirrors meant to baffle and bewilder? I headed the first one THE PLACE OF BLAME. From the start, this had been Papa Bulgaria. Even Mirela believed that, but it still wasn't clear to me if Kizzy had left the takeaway and fallen into trouble, or left the takeaway because it *was* trouble. With my new information about the *Mutri* and Mirela's half-suspicion that they couriered drugs as well as food, I was becoming convinced that Papa Bulgaria was to blame for an awful lot of things. I bullet-pointed everything I knew.

THE PLACE OF ABSOLUTION. I was sure this was the Agency of Change. If anything, Fergus had known Kizzy better than I ever had. He'd sat through an interview with her and her sister. I chewed my pen. Absolution. The only good place, so far, on my list, although, when I thought about it, Fergus had not actually been of any real help to the Brouviches.

THE DARK PLACE. I wrote a short description of our experience at Belinda's Bunnies. It was a guess, that the massage parlour was the dark place. *You will find little in some, and nothing in others*, the wolf had said, but Belinda's had been more a total curveball.

THE PLACE OF NO ESCAPE. Reading the translation of Kizzy's letter had made me wonder all the more what Kizzy had meant by telling Mirela she was not to trust the man with the snake. Was that anything to do with Anaconda, or was I becoming obsessed with journey images?

The greeter at CORE had quoted words from the Bible: *the place of no escape*. I'd recalled how I'd met Drea for the first time only hours after I'd met Kizzy, and even though this connection seemed tenuous, it could be important. Connections in the otherworld were as crazy as that child's game where you join random dots without crossing previously drawn lines—I only had to think of Lettice to demonstrate that.

I headed a fresh flyer DREA COMER and put her story into bullet points. I'd written about her in my shamanic diary, and in the letter that had had such dire consequences, but now I tried to encapsulate what I knew about her life and the misapprehensions I'd made, before taking a new flyer and summarizing my relationship with Andy. Finally, I started on everything I knew, or guessed I knew, about CORE leader Eric Atkinson.

I was creating an index of possibilities. I chewed the end of my pen, wondering if there was anyone I'd forgotten. But before I was able to think any more, the door bell chimed. Rey slid into the hall and wrapped me in his arms.

Writing down my thoughts had made me actually forget about Rey for an hour or so. Shock passed through me, a gasping weakness that left me as helpless as a newborn.

"Hi," was all he said.

I wanted to reply with something clever or funny, but I was struck dumb. All I could do was kiss him. It was glorious to do that; to kiss him *back*.

He passed me a bottle of something Australian. "Just for an evening, I want to forget all about work."

"Brilliant. D'you want food with this? Only I don't have much above bread and cheese…"

"Er… maybe later?"

It's funny what a couple of words can do to your flesh. One thought of Rey in my bed and I was as squidgy as the dough that goes round and round in my bread machine. You could've moulded me into any shape. We wound our way up the stairs and around each other at the same time, flinging ourselves onto the bed, tugging at buttons and wriggling out of underwear. We kissed every bit of flesh as it was uncovered. I could feel Rey's heart thudding against mine. I could smell his spicy aftershave. He'd showered right before he'd set out. But I didn't care about scent. What delighted me was that he'd come, unbidden, to my door.

"God," he grunted. "You are so bad for me."

"Bad girl, that's what I am." I wrapped my legs around him. "Deserve a spanking." I needed to wipe his words away before they could be added to a growing list.

I'm not going to be good for you. We can't be lovers. You are so bad for me.

To Hades with work ethics. I just wanted Rey, no complications, no strings. His hands were all over me, his lips following their course. He wanted this as much as I did. I put my mouth hard over his and tried to forget.

———

It was late when we finally made it downstairs, and we'd both worked up an appetite. Rey uncorked the wine and I put some cheddar and what was left of a loaf onto a wooden board. There were last year's pickled onions and a half tub of olives from the back of the fridge.

"At last! You're taking some action."

I turned to him. While I was finding clean glasses (all right, I confess, while I was *cleaning* clean glasses), Rey, being the detective he was, had unearthed my back-to-front therapy flyers.

"Yep, I'll be shooting them through doors as I proceed."

"Well done." Rey dug deeper. "And what're these?"

"Mmm? Oh, just some stuff I was jotting down. Always re-use paper, is my motto."

"So, is it okay if I read them?"

"Well, I guess so. Grab a stool, let's eat."

We sat opposite each other at the breakfast bar. Rey used one hand to stuff bread into his mouth while the other flicked through my index of possibilities. I tried not to be annoyed. There was no reason to hide the things I'd written, but the silence was disconcerting. Rey was absorbing material as if he was at work.

"Talk to me, Rey," I muttered.

He looked up, not the least fazed. "These look like the Sabbie Dare answer to Avon and Somerset central computer files."

"Is that a criticism?"

"Not one bit. See, I don't know all of it, do I? It's a fresh perspective. Your—sort of—shamanic perspective." He tapped a finger on a page. "You write a lot about blokes."

"What? I do not!" I could feel my cheeks warming.

"Okay, I can see you don't have the hots for Mr. Papazov. Great record of him, though. The team's already got their beady eyes on him, et cetera."

"Is he up on your board?"

"Sorry?"

"Like on telly. They have a whiteboard, and they pin pictures of suspects on it. Do you do that?"

He raised his eyes in despair. "There's a lot on our Mr. Quigg. I see he gave you a translation of Kizzy's letter."

I mentally kicked myself for writing that down. "What it proved to me was that Mirela didn't needlessly lie to me. I'd been worrying about that."

"Tell me more about this Jimmy Browne. Your gut feelings."

"He's sweet. He's a cook. Well, he'd like to be a chef one day. He knew both the girls, but…" It was stupid to point out that he could surely not be a killer. Most probably, no one I knew was Kizzy's killer, except perhaps Petar the lanky slime-ball who I'd already clocked as a thief. I'd happily see him taken in for questioning.

Rey took a slow swallow of wine. "How is he with a knife?"

"What?"

"This Browne. He's a chef. Wants to be. Is he good with a knife?"

The room suddenly felt depleted of oxygen. The police had been keeping very quiet about the killing, and the news sites had been going ballistic in search of information. Some wild rumours had been circulating.

"They're saying…" I took a deep breath. "That she was slashed. Ripped."

"Yes, they are. But we're not going to jeopardise our enquiry by filling the heads of the public with unnecessary hypotheses. We've got lines to pursue and things are coming together with solid indications. Best start of all, your ID, which gave a name to the victim. But there's also a good basic forensic report because we found Kizzy while she was still caught on the cooling tower."

"Cooling tower?"

"Yeah. Part of the Hinkley Point nuclear power station, but slightly out to sea. It's where the witness spotted her. If she hadn't, the body would have been lifted on the following high tide."

A stunned feeling was creeping through me, as if someone had injected me with curare poison. "How did the witness find the body?"

"She walked out there. She was a complete idiot. The tides are treacherous and the mudflats can give way."

"This woman…" I was thinking as I spoke. "Could I talk to her?"

"She's told us everything she knows."

"It's just… you mentioned the shamanic perspective."

"True." Rey crunched down on an olive. "I can't pass on her details, but I could explain to her about you. How you've helped us before. Give her your number."

"Tell her about me, Rey. Tell her I'm free most of Thursday. I'd want to meet her near this cooling tower."

"You can't do anything conventionally, can you? I mean, you could chat to this woman on the phone. But no, you want to go all the way to Hinkley."

"That's my *method*, okay? I work through the spirit world, and the spirits are as much in the land as they are in more subtle spaces."

"I've always wanted to ask," said Rey. "Where *is* the spirit world."

I took a breath. I was not going to get rumpled. "It's beyond the dimensions we can perceive." I watched him smirk and ploughed on. "Solid things… material things… exist on the slowest level of vibratory life. But not everything vibrates like a block of wood. Sound and colour vibrations are faster. We can't hear ultrasounds or see ultraviolet. I believe some things vibrate so fast, people are not keen to admit they exist at all. Our physical body is solid; it vibrates quite slowly, but it has subtle parts that are like light and vibrate at such a rate, we don't know they're there. Not by looking or touching. That's the part that tells us we feel wretched, or great, or whatever."

Rey grinned at me. "Hunches?"

"Yeah, why not? Working with these extra dimensions can help us think laterally. Feelings move through your subtle body. Sensations that transmute into intuition, even into premonitions. The more you link with the subtle planes of existence by meditating, journeying, Tai Chi, chakra work … the more it happens."

"But how does it work?"

"In an often perplexing way! Things get twisted round, mixed up. Spirit connects the paths of every journey I take. The links I follow are on the landscape of the spirit world. And in the Tides of the World of Spirit," I added, hardly meaning to. "But when things feel clear in that world, they often become snarled up in this one. Or vice versa. Say, the spirits tell me something, but I don't interpret it right."

"Wonderful back-out clause, Sabbie."

I laughed. We found each other's feet under the table. Rey's were bare. Mine were in sloppy slippers; I kicked them off and we made love with our toes.

"Remind me, who is Andy?" he asked, all casual, flapping the flyer.

"I'll give you the full story, shall I?"

His toes squeezed mine. "Can you make it a bedtime story? When I was a kid, my mum would always tell me a fairy tale as she tucked me in."

Aw, the man was a romantic after all. "Fairy tale? Andy and Drea's is the bad witch kind, I'm afraid."

"They're all like that," said Rey. "Fairy tales. They're all somewhat Grimm."

TWENTY-THREE

THE ROAD TO THE power station was as straight as the Fosse Way. In the slow-failing light, all I saw was a single fox. Its amber eyes flashed like a warning.

Hinkley Point loomed out of the growing darkness, defying the desolation of Bridgwater Bay. From a distance, it resembled a scattering of squares, like discarded Lego bricks, but it still provided electricity in the Somerset region.

I'd been watching for a turnoff, but the road carried on past a sign telling me I was now entering British Energy property. Buildings overshadowed me on either side, the gates secure.

Ahead was a luminous sheen of grey. The Bristol Channel.

My scooter bounced over the rough grass that fronted the beach and came to a stop. I pulled off my helmet and immediately the wind hit my face, lifting my sparse hair and biting at my scalp.

I stared at the grotesque buildings standing so close behind me. There was a gentle hum coming from somewhere. Did nuclear power make a noise as it generated electricity?

The only other vehicle parked on the scrub-grass was a carefully washed-and-waxed Mercedes. Although the lights were off in the car, its radio was beating a tin can rhythm from inside. I went over and tapped on the window.

The woman jumped, as if surprised that anyone had bothered to turn up. As if I might not be the person she'd agreed to meet. The window descended by a fraction.

"Ellen?" I said. "I'm Sabbie."

"Oh, yes." She got out of her car. She looked to be about ten years my senior. She was neatly made up, her lipstick perfect, with hair styled in a bob that had been so lacquered into place even this wind wasn't moving it. She was sensibly coated in a padded jacket with fur around the collar, but her footwear wasn't sensible at all … here was me in walking boots and socks and there was she in calf leather with four-inch heels.

"Thanks for coming here like this," I said.

"I wanted to. Think I needed to come back." She gazed out across the beach. The water shone like pewter in the dull light. She spoke in that direction, as if addressing the sea. "Can't believe it happened only ten days ago."

She began walking towards the beach as if it was beckoning her. When she got to the fence, she stopped and gripped it, her hands encased in soft leather gloves.

Like Ellen, I examined the desolation of the bay. The tide was low, and the stone causeway could be seen clearly, a formation of flattened boulders with a squiggly pattern across the far shore made up of shingle, rock, and mudflat. At its far edge was a ridge where hardness fell away into sea. A cold wind blew in, but the water only rippled slightly, as if it might be on its way to freezing.

From the deep water beyond rose a skeletal structure, ragged with seaweed. It felt as bare as bones, and the wind moaned through it. Or was it the cooling tower that moaned, in sheer misery of its location?

The cooling tower could have been a gallows, a complex gallows. I could see how it might trap a victim, cling on to her. I kept staring over the bay as the light failed, desperate to get my thoughts into shape, but my heart was racing too fast, keeping in time with the wind that flapped in my ears.

"This beach looks almost alien," I said. "Like a moonscape or something."

"Yeah, well it's the submarine forest, isn't it?"

"Whatever's that?"

"Some sort of prehistoric thing." She waved a hand to demonstrate her lack of expertise. "Where a forest grew millions of years ago, something like that. We used to take home some great fossil finds when we came here as kids. We'd dig around in the mud for them."

I nodded, caught up in the idea of how landscape changes. Neither of us spoke for a while and in the silence the sun fell below the horizon to our left, painting the water with a spectral purple glow.

"It's odd," said Ellen, "because I didn't think about it, when we agreed a time on the phone. But this was when I came here. The light was almost gone."

I nodded. I'd known that. It was how I'd wanted it. "What were you doing?" I said, desperate to ask if she'd come in stilettos on that occasion. "Walking the dog?"

"They didn't tell you?"

"No. The police never pass on personal details."

"Looking back, I can see just how crazy I'd got. But it was a day out of hell. Complete hell. Had some hell-like days in my life, but God, not many worse than that."

I stood next to her, also leaning onto the fence. "Do you..." I paused. I didn't want to sound like a therapist, because Ellen was not my client. Even so ... "Do you want to talk me through it? From the beginning?"

Ellen gave a damp sniff. "She was younger than you are, probably. Straight from university and so keen."

"Sorry. No ... she was from Bulgaria. A Roma."

Ellen took at my perplexed frown and yapped a laugh. "God, no, I'm talking about Coriander."

"Coriander?"

"You said start from the beginning."

She was right. She'd tell the story in the best way for her. If we'd been in my therapy room, I wouldn't have queried her at all. She needed to have her head.

"Would you believe I actually took Coriander on? I had to persuade Keith. We'd always said we'd use graduates, and she looked ideal." She paused, forming the story in her mind. "She was nice, friendly, you know, and I guess I made a friend of her while I showed her the ropes."

"And the ropes are?"

"Conservatories. Small firm—Keith and me started it. Coriander had done business studies and marketing. We wanted to expand our client base. We gave her a brief to see how she could do that as effectively as possible."

"And..." I struggled for the right prompt. "Did she fulfil her brief?"

"She'd been sleeping with my bloody husband. I think he fulfilled hers!" She brushed her hands across her eyes, but she wasn't crying. It was a gesture of rage. "I did think it was odd, the way Keith kept encouraging me to take time off—go out more. 'Now we've got Coriander, you ought to take advantage.' Those were his very words, and believe you me, I should know, they're engraved on my heart."

I *could* believe that. People often give themselves away with their words. "So he … took advantage … while you were out."

"The knitting and stitching group in Stogursey. Every Sunday afternoon from two in the afternoon. I'd finished a tapestry and I'd been too shy to bring it to show them. They made me go home and fetch it."

"And when you got back," I said, light beginning to dawn.

"Yes. They were so bloody absorbed in what they were doing they didn't even hear my key in the door. And do you know, I might have come in and gone back out without ever knowing, if my tapestry hadn't been in the bedroom." She brushed at her eyes again, but still no tears. "At least they had the duvet over them. I should be grateful for that."

"Was that why you came here?"

"This is a good place, if you want to scream or something. It was where our gang chilled out. Played make-believe games. *Dr. Who*, it was back then, that and *E.T.* Expect it's something different now, though who knows?"

"You've always lived round here?"

"Yep, it's Keith who's the newcomer. When he left Universal Windows we set up our own company in a unit on that commercial estate on the Taunton Road. We had a starter home in Minehead and we remortgaged it to the hilt. It was prosper or perish. Luckily, by time the banks were all failing a few years back, we'd more or less got established. I wanted something better than the terrace in Mine-head. I spotted this nice detached cottage outside Stogursey … be-spoke kitchen, antique quarry tile floor, everything. We bought it this summer."

She was crying now, looking away from me into the wind. *Poor Ellen*, I thought. *She's poured her life into things that could be snatched away with one hump under a duvet.*

"And I love it. I'm right back at my roots. Mum lives a mile away." She gave a bleary grin. "You'd think I'd have driven over to her, wouldn't you, but no way. She still doesn't know. We're that sort of people."

Ellen swung round, away from the sea, and leaned her back against the fencing. She was quiet for over a minute. She was regain-ing her composure. "We'd tramp here of a school holiday," she said eventually. "We thought the power station was a scary place. Dared each other to get over the fence and explore it. The Dark Places of the Inside, we called it. Got chased off a load of times. But actually, it's the sea—the beach—that's really dangerous." She gestured towards the sea. "The other dare was getting out there … to the cooling tower."

I imagined a gang of youngsters, picking their way across shingle and flat rock, listening to the hum of the monster building. Better than an adventure playground.

"But no harm came to any of you?"

"Nah. We were fine. The boys used to chase each other out to the sea. The girls were more circumspect, I'll admit. I never went right out. I wasn't that keen on mud."

I looked at her careful makeup and her nut-brown Jimmy Choos and nodded. "So you came here … ten days ago … to have a good scream?"

"I dunno." She dug her hands into her pockets. "I don't know how I felt, except I knew that I would go all the way. Right to the ridge. I'd never done it before, but I was determined. I didn't care what might happen."

I touched her arm, a tiny brush of my fingers. "I can believe how you could leave it to fate."

"Yes," she said, fiercely, "that's it, exactly. If I made it out there, had a good scream, a good, good, scream, then made it back … that would be how it was. If I didn't, well, that was in the lap of the gods. Or *that* thing."

I looked at the looming buildings, the glow from their windows almost cosy. In the silence the hum I'd heard as I parked became louder in my ears. "I was surprised you can get so close," I said. "Security seems a little lax."

"Not for much longer. They've got the go-ahead to build Hinkley C. Twenty-first-century nuclear power. They're going to stop traffic coming anywhere near this place. Quite a lot of villages will be affected too. Everything will change."

"It always does, doesn't it?"

She looked at me as if I'd made a deeply profound statement. "I still don't know why he did it. He tried to explain, but frankly, I didn't believe him. I think it had something to do with … being able to … you know?"

I certainly did. But we'd moved far away from Kizzy. I could almost see her, hanging across the bars of the tower, the grey sea tugging at her hands and feet and hair.

"You spotted the dead girl's body, didn't you. When you arrived?"

"Not then." She put her hand over her mouth, as if she'd forgotten the actual reason we were here, she was so caught up in story of Keith and Coriander. "I was concentrating on my dare." She snorted through her nose. "Not that anyone had dared me, but … I had dared myself, I guess. See, I was looking at my feet a lot. Even the flattest boulders are slippy and in the dusk the mud doesn't look much different."

"Were you wearing those boots?" I *had* to ask.

"I had on the stuff I wore to the knitting and stitching group. Light casual. Sneakers."

"Right. Good dare gear."

She tried a laugh. "Yeah. Those shoes got me quite a way. They were totally wasted, but I didn't care. I was doing the dare and spiting Keith, if only he knew it. Actually, he was already ringing round looking for me. Even my mum. Later we had to make up some story about walking a neighbour's dog."

"You're still together?"

"Oh yes. Of course. Coriander's out on her ear. Well, we couldn't *sack* her as such, but we've persuaded her to go. We're sole partners in the business."

She said this as if it explained everything, and I guess it did. It allowed me a peek into a world I'd never known—the world of the couple that present a solid face against all adversity and rely on each other to shore up the nest they've built with fragile twigs.

"I s'pose I was about three quarters of the way to the ridge when I looked up properly for the first time and took stock of where I was. That ridge seemed touchable. I knew I could do it. My plan was to sit on it, dangle my feet off it. I don't know if that would've been easy, but I could remember the boys jumping all over it. *Sit on it*, I thought, *and think things through. Have a scream.* I'm staring at the ridge, really. Not the cooling tower. Then I look up, and there's this pale bit. I had a … sensation … you know? I kept walking forward, but I was looking at the cooling tower, not the ridge." Her voice had gained enthusiasm, as if telling this macabre side of events took her further away from the desperation of adultery. "Now I'm looking so hard, I keep missing my footing. I'm up to my ankles in bloody mud. I'm on my knees, scrabbling forward. By then I knew."

"That all was not well?"

"I felt like shit, but this was separate to that. Above it. Like the music from *Jaws*. That pale bit. I couldn't believe it. I didn't want it to be…"

"Her face?"

"Yes. Her poor, dead face." She screwed her eyes tight, clutching the fencing, as if Kizzy was still out there. "Like a moon was caught in the bars, with eyes, as big and dark and hollow as craters." Her body convulsed. She wrapped her arms around herself as if it had been the cold. "They're talking about her being slashed. When I think about it now, I keep seeing blood. I'm imagining it, really. It's the way the light goes down out here. It catches things. Like the rocks, now."

She was right. The mud flats and boulders that rose out of the fingers of water gave off a glow, as if they were alive with nuclear energy.

"But honestly, I didn't do that 'good citizen' thing at all—take note of the crime scene, whatever. I was way too spooked. I backed off, totally forgetting about the mud. Covered in it. Pulled myself flat onto a bit of rock and didn't move for a very long time. Then I realised that my mobile was in my back pocket, where I'd dumped it after switching it off the first time Keith tried to call me. It was mired; almost slid out my hands. I didn't think, *must report a murder*, anything like that. It was more…"

"Please help me?"

"Total hysterics. And I was cold, very cold and frightened and mad with myself for being so utterly stupid. I could hardly dial. I think I sort of lost it. Because behind me was a dead girl and in front of me was the power station. I know I was screaming by then, on and on. Got myself right freaked out until I couldn't move at all, like we did as kids, imagining Hinkley Point was the Dark Places of the Inside, where the Mara lived. We loved to scare each other with that *Dr. Who* stuff, say the power station could transmit telepathically, and that the Mara was manifesting as one of us. We'd point to one of the gang and run screaming from them—the pure hatred and greed of the Mara and all that. It all came back to me. I was stuck there remembering that when the Mara manifested into its snake form it would destroy me. Like her. I'd got it in my head *that* was what had happened to her."

She stopped, and wiped her mouth. "Madness. How your mind plays tricks."

"What did you say?"

"That I went quite mad, really. Screamed so hard, I couldn't use my voice for days, after—"

"No. Not that. The thing about Hinkley. What did you say about a snake?"

"Oh, I was just *frantic*, totally back to when we were kids. We loved scaring each other. We *knew* about nuclear power, but we *didn't*, if you get me. We made things up. Even the signs are scary. DO NOT ENTER. To us, that meant, *enter at your peril*. It was Rick who started saying the power station was the Dark Places of the Inside. Said he could hear purring, but it wasn't a cat, it was the Mara, who was, I dunno, this snake; a representation of all evil from another planet. It was what was on *Dr. Who* at the time."

"The power station is…"

"I'd half lost my mind, Sabbie, be fair."

"Yeah, I understand." I did not understand at all, except to recall how the spirit wolf had spoken of a dark place. Was this the same? He hadn't mentioned a snake. But, by then, I had already I met a spirit snake. Anaconda. Like I'd explained to Rey, the spirit world is full of twists and tangles.

"I don't remember much after that," Ellen was saying, bringing me back to the biting wind and bleak seascape. "I don't know how long they took to come, and I made a complete prat of myself when they arrived. There was this nice copper who took off his jacket and covered me with it, mud and all. I made an awful mess of the lining. I must have given them my name because Keith was at the hospital; he was there when they got me out of the ambulance."

"He was sorry," I said. "That's lovely."

She gave me a look. "Yes. He was sorry all right. He'd made a suicidal business decision. Of course he was sorry. I could've have nailed his ass."

———

There were paradoxes and confusion. Tangles and twists. I had to return to the spirit world to unravel the puzzles.

"Trendle," I called.

I could still faintly hear the drum, beating on the CD in my therapy room. Vaguely, I knew I was lying on my back, my hands clasped. My stomach was tensed. My heart raced. I didn't ever want to meet Anaconda again, but I needed to find out where he came from. Was it a dark place… the Dark Places of the Inside? I had to know if there were links between Drea's ice temple, the spirit wolf's directions, and what Ellen told me about the power station.

"Trendle?"

Silence.

Winter had finally arrived at my spirit portal. The grass crunched beneath my feet. Hoarfrost decorated the trees and bracken as prettily as any window display in town. A sheet of ice covered the stream, a couple of centimetres thick. The landscape was soundless and still; frozen into place. It felt like Santa might be delivering presents from his sleigh across the next field.

Trendle was probably curled up in his hole with a good supply of half-frozen fish. But I could do nothing without the guidance of my spirit animal. I would certainly not leave this portal. I lay on the floor cushions in the therapy room only half into my trance, wondering if he'd chosen not to come because he thought my journey foolish. Ellen had watched *Dr. Who* as a kid. Who hadn't? So it was some snake that they'd focused their scary game around. It could have as easily have been Daleks or Cybermen.

Tangles and twists. Mist and mirrors.

In my head, a design took shape, a web of connections. In the centre was Kizzy's face, swollen and frozen in death. Around her the random symbols connected to my search for her. Except, I began to understand, they were not random. They were part of the Tides of the World.

"Trendle?"

A thin snake oozed its way over the frozen grass. Its green body passed my feet, nudging at my bare toes. I tried not to leap back in alarm but let it go on its way. It was heading towards the frozen brook. I watched as it reached a stick that lay on its path. It was the wolf stick, but it had changed subtly yet again. It had fully become a wand with notched carvings along its polished length. I had the feeling they were letters, words. I took a step to try to make them out, but the wand began rolling, as the snake poured his body over it. The momentum increased. The wand rolled down the bank and lay on the ice. The snake slithered away, but I kept my eyes trained on the wand. It seemed to give out heat. The ice sizzled under it. By the time I reached the bank, it had melted a thin slit of ice and sunk to the bottom.

I looked down into the water. Under the ice, weeds moved with a slow ripple. I saw the wand, a pale line along the stony bottom. And something else. Something glinting. Two silver clasps. I knelt on the frozen bank and peered closer. It was a case with shiny metal fasteners. A suitcase, dropped into the water by error or design. Mirela's suitcase.

I pushed at the ice layer with the heel of my hand. It didn't budge. I got up and balanced over the water, slamming my heel down on the thin break the wand had created. The ice crashed open and I toppled into the brook. The water hit me like a returning fist. The cold burned into me. I grabbed the handle of the case and struggled back to the bank. For several moments, I could only gasp and wheeze. Water was dripping from my chin, my fingers, the hem of my long dress. Its arctic touch closed my lungs and stopped my blood.

I turned to the case. My fingers shook as I forced open the clasps and the lid sprang open.

Like her life, Mirela's packing was haphazard. Her clothes lay knotted together, fusing into a sort of beige colour. Despite the soaking in the brook, everything was perfectly dry and the suitcase radiated the sour smell of dirty underwear. Lying on top was the tiny picture of Mary I'd used to find the spirit wolf. Below it, I could see the envelope that contained the letter from Kizzy.

My body convulsed with cold. A wind was forcing its way in from the north; Boreas, it was called. I sometimes summoned it when I wanted an answer to questions that were earthy or dark but not yet solid in themselves. I stood and stared up at the stand of beeches on the summit of the first hill behind the meadow. Would my northward guardians help me to make sense of this? The wind slapped my wet dress against my legs. I grabbed at a matted wool jumper from the suitcase, pulling it over my freezing shoulders.

Something bumped and fell from the folds of the jumper into the soft whiteness of the frosted grass. It lay there, shining and dark, like a polished piece of jet.

It was a mobile phone. Funny, because Mirela didn't have one; the only number she'd given me was for the telephone that had rang like a church bell in the hall of her lodgings.

I stooped to pick the mobile up, turning it over in my hand. Immediately I knew I'd held it before. Awareness coursed through me, followed by a deadening feeling of alarm. This was the gift of the spirit world. The iPhone that Gary Abbott had dropped on the night he was killed.

I was instantly returned to the therapy room. My eyes were wet. I couldn't tell if they were running from the cold or if I had been crying.

Bundled into a fleece, I wrote in my shamanic journal, scribbling things down before the images left me. There were so many images and symbols now, I was afraid of becoming confused.

I recalled the web I saw in the journey. I rummaged around until I found an old roll of wallpaper under the stairs. I cut off a piece slightly longer than it was wide, and pinned it down on the kitchen worktop with an empty mug on each corner. I propped my journal beside it and fished a set of coloured felt tips from a drawer.

I took my time with the images. I wanted to make this look good. I used all the colours in the pack, leaning right over the surface with my tongue peeking from my closed lips as it had when I'd drawn as a child.

There was much to depict. I placed Kizzy's face centrally, as I first remembered it. Her bright black eyes, glittering earrings, and curtain of hair. Around her, I placed all my otherworld images: the gypsy dancers, the violin they'd danced to. The wolf's howl against a full moon. The stick he'd dropped at my feet and the way it had changed into a wand. The four places he'd directed me.

There was Mirela's suitcase with her letter, the icon of the Madonna, and the iPhone. The girl on the shelf in the vast ice temple. The megalithic structure of the power station which was the Dark Places of the Inside. The beach of rock and mud that led to the cooling tower and the cave that led to Hades, the candle flickering in the dark and my haunting cry, *Don't look back!,* from the dream I had the first time Mirela came to my house.

Spiralling through all this, I drew the sinews of Anaconda, his body longer than sleep.

It was gone eight by the time I'd done, and I'd had nothing since my lunchtime sandwich. I had lost my appetite of late. I chopped up one of the apples from my veg store, tossing the good bits in a pan of porridge. It bubbled away. Doing something practical often helped jog my thoughts when the messages from a journey overwhelmed me.

I whipped the porridge off the heat and poured it into a bowl, drizzling over a spoonful of honey. Like the three bears, it was too hot to eat, but that was just as well because I was desperate to take a metaphoric walk in the woods.

I tacked my wallpaper diagram to the kitchen door. I wrote in red, *Everything is connected.* That's how the spirit world worked. *Spirit connects the paths,* I'd told Rey. *When things feel clear in that world, they become snarled in this one.*

I used a thick black marker to draw lines of connection.

The ice of the brook, the shelf of ice. The ice temple, the power station. The icon of the Madonna, the Lady of the River. The dark place, the Dark Places of the Inside. The length of wolf wand, the length of the snake.

The symbol of the snake was universal. Snakes had represented certain things for millennia: wisdom, intuition, evil, cold-bloodedness, fear, and of course danger. Drawn with its tail in its mouth, it depicted eternity; drawn as a caduceus, it represented the healing energy of the chakras. Because snakes shed their skin, they symbolised rebirth.

I'd seen it in my spirit journey, and on the banner at CORE. Ellen believed it lived within the power station.

I stared at my diagram, but nothing made any further sense. I swallowed up my porridge and hoped it would help me sleep tonight.

TWENTY-FOUR

By Saturday, Mirela had been missing for thirteen days, a dark trench of time that made my stomach curl each time I thought about it. And it was five days since I'd seen Rey. He hadn't given me as much as a text. I knew Rey wasn't going to be running, except after the bad guys, but I had thought he'd get back to me to ask how my interview with Ellen had gone. In fact, I had almost nothing to report back. Somehow, I didn't think he'd be interested in *Dr. Who* characters. Before setting out for my shift at the Egg, I'd texted him: Fancy quick pint? A nice casual invite, no pressure, no hint of the screaming female raging inside me. The illogical terror I'd felt as I'd looked down on his sleeping form hadn't left me for one moment. It wouldn't just be hard to keep Rey as mine; it would likely be impossible. That thought weakened me.

By the time Nige and I were hanging the damp tea towels over the beer taps and pulling on our coats, I had bitten my knuckles raw over the silence of my phone. He was busy. He had murders to solve and missing Romanies to locate. Why would he even reply, let alone turn up?

Fergus hadn't come to drink ale on his usual bench, either. That might have been because the group tonight had been punkish, way too loud and brash for the sensitive Fergus Quigg. But the idea of chatting to Fergus filled me with dread anyway. He hadn't had the same relationship with Mirela as I'd had, and his response to Kizzy's death had been, well, too "professional" for me. He was sorry, but not *sorrowing*, and right this moment, I really didn't want to pull the Brouviches to pieces. And last Saturday, he'd invited me to his flat. I hadn't stood Fergus up ... had I? Truth was, Rey was the only bloke I could think about.

"I'm shattered," I told Nige, as we left the pub and headed towards our late-night taxi. "But I won't sleep, I know it. I haven't slept all week." I didn't mention that I'd hardly eaten all week, either, and that being sick in love was at least partly to blame for both situations.

"Want to come back to mine? Watch a DVD?"

The invite caught me off-guard. Was Nige just being a mate?

"Sorry," he said, lighting up. "You're probably seeing your boyfriend. The one that was talking to the boss."

"Rey? Was here? Talking to Kev?"

"That his name? Anyway the Irish one. I was out in the yard, having a puff. They were by the corner gate. Kev was passing him paperwork, something or another. It was probably not him ... someone like him, you know?"

"Yeah, Nige. It couldn't be Fergus, he'd've stopped for a chat with me."

"Whoever, man," drawled Nige. "He was deep with Kev, anyway. Talking low, meaningful, you know?"

I didn't reply because I was suddenly aware that a Nissan was parked right behind the taxi. A man stepped out of it.

I pointed. "That's my boyfriend." I could feel my chest puff with pride as I said the words.

"Looks like Daniel Craig after a heavy stunt," said Nige, casting an abstract eye over Rey. "Is he the copper?"

"Yep."

Nige burst out laughing. He had an incongruous sense of humour. Clearly he thought I was the wrong sort of girl for a cop. Probably, he was right. I didn't stop to work it out. I was running over the cold pavement. I desperately wanted Rey to hold me, but I stopped a metre short of his arms.

"Thought you'd be too busy."

"Even I've got to eat sometime." He slid his fingers under my open coat, probing my ribs. "I want to feed you up. Steak or something."

"Rey! I'm a vegetarian."

"Or something then."

We picked up a Chinese for two and some Cokes and drove to mine, where at least there was a breakfast bar to eat at. I put on some of the Dolmen's music I had on download because Taloch's husky voice and pensive lyrics suited my mood. We shared out the foil containers—the meaty ones for Rey, the veggie ones for me. I sat opposite him and kicked off my shoes, ready for another game of naked footy, but he didn't notice; he still had his big policeman boots on. "We ordered too much," I said, waving a hand at the food.

"You are going to get your share down you," said Rey. "I want you safe from malnourishment."

I took a big gloopy mouthful of mushroom chow mein, trying (unsuccessfully) to suck the noodles off my chin and so remain appealing. Rey was pushing his black bean beef around the foil container. He had stuff on his mind, I could tell.

"We did a check on that chap you told me about."

My mind raced. "What chap?"

"The fairy story? The Grimm one?"

"Andy?" I felt my mouth sag, noodles and all. "You did a check on Andy Comer?"

"No, of course not. I'm talking about the preacher."

"Wow—you actually listened to something I said!"

"I wouldn't say that. And we don't have a lot a spare time at the moment for chasing bigamists. But a crime is a crime, so I got a uniformed constable onto it. Turns out he is as clean as a baby's bottle. Perfect upstanding member of society."

"He's married to three women Rey. I saw them, and the two babies he's had with them."

"He's not married at all, Sabbie. You can go through a religious ceremony without actually applying for a marriage certificate. There are no records of Eric Atkinson ever getting hitched."

Relief washed over me. Drea was free. If Andy could persuade her that she'd been tricked into believing she belonged to Atkinson by law, she might finally agree to leave him. I needed to tell Andy. But that could wait for a while at least. I had other thoughts in my mind.

"I was wondering," I said, trying to stay cool, ease the information out of him, now he was in the mood to talk, "if you ever found Gary's iPhone."

"Of course not," said Rey. "The gypsy took it. And she was pretty bare when we found her. No pockets full of useful clues, I'm afraid." He eyed me. "Why are you asking that now?"

"It made an appearance in one of my shamanic journeys."

Rey lifted his hands clear of the table. "Oh, for God's sake, Sabbie! Please grow up!"

I felt my neck glow with warmth. I tried to swallow a mouthful of fried rice; it grated at the back of my throat. "I thought we'd agreed. Spirit world messages can be important … in their own way."

Rey was scrabbling in his pockets for cigarettes and a lighter, clearly desperate. "You're beginning to think you're part of the investigative team."

I exploded. "Don't be an idiot! After the way Abbott treated me back in the spring?"

His look was raw. "Gary was a good cop. A great detective."

"Yes, of course." Rey was stricken by his death. There was no point now, examining his flaws. "But I was wondering if Kizzy might have been in St. Mary's Lane *because* of Abbott, rather than by coincidence."

He tried a grin, but it didn't really work. "Unbelievably, we've already thought that through. Surprising though it might sound to you, Bridgwater CID are way ahead of the lay shaman."

"Okay. I'm sorry."

Rey shrugged, not the answer I was hoping for. "I'm going out for a fag." He strode off without looking back. I stayed perched on my stool.

You are bad for me. Too nosey by half, I fired up my stressed-out detective at the least opportunity. Rey was dealing with three murder enquiries and, as far as I was aware, none were getting solved.

I felt the chilled evening air on my face, fingering through the open door. I'd dreamed for months of having Rey in my bed. I wasn't going to shatter that dream over one tiny issue.

He was on the park bench by my hut full of wrinkling vegetables. He could not sit on it in a conventional manner; he'd perched his bum on one wooden arm with his feet resting on the slats. I climbed up, copying him in mirror fashion, so that our feet touched in the middle. Mine were still bare.

"Didn't mean to pry," I said. "Of course you can't tell me everything. Need to know, and all that."

He blew smoke into the night. "I'd be dancing if I could find something that connected Kizzy Brouviche with Gary's death. But it's not going to happen. The MO's ... well, Kizzy was killed in a very specific way, and the pathologist has been able to work backwards to the other girl, re-examine the previous forensics."

"Has that given you ... leads?"

"Yeah. Difficult to follow up, mind you, but we're trying." He leaned down and took my foot in his warm hands, caressing it. "Sometimes you have to be circumspect. Diplomatic."

"We're not talking buccal swabs here, then."

"I fancy those are going to be a slightly different line of enquiry."

I waited for him to elaborate, but naturally he didn't. "Was Gary on that investigation?" I asked. I was wondering if the girl found at Dunball Wharf might have been "watching out" at some other shooting. But this was Bridgwater. Abbott was the first person to be shot in this sleepy town for a very long time.

"Yep, alongside me." Rey frowned. "He was odd about that case."

"Odd?"

"Almost over-keen, which is not how a cop should be ... emotional. Objectivity is how we work."

"Gary Abbott, emotional? As in caring?"

"Almost." He paused. And then he told me what had happened when they'd hauled that first dead girl from the wharf. How Gary had touched her hair and spoken sharply to the technicians about her treatment. How, in the months after, he'd been touchy, almost urgent about the case, and yet less than keen to share.

"Was there something he wasn't telling you?"

"He would never have retained evidence. Never. But it was as if the girl meant something to him, even though he clearly did not know her."

I had a sudden thought. "Or Kizzy? He couldn't have known Kizzy, could he?"

"Can't see how. Okay, that theory would tie up lots of loose strings. It would explain why Kizzy was at the location. It would even explain why he was so wound up about the first death."

I felt my stomach lurch as the pieces fell into place. "It's the hair, isn't it? Kizzy had long, dark hair, like the first girl."

"Good try, Sabbie, but 'long, dark hair' is not a line of enquiry that's going to take us any useful place."

"You said the forensics were the same," I mused, working backwards through the things Rey had let slip.

"That's not what I meant," said Rey. "It's simply that the pathologist can now make some deductions, looking at what Kizzy's shown us."

"A DNA link to the same killer."

"Not so much. The killer wears gloves. The girls were both clean."

"I can't blame you for not wanting to count me in, Rey. Not exactly empirical, the way I think."

"But then there's how you hit the nail on the head last time. And that's the sticking point."

"Why?"

"You end up in such *scrapes*."

"Jolly good scrapes," I said, using Lettice's crystal tones. "But is there one killer? Someone who's done this to two women? And might do it again?"

Rey took the cigarette out of his mouth and examined it. "God, it's hard not to tell you things, you inquisitive minx. But I won't have to fill you in on the DNA result; it will be public knowledge in"—he checked his watch—"exactly five hours."

I gasped. "You're about to make an arrest?"

Rey nodded, the tiniest movement. "Yeah. We're hopeful. 'Course we are."

I stared upwards. The sky glittered with stars. I could see Saturn clearly, a fat pinprick of white light.

But Rey wasn't looking at the stars. He was digging his fingers into his scalp so that the palms covered his eyes. A flash-flood of pain rushed through me. Like a heroin rush it was, although, even in my bad old days, I'd never been that daft. The electric pain of love. I put my hand to his night-chilled cheek. My action seemed to explode in him. He wrapped his arms round my ribs, crushing the breath from me and we were kissing, kissing, and all around us was velvet night, swirling stars, and scented breezes.

I thought I heard nightingales, although it was more likely to be distant sirens up on the dual carriageway.

———

Rey took a shower and was gone by five on Sunday morning. He left me tossing about my bed, unable to get back to sleep. I wondered how long it would be before details of the arrest were made public.

After an hour of letting this revolve in my head, I dragged myself under the shower in the hope it would clear my mind. Luke-warm water trickled down on me—the last, dripping straw. Rey had used up all the hot. Why was it that when the weather was coldest, my shower was at its least proficient? I rubbed myself dry and, for a treat, lavished some rose-scented oil over my body. By then, I knew I wasn't going back to bed, so I let the hens out at the first glimmerings of light, fed them their pellets, and checked their water. I downed a cup of tea and slurped my way through a bowl of Weetabix drizzled with honey, almonds, and warmed soya milk.

I opened the blinds in the therapy room. Andy Comer was walking down to the paper shop for the Sundays, his shoulders hunched. I waved, but he didn't see me, so I tapped on the glass. He came to a halt, trying to isolate the noise. I tapped and waved again. He crossed the road to my gate.

I needed to pick my words carefully. I wanted him sitting down before I explained Atkinson's marital status. "Do you fancy a quick coffee?"

He gave a brief nod and I let him in.

———

"I haven't found her," Andy said, as I made coffee and Barleycup. I didn't tell him I could already see that, in every movement of his body.

"You went down to Exeter?"

"Yes. They wouldn't let me through the front door. I don't even know if Eric was there. She'll be where he is; he takes his wives with him when he travels."

I had him in my mind's eye, the big navy four-by-four full with wives and children. "I'm so sorry, Andy."

He looked out, across the room, into the past. "It's kidnapping, surely? I've reported it to the Exeter police. They were nice about it. Sympathetic."

"But they couldn't do anything," I sighed.

"Friday, I went to Charter Hall again. I didn't get past the welcoming committee. I tried to sneak in, but…"

"You didn't get into a fight, did you?"

He half grinned. "A silent one. On their side, at least. They don't want the nearly converted to see what their underbelly is like. I was hoping to catch Drea as they all left, but this time Eric brought the car to the hall and they piled in from the entrance. I didn't stand a chance."

"I wish I could do something to help. To right all this."

"It's not your problem. I don't want to moan, not really. I thought I'd bring you up to speed, that's all." His fingers were gripping my mug so tight I was worried he'd snap the handle. "I can't give her up. And Zachariah. I went into town and got a load of toys from a couple of charity shops, just in case he comes back and has to leave all his behind." He took a sip of coffee. "Zac used to call me Andy Pandy. Perhaps he's forgotten me. Eric would encourage that."

"There is something I've discovered about Atkinson."

His eyes sharpened. "What?"

"He's an unmarried man."

"What d'you mean?"

"There are no marriage certificates for any of the weddings. Which means although he's told Drea she's his wife, she's free to leave him at any point."

319

Andy looked almost unsurprised. He shook his head. "That wouldn't convince her. It's God she's married before, not a registrar."

"Even so, she lived with you when she thought she was properly married to Eric…"

"You don't understand our religion. She feels she was tempted by the devil to give in to sin. She believes she *had* given in to sin."

"Do you believe that?"

He stared at his feet, shaking his head monotonously. "I don't know what to believe."

"Maybe there isn't a devil at all," I said, keeping my voice calm. "I don't think there is."

"But you must believe in evil."

I thought about Kizzy and the other dead girl, and about Abbott, shot directly through his skull. "Rey—the policeman who investigated Atkinson—he believes in change and status quo. But I think a lot of evil is actually madness."

"Eric's not at all insane."

"Then he knows what he does is wrong. He contravenes his own beliefs. I heard him go on and on about holy union at Charter Hall, but he didn't even bother to marry his wives."

"He's more evil than that, Sabbie." Andy took a deep breath in through his nostrils as if to steady himself as he thought about Eric. "Zachariah was a difficult delivery. Long. Protracted, they called it. Naturally, I was not allowed anywhere near the maternity unit, but Eric paced the corridors for most of that time." Andy gave a humourless grin. "He assumed he was the father. Maybe he is. But Drea and I knew Zac might be my child, and she would have given anything for me to be there with her."

"I didn't realize," I said.

"She came home when Zac was four days old. They had warned her to go easy. She told me that in confidence, but ..." I watched as Andy's fists clenched until the skin on his knuckles was as white as the bones that lay beneath. "Within two months she was pregnant again."

Bastard Atkinson, I thought, but I didn't speak the works.

"It was an ectopic pregnancy. She was rushed into the Royal Devon. It had to be taken away. They grow in the wrong place, you see. And after that, they said the chances of conception were very low."

I remembered the weakness I'd picked up the Reiki session, the trauma I felt in Drea's groin. "I'm so sorry."

"I wasn't. Not at the time. Thinking Drea would be Eric's second wife forever, thinking one child was enough with a husband like him. Drea admitted, quietly to me, that she had such thoughts too. But thinking them was the sin of pride and of unnatural womanhood. That made her guilty twice over."

"Twice?"

"Once for the prideful relief that she'd never have more babies. And once because the Lord had struck her down with the ectopic pregnancy because she had already sinned. She had lain with me."

"Oh, Andy," I said.

"Eric couldn't have been sure about us, but I think he suspected something, for he punished her iniquity cruelly. He rebuked Drea by taking Naomi to him."

"Is this the girl with the baby?"

"Yes. Almost as soon as Drea was out of hospital that second time, he married Naomi. She was carrying inside weeks. It makes me shudder."

"Was that when you and Drea started to plan ..." I didn't want to use the word *escape*.

"We were offered some luck. He went up north to confront Naomi's parents. Understandably they were trying to convince her to leave CORE. While he was away, we moved fast. I went out and bought tickets for the train to Bristol. But at Taunton, we thought it might be a good idea not to use the right station. So we got off. We spent a few nights in a B&B. I found some work. At work I had access to a computer and we found this house."

"The rest is history," I said, trying for humour.

"Eric acts like a god. He knocked on our door. I opened it. He shouldered me out of the way and stormed into the house. He started yelling. You haven't heard him yell. It's agony. He told Drea I'd seduced her in her weakness and stolen her away from her rightful place. I threatened to call the police and at that point he left. On Tuesday, I came home to find she'd gone."

There was a long silence. I said, "You were right, Andy. What you said to me in the street. I should have stayed away from Drea. I should have been warned by the messages coming off her. I should have said *no, not right now, make an appointment. Think about it and come back when you're sure.*"

"It wouldn't have mattered. Okay, you told Eric we were up the street. But I reckon he would have knocked on every door in Bridgwater, if it meant finding his God-given wife." He stood, brushing down the knees of his Sunday jeans. "I can be just as stubborn. I can keep going just like he did."

"Why not give it a rest for a week or two? Allow his guard to drop a bit?"

"Yeah." Andy nodded. "Good advice. Good advice."

"Don't go to Charter Hall again," I said. "They'll only chuck you out."

"I need to keep trying. It's what's keeping my soul inside my body."

"Okay, look; promise you won't go without telling me. You won't go without *taking* me."

"You're a pretty damned kind person, to say that."

I didn't explain. It was the way I recognised a kindred spirit in Andy. We were both in separate capsules of lamentation, sorrowing for things that were wrong and people we had failed.

TWENTY-FIVE

I PULLED ON MY black dress and my belt of shamanic tools. On the floor of the therapy room, I spread a black silk scarf. I sat beside it, cross-legged on a floor cushion, a fleece around my shoulders. I shuffled one of my Tarot packs. I didn't intend to do a reading; I wanted to bring the symbols I'd arranged on my wallpaper diagram to mind.

Every time I walked past the chart pinned on my kitchen door, I stared at it, looking for patterns. Some symbols didn't seem to connect. The mobile phone was the most puzzling. I had no idea what it was doing there, or what it represented. The otherworld was sending me pop-up messages and it was my job to interpret them, but I knew there was no point in forcing things. Symbols were like lottery balls; they would fall into order when they were good and ready.

My shamanic mentor Wolfsbane used the stars to explain difficult times. He would say that right now, I was passing through bad astrological aspects. I preferred reading the Tarot to gauging the movements and positions of celestial bodies.

I'd chosen the Rider-Waite, a good orthodox pack. I wanted to remind myself of long-acknowledged meanings to begin this work. I shuffled slowly, pulling out cards linked with the various symbols, arranging them on the black background. Snakes alone gave me several images: The Magician, The Lovers, The Wheel of Fortune, and both the Two and the Seven of Cups. That made me sit up. The Seven of Cups indicates disorganisation in your life, warning that you're not focused enough. This was only too true, but being told didn't help, especially as the Two of Cups represented harmony and togetherness.

I turned my attention to the mobile phone. Why had my journey taken me to this? The otherworld usually deals in ancient symbols, not techno-gadgets. What might an iPhone symbolize? Communication on the move, perhaps? There were Tarot cards representing that, but Abbott didn't strike me as communicative, and he'd never been interested in the otherworld. On the other hand, minutes after I'd found his mobile, it was in Kizzy's possession. I had brooded over the oddness of her being in St. Mary's Lane.

It seemed almost deliberate, the way Kizzy had approached us from the shadows, as if to prevent us going farther. As if she was some sort of look-out. As if she knew precisely what was going on in St. Mary's courtyard. Rey had dismissed this out of hand. I could remember his exact words: *Kizzy was killed in a very specific way.* I had no idea what that mean.

I shrugged. There were plenty of other symbols on my wallpaper web to examine without getting screwed up about phones. I was transfixed by the image of the wolf baying at the full moon. The Moon card came up in readings where psychic or intuiting abilities were important.

The faint chirp of my own mobile floated in from the kitchen. I sat back on my heels. A pulse throbbed in my neck. Bad news. I knew it. It could be nothing else. I repressed a shudder as the phone stopped. I went back to looking at my Tarot. The phone started up again. I could not bear the blithesome tones. I stormed into the kitchen and snatched it up like it was to blame.

"Sabbie *Daar*?"

"Stan," I sighed.

"I want you to come in to Papa."

"It's my day off." *Fuck you*, I thought.

"We have a staff crisis."

"You've always got a staff crisis." The thought of spending a single extra moment on that scooter made me nauseated.

"Max is having to deliver. He's rubbish on a scooter!"

A grin spread over my face. "That's your fault for paying buttons. All your Cinderellas have gone to the ball." There was silence. He didn't intend to get my gag. "I'm busy, Stan," I said, deliberately making my voice sound weary. "I am actually working at my other job. You'll have to find someone else."

"Please. *Please*, Sabbie. Jimmy is missing."

"Missing?" I pulled the phone away from my ear and stared at it. "What, like Mirela?"

"No. Like police custody."

"*Jimmy*? Are you kidding me? He wouldn't nick a Mars Bar."

"It's Kizzy." Stan sounded shaken. His voice actually wavered. "It's on the news. He's under arrest for her murder."

The bad news I'd foreseen. Rey's dawn raid. The DNA. But Jimmy? It didn't make sense. No one would suspect he was hiding any sort of dark secret.

I brought to mind my first sight of him, how he knew the blow to his head was coming but hadn't even ducked, as if Papazov had a right to consider him a personal gym. In other words, an underdog. I bet he still lived with his mum—a bit of a wimp, quiet, no proper relationships. A loner. The sort police profilers always think are the culprits.

Arrest first, Rey had explained. Twenty-four hours allowed for questioning, unless a magistrate agrees to an extension. Ninety-six hours maximum. Then the charge must be laid, and the DPP must approve it, or the suspect must be released.

"Sabbie!" A tinny voice in my ear. "Sabbie *Daar!*"

"Stan—I said I'm working at home today. What part of the word *no* don't you understand?"

"Okay-okay!" He exuded a hissing sigh down the phone. "Okay. Double time."

"What?"

"Tomorrow? Eleven to ten, double shift, double time?"

"Take a hike. You'll just deduct a heap of imaginary expenses."

"It's Christmas! People are holding parties, wanting lots of food. I need you bad." I couldn't help but grin. What had it cost Stan to admit that? "Cash! I'll pay cash!"

"Triple time. And I want to be paid for all my work. No loan. No excuses."

There was a long pause while on the other end of the phone I could hear Stan cringe at the thought of passing money into my eager hand.

"Okay," he squeaked. "Triple. Could you do double shifts on Tuesday and Wednesday, too?"

"Jimmy should be back by then, surely."

"Don't think so. Ask me, he's guilty as sin."

"Stan! Jimmy wouldn't hurt Kizzy. Not any woman. He hasn't been charged, has he? They had to be seen to make an arrest!"

"You check the news sites. They're taking bags of stuff from his house."

I closed my eyes. Not Jimmy. Please not him.

"Sabbie? Okay, then?"

"Okay, Stan."

I wasn't listening anymore. I didn't care what I agreed to. A thought was building in my head, creating pressure, making me reel.

"Thank you, Sabbie *Daar!*"

The line went dead. The phone dropped from my hand. The thought exploded. I gripped my kitchen worktop. My stomach convulsed.

Jimmy had handed me an unwanted order, pushed it at me. *Go on*, I think he'd said. *Enjoy…* And moments after finishing it, I was collapsing in the loo. Too fast a reaction for food poisoning, the doctor said. Pressure of work. I was working hard. I was under pressure. It seemed a reasonable diagnosis. Who would imagine that something had been added to the foil container—sprinkled over the spicy food. But what would Jimmy put in my food? And why would he want to do that to me?

Rey had asked a strange question. *Is he good with a knife?*

I gave myself a shake. These were ridiculous thoughts I didn't have time for. I couldn't afford to feel discombobulated, as Gloria would've put it. I had to concentrate on my work. Two clients today: a reflexology at four p.m., and, before that at half past one, a first consultation with someone who wanted to see me as a shaman.

I folded the silk scarf around the Tarot pack. I would have to return to this later, when I was in the right mood.

I gave myself a little manicure for the second appointment (nothing worse than having your feet rubbed by someone with snaggy nails). I lit a charcoal disc and let a small branch of sage burn, the smoke spiralling slowly upward as I walked it round the room. As I called power in, I found my voice lifting and bursting into song, as if my throat could not contain the words by simple speech. I was no karaoke star, but singing in the north, south, east, and west filled me with sudden joy. I'd almost forgotten about joy; how easy it was to find moments of it, how easy it was to lose again. I sat cross-legged in the centre and went on singing, trying to stay in the moment of ecstasy, until the door bell chimed. I rose slowly, giving myself time to get back into the apparent world, because doing this too fast can result in a shock.

Then I opened the door and—bang! There was my shock. Smiling rosily from behind his golden beard was Juke.

"Hi." He thrust a narrow bunch of lilies at me. "I have an appointment with you?"

"You're my new shamanic client? Justin Webber?"

He tried to look sheepish. "Sorry. I got Cath to phone in case you thought I was mucking around."

I was pretty sure that he *was* mucking around. Reluctantly, I took the lilies from him. "These are lovely," I lied, turning away to find a vase. I hate hothouse flowers. They last so long they might've been genetically engineered and smell like they'd doused themselves in some cheap market scent for a night on the town.

"I don't suppose you remember from my party, but I did say I was sort of interested in how shamanism works."

"I do remember."

"You ... you thought I was coming on to you, at the party, didn't you? That's why you left, isn't it?"

I stuck my head in a cupboard, hoping he'd think I hadn't heard him, and found a jug which I filled with water, sliding the lilies in and letting them find their own spaces. Bless them, they couldn't help their start in life. They were like ex-bat hens.

"You said you'd read a lot of books, Juke, but to be honest, that don't impress me much. Books tell you stuff, but only your own spirit world can show you what shamanism can offer."

"Yeah," said Juke, "I get that."

"Come and sit down."

I led him into the therapy room and offered him one of the wicker chairs, taking the other myself. I didn't grab a notepad. When a new client arrives, I try to fix what they say in my mind, ready to make notes after they've gone. That has three benefits: I keep alert because I don't want to forget anything; I focus on their physical presence, which can tell me loads about them; and it feels to them as if they have my entire attention, which they do.

"Explain why you made this appointment," I said, thinking that I already knew the answer; Juke had met a shaman at a party, simple as that. No doubt he already planned to use the experience to show off in pubs.

"I have this shoulder pain."

I blinked. "Oh. Right."

"I've had it for ages. Years, when I care to work it out."

"Juke, can I presume you've seen your doctor?"

"Yep. GP sent me to a physio, who sent me for an X-ray and gave me exercises that did nothing. I cried off then, told them it was only a slight ache."

"Was it a slight ache?"

"It did start out as an ache, but over the years it's grown more intense. Since then, I've seen an osteopath, a chiropractor, and had numerous massages. Nothing works."

"Has anyone been able to give you a diagnosis?"

"Yeah, I went back to the doctor's and finally he told me I probably had a frozen shoulder. So I looked it up on the net... as y'do... and it sort of means inflammation of the shoulder."

He raised his arms and squeezed the opposite shoulders, hardly noticing his gesture, wincing as he rubbed the muscles. At once, I recalled seeing him do this at the party. I leaned towards him and put my palm on his knee and words fell out my mouth without my bidding.

"It's all right. You don't need forgiveness. You don't need to be absolved. You don't need to feel guilt. You are innocent."

It was one of those moments that arrive unbidden in my mind... images, symbols, words. They sound like gibberish. Only the person listening can tell me if they *are* gibberish. Partly it's experience. As soon as Juke told me he had shoulder pain, I recalled the way he did stoop a fraction... the way he'd held and squeezed his shoulders a lot at the party, and the way I'd empathized with the lilies that could not help what they represented.

Juke's face blanked momentarily. His eyes widened as his mouth worked, battling a surge of emotion. His whole upper body jerked in the chair.

"Wha... what d'you mean?"

"Shamans rarely know what they mean."

"Then why did you say that? That I'm innocent?" He gave an abrupt laugh. "'Course I'm innocent."

"Of course you are. But your body is not agreeing with you. You're all bowed over as if in shame. Your shoulders have ached for years, as they would if you were carrying a terrible burden you couldn't shift. Finally you come to see me, because no one else can help you." I shrugged. People often came to me as a last resort. I was used to it. "And, for some reason, you bring lilies."

"There was no reason," said Juke. "I was halfway here, driving past this little florist, and it came into my mind that I ought to bring you flowers, to say thank you. I saw the lilies as I walked into the shop. A massive bucket of them."

"They asked you to buy them?"

"Yeah, guess they did."

"For me, Juke, lilies often represent innocence. Whatever burden you're shouldering, you're not responsible for it."

"But—what're you talking about?"

"I don't know. Maybe you'll have more idea than me. Or maybe, when I journey for you—as I'll do between this appointment and your next—I'll find out for you."

"Are you talking … do you mean …"

I waited.

"No. That's crazy."

"Say it."

"My brother. Mark." His hands grasped each other. "It's my brother."

I didn't reply. Juke would sort the story out in his head.

"He's a year younger than me. Not much of a gap. I guess that gave us a tight bond, as kids. But we're not alike. He's always been the—well, the impetuous one. Easily sparked off, you know?"

I nodded.

"We were seventeen, eighteen at the time," he went on. "It was before I left for uni. We used to hang out together a lot. We were still sharing a bedroom at Mum and Dad's. We spent most nights in the Hamp Tavern." He laughed. "I have no idea where we found the money, but whatever we had, we spent it there. Nissed as Pewts from eight o'clock on."

"Believe me," I said. "I remember those times."

"Nah," said Juke. "If you remember them, you weren't there, right? Getting pissed-up from eight o'clock; getting pissed-off by ten. Getting into a punch-up as we finally fell into the street."

His hand crept towards his shoulder but jolted to a stop before he could grab it. Instead, he brushed his fingers over his beard, like you can with waist-high wheat.

"Mark was always first. Very keen." He managed a grin. "Back then, it was like he lived for it. 'Saturday Night's Alright for Fighting,' yeah? I was always pulling him off people and patching him up. Cleaning away the vomit before Mum saw."

"You were a good brother."

"I was too late that one night. Came out of the Hamp to find him standing over some older bloke. The fight had been about a watch, apparently; I never got the full story from him. But the bottle was in his hand. Those jagged edges have not left my mind, or the way the blood seeped onto the tarmac. It was thick." Juke shook his head, as to disperse the image of redness and sharpness. "There was no one about; it had been between the two of them. I grabbed Mark and pushed him along until we'd turned a couple of corners. I flung the bottle into a hedge. It caught the streetlight as it fell. It was a Stella. He always drank Stella."

"Do you ever talk about it?"

333

"He'd forgotten overnight. Couldn't recall a thing. Didn't believe me, until it came on the news."

"Was the other guy okay?"

"He recovered, but what Mark did might have got him ten years. I was about to go and study law. I already knew he'd unlawfully and maliciously inflicted grievous bodily harm. That scared him. Yeah, he was terrified all right—terrified I'd report him."

"And..." I closed my eyes, trying to imagine. "That is your guilt. You didn't report him."

"I haven't thought about it properly for years. That feeling of wrongdoing that taints the good times. I didn't even call an ambulance. It was no thanks to me that the guy hadn't died right there in the gutter. That's never gone away, you know?"

"It's buried deep in your shoulders," I pointed out.

"What can I do?"

I took a moment, thought about the best way to offer Juke something positive.

"It will help knowing why your shoulders hurt. But you said you were interested in shamanism. You may gain more benefit if you learn to take shamanic journeys yourself."

Juke sat up. "Become a shaman?"

"No," I said. "That stage would grow over time, when you're ready and discover you enjoyed the experiences. To start with I'd show you techniques to help you understand yourself. Help you cope with life."

"That would be amazing."

"Yes. Shamanic practice is amazing. It changes your life. There's a warning on the bottle, though, so beware."

"I'd like a life change. I'd like to stop feeling every happy moment is clouded."

Rey would say Juke had "perverted the course of justice." Juke knew that; it was part of his longstanding guilt. He'd put his brother above the law. Then I thought about lilies, small flags of purity. Blameless.

Surely they were a start.

———

I gave Juke too long. I was so relieved that he hadn't come to mock or revel in my "outsiderness" that I forgot the time as I led him through the preliminary steps of a simple spirit journey. I explained that he should first find his totem, his power animal, telling the story of how Trendle had been waiting for me to contact him for most of my life. I think that's true of everyone, that there's a totem waiting if you care to look. And I had to make it clear to him that if I took him on as a shamanic student, rather than a client, he would be paying me by the hour for months, rather than for a set of sessions. I might be broke and desperate for work, but I needed to be sure it was what he wanted and could afford.

"We're going to miss Fergus, aren't we?" Juke said as I opened the front door.

I paused. "What d'you mean, *miss*?"

"He's off home soon. Sorry, I thought you'd know. You're not still seeing him, then? None of my business, naturally."

"Home? D'you mean Belfast?"

"Yeah. He's on a year's contract."

"Right. I just assumed he was permanently with you."

"No, time's nearly up. Be heading back before long."

It took me a moment to grasp that Fergus had made a play for me—and that, if it hadn't been for Rey, I would have responded—

even though he knew our relationship would burn on a shorter fuse than a carnival squib. Juke had no idea what he'd revealed. He was still nattering on. "Gonna be manic without him. And he's fun to work with. He thinks in swerves, you know? Gets round the back of things."

I tried to get this into perspective. I knew that Fergus was an operator, a wolf. He liked to chat the girls up, take them to parties. Neither of us had sworn undying love. I wasn't the settling down kind, anyhow. I had a sort-of boyfriend, for goddess's sake. Why should I care if he was heading back to Belfast? Why should I be the least upset about it?

"Shame, though," Juke said. He put out his hand to shake mine. "Said things were going good for him over here. Taking off, like. He's not one to chat about his life outside work, but he did say that. Said he was planning something to mark going home. Something big to remember him by. Go out with a bang! He hasn't mentioned a party to you, then?"

"No." I tried not to sound curt. "He hasn't mentioned anything at all."

TWENTY-SIX

HALFWAY THROUGH THE REFLEXOLOGY treatment, Gloria let herself in through the back door and started rummaging around in my kitchen. At least I hoped it was her, as I was not planning to investigate my intruder until I'd finished. I finally waved bye-bye to the client and found Gloria stashing dishes in the freezer. She straightened her back, pushing her knuckles into her lower spine.

"Have you finished for the day?"

I nodded. "What's the thing in my oven with the heavenly smell?"

"Sweet potato casserole, and I think it's ready." She wrapped her arms around me (quite a feat when you've got short arms and a generous middle), easing me onto one of my bar stools where cutlery was already laid. "Sit down and behave."

She tossed a bag of mixed salad into a bowl and added some dressing. I loved to watch her work around the kitchen. Whenever she dealt with food, there was a gracefulness to her body you wouldn't have guessed she could possess. While I was still kid enough to listen to her, she'd taught me everything I know about cooking. Luckily that included a lot of egg recipes.

She brought the dish out of the oven and sliced it through, serving generous, Gloria-sized portions onto both plates. She added salad to hers and passed the bowl to me. I tucked in, trying not to catch her eye. There was something she wanted to say, and she would get round to it when she was ready.

Finally she put down her fork. "D'you know the date?"

"Yeah," I said, in surprise. "Er ..."

"It's six days before Christmas." I gawped at her. "You had no idea, had you? Thought not. Don't know what's going on in that mind of yours, but it isn't the festive season, that's for sure. You haven't even told us if you're coming up for your Christmas dinner."

"Of course I am," I said, my voice failing. "I've just been mega busy, Mum, trying to pay my mortgage, you know?"

"There's something goin' on that accounts for way more distraction than 'busy'," she accused. "Something I'm not gonna like."

She bent down from her stool and slapped a pile of Papa flyers on the working top, which she'd secreted at her feet. "I was packing a few things away for you—"

"Which you shouldn't have been doing in the first place!"

"—and I came upon these." She turned them over, one by one, to reveal the notes I'd made on Kizzy. Then she raised her hand and pointed to the kitchen door, where my wallpaper diagram was tacked up. "Only the good Lord could guess what that is. But you're gonna tell me."

How could I tell Gloria the story of two sisters who had arrived in Britain with high hopes? Kizzy wishing for great riches, Mirela wanting horses for Itso. I didn't want her to know how involved I'd become because everything had ended in death and sorrow. Gloria believed being a shaman got me into trouble, and if I was honest with myself, she was bang on the money here.

"Come on." Gloria glared at me. "Tell."

"Bouquet garni," I said, and smiled at the look covering her face.

I'd constructed a question for Jimmy, which I wouldn't be able to ask him unless... *until he was released. Are you ever asked to put sachets of herbs in certain dishes? Like a special bouquet garni?*

There had been something wrong with the veggie moussaka I'd eaten the day I'd collapsed. Just because Jimmy had cooked the food—just because he'd offered it to me—didn't mean he'd doctored it, or that the substance that made my head spin had been meant for me in the first place.

Had I swallowed a sachet of something illicit, hidden between layers of aubergine and tomato?

No wonder Stan had been so quick to call a doctor. No wonder he'd been so concerned.

"The place I work, now," I said, trying to keep my story simple and non-threatening, "I think there might be things going on there."

"If there is," said Gloria, "your nose will smell it out, girl."

"At first, it was just the way they treat their staff. Badly, to sum it up. But then I heard something from another employee about hiding drugs in the deliveries. Rey said they'd done a stop and search on the Papa Bulgaria scooters, but, Gloria, how could you do scrupulous forensics on bikes that all belong to different, seemingly innocent people? Not that anyone at Papa has ever asked me to carry something that wasn't food, but I've been thinking: Would we know? Once those cardboard lids are firmly on, no one checks the contents. That'd be poor hygiene. Let the heat out. And guess what? Each container's finished off with a label stating what's inside. Ever known that before? I mean, it's a nightmare, isn't it, trying to work out which order is which from the penciled scribbles you usually get. It's a nice Papa touch—customers with big orders appreciate it. But what if there's a special sort of label—one with a hidden message?"

I stopped for breath. I'd run on and on, my thoughts teeming into my head and tripping out over my tongue. Gloria took a few moments to process the entire outpouring. Then, being Gloria, she asked the one vital question.

"Who is Rey?"

"Right. Yeah. He's a guy." I couldn't speak then for an age. My mouth was stretched into such a cat-and-cream grin, it was impossible.

"Hang on. He's the detective?"

I nodded, trying to control my face.

"Okay. Well, he might do you good. Rein you in. Stop your brain runnin' off in all directions that's not good for it." She waved a forkful of sweet potato. "Every which way. Trying to convince yourself of this and that. Crazy theories that don't stand up 'cause they got no bottom."

I knew there were flaws in my theory about Papa Bulgaria. I'd been imagining foil containers fully pre-packed with sachets, secreted into the general mayhem of the busy kitchen, marked by their special labels. But in that case, how could I have swallowed a single one in a dish of moussaka? Jimmy was known for his errors. Maybe Stan had spotted what he'd done and told him to ditch the container. Instead, Jimmy had passed it to me.

What pleased me about my theory was it let Jimmy off the hook. I was able to pass the blame for my collapse at work straight onto the Papazov dynasty. I knew it didn't absolve Jimmy of the murder of Kizzy Brouviche, but I could convince myself that if he wasn't a poisoner, he couldn't be a murderer either.

"I'd never thought you'd turn out to be a healer," Gloria went on, unaware of how far my thoughts had wandered. "You didn't show a sign when you were a kid. One minute you were leading Dennon down paths of iniquity—"

"You are joking! He was dragging me!"

"There was drinking and smoking and thievin' too, don't tell me there wasn't. And there'd always been fighting. If you didn't have blood on your lip, you'd have it on your knuckles. And lying, even," she added, as this was truly the worst thing. "Then the next minute you're all greenery and therapies and calling up old gods, who if you ask me—which you don't—would be best left alone." She sniffed. "Was hard for me to understand."

"But even when I was a kid, you'd say I went away with the fairies."

Gloria gave a reluctant nod. "There was that time, one walk we did, when you came screaming out of some trees, yelling about gnomes. You dragged us off to show us this odd-shaped stone you were so sure had winked at you."

The memory was enshrined. A malevolent spirit, I'm sure to this day, inhabited that stone, or had turned itself into a stone shape because humans were near. I had seen the stone move—expand and reshape—and into my head words arrived, unbidden ... *dance around me, dance until you fall ...*

I felt like that was happening now. Something was beckoning to me, something that had not yet taken its final form. I did not think its final form would be a pleasant experience.

———

We'd finished our meal and were well into the gossip that comes afterwards when the doorbell chimed. Gloria roused herself first.

"Send them away, whoever they are," I called after her, only quarter joking. It was lovely having Gloria all to myself, and she'd probably have to leave in an hour or so.

I heard a muttered exchange of conversation that grew louder. She'd let them in, whoever they were, and I just knew it would spoil things.

I was right. A stupid trill of fear passed through me as my aunt and her daughter were shown into the room. I couldn't help do the housewife thing of looking round my kitchen with outsider-eyes; it was sprayed with dust and dirty crocks. I contemplated crawling under the coffee table.

Both of them were wrapped against the cold. Mrs. Mitchell's Russian hat was pulled firmly over the corona of her cobwebbed hair and Laetitia was zipped into a padded fleece with a tirolean fur-lined snow hood and cute matching hand muff.

"We can't stay long," Mrs. Mitchell began.

"I'm on my way to a Christmas Concert," said Lettice, trying to soothe her mother's words.

"Lovely!" I smiled at her. "Have a great time."

"Lettice is a flautist," said Mrs. Mitchell. "She plays in the school orchestra."

"These are the people I told you about," I said to Gloria, mostly because my aunt had totally ignored her since arriving in my kitchen. "Mrs. Mitchell and her daughter, Laetitia."

Gloria flashed me a perplexed look and I realized she had no idea who they actually were. To be fair, the only time I'd mentioned them was on the walk at Brean Down when Lettice had sent me the text, but Gloria put out her hand towards my aunt. "I'm Gloria Davidson."

"Well," said Mrs. Mitchell. She observed the hand and used a finger and thumb to shake it briefly. "I can see you're both involved in something already. We won't keep you." She armed herself for the retreat by clamping her Gucci bag to her chest.

"Ma!" Lettice glowered at her mother. "You were going to say something, weren't you?"

"Ah. Yes. Indeed." The fur hat made her look like a figure from a Russian film. I expected a steam train to pull in behind her at any moment. "We are having a very small post-Christmas gathering at the Hatchings towards the end of the month..."

"The twenty-eighth," said Lettice. "From sevenish."

"Cocktails and canapés," said Mrs. Mitchell, as if she hoped that I'd be put off by posh drinks and finger food. "Lettice wondered—"

"*We* were hoping," Laetitia interjected, "you might come and meet Grandma."

"For just an hour, perhaps?"

"And your grandma," I said, speaking to Lettice. "Does she know? Is she happy about this?" I had a horrid thought that she might keel over with unexpected heart failure if I was introduced to her. After all, Mrs. Mitchell's reaction had been pretty heart-stopping.

"I'm glad you understand that," said my aunt. "We felt it was pointless to put this to her until we knew you were coming along."

I couldn't make out what this was about. Why wait until all her friends were milling around in cocktail dresses and cummerbunds before introducing me to my possible grandmother? Surely it would be better, if I was going to meet Lady Savile-Dare at all, that I did so quietly, not in the glare of some Christmas party spotlight. Anger flared in me as things fell into place. Peers Mitchell wanted to find out how I would behave in good company. It was a test.

"I dunno," I said. "I hadn't thought about pursuing this." I glanced at Gloria. She was trying to pick up on the full implication, sending me laser-beam messages from below lowered eyebrows. I quickly decided it would be better if she didn't know what was going on until the Mitchells left, and my spine was pricking with an urgent need to get this upper-class twit out of my house. "I think I'd like to discuss it with my mum first, and let you know."

"Your *mother*?" said Peers. Her voice had dropped and she sounded a lot like old tapes of Maggie Thatcher.

"Gloria," I said, flapping my hand in her direction. "She's been my mum now for—"

"This woman is your mother?"

"No," I said, catching on. Then I stopped, shut my mouth and nodded. "Yes. This is my mother."

"Of course." Mrs. Mitchell smiled quite pleasantly. Well, she *had* received very pleasant news. "I can see the resemblance. Quite a similarity of … skin tone."

"Ma!" shrieked Lettice. "Let Sabbie explain properly."

"I don't think I want further explanation." The handbag shifted again. Its gloss and pattern caught the ceiling lights. I wouldn't know crocodile skin if it regrew teeth and bit me, but I wouldn't've swooned with surprise if this had turned out to be the genuine article. "I've suffered sufficient discomfiture from my dealings with your new friend, and I don't plan to continue this connection."

She swung from the room. She didn't actually say, *Come, Lettice,* as she left, but the words hung in the air.

Lettice didn't move for a long time. She seemed to be practicing breath control for her flute performance. Her eyes were large, unblinking. She said nothing, and I knew that was because she was afraid of crying.

"You'd best go, Lettice."

"I hate Ma."

"No, you don't. When you reflect, you'll agree with her. I don't want to meet Lady Savile-Dare. I have enough things at the moment to shake up my life. If I can avoid another, I will."

"But..."

"I understand. We're cousins. That counts for a lot. But we've been quite happy not knowing up to now, haven't we?"

It was a blunt thing to say, and for a second or two Lettice looked as if I'd slapped her. But I didn't soften my words. I wanted her to feel a bit slapped around, if it meant she'd scuttle quietly after her miserable mother and never contact me again. I could not take any more messing with my personal life, and I was pretty sure that allowing me into hers would have the same messing-up effect. I didn't want that for her. She was way too nice.

Lettice ran from the room with tiny steps. I didn't move. But after the front door's slam, I felt Gloria's arm round my shoulders. There is a warmth in that arm that can reach right into a girl's heart.

TWENTY-SEVEN
WINTER SOLSTICE

I LEFT EARLY FOR work the following morning, pulling the scooter out into rush-hour traffic. The morning was bitingly cold with a wild wind that had picked up during the night. The scooter didn't like crosswinds. I almost came off a couple of times. And that wind was icy; it got inside my bike gear and under my helmet. Every part of me trembled with cold.

I'd been mad to agree to these long shifts. Tomorrow morning I'd be up before dawn because Tuesday was the winter solstice, and six of us were meeting to celebrate Yule. I glanced up as I waited for traffic lights. The sky had disappeared below a grey layer of nimbostratus. I was already worrying that the ritual we'd planned was going to be a letdown.

I knew I'd find Fergus in the Polska Café. I knew he'd be at his usual table, drinking his usual latte. Kate was also eating breakfast at a table close to the door, and I lifted my hand in a friendly acknowledgment as I bought a mug of tea from Maria.

I carried my tea over to Fergus and stood awkwardly with it. For a moment, he didn't notice me. His head was bent over his notebook. He was using a fine fountain pen to write, slowly inscribing the words in his head onto the page. I gave a cough. He looked up. My intestines knotted as I realized he didn't look all that pleased to see me.

"How've you been?"

"Ah, I've been just tops, thanks, Sabbie. Er…busy. And yourself?"

I sat down, uninvited. "I wondered if you'd like to know about the developments at Papa," I said, keeping my voice in "professional meeting" tone. I launched into the story of the nonexistent pay cheque, the offer of a loan, and my recent opportunity to earn triple cash in hand.

He screwed the cap on his pen and rested it on the cover of his notebook. "Interesting."

I took a sip of tea. I needed a dramatic pause before I revealed my stunner. "You have heard about Jimmy Browne?"

"He's the man under arrest?"

"He's more of a boy, really." I lowered my voice. "Remember those buccal swabs? He came up positive."

"Glory b'Jesus. Never."

"He works for Papa Bulgaria."

"Glory b …" he trailed off. "He's Bulgarian?"

"No, he's as local as they come. And as innocent as they look."

"He surely can't be. He's a DNA trail leading to him."

"Anyway, they won't take any more samples, Fergus. And they destroy evidence once it's not needed."

"Unless you're a Catholic from Belfast."

"I don't believe that."

"Because you have no idea of my world. It's as alien to you as ... Bulgaria." Fergus picked up his coffee. There was almost nothing left, but he took several tiny sips, staring over the rim as he did so. "It's *him*, isn't it? The cop. He's the fellow who's taken your heart." He put down the cup onto its saucer with a chime that seemed on the verge of a crack. High spots of heat were brewing on his cheek bones. "It's that DI Buckley who took my spit."

My insides did one of those inversions that make you feel you've been yanked inside out.

"Fair chances." Fergus shook his head and his barley-coloured hair flew away from the elastic band that gripped it. "We must take our chances when we have them. You came to the party with me, but I didn't take my chance. We can't always have the thing we want the most."

I thought about the difference between us, when he said that. The thing I wanted most—I didn't have to think about it—was to see Mirela to walk into the café and wave across at us as if she'd never disappeared. I wanted that far more than I even wanted Rey.

"I thought we had something, for a minute there. I liked you, Sabbie." I heard the past tense; he hadn't noticed he'd given himself away. "Have I missed my chance with you now, is that it?"

"I don't know. I don't know how chances work." I called to mind how he had never told me that he was at the end of a contract here and would be going back to Belfast soon. He was an operator. A wolf. The nerve of the man sparked me into candour. "You're going home, aren't you?"

He tugged at his earlobe. "I should have let you know."

"Yeah, you should have let me know a long time ago." I took a breath. I had no idea why I'd got so strung up over this, but gut feelings were usually what I went by. "Or at least invited me to your party."

"What party?"

"The farewell party your workmates think you're going to hold?"

Fergus looked genuinely confused. "I certainly hadn't planned anything like that."

"I—I bumped into Juke. He says you wanted to go out with a bang."

Light came into his eyes. "That's right, Sabbie. I do. I do hope to do that. Isn't it what every fellow dreams of, going out with a bang?" His mouth twitched. "I would love it now, if you'd share that with me."

"What?

He steadied his gaze. "I'm surprised that you haven't an inkling."

"No," I snapped. "I can't guess. What?"

"I'd be honoured to show you. I could show you on Friday evening."

"I dunno, Fergus. I might have something on."

"I apologise for asking," he said, his voice too sharp to be an apology.

"I've promised a mate. I can't let him down if he needs me. He's lost his girlfriend; his lover. He's lost her, you see."

"What, dead?"

"No, love-bombed."

I started to unravel the story of Drea. I needed to properly explain that I had a good reason to decline his invite. Anyway, Fergus came from a religious background, so he might have a good take on the problem. I was also longing to move onto a fresh, unrelated subject that would help us forget the shadow that had passed over the table.

I told Drea and Andy's story without mentioning names, describing the way I'd been peremptorily tossed down the steps of Charter Hall and into the street. I hoped that would make Fergus smile, but he was shaking his head.

"No two ways about it. The power faith offers can turn you into a controlling beast."

"Obsessive," I agreed. "And you have to let go of reason a bit, don't you? The entire point is to believe something unbelievable, and know it's true."

I thought about my rattle, broom, and wand; the moon water Marianne and I made each month. Looked at rationally, these things seemed quite mad, but when I worked with them, they felt necessary, important.

"And then there's the opposite effect," said Fergus.

"What opposite?"

"Strong faith attracts people who are on the edge."

"That's so true!" I chuckled at my thoughts. "Glastonbury is full of zany people. It's hard to sort the eccentrics from the certifiable. But something different's going on in CORE. Eric Atkinson enjoys the power, the hold he has over people. Especially vulnerable women. He tells his followers that everything he does has goodness at its heart, but he's holier-than-thou, obsessed with sex, and absolutely sure he's right about everything."

"Using madness. Desiring authority. Evil intent," said Fergus. His eyes flicked around, like he was about to lie. "Sin."

"Yes, they're obsessed by it. This poor girl who's gone back to CORE thinks she's committed numerous sins, but she's harmed no one."

"I bet this priest truly believes he's doing the Lord's work." Fergus's eyes had an uncanny brightness. "Many people live for years with a little voice at the back of their mind telling them to make sure they're not enjoying their life."

"That's very profound." Something, some block held me rigid, prevented me from looking directly at him. I shifted in my chair and dropped my gaze, noticing how his hand moved to his notebook, caressing the cover. He picked up the pen and turned it round in his fingers. I looked at the picture on the cover again. The Celtic knot, a ceaseless cord that twisted its patterns round and round into infinity.

Except, this knot did have an end, of sorts. An end and a beginning. A lot of Celtic knotwork takes an animal shape, often animals twined perpetually. Now that I looked closer at the cover, I could make out the beast. It was a common one used in such knotwork. It was an ouroboros. A twisted snake with its tail in its mouth.

Do not go with him, if he comes for you, the man with the snake.

I glanced up. He'd seen me staring. I tried to smile, a bogus stretching of lips. I felt like an animal trapped at the kill.

Rescue came in a surprising form.

Kate had got up from her table and was headed towards the loos, swinging her handbag. She paused as she past us.

"Hi."

"Hi, Kate," said Fergus. "You good?"

"Yeah, okay." She turned towards me. "Can I have a word?" And then she walked on, disappearing into the Ladies. "I'll see what she wants."

"I'd best be off to work. But Sabbie?"

"Ugh?"

"I'll give you a call about Friday, okay?"

I watched him go. The feeling flowing through me was like an ebb tide. It forced my thoughts in all the wrong directions.

I pushed through the loo door. "Kate?" She was by the basins, brushing her long hair. Her face was full of misgivings. She looked tired ... sad. "How have things been?"

"Okay. I am okay." She put her brush away. "I would like to talk to you proper. Somewhere where we can be private, do you know?"

A pulse, which had set up in my temple while I'd been with Fergus, still throbbed under my skin. "Is this about Fergus Quigg?"

"No," said Kate. As she spoke, she moved along the basins, away from the door, until she was squeezed in between the wall and the tampon machine. Her voice was dropping, as if microphones were concealed in the light strip above our heads. "But it is very important."

"Can't you tell me now?"

"Here? No, not here. Please, it will be better at my house."

"I'm working all today. Till Thursday, in fact."

"You cannot do it sooner?" Her voice had sunk away to nothing. In the silence came the sound of the wind, moaning and rattling the open window.

"Are you sure this has nothing to do with Fergus?"

"Of course not. But it is also something I cannot take to him. You look ... like the person I should tell."

That made me smile. "You could always order a Papa Bulgaria meal. I'd be the one to bring it to your house."

"I can do that." She'd taken me seriously. "Will you come? Please? Sabbie?" Her voice suddenly peaked, echoing in the bare room. I looked around. We were still alone, but anyone could come in at any time. She was right; this was not the place for a confidential chat.

"Of course I'll come," I said.

———

Popping round Bridgwater and environs on a Papa scooter gave me time to contemplate things, and those things made me feel horribly exposed, as I travelled on my torpid bike.

In my belly was a feeling of sickness, the feeling you get after a nightmare you can barely remember. If I hadn't been in the middle of a constant stream of deliveries, I would have gone home and showered, then had fifteen minutes of meditation to clear myself of my sinister suspicions. Fergus was many things, more things than I'd first suspected, but I was already praying I was wrong about this.

Using madness. Desiring authority. Evil intent ... sin.

Kizzy hadn't trusted him, but she might have had things she wanted to hide. What had Fergus said about Kizzy? *Raw with sexuality ... difficult to resist ...*

I took the scooter around a left bend, leaning into the wind. I reasoned and re-reasoned as I delivered Papa takeaway to the good folk of Bridgwater. All my faith had been in Fergus. How could I swerve so way off course in my presumptions? I trusted my skill at seeing inside people; what I'd seen was that Fergus was a principled man, full of good intentions. He could be a little bombastic. He sentimentalized his opinions at times. Okay, Mirela, suspicious of all authority, had never taken to him ... *he'd lick your hand then bite your hand.*

I didn't always understand the things Fergus said, and he was choosey about what he told you.

Some people like to keep secrets. There was the way he gently closed his notebook when people came up to him. It looked like a polite gesture ... *sorry, you have my full attention now ...* but it was also a secretive one. He wrote songs, he said. But I'd never asked the right question.

What are your songs about?

People live for years with a little voice at the back of their mind …

Why had it never occurred to me before? Fergus was in the perfect position to gain the trust of girls with no name, no identity. He must have arrived in Bridgwater before the girl in the Dunball Wharf had died, and now I was wondering if he knew where Mirela was right this minute. And what had happened to Kizzy.

The nausea erupted, swept over me until I was sure I would vomit, right there on the road.

Change and status quo. Rey's definition of murder motives.

Isn't it what every fellow dreams of, going out with a bang?

Sweat pricked me like pinheads and dried in the wind that blew into my face. I was terrifying myself over nothing. I should not be thinking of pinning evil upon anyone I knew. I took in a deep, long breath—the first since my mind had dropped into a chasm. I forced myself to be reasonable. I was imagining these things. I had to be. I had kissed this man. Listened to him try to change the world for the better. They had taken his DNA and arrested someone else.

He had never told me what he'd done before, back in Belfast. Why should he? But now I couldn't get the question out of my head.

What secrets had Fergus left in Ireland?

———

Kate lived in a brick-and-concrete maisonette on the edge of town. I parked away from the double yellow lines, seeing as I didn't know how long I'd be, and found her door on the long corridor of other doors. Hers was blue with a flat white button for the bell, which buzzed in my ear as I pressed.

She came immediately, swinging the door wide. I lifted her paper carrier of food. "Takeaway for Miss Siminski?" I'd only learnt her last name when I'd picked up her order from Max.

"Please come in." She sounded formal, as if she was a little scared. "Are you having a good shift?"

"Yeah, fine, thanks." What else could I say? That I had massive, brooding suspicions about a man who worked upstairs from the Polska Café? That I was war-weary from being up since dawn and that controlling the scooter in a gale was making every muscle in my body cramped and stiff as cardboard? "What about you?"

"Yes, thank you. It was nice to see you again at the café. It is good food there, yes?"

"Lovely."

"I have breakfast there most days. It means I get to chat with Maria, and see other people from home too."

"Nice," I agreed. She'd led me into the kitchen. I put her carrier of food on the table. Arms free, I stood, wondering what she was planning to tell me.

"It is good, in Bridgwater. The Poles here stick together."

"You've needed that, am I right?" I was thinking that if Mirela and Kizzy had received the sort of homeland support that Kate had been offered, they'd've had a better experience of Britain. Maybe even, Kizzy would still be alive.

"Four years, I am here now. My husband came over first, to work in the building trade."

"Oh, right." Rey had told me something of Kate's story, how she'd ended up with Abbott. "You didn't come over together?"

"No. I was having my baby when he left Poland. My son, who is now in his first class at school. Dawid was supposed to get back in time for the birth. But he didn't come. He'd disappeared."

355

"What?" I must have looked stunned, because she touched my hand in its glove.

"Once the baby was big enough, I came here to look for him. Agency for Change helped me trace him, but all Dawid wanted from me was a divorce. He'd found someone new."

"Kate, that's dire!"

"Me? I could have killed him. Right there in the Polska Café. But I just got up and walked out." She looked at me, holding my gaze. "At that moment, I had nothing. In England, money goes faster than in Poland."

"I bet that's true."

"I needed food for my child. I needed the fare home. And for the divorce, that costs too much money."

I nodded. I didn't think there could be much that is more scary that being broke and alone in a foreign country. "But, in the end, you stayed on? Found Gary!"

"Yes, in the end. But that is not what happened first."

Kate shook her head, and her hair swung. She lifted a pale hand and brushed it from her face. The action rang a bell; a thing Rey had told me. The way Gary had gone a little crazy over that first dead woman's body.

"Did Gary … did he ever talk to you about the murder, the woman they found in the summer, that turned up in—"

"Yes. Please—I know this. It is this that I want to tell you about."

I looked at the chestnut shine of her hair. "She reminded Gary of you, didn't she?"

"He had pestered the doctor. The woman who had done the autopsy. What is she called? Path …"

"Pathologist," I said, wondering where this was taking us.

"The woman's stomach, it was all opened, when they found her. You know?"

"Sort of. Well, no, I don't."

"Gary said … that it wasn't fishes. He told the woman, but she didn't listen, I don't think. Now, he is dead, and another woman is dead!"

"They're talking about connections, aren't they? Between Kizzy Brouviche and the other woman. Slashings. A ripper."

"Slashings, yes." Her face was as white as paper. Even her lips were white. Like Kizzy's face, through the window of the morgue. "I have been reading. Everything in the papers. I have been trying to do it for Gary. In his place."

Waves of assumptions suddenly formed into a single solution.

"Gary knew who killed that woman, didn't he? He knew who was going to kill Kizzy, even before she died."

"Perhaps. I don't know. Not who this person is or even if Gary knew. Not a name, or a thing like that. But one thing is sure. The person who killed the girls—they killed my man. They shot him."

Neither of us spoke. I shivered, the cold of the open window getting to me. "How?" I asked, at last.

"Because … I survived."

"You? You encountered this man? The murderer?"

"Yes. I encountered."

"Did you see him? Is it a him?"

"It is a man. I know this. But I didn't see him. His eyes only. I didn't see his face. I didn't see anything much."

Kate turned from where we were standing beside her table full of cooling Bulgarian food. She closed the kitchen window. She worked at the plastic string and the roller blind cascaded down. It was rose pink, with a scalloped edge, trimmed with lace. She pulled it right to the sill. She moved to the kitchen door and shut that tight too.

I felt a tremor on my lips. I sucked them in to stop it showing. She shook her head, as if it was too difficult to tell. She wanted me to draw her story out of her. "How did you get away, Kate?"

"I woke up, I was paid. They paid me less than they had promised, but I was too weak and in pain to complain. I was put into the blindfold again, as before. I was driven to town. Then I walked. I walked home."

"What?" There was a ringing in my ears. It was in my heart too.

"They say you will be paid. Good money. Make you rich. But in this country, money goes like pee from the bladder."

"Rich." I settled on a phrase. "Great riches."

"No," said Kate. "Just a package of used ten-pound notes."

Not really riches offered …

"They leave you, they push you out the car with the blindfold still on in the middle of town, and you never see them again."

"Kate?" I said, unsure. Because Kate had begun fiddling with the buttons of her cardigan. She peeled it off and folded it over the back of the chair that was tucked under the table. She crossed her arms to grasp the hem of the long-sleeved top she wore underneath and pulled, so that it rose over her head. I saw goosebumps in the spot-lighting. Now, all she had on above her waist was a flimsy, slightly greyish sports bra.

"Kate?"

She raised her arms away from her body. Then she turned. A full three-hundred and sixty degrees, slowly round, as if she was modelling something.

From her bra strap, round the side of her ribs and down towards her navel, was a scar. It wasn't new, but it looked as if it hadn't finished with her yet, as if it would always be there to remind her of a terrible day in her life, when she sold herself for great riches. Riches to feed her son and return to her country free of a man who had betrayed her.

When she'd finished turning, Kate pulled on her clothes in silence. She left the blind down so that the dark Bridgwater night couldn't get in, couldn't disturb her fragile peace. She stood completely still, watching for my reaction, waiting for my questions.

I was unable to piece together enough words to make a sentence. I could only look into her face as she stood motionless beside me. I couldn't read her expression. There was nothing in it, as if the dreadful incision around her body had sucked emotion out of her at the same time it had taken her kidney in return for a package of crumpled ten-pound notes.

TWENTY-EIGHT

THE BURGER VAN WAS closed, the shutters as tightly pulled as Kate's roller blind. Rey was leaning against it.

"Hi," I said. "Thanks for answering my SOS text." There were smudges below his eyes that looked like he'd been experimenting with his mama's makeup bag. "You haven't slept in days, have you?"

"That is about accurate. Your trusty detective never sleeps. He never pauses in his investigation, which is why I hope you've pulled me out here for a good reason."

"So do I." I was all over the place, bone-weary, and beginning to feel useless. It must have shown, because Rey leaned in and pecked a kiss. On the cheek, but I guess we were close to the station and he was on duty. He put his arm on my back and led me to the low wall. This was the place it had begun, the Saturday morning after the carnival.

"I've had a bitch of day," I said.

"Join the club."

"But, I've learned something. And—well—the police are always asking us to share our suspicions, aren't they?

"No, we are not." He ground his first cigarette underfoot and lit a second. "We ask the public to report anything they feel may have a bearing on a case, however slight. Anything suspicious. Not *their suspicions*."

"Okay. Well I'd better go with that, hadn't I?" I gripped myself tight, balling my fists and pushing my elbows into my ribs to prevent him from seeing that I was trembling on the wall beside him. "I know what happens to the girls."

"What girls?" said Rey, blowing smoke into the wind.

"Kizzy…the other woman. They died under anaesthetic, didn't they? They died having organs removed."

"Humph," said Rey. He shifted slightly on the wall.

"The reason Abbott got so uptight about that first body, was because her hair reminded him of Kate."

Rey's jaw padlocked down. I watched him process what I knew, and correlate it against what he knew. He wasn't dismissing my words, so I battled on.

"Because the dead woman wore her dark hair long, but also because she was from somewhere else, and no one missed her. No one knew she'd gone, except the people who ply their trade selling organs. Black market, I guess. Who wouldn't pay for a kidney, to keep their life, if they had the money? Kate needed money. She was approached by someone on the phone. She was picked up in a car. A blindfold was placed around her eyes and she was driven some miles. Can you imagine how terrifying that would be?"

Rey didn't respond. But he was looking at me, his attention so tightly held that he hadn't noticed the ash had burnt long on his cigarette.

"When the blindfold came off, she was in an operating theatre. The lights were on overhead. The surgeon was all in green; mask, gloves, everything. He put an injection in the back of her hand and the next thing she knew, she was being tumbled out of the same car. She'd sold her kidney for a few thousand pounds. She had to walk home with a dressing dripping blood down her thigh."

"Fuck," said Rey. "Why didn't Abbott tell us?"

"It happened some years before she met him. But he knew. He'd seen the scar and heard the story. When that woman was found at Dunball, he started following his hunch. Because it couldn't be more than a hunch, could it? The woman was clean. There were no forensics. You said that yourself."

"He did like to hold his cards. Scout round first before presenting his hypothesis. That was just Gary. The way he worked. I respected that, didn't push him." He was staring away from me, his shoulders hunched. "What if I'd pushed him? Would he be alive?"

"Didn't you know any of this?"

"I didn't know about Kate."

"Oh, Rey, if you have to bring her in, treat her gently!"

"Christ, Sabbie, where d'you think we are? Chile?"

"But that's the link, isn't it? Between Kizzy and the other girl. It's what happened to Kizzy, isn't it? She donated her kidney. But it didn't work like Kate. She didn't wake up, get off the table, go home."

"No."

"Kizzy told Mirela she knew where there was a lot of money to be made. But she'd scared Mirela enough to make her say no. Mirela told me that the very first time I met her, but I didn't understand. I'm not even sure Mirela truly understood. So Kizzy went off on her own. Middle of the night to exchange a kidney for a sum of money."

I took a deep breath. "That's my theory. I've been working on it as I finished my shift."

"I see," said Rey.

"Horrid."

"Yes."

"And the first girl? Is that the link?"

"Maybe."

"Oh, come on, Rey! I'm not going to go blabbing this around!"

"I'd love to share with you Sabbie. Love to. Don't know if I *would*, but I'd love to have the opportunity. Truth is, we don't know. It's all surmise—the weakest of the Criminal Investigation Department's tools. Supposition. You've laid out events nice and simple, but something more is going on. Kizzy Brouviche disappeared on November sixth and reappeared weeks later. In the meantime, she writes a letter to Mirela. Not quite so simple, is it?"

"So you need to know who 'he' is. The bloke she stayed with. What she was doing between her disappearance and her death. Where she was hiding all that time."

"Huh," said Rey. "Yeah."

"In my journey for Mirela, I was met by a wolf. He told me to look for Kizzy in four places. I've isolated three of them. The fourth was the place of no escape. I'm sure that is where Kizzy was held, by the man with the snake, the man she warned her sister of."

Rey smiled and wrapped his arm around me as we sat on the wall. "That's my Sabbie," he said. "I talk about pathology, interviews, forensics, footwork, Internet searches. You talk about wolves and snakes."

"I've seen Kate's scar. That was solid enough. And I can guess that both Kizzy and the first girl started off with massive wounds like that. Slasher wounds, the press are saying. Are you letting them say that to keep them off the true mark? That the girls were missing a kidney?"

"The first one, we think, yes. But Kizzy..."

"Kizzy what?"

I'd noticed that Rey needed to build up a head of anger before he told me things. As if they had to burst out of him. "What? Whatever! Whatever they pleased to take from her!" He tried to quiet his voice; the back lane was empty and dark, but the police station no distance away. "With that first girl, there were traces of abdominal organs intact. The fact that some might originally have been missing couldn't be detected, not back then. But that wasn't so with Kizzy Brouviche."

A frisson caused me to shudder, as if the cold of King's Sedgemoor Drain had washed over me. "Rey?"

"All her organs. Her heart. Her lungs. Her liver. Her eyes. Both kidneys. Almost all her organs. Gone. Swiped away. Packed in ice, yeah, you're right. Packed in ice and shipped out of here." He ground his second cigarette under his boot, gripped his hands together and shoved them between his knees, as if already struggling against lighting the next.

"Oh, goddess," I whispered.

"So, yeah, Sabbie. You've hit the bull's eye with this one. No point in taking out organs that don't have a recipient waiting; can't sell them later. And if you're planning to sell a human heart..."

"It's clear your donor patient isn't going to survive."

"That you don't have any intention of letting them do so."

I heard a moan, a cry of distress. It was me, the moan coming out of me as I remembered Kizzy, calling out to me. *Not good boys-friend lead to danger. Lead to death!*

Kizzy's prediction hadn't been about my future at all, but a certain one for herself, starting with a fist filled with money but ending with death.

"We have a hypothesis. You might as well know; no doubt some wolf will tell you if I don't. She was involved in the murder of Abbott. Because of that, she willingly hid away. She probably didn't realize that as a witness, she needed to die. Possibly as a legit client, they'd already taken one kidney, to weaken her. There was blood on the letter to Mirela. Wherever she was, she was kept there while they cross-matched her up to sick people across the world and sold a whole shipload of organs."

"How many people could do this sort of thing and stay below the radar? After all, you need the right place. Taunton Hospital?" I recalled what he'd said about interviewing the surgeons. "If you knew this, why haven't you made an arrest?" Jimmy's knife flashed into my mind, slicing swift and clean through meat. The generous smile on his face as he handed me the leftover takeaway. "Is Jimmy involved? I mean, he can't be doing the operations, can he?"

"No," said Rey. "He's not capable of that."

"So, would it be, like, a medical student or something?"

"We're assuming the main perpetrator of this ring is experienced. Barbaric, cold-blooded, implacable, and probably not practicing as a surgeon any more."

I took a long swig of the water bottle I'd brought from my scooter. My mouth was dry as ash. "So if there was someone...whose background we don't know...who works with people that are hardly more than refugees...would they be a suspect?"

He gave me a hard stare. "Best leave the investigating to us, Sabbie."

"I think Kate showed me her scar knowing I'd come to you." I paused, trying to put my thoughts in order. It was an impossible task. "But I do have my suspicions. They're crazy. They're off-beam. But…"

"Are there wolves or snakes involved?"

I checked his face. He was grinning, which was good to see. I'd decided it was my task to add lightness and laughter to his life. Well, and love, naturally.

"If Kizzy's captor carried with him—everywhere he went—a book with a picture of a snake on the cover—then wouldn't that be how she might describe him? I'm having these massive, gut-wrenching suspicions about someone. But you said you didn't want to hear about *our suspicions*. And now, here, sitting on this bloody cold wall, they don't feel very solid."

"Even solid's doing us no good, Sabbie. We've got enough possible suspects to fill the River Parrett, except drowning's too good for any of them." He put his hand on my knee. "Is there a shred of evidence, Sabbie? A single indication of proof?"

I had to breathe for several seconds before I could answer. "Not really."

"Then I don't want to hear it."

"And I don't want to articulate it. Anyway, I recognise the statistics are off the sheet—the chance of me bumping into a killer is a million to one. And I've already done that before, haven't I?" I could hear my breath in my ears. I was exhaling in relief. I didn't want Fergus to be a killer. "Everyone thinks you've arrested Jimmy because you've got to be seen arresting someone. You're not sure if you can charge Jimmy, are you?"

"Who knows? I sure as hell don't." Rey's eyes swivelled away from me, but his hand was still warm on my thigh. "At the moment, all I want is for Jimmy Browne to cooperate with us. He's making less sense than a chimpanzee on cocaine." There was an edge to Rey's voice. Urgency? No. Panic. "Would you do me a favour, Sabbie?"

"What?"

"Will you speak to Jimmy? I mean, as a shaman?"

"You want me to question him? Without knowing any details about his arrest? Do you think I'll be of help if I only work with half the evidence you've got?"

Rey nodded, once. "Of course I do. Because how you work is *not exactly empirical*. That's what you said, wasn't it?"

"So, when do you want me to talk to him?"

"We can't hold him much longer. This investigation has got more worm holes in it than an episode of *Star Trek*. Jimmy Browne was down one of those holes, but it's not the right one, which is a bloody annoyance. There has to be another hole waiting for us to shine a torch down ..."

I put up my hand. "Okay. Enough of the hole analogies."

"Can I text you when we let Browne go?"

"Please do. I'd like to see Jimmy anyway." I had reasons of my own to see him. I needed to ask him if he had poisoned my food.

TWENTY-NINE

THE FULL MOON HUNG low in the west, glowing like a Christmas bauble, outflanking the real baubles in every shop window. It was bitter cold in my garden as the moon sank on its steady course. Six of us stood on my lawn, holding hands through our gloves, our faces raised to watch the moon set. Magically, this full moon would drop below the horizon just after the winter solstice sun rose above it.

We'd set up a pagan circle under the dying moon, in almost the same way as I set up my therapy room. We cleansed it with a besom broom, smoking incense, and a sprinkling of Glastonbury water. I took my wand of yew and cast a circle that would enclose us and keep us safe. We called in the powers of the four directions—north, east, south, west—and the central powers that come from a place and time so sacred, it existed before any place or any time. The centre of our circle was marked by a lantern (didn't think a candle would last the event), which let out enough light for us to see where we walked while the sun rose.

It was already getting lighter in the garden; dawn was arriving long before we would see the sun rise over the rooftops. But we could see into the west, where the moon's last light was fading as dawn broke. I thought about the way the solstice sun would hang at its southernmost latitude for three or four days, where its path from horizon to horizon was so short it offered nothing more than a glimmer of warmth and a few hours of light, making the night interminable. Once those three solstice days were through, the sun would begin to move northwards. It would grow warmer, week by week. And every day, the sun would rise earlier and set later.

We'd put the patio table to the north of our circle and draped it with the Celtic throw I use in my therapy room. Once we'd called in the directions, each person had brought something to the table, something that was dear to their spiritual lives.

Marianne had brought a shell she had found on a beach in Zeeland, close to where her family lived. On the day she'd found it, she'd made her decision to come to England to live and work. She told us this small story and placed the shell on the table. Stella and Garth had brought one thing between them. It was a small framed photograph, but from my position in the circle, it was hard to understand what the picture was. "Our baby," Stella said. "Twelve-week scan." Garth, in his usual way, gave a solemn nod.

Marianne's friends, Avalon and Teddy, who I'd not met before, went to the table in turn. Avalon brought from her belt a black-handled dagger and raised it above her head. "The Temple of Elphame!"

We all called out in response. We'd decided to call our new gathering the Temple of Elphame, in honour of fairy energy, which I know I've got plenty of among my flowers and vegetables. Avalon had suggested our name, an old term for elf land, and the rest of us had loved it. In fact, so far we'd got on well. Two shamans, two Wiccans, one new-age traveller, and his open-minded partner.

"This is my athame," Avalon began. "I have used it since I became a priestess of Wicca—an extension of my own magical power—a way of directing my energy. I dedicate it to this new gathering."

Teddy came next, holding a chalice made from pewter. It was the sort of thing you can buy in half a dozen shops along Glastonbury High Street, but no worse for that. He placed it onto the table with care. "We used this in every ritual our coven held. But that company was not to be. I bring it to the circle in the hope that this gathering will be strong into the future."

I'd brought the little china otter that stands on the altar in my therapy room. I placed it facing the north and told the story of how Trendle had forced me to open my eyes to the otherworld. "Perhaps, as time goes by, all of us will have our totems added to this altar."

We joined hands, singing chants to keep ourselves warm as full light came into the sky and colour came into the garden. There were some clouds but they were high; the skyline was clear as the sun rose. It was a red dawn, suggesting bad weather today.

"The longest night of the year has passed," said Teddy with quiet intent. "The shortest day will follow. The sun is at its lowest point, but from this moment onward, the year will open out. The land will stir and before we know it, spring will arrive."

From the table I took a basket of my bread. Marianne poured the grape juice she'd brought into the chalice. We passed round the food and drink to celebrate the solstice dawn.

We stood for a while, just enjoying the rays of the sun, before clouds passed in front. Then we took our circle down, hugging each other over and over. The first ritual of the Temple of Elphame was closed, leaving simple, magical memories in our hearts.

———

It was warm in the kitchen. As we pulled off gloves and hats, a low-volume chatter started up. Marianne got into the business of making everyone hot chocolate. I couldn't wait to congratulate Stella and Garth on their new baby. Garth had got into a conversation with Teddy, but Stella was keen to tell me how things were going.

"Garth's got a job now. He's working at that big garden centre outside Taunton. He likes it a lot. I'll carry on in the office until I get my maternity leave, and Mum's still having Aidan after school."

"How is Aidan?"

"He's as bright as a button. He sometimes talks about the time he was away from us. The counsellor suggested we just listen, without showing anger. That's hard, but we manage it. We've got to pick our moment to tell him he's having a new brother or sister. But I think he'll like it." She smiled. "Things are good. They feel back to normal, but better, y'know?"

"As if things have shifted into their proper place?"

"Exactly that."

We cupped our hands round mugs of chocolate.

"Watch the time," Marianne said to me. "I'm very aware you must be at work at eleven o'clock. We need to get out of your hair so that you are not late."

I pulled a face. I was not going to confess to Marianne that I didn't care how late I was. She wouldn't understand. I had a long shift ahead of me out on the road until gone nine tonight, then there was cleaning the kitchen and shop ready for the following day. An image of Stan grudgingly passing over my full pay was all that kept me going. I was going to stand there until he gave me every penny. I was going to demand a payslip that showed all deductions, even if he had to write it out by hand.

I raised my chocolate and smiled around at everyone. I wanted to properly get to know both Teddy and Avalon before they left, and talk a little to Garth, if he'd let me. Frankly, I didn't care how late for work I was; they were desperate enough to forgive. "Happy Yule, everyone," I called, and everyone called back in their individual ways.

"Merry Midwinter!"

"Happy New Year!"

"To the rising of the solstice sun!"

In the tiny pause of silence after our cries, as we sipped our hot chocolate, my phone beeped a text in.

"Do you need to get that?" said Marianne.

"Not right now. I can guess what it's telling me."

———

"You must be Mrs. Browne."

The woman at the door nodded. She was shorter than her son.

Mrs. Browne possibly boasted the same centimetre width round her waist as Jimmy had in height. Her wild hair was streaked blonde and although she wore hardly any makeup, the slash of geranium lipstick managed to make her look a perfect tart.

"Is Jimmy in?"

"Come on through, he's in the back."

I was grateful that Mrs. Browne was the one at the door. She hadn't asked me any awkward questions. She'd assumed Jimmy had told me where he lived. I was hoping Jimmy would think Stan had given me the address, rather than confess it had arrived in Rey's text, shortly after they'd released Jimmy this morning. The address was in capitals, followed by a single lowercase *x*. A peck of a kiss that broke my mind into pieces as I remembered the last time he'd kissed me properly … Sunday morning, as he'd left my house to arrest Jimmy. I was trying to get used to the way Rey conducted his relationships. I had dropped into the same position his wife had been in, when they were together. I was gaining sympathy for the woman.

Jimmy was curled like a girl into a fat armchair right up close to a flaming gas fire. The heat in the room hit me as I moved into it, along with the smell. I was reminded of the odour of the varnish they had used on the doors and windows in my old children's home. It wasn't a bad smell, but it was so chemical that it hit the back of my throat and made me want to gag.

"Hi," I said. "Nice to see you back in the land of the living."

It was my prepared start, to ease me into the visit, but it hardly bordered on the truth. Jimmy looked as if he'd returned from a Stasi torture cell. His face, always pale, had lost every trace of colour. His nose looked pinched and his pale eyes were bloodshot.

"I thought I'd pop in. You know, between deliveries. We can't wait to have you back, Jimmy, they're making us all do double shifts."

He hadn't spoken at all, not even a brief "hi." I let a silence settle, then I asked, "Were they hard on you?"

"What?"

"The police? Didn't they treat you okay?"

"They were all right, yeah."

"It's the cells, isn't it?" I had a sudden and unwelcome flashback. The sound of a crashing door. The dim light you can't control. Tiny place to lay your head. Wee staining the floor. "I spent a night in the cells once. Sobering, huh?"

"You were drunk?"

"No … I …"

"They think I slit open them girls."

"They've released you," I said, softly. "They haven't charged you." There was no point in adding … *yet*.

"Yeah." Jimmy shifted in the chair so that his bare feet lodged on the edge of it. He began to pick at a toenail that was yellow from a fungal infection.

"Everyone at Papa asked me to send their love. Can't do without you. Even Stan!"

"Yeah, right."

"No, honest. Stan is cooking, would you believe!"

He wasn't listening. "I never liked her much. Pushy. Screechy. I was glad when she went, to be honest. I wished she'd gone sooner. But I never wished her dead."

"I believe you, Jimmy. I was sure they'd got it wrong. The police do get things wrong. They've admitted their mistake, haven't they?"

Jimmy began to shake. It started in his shoulders. Surely he couldn't be shivering. The room was so warm I could feel sweat pricking under my arms. Jimmy had a film of it across his forehead.

"What they said, it was a shock." He paused. He was trembling all over now, as if he'd contracted a bad case of flu while he was in the cells.

"Jimmy, are you all right? Shall I get your mum for you?"

374

"She ain't no help." He tried to smile. "I mean, she don't know what to do. She wants me to be brave an' all."

"I think you are being brave. We're all brave in our different ways, aren't we?"

"No, she's right. She don't know it, but she is. I can't tell her. I—I want to tell her, but …" He hunched his trembling body as he picked at his bare toes. The scent of unwashed feet rose up and joined the chemical varnish. I found an old tissue in my pocket and pretended to blow my nose. The tissue smelt faintly of imperial mints. I inhaled, my eyes almost closed in rapture.

I was sure that days and nights of police interrogation might easily bewilder Jimmy. At work, he didn't even dodge the blows. Under the powerdrive eyes of DI Reynard Buckley, he'd cave completely. I tried to formulate a question that would take us to the point I wanted to raise—did Jimmy know what had been in my moussaka? But he was a wreck. Rey had turned a gentle sous chef into a gibbering jelly.

"See, they talk to you like they've already told you what they're on about. Then they shout at you if you don't understand. They get you all relaxed, then they jump. Right over the table. They jump at you and say, *You did it, Jimmy Browne. You killed her, didn't you?* And I'm saying, no … no … Over and over, no … no … But they whisper things and they're true things, and then they whisper things that are lies. That can't be right. Can't be!"

"What? What can't be right?"

"I didn't kill her, Sabbie."

"Jimmy, you look really cold. I'll tell your mum to bring a blanket."

He shook his head. "I wish I hadn't done it."

"But you said you didn't …"

"She made me feel sick. But desperate. Both. She was…" Jimmy doubled forward. He was trying to hold back tears. No—not tears. More the juddering breaths you get when you begin to howl.

I stuffed the mint-scented tissue away. He was not their man. The police knew he was not their man. They were looking for an experienced transplant surgeon, for goddess's sake.

"What about after she went missing? After the carnival? Do you know where she went to?"

"You aren't the police. Why should you care?"

I put my hand out to touch him and my fingers landed on the sole of his bare foot. It felt like something from the fish counter. "I'd never tell the police anything to hurt you. But, Jimmy, there was something in my moussaka, wasn't there."

He looked up. A line of drool led from his bottom lip onto his jeans. He seemed to have no idea what I was saying. "Do you remember? How I fainted in the loo? What had you put in the food, Jimmy?"

"What?"

"Did someone tell you to do it?"

"Do what?"

"Put something in my food?"

He swallowed hard and swallowed again, like there was shingle in his mouth. He was still holding on, being brave for his mum.

"She came on to me so strong." He hadn't understood my question. Perhaps he hadn't heard it.

"Strong?"

"She came on to me, out by the scooters. I know she's dead, but I have to say it. She was a scrubber."

"Scrubber?"

"Yeah? Never heard the word? Not from Somerset then."

My mouth opened ... closed again. Not from Somerset. This wasn't the time to explain I was exactly that. Instead, I stared at him, my heart thudding like a shaman's drum, waiting for him to confess.

"A scrubber's someone who gives her favours easy. Like, not even a prostitute. A scrubber will do it with anyone for nothing."

"Not even a ..." It was a dreadful thought. "What about being pure? Staying pure for the big gypsy wedding?"

"Don't believe it."

He turned his hands into loose fists and thrust the pulp of his thumbs into the corners of his eyes. I couldn't help thinking that their redness might be due to infection; he'd passed his foot infection to his eyes.

"Jimmy," I began. My voice failed me and I stared again. "What did you do to Kizzy?"

"What d'you think? She asked for it. She was panting for it." I watched his eyes open wide as he remembered.

"Asking? To be killed?"

"I didn't kill her," he said. "I wouldn't kill her, would I?"

"No," I whispered. I remembered Mirela's frothing red bra that peeked from beneath her overall. Both the Brouviches could wind a boy up, but Kizzy was older, more sexually streetwise.

"You had sex with her, didn't you?"

"I never thought it would end up like this. Not like they're saying. She was ... it was ..."

They had found something on Kizzy's body that had traces of DNA. Forensic evidence. I had wondered if Jimmy's sperm had matched what they found inside Kizzy. But if there was still sperm inside Kizzy, it must have got there not long before she died. If

Jimmy'd had sex with Kizzy before she disappeared, all trace of that would surely have vanished, and even if it had been a recent event, wouldn't the dousing in water wash the traces away?

Something solid, traceable. Undeniable.

I imagined Jimmy as he was questioned, his fists bunched on the interview table, his pale brow furrowed, as Rey thrust questions at him. I took a breath in. I'd stopped breathing for long seconds.

"She was having your baby, wasn't she? Jimmy? Was she?"

There she was. In a temple of ice, cold as a morgue. Her belly swollen as she lay on the slab, the snake preventing me from seeing her face.

That was the way with the otherworld: things got twisted round, tangled up. Mist and mirrors. I had met Kizzy. She had taken my hand, held my gaze with her black eyes. Already pregnant. Hours later, I was in the ice temple, the words she called across the empty-ing High Street still hanging in my mind. *Death! Danger! Do not go with him, if he comes for you, the man with the snake.*

"That's why they wanted DNA samples. To find out who the father was."

Jimmy's thumbs were still squashing his closed eyes but doing a poor job of stopping tears from oozing out. He sobbed wildly.

"Getting her pregnant's no proof you killed her. If it happened before she went missing. Did it, Jimmy? Is that all they are saying?"

Jimmy didn't reply. Words weren't coming from him.

"It's all right, Jimmy. They worked it out. There's no shame in being the father of a dead girl's baby. They'll take you off their list, now. I'll make sure it's all right."

"You?" Jimmy raised his head, as if suction had forced it up. "How can you make it all right?"

"Well, of course, I can't, but ..."

"She was having my baby." His shoulders juddered. His whole body pulsated with sobs. "My baby's dead. My baby's dead!"

"Jimmy?"

He didn't speak again. He hardly knew I was there.

I crept from the room to find Mrs. Browne and ask for a blanket.

THIRTY

I DIDN'T BOTHER TEXTING Rey back. I had nothing to give him about Jimmy—nothing he did not already know. I had a suspicion that a baby in the womb had to grow to a certain size before the father's DNA could be detected. Kizzy might have been pregnant by Jimmy weeks before she'd disappeared.

But the time I'd spent with Jimmy had shifted something inside me. I was fed up of working in an environment that made its staff weary and troubled and sucked dry. At twenty-five to ten and almost dreaming of my bed, I parked the scooter around the back of Papa Bulgaria. It was crunch time—I was going to walk away from the job. But first I had to wrench my pay from Stan's sticky fingers.

In the kitchen, they were sluicing down for the following day. Vittoria and Max were at work with buckets of soapy water, their cloths steaming. Stan worked in their wake taking the soap off the ceramics and buffing it dry.

"Don't come in here in your outdoor clothes!" Stan yelled at me. The other two turned to stare, as if they'd never commit such a crime. "Get changed!"

I stepped back to his precious threshold. "Jimmy's out," I called. "Give him a bell, he can come back to work. He's feeling a bit rough—okay, he looks totally wrecked—but after a few slaps from your dad he'll be as right as rain."

Stan's heavy eyebrows reminded me of his father, who no doubt one day he would fully resemble. "How do you know?"

"I saw him earlier, at his mum's. He's been released, free to go. And, hallelujah, so can I. I want my wages. All of them."

"What?"

"Despite the wonderful pay and conditions, I'm leaving your employment."

"Not yet," shrieked Stan. "You have to stay until this crisis is over."

"Jimmy can be back by tomorrow. And I quit. As of now." I grinned at his shocked face. "I want cash or a cheque and a full pay-slip, showing all deductions."

"That's a tall order for ten at night."

"It could be midnight for all I care. I'm not leaving without it."

"Are you going to walk out of here and leave us in the lurch?" said Vittoria, as if she suddenly cared. "We've lost three staff, two permanently."

"Three permanently," Stan flung at her. "I don't want Jimmy back."

I gawped at him. "The police screwed Jimmy to the floor. He just needs some encouragement to recover."

"I don't want wrecked cooks. They might poison the food."

I laughed. "Hah! Wise words, Stan."

Stan strode across the kitchen. I thought he looked comic, with his J-cloth in his hand, but his brows were thunderous. "How come you knew he was out before we did? Have you been talking to the cops?"

"Why would I do that?"

"I heard rumours."

"What does it matter who I talk to?"

His voice was very low, lips hardly moving. "The police arrived minutes after we heard Jimmy'd been arrested. All Sunday, they were up in the office. My poor father had to go down to the police station. Make a statement. You were unable to help us out that day, weren't you? So you missed it all. Running this shop is fucking hard enough without all that crap."

"The police were bound to investigate the suspect's working environment, weren't they?"

"See?" His cocktail stick flew from his mouth like a poisoned dart. "You even talk like a fucking cop."

"Well, if you want rid of me, fine. I want rid of you. Pay me and I'll go."

"Not until you finish the jobs for this shift. You can clean the shop. Counter then floor. I will sort your pay. Okay?"

"*Thank you so much, Sabbie, for helping out at short notice,*" I said, hoping Stan would not detect the quake at the edge of my voice, the weakness in it. I shouldn't let him see that I was scared, but my heart was banging against my ribs like it was desperate to be let out of a cupboard. I turned my back on him and stormed over his clean floor into the shop area, the kitchen door swinging behind me.

I pulled down the shop blinds and locked and bolted the door. I picked up the gaily sequinned cushions, plumping them and arranging them along the bench. I flicked a rusty-looking J-Cloth over the counter. I took three minutes to mop the floor with the dirty water from last night then put the mop and bucket back under the stairs.

My gaze followed the stairs to the office above. I'd only been up there once, when I'd had my interview with the elder Mr. Papazov. But I'd always longed to take a second look. Rey hadn't bothered telling me the cops had searched the office. I was a cop's girl, not a member of the team. I didn't think empirically. I was all wolves and snakes.

Every tread of the stairs groaned as I sneaked up. I took my time moving across the office floorboards, which were painted black like the stairs. I was above the shop, the original lock-up building, so Stan wouldn't hear from the kitchen, which extended out into the yard. Besides, he was not going to come searching for me. He'd be expecting me to finish cleaning then nag and plead once more for my pay. It crossed my mind that if the cheque book was hanging about, I could take it down and slap it in front of him. I'd take a pen, as well.

I went over to the window to let down the blinds. My hand froze on the cord as I heard voices in the yard below. It was Vittoria and Max, both finishing early. They got into the same Smart Car, which I'd learned had been a present from Vittoria's daddy. The headlights illuminated the gaping back entrance as they swung into the road. Only Stan was downstairs now, and I hoped he imagined I'd scarpered through the punter's entrance, leaving work without my pay. I'd inform him of my continued presence when I was finished.

I closed the blinds. Unlike a proper prowler, I'd neglected to bring a torch but I felt fairly safe as I flicked on the desk light. Dust swirled in the beam. Stan hadn't told me to clean up here. He hadn't told me not to, either, but everyone knew the office was out-of-bounds to staff.

I cast my eyes over Mr. Papazov's desk. There was nothing of interest covering the swirls and knots of its surface apart from a thin smear of dust. I tried the drawers on either side of the desk several times before giving up. I was sure that whatever I'd hoped to find, it would be in those locked drawers. Somewhere, there had to be a key. I searched the ashtrays (which was daft, they were overflowing with ash), lifted the decanter that stood on the windowsill, and inverted the sad-looking vase that was next to it. A button jangled out.

I moved to the filing cabinet and gently tugged at the top drawer. This was not locked, but it wasn't what you'd call tidy, either. I'd presumed there would be a file on each employee, but everything was in disorder; reckless piles of receipts, letters, and invoices. Perhaps the police had tossed them back in like that, but it was more likely that no one did filing for Mr. Papazov, and he wasn't up to doing it himself.

I couldn't help smile. This must have been a headache for cops sniffing out any sort of lead. The thing that would have made their eyes glint—Papazov's laptop—was noticeable by its absence, but the old cassette player was still standing on top the filing cabinet. I checked under it and a woodlice scampered over the metal surface.

I moved to the second file drawer. Sweat was growing on my forehead and neck as I worked. Each pile of documents I examined had to be brought out and positioned directly under the desk light, a skeletal structure in bright red, although the paint had begun peeling long ago, revealing the dull grey metal beneath.

Most of the paperwork was mundane—bills from suppliers, especially those with OVERDUE stamped on them. But in amongst these was a manila envelope full of passports. I pulled them out, wondering if Mirela's or Kizzy's was still here. Mirela would need hers to get home, after all.

I flicked through each passport. Standard EU issue, but undecipherable, nevertheless. The names were too Bulgarian to read. I peered hard at each photo, but neither Kizzy nor Mirela were among them.

It seemed futile to sift through yet more final demands for payment in the third drawer, and my time was probably running out. But after finding the passports I decided to give it another five minutes. I lifted the entire pile out and took it the desk.

Behind me, I heard a clunk. Something had fallen onto the metal base of the drawer.

I peered in. A mobile phone lay there. Smeared over its back was a massive blob of Blu-Tack. It had been stuck to the drawer top. Shifting the papers had dislodged it.

I was winged back to my last shamanic journey; the suitcase under the ice, the layers of clothes hiding the iPhone Gary Abbott had dropped before he lost his life.

I peeled off the Blu-Tack and examined the phone more closely. Apart from knowing it was a very similar model, I could not be sure that this iPhone was the same one I'd picked up on High Street. But it had been deliberately hidden—okay, in a ludicrously amateur fashion, but I guessed that a routine search after arrest wouldn't include running your fingers around the tops of filing cabinets.

I turned it over. It did look like the phone I'd found the night of the carnival. Seeing it here made me sure that Kizzy had nicked it out of my pocket. Maybe she nicked things out of pockets all the time. She must have taken it to the room she shared with Mirela. Perhaps she thought Mirela could do with a phone. For some reason, it had ended up here. In fact, it might have been Mirela who'd stuck it out of sight, which would explain the crummy hiding place.

I held my breath as I forced the phone into life; it possibly hadn't been used for the entire six weeks since I last held it. I peered at the screen. There was a good signal, but almost no battery life. A messaged popped up asking me to enter my pin.

I longed to discover what was hidden inside this mobile, but as I didn't know who it belonged to, how was I ever going to crack the pin? Naturally, the most obvious solution—take it directly to Rey— didn't even occur to me. How would Gary Abbott choose a pin?

I keyed in 4279. The screen swirled. *Have a nice day* appeared in a magical way. I grinned. Gary had used the numbers that represented his own name.

I went into the call log. The first named number to spring up was *R.B.*

Rey Buckley, as I live and breathe. I pressed to dial and didn't have to wait long.

"Who is this?" Rey's voice was sharp with nervous edges. "Identify yourself please—"

"Rey, it's Sabbie."

Thin bleeping sounds came between us, warning that the battery was at its lowest ebb.

"Sabbie? The fuck? What is this? Fuck Sabbie, this is fucking Gary's phone—"

"Rey, will you calm down?"

I trailed off. Lights arced across the office walls. I went to the window and used my fingers to prize a peeking space in the slats of the blind. A hefty vehicle was pulling into the yard below me. It was glossed to a high finish and its dark paintwork gleamed under the streetlights. I trained my eyes on the car because, for some reason I could not pin down, I knew I'd seen it before. I could not quite make out the driver, but I could tell it was a man; hefty, like his car.

Stan strode towards it, his hand raised, bringing it to a slow halt at the top of the yard. The driver's window rolled down and Stan stuck his head in through it.

On the phone, Rey was hissing curses at me. "Rey!" I yelled. "Rey guess wha—"

Two things happened. The phone died and Stan, talking fast to the driver, pointed back to the building and looked up at my window.

I let go of the blind as if it was red-hot. I turned on my heel but could not think of my next move. In fact, any move was impossible. I was rooted to the black floorboards, knees locked, brain in shutdown. I stared like a dummy at Abbott's phone. Moments later, a voice grated up the stairwell.

"Sabbie *Daar*!"

The treads creaked in fast succession, like gun shots. I finally managed to stuff the iPhone into my pocket and whip out the J-Cloth.

Yellow light burst into the room as Stan opened the door.

"What're you doing?"

Attack is the best form of defence. I strode towards him, shaking my J-Cloth, which mercifully, was full of dust.

"Cleaning. Like you told me." I could feel a scream building, pushing up from my chest into my throat. I forced it down. "Cleaning your fucking shop, like you said, after hours of mindless fucking work. And I don't even know what I'll get; you said triple-time, but I've only got your word for that and frankly, Stan, I don't think much of your word."

Stan's gaze settled on the pile of documents I'd left on the desk. "You look for your cash?"

"No," I said, before realizing what a good excuse that was. "Well, yeah, but I wouldn't have just taken it."

He put his hand into his back pocket. When he drew it out, it was fisting a wad of twenties. At no point did he take his eyes off me. When I opened my mouth to ask for a payslip, nothing came out. The big dark car was still purring in the yard—the headlights seared round the edges of the blind. I wanted out of Papa Bulgaria forever. I watched Stan count twenties and realized I was about to be royally shafted. I reached out to take what he offered. My fingers shook. As I touched the money, he yanked his hand away.

And then my mobile rang. It was the thing that I should have predicted and planned for. Of course Rey would get straight back; I hadn't even told him where I'd found Abbott's phone. I had to poker up my face and cancel the call. I took just one second too long. Stan stuffed the money back into his pocket. He hurtled towards me. His body slammed into mine, and we powered across the room. The breath was crushed from my lungs as he pinned me against the filing cabinet. My spine shrieked in pain as I hit the drawer handles.

I tried to inhale, but all I could do was cough and gasp. Stan's arm was crooked around my neck, his other hand searching pockets. He found my phone, buzzing and chirping away. He stuffed it in his jeans pocket. The ringing tone went on, muffled by denim. Stan went back to his search until he'd extracted the iPhone. His grin widened. I realized that he hadn't been staring at the documents on the desk. He'd spotted the innocuous blob of Blu-Tack.

"I knew you were trouble," he said.

Stan had been saying this about me from day one, but suddenly it seemed to mean something. I didn't want to learn what. The answer was not going to be in my favour. His hand was still round my neck. The pressure was making me gag and it was clear my relationship with my former employer was in the process of terminating due to bad feelings on both sides. Finally, my phone stopped ringing. The silence was terrible.

"Let go of me." I swallowed hard, trying to keep my voice from croaking. "Give me my pay and I'll be out of your hair."

He hung on, his face so close to mine I could smell the lukanka he'd had with dinner. "You'll get exactly what you're owed, darling. *And* be out of our hair." His steady gaze caught and held me. There was a glitter in his dark pupils that penetrated deep, forcing me to focus on him. We were staring each other out. Like, if he looked away first, he'd release his iron-man grip and let me collect my winnings. But if I looked away …

I did not believe he knew why he was holding me there. It was all to do with being boss, with not showing weakness. He'd caught me prying, and that was unforgivable.

I started to struggle against the grip round my neck. Stan was maybe twenty pounds heavier than me. If the guy wanted a cat fight for his money, he was welcome. I went for his eyes and he yelped. A space grew between us and I felt the pressure go off my spine. I pushed hard. He stumbled. Stan had the upper body power that might be useful if he had you pinned on the floor, but his legs and hips were lean. I took my fingers from his eyes and pushed hard against the tops of his shoulders. His grasp on me slipped as he lost his balance. I was free to make my exit. I bolted towards the door.

I felt my arm wrench with a shock of pain. A jolt spun me round in a full circle. Stan had caught and gripped my wrist. He was grinning. He was enjoying this. He liked a bit of rough with ex-employees. It cut the cost of wages.

"Let go of me." I tried to keep my voice strong. "Give me my pay. Stop acting like a dumb fool."

"Nobody calls me that." He raised the flat of his hand.

A deep boom sounded, like something had been detonated. The slap whipped my neck back.

"You hit me!" I was more stunned than frightened. A month of having to put up with my insolence had gone into this misplaced attack.

He used his other hand on the other side of my face. With the second slap, my jaw shifted. Pain exploded over my head. I felt each joint of my body give way as I crumpled.

I was on my back, staring up at the ceiling. It turned from white to a darker and dimmer grey. The air I sucked in was thick and ashen. The world was ash, with sparkly dots of black around the edges. It was hard to see. It was hard to move. My body was inside a fog that was turning to black night.

Stan disappeared from my sight. I heard the door slam shut.

The air was so thick now, I struggled to breathe. The dimness closed over my eyes, and with it, all other thoughts.

THIRTY-ONE

Out of the thick murk of fog, a creature with scales as green as bile undulated towards me.

Miss Dare, it hissed.

A whimper juddered out of me. I wanted to step away from its never-ending form, but I was surrounded by floorless, airless lint.

The creature rounded on me. I saw its yellow head. Its eyes blinked once. A thin, black line shot out and disappeared in a pulsing motion. A serpent's tongue. Anaconda.

The snake's jaw stretched wide, its forked tongue ready. A firework of spirit poison sprayed harmlessly into the air, falling like the sparkles of a squib.

———

I was out for only minutes, but coming back into the world of Papazov's office made me wish I could sleep forever. My ears pulsed heat and stung with pain. I took a breath that made me cough and gasp.

I was propped beside the filing cabinet. I shifted my legs, pushing myself up. I looked down at my feet. I was bare footed. Had Stan made off with my footwear in the foolish belief that it would prevent me from fleeing Papa Bulgaria and downloading everything to the police? I was so groggy it took me several more seconds to realize that I didn't have my coat. In the pocket of the coat were the keys to my scooter. I felt bereft without them. It came back to me that I didn't have a phone, either.

I careered towards the office door, my only route of escape, keeping my sights on it. It was locked. I yanked the handle. I kicked the frame. I screamed at it. I felt like sliding down it and closing my eyes. I turned and used it as a leaning support. My breath seared the back of my throat.

There had been a phone on the desk the first time I'd come here, to be interviewed by Papazov. But I'd searched the entire office minutes ago, when I'd still been a working member of the staff here. I stared at the surface of the desk, as if hopeful it might rematerialise. It was only then that I saw the other thing that was in the room with me.

The bundle was by the desk, small, dark. Like a sleeping hound. I remembered seeing Mirela curled into my porch, waiting for me to come home and solve the mystery of her sister's disappearance. My body stiffened as I took in the inert heap, hair spilling over the floor like treacle. I tried to breathe, forcing the blur and grey thickness from my head. After my descent into Anaconda's world, I was capable of believing that Stan could produce the girl by magic.

I was on my knees seconds later.

"Mirela," I whispered. I had no idea how she'd got here, or why. I was still groggy round the edges, so much so that it was only just beginning to occur to me that she was lying on the floorboards because she could not get up. I rolled her gently onto her back so that I could see what was happening. I heard her sigh and felt a wash of relief. Her breath smelt like those pear drops no one sucks once they've passed the age of puberty.

I stroked her small hand. "Mirela?"

"Mmm?"

"It's Sabbie, Mirela." I didn't think it mattered what I said, so long as she could hear my voice. "Where have you been? Everyone was searching for you. We were all so worried."

I got up and re-angled the desk light so that it shone on her face. She was alabaster pale. Her face had thinned. She seemed even more breakable than before.

"Mirela, wake up."

I didn't want to hurt her, but I took her shoulders and tried to shake her awake. She moaned. I felt like moaning with her. I was locked in a room with a half-comatose girl and downstairs was a manic Bulgarian who could slap like a door in a gale. The pain from Stan's double slaps still rang in my head. A wave of nausea took over my body, making me double up. I stood, breathing though my nose until it passed. Then I put my hands under Mirela's arms and slid her along the floor until she was propped up against the wall. She looked like a rag doll.

For the first time, I saw Mirela as I should have always seen her. She was a child. I'd always thought her to be child*like*, I'd always been concerned that she was little more than a child. But her makeup and frothy bras had hidden the difficult truth: Mirela *was* a child, a girl in her early teens, not old enough to know what she was doing when she signed up to Stanislaus's regime.

There was no water in the room, but I pulled the top off the decanter and sniffed. Brandy? Probably some evil Bulgarian substitute.

I poured a little into the glass that formed its lid and wafted it under Mirela's nose. Her eyelashes fluttered.

"Mirela? Take a sip of this. It might fortify you." I poured a tiny drop onto her tongue. She half-swallowed, half-coughed. "Mirela! Please tell me you're all right!"

"I don't find my sister." The words blubbered out. Her eyes opened for a second and they seemed even larger in her head than usual, the whites scratched with red and the pupils big, black lakes.

"Oh, Mirela . . ."

I would have to tell her. Why was it always me? But not yet. Explaining that Kizzy had died might shock her. Explaining *how* she'd died—a surgeon had removed her organs, leaving her little more than bones and skin—might kill her.

"Have you been hiding, my dear? Or did someone hide you?"

"I wait for Kizzy," she said, and her head drooped.

The dullness that two slaps can leave you with was preventing me from thinking fast enough. Stan must have brought Mirela to this room. He'd thrown her in and locked the door on us both, and he'd managed to accomplish this trick in just the few moments I'd been out cold. So Mirela had been in the building all the time. I glanced over at the window. No—Mirela must have come in the beastly vehicle that I had seen somewhere before. An urgency gripped me. I had to get us both out of this place.

I put the glass down and went back the window. I lifted the blind, trying to be discreet.

The car was still there, but its nose was now pointing out of the yard gate, the engine ticking over and its big back door lifted like a shark's jaw. In the shadows within the yard, two men worked together. They were shifting one of the scooters. I heard them grunt as they lifted it into the open back, laying it on its side.

I could make out the forms of both of them, even in the darkness. One was Stan. His tight jeans and pumped shoulders stood out clearly against the red glow of the rear lights. The other man was taller and seemed to have taken charge, but it was impossible to make out his features. Even so, a perception crawled in me. I'd seen this man before.

I saw Stan throw things into the boot. The items landed haphazardly on top the scooter. *My scooter,* I realized. *My coat. My trainers.* He tossed another item, something small that landed hard. *My mobile.*

The door to the big boot was slammed shut. Stan hopped into the driver's seat, signalling and turning onto the narrow road with care.

The taller man was left in the pitch dark of the yard. I have a good memory for faces and a reasonable recall of cars, but nothing jogged into place. It was likely that this guy was on the very periphery of my contacts. Someone I'd bumped into. Someone who'd come into the shop as I was leaving, a mate of Stan or his father, perhaps.

He walked into the scooter shelter. It was dark in there, for the shop lights had been doused. That made me wonder about Rey, if he was looking for me after the aborted phone calls. Would he have sent a patrol car round to my house? Would they think to come here? If they had, it would be clear everything was locked up and in darkness. Most probably, he'd assumed I'd got pissy with him and was refusing to return his call.

Streetlight crept in through the open gates. I could follow the glow of the man's pale trousers as he moved about. He went up to the big bike that I'd first seen during my interview with Stan. A Yamaha, I remembered, fast and heavy and lavished with chrome. I peered through the blind, thinking that he was planning to leave too. But he opened the panniers on either side of the bike and pulled out the containers inside. Holding them by their chunky handles, he carried them into the kitchen.

My mouth formed a word. "*Mutri.*" Mirela had thought they were moving drugs on the scooters. That idea was ludicrous, but she had been so close. The powerful bike, always parked in the shelter, was what the *Mutri* were using. No wonder Stan had been so tetchy about my interest in it.

Mirela let out a sort of grumbling sigh. I swung round. She had slumped over and crumpled onto the floor. Her pale face had continued to whiten; even her lips were white. I pulled off my jumper and put it under her head where she lay. I didn't have a first-aid bone in my body—I had no idea how to deal with this. Should I let her sleep or try to wake her? For the first time, I realized Mirela might be dying.

I went to the door, tried the handle again. It was a futile thing to do, I knew it was locked, but I was the only responsible ... the only *conscious* adult in the room, and it was up to me to get us out. I backed off and charged the door, thumping all the power of my shoulder into it. The pain that drove up my arm was unbelievable. I had to cover my mouth to stop myself crying out. My weight had done nothing. The door hadn't budged.

I went back to the window. Now there was no one in the yard, I dared pull up the blind. It was a single floor drop onto the kitchen roof. I tried to move the sash of the window. It was stuck by years of paint and damp weather. It was stuck, and so were we.

It hadn't occurred to me to wonder why there was no one in the yard until I heard the key turn in the lock behind me. I spun round to face the man in the doorway.

He stood with the purpose of someone about their business. Someone in control. He was neatly dressed in chinos and an open-necked shirt. He was smooth shaven.

At the sight of him came the recognition of my fears. I could hear my breath take off, fly off. I knew any moment I would not be able to control my breathing at all. My mind moved towards the shutdown that comes with absolute terror.

I had pieced things together badly. I thought Stan was a loose cannon with a central core of careless malevolence. I knew he could slap a woman down and lock her up. But it turned out Stan was a tiny cog, the no-one guy who ran around for the top cats. I should have guessed from the start. If you deal in prosperous illegal activities, you have to be like ice. Rey had said it—*barbaric, cold-blooded, implacable.*

The man smiled and the wrinkles at the sides of his eyes creased up. His voice was full of compassion. "Good evening, Miss Dare. I hope Stan hasn't treated you badly?"

I'd been right about one thing. I had known the man who had been in the yard, even from only looking down at the top of his head in the darkness. I had met him on my first delivery for Papa. I had met him again in the changing room below. I did know him, and I did know his Toyota Land Cruiser.

It was Dr. Grace.

THIRTY-TWO

I DIDN'T SCREAM. THERE was no hope for screamers. Papa Bulgaria was closed and empty downstairs. And in this part of Bridgwater, people were used to screams. Hordes of girls with too much bad white wine inside them screamed their way down the streets regularly, even on Tuesday nights.

Beside, I had no breath to scream. I could feel my lungs trying hard to work, panting tiny, useless sobs in and out.

I had time to look at Grace, at his benign, almost genial face. His hands were large but fine, long, tapered. Once they had gentled the sick. Once, surely, they had used their skills to help people get better. To cut out disease. His eyes still seemed to smile, as they had when I passed him his order in the driveway of his house and again in the changing room downstairs.

He closed the door behind him and moved towards us. He stepped like any doctor, that reticent tread, as if we were his patients. As he shifted his stance, a shade fell over this face. His otherworld image revealed itself. My panting fear had left me giddy and for a few appalling moments, I witnessed his subtle body, distinct and bright as buttercups, so bright it made me blink. This sort of yellow was not a good sign. The man was struggling inside himself. He longed for respect and prestige, and was terrified of losing it. I steadied my gaze. Rising from the base of his spine and coiling around his body was something serpentine. It reached the crown of his head, and at the place the aura glows most brightly, I saw its head. Yellow, flecked with green. At first I thought it was a spirit intrusion. I'd seen these many times before—misplaced energy from opportunistic spirits that rub off on those who are low in energy. His patients, who came to him desperate—not because they were sick, but because they were dead broke—would perhaps leave such intrusions behind. My own spine convulsed, as if I might become infected. But this wasn't an intrusion. It was the man's totem. A wave of nausea forced me to swallow bile.

Grace shifted stance. My view of his energy field was lost as he closed down the chink that had allowed me to see his true self. He looked across at Mirela.

Immediately, I ran the few steps from the window to where she was slumped. I stood in front of her. I had no idea what sort of protection I offered her, but I couldn't help myself. I stared up into his untroubled, guiltless eyes. There was no use in cowering. This had been planned for a long time. I'd been flagged—too curious, trouble. I'd dipped my toe and found the water was poison.

"You shot Abbott." A tremble was in my voice. It was spreading through my body. But I spoke on. "Abbott was getting somewhere. He had his sights on you. You lured him into the alleyway. Kizzy helped you."

As I spoke her sister's name, Mirela gave a tiny gasp, almost a whisper of sound. Her eyelids fluttered. "Where is my Kizzy?" I imagined how she'd asked that question every time Grace had come near her. Every time she woke and was sedated again.

"Kizzy died," I said aloud and clearly.

I could feel Grace's eyes on me now. I'd been worried that Mirela would fall apart when she heard the truth about her sister. But she didn't stir. She probably hadn't even heard me, but even so I wondered if the news would really come as a surprise. Perhaps she'd known her sister was in mortal danger since she'd read the letter.

"She died when you took out her organs." My heart was pounding. My entire body beat with the same fast *thud-thud*, but I didn't take my gaze from the doctor's face.

Grace sucked an impatient breath in through his nose. "All surgical procedures pose a slight risk. We do this donation surgery three, four times a week. A single kidney, sold to someone in desperate need. The risk is slight. Very slight. Sad about Kizzy, of course."

"But you're not sad, are you?" I tried to keep my voice even. *As long as he's answering my questions*, I thought, *he isn't cutting us up.* We were in an office, far from operating theatres. If I kept Dr. Grace talking, I might yet get us both out. If we all just kept talking. "You don't know what sadness is. Or pity. You don't know pity or love or healing. All you know is money."

I thought of the narrow scar that ran around Kate's ribs and belly. The girl they'd found at the Dunball Wharf had no one, but Kate had friends, a community she belonged to. So with Kate, they took a kidney and left her, dripping blood through her dressing, clutching her wad of notes.

And Kizzy, hanging on the gallows at Hinkley Point, had a sister who had never given up the search.

Not one kidney, Rey had told me. *Almost all her organs. Gone. Swiped away. Packed in ice and shipped out of here.* Biological gold, sold on the black market to people hoping for life.

"You took everything." The trembling had penetrated my entire core now. I looked into the doctor's unruffled face and imagined my body floating out on the tide. Tiny gasping cries came out of me. And then I was screaming. "Every organ! Even her eyes!"

Grace didn't like the truth yelled at him. He lurched forward, his hand raised and his fist curled. I flinched from the memory of Stan's slaps, which were still ringing in my ears. The thought of being hit by this man buckled my body. I doubled up on the floor beside Mirela, holding my ribs as if they were about to be torn open.

I could feel my heart, beating so fast and weak it felt like the heart of one of my chickens when I put my palm over its breast.

The doctor unclipped his black bag. I had not even noticed he had carried it in; the ubiquitous, invisible medical accessory. He lifted the lid. It was neatly arranged. A selection of vials and syringes, tourniquets and sterile needles. And, carefully wound into the lid like the snake around his otherworld image, was a stethoscope.

He stood erect for a moment, his eyes on us as he unbuttoned his shirt sleeves. He rolled up each sleeve, as if to get to get on with the job. A tattoo was worked along the entirety of his right arm. I remembered the tiny end to this tattoo, from the time he'd come to me in the changing room in his gleaming Italian suit. Its hidden edge had peeked from the cuff of his shirt. Now I saw it all. The colours had faded, but the tattoo was recognizable. A rod of brown with tiny sprigs of white blossom decorating it. A snake in shades of green entwined the length of the rod. As the doctor finished rolling his right sleeve, the snake's head was revealed, the ink as bright a yellow as it had been on the day the tattoo had been given. Its single black eye was the strongest point on the tattoo.

It was a caduceus, the rod of healing.

At some time in the distant past, he had sworn to uphold the Hippocratic Oath. He had been young and impassioned and liberal enough to imprint his beliefs upon his arm. That must have been a long time ago. But Dr. Grace still gave the same performance of being a doctor as he had then. I recalled his crinkly smile as he'd told me he'd given me a tonic.

I understood with a jolt that I had not collapsed in the changing room because I'd eaten something that Jimmy had mistaken for bouquet garni, or because of any kind of mistake. The entire episode had been engineered; Stan slipping a simple sedative into a well-flavoured dish to make me sick enough to call a doctor … sick enough not to notice that the needle in my arm hadn't given me a tonic, it had taken something from me—my blood for cross-matching.

I might even have been sent to his house in Westonzoyland that first day for him to cast his eye over me. Even then, somewhere inside his house, Mirela's sister had lain, waiting for death. *Do not go with him, if he comes for you, the man with the snake.* I could not believe that I had stood so close to where Kizzy was hidden. Grace's charmingly pink house. The place of no escape.

He worked out of his doctor's case with an unruffled calm, selecting a syringe, fixing on the green-tipped needle. His smile seemed to be full of humanity, but that was a trick of the wrinkles around his eyes—an ingrained professional response. It wasn't empathy. It was satisfaction with his work. He wasn't sorry for what he did.

The doctor snapped the head off an ampoule. It seemed minuscule in his large hands. He began drawing the colourless contents into the syringe, working with measured care, a doctor taking his time, like he was concerned to get the dose accurate. The drug would be for Mirela and I had to think now of the best course of action: protect her or attack him?

He walked steadily. I watched his shoes approach. Black leather, highly polished. "Please don't worry. This is just something to keep you calm." He was standing over me, as if quietly waiting for my consent.

I tried to speak. My jaw wouldn't let me. My tongue felt swollen in my mouth, as if I'd already been administered a lethal dose. Panic knotted up my stomach, annihilating thought for precious seconds.

Vein. After a vein. He was after my vein. My whole body convulsed in terror. He bent towards me. Every muscle fought against his professional touch. I screamed along a dried throat until my lungs were screwed up like a rung-out flannel.

"I didn't know anything! I don't know anything!" I was making no sense even to myself. "I am not your PATIENT!"

My entire body was screaming, lashing out with arms and legs, feet and fists. I had to get out. Get past him. The sudden hope that he'd left the door unlocked ripped through me. I caught the side of his nose and he rocked on his heels. A slow smile spread over his mouth. "I really didn't want to hurt you unnecessarily." He hadn't raised his voice He didn't have to catch his breath.

I'd become an expendable nuisance, like Kizzy. I was a bag of costly merchandise ready for sale.

Grace fell onto his knees and pinned me to the floor. One knee was in my chest, stopping my breath. The other was trapping my hand, the one he didn't want. Both his hands were free to work on me.

I squirmed under him, taking breath as best I could. I fixed my gaze on his hazel eyes. He smiled. It was his way. He'd probably been taught to smile in medical college, and it had become ingrained. He smiled encouragingly at his patient, while beneath him, I was a helpless puppy, chastised for messing on the rug. He tightened a tourniquet around my arm. I felt the numbing grip as he twisted it tight.

I was never going to give up. If I gave up, I was dead. Dead and empty. I kicked with my stockinged feet and with my knees. I heard him swear under his breath. But the muscles in his right arm hardened as he held my hand firm and flat to the ground.

The movement of muscle seemed to turn the head of the tattooed snake. It looked directly at me with its one bright eye. It was so close to me now I could read the words that were inked along the body of the snake in letters which might once have been a navy blue: *Primum non nocere.* The words were Latin. I couldn't've deciphered them, even if I'd been given a clear head and a book of translations, but I could hazard a fair guess at what they meant. *First do no harm.* Creed of magician, witch, and shaman as well as physician. I knew it well.

The sharpness of the needle caught me, scratched at me. I heard the snake hiss, *I will get you.* The hiss took over my thoughts. I was sliding down, down to a different place.

———

A dim-lit room with panelled walls, high metal-framed windows, and an ornate ceiling stained smoker's yellow. My feet were on solid parquet and a polished wood bench ran along the wall, filled with rows of test tubes and roaring Bunsen burners that let off a smell of gas.

Coiled on the surface a hand span away from me was Anaconda. His head reared and he eyed me blackly.

"This is where I was given life."

I had no idea where anacondas lived as a general rule, but an ancient laboratory didn't seem any more ideal than an ice temple. I summoned up a drip of energy to speak to him inside my mind. "You belong in the jungles."

"Time and place must change. Home may change." The plaintive tone in his voice was not a sham. He was sad. That made me sorrow for him.

"You are Dr. Grace's totem."

The snake blinked once. "I am the embodiment of his physician's oath."

"First do no harm. He had you tattooed down his arm."

"And so can never be rid of me."

The only way the spirits know to communicate is through mirrors and mist, conundrums and connections. But I hadn't unravelled the mysteries fast enough. The spirits had walked me into mortal danger and left me with no defences at all.

Sabbie.

Trendle's voice came to me.

I can't lift my head, I told him. *I can't move my arms. I can't breathe!*

You must try. You must fight!

———

I was sucked back to the world of knees and syringes. I'd been away less that a second in real time, but Grace had found my vein; there was blood in the barrel of the hypodermic. He began to ease the venom into me.

I powered my body into one last effort. I hurled myself about, flailing my legs to shift his weight off me until I dislodged his knee from my pinned hand. For a few precious seconds, his smooth action stuttered. I drove all my failing strength into my free arm. The syringe wobbled as my arm jerked. The doctor's grip loosened as he tried to catch its fall. I used my free hand like a bat and hurled it across the room.

His face paled. The tip of his tongue darted. He glanced to where the syringe had landed. It was spinning like a top. Both of us watched the spin decrease until the needle pointed like a compass, towards us.

I'd given him a dilemma. He would have to release his hold on me if he wanted to fetch the syringe and put me out.

"You fucker," he said, the word sounding even more foul in his cultivated accent.

He raised himself clear of me and his fist came crashing towards my face. But he was not well balanced, he had no purchase. I saw the blow almost before his fist was clenched. An image of Jimmy, holding fast under his assault flashed into my mind. I yanked my head sideways. The blow glanced off; I felt it tug my hair as it passed my scalp and hit the floorboards. I heard the crunch of sinew and bone.

Grace howled and rolled with the pain. I gasped a blessed breath of air. I scrambled out from under him, exploding into arms and legs, pummelling and pounding with my smaller fists. He snatched at my ankle, but I had all the momentum now. When I'd tried to tear myself away from Stan, I hadn't wholly believed in the seriousness of his attack. Now I knew. If I did not fight with every drop of my strength, I would die under this man's knife. I used the heel of my foot on the soft middle between his legs. He howled again. Strange that he did not like pain.

But the venom of the snake had entered my body. My spine was growing numb. My eyes were unfocused. My legs were like bags of fishing maggots. Soon my mind would close down. I fought against the drug, struggling to stay in one piece while Grace was still knocked off balance. I threw myself across the room. I grasped the handle of the door. Had he really left it unlocked? My palms were wet with fear as the handle slid down.

The door swung open. I fled through it and slammed it behind me. In the keyhole lay the key—shiny, black with age and use. It took me almost too many microseconds to recognize my good luck. I felt the handle on his side press downwards. Grace had reached the door.

I turned the key in the lock.

I snatched at the banister to hold myself up. I was staring at the door, unable to move. I had left Mirela, unconscious, in that office. I'd left her to Grace's mercy, which was none too generous. But there was no other way. If I could get clear of this barbarous prison before Grace broke through the door, I could get help for Mirela. And I had no time to lose; I didn't know where Stan had taken my scooter in the Land Cruiser, but I had to assume he would return.

I started my descent of the stairs. My numbed legs were out of control. I was stumbling, falling. Above, Grace was hammering at the door and yelling for Stan. I was on my hands and knees but had the exit in my sights. I could vaguely remember leaving that key in the lock when I bolted the door, a million light years before all this. If the key was there, I'd be out of this madhouse in seconds.

But the key was gone, leaving the front door locked and bolted.

I thought wildly about smashing a window or crawling into a kitchen cupboard. But first I should check that Grace had not left the place open at the back. I was betting he had. I was praying to every goddess that had goodwill for me. Surely, he would believe he could deal with a couple of silly girls.

I could barely keep upright. Something was swirling in my brain, heavy as poppy juice, drifting me towards lethargy. I blinked several times to keep my vision clear. The only way to propel myself along was to lean forward and sprint, even if that meant sprawling on my nose at the end. I just had to keep going until I was out in the road. I flung myself into the—

Kitchen.

Kitchen? This was not the kitchen. I stood on the glossy tiled floor, sucking in fiery breaths. My knees went and I grabbed the nearest worktop for support. It must be the drug Grace had injected. It was giving me hallucinations. Because I couldn't be seeing this. Not this place.

This was not the Papa Bulgaria kitchen. This was no kitchen at all. It was a damned place. A place of Hammer Horrors, of worst nightmares.

A place of blame.

THIRTY-THREE

THE KITCHEN HAD GONE. It had been transformed. Surgical instruments were laid out on sterile paper spread over the pristine steel surfaces. Their sharpness caught the overhead lights. Industrial pans were boiling on the hobs. The central island was covered with green cloths. A table for a patient.

I had never visualized this. Killers do their bag of tricks in some dark alley, or a locked basement, or a clearing in deep forest. But black-market surgeons need a place like that too: dark, locked, isolated. A black abode that could absorb malicious intent.

I was focused on the horror at the centre of the kitchen. But closer to the outside lobby, the fridge door was hanging open. I focused on it. As I tried to get my feet moving, the fridge door closed and I saw Stanislaus Papazov, a wide bowl of ice cupped in his hands. I thought he might drop it seeing me sway behind the worktop. But Stan put the ice down carefully. His grin widened. He cocked the point of wood in his mouth and spoke in a measured, dramatic manner.

"Boy, have you been a nuisance, Sabbie *Daar*. Prying into every corner for Kizzy. Lucky for us, Mirela never could keep anything to herself. Soon as she'd spent the night at your house, she was blurting out what you were, what you planned to do. Want to know why we employed you? We make friends of our enemies."

My fingers hurt, I was gripping the worktop so hard. "You let this go on?" My voice came out slurred. I gave a little cough, right in the back of my throat.

"Think I enjoy boiling all day in a hot kitchen?" Stan's image rippled as he moved, as if he was underwater. "It's why I bother to come into work."

My head drooped. I tried to pull myself up to my full height. *Fight the sleep. Fight the drug. Don't let yourself slide away. If you do, you'll be dead.*

Above our heads, Dr. Grace was trying to break his way through the office door. The steady noise thudded in my head. Stan glanced upwards and walked past me, nudging my shaking body with his neat hip as he went, sending me finally off balance. I felt myself slipping. I so longed for sleep. I was drowning in the need to close my eyes and let myself go. I was on my knees, clinging to the handle of a drawer. The world was blotched with a slow loss of consciousness.

And then I felt arms lift me, as if I was in a small boat on high waves. Stan and Grace, hauling me onto the green-draped surface. They rolled me on to my side, took my arm, and carefully moved it out of the way of my ribs.

Kidneys first. Then, perhaps corneas, pancreas, liver? Finally, the things you could not do without, for once the heart was gone, you were dead.

"I need to scrub up."

410

I heard the voice. It took a long time, minutes perhaps, for the words to sink to a place where I understood them. It took all my strength to see round the edges of the black blotches that seeped across my line of vision. I was a mess, almost gone, using the last of my will to force my eyes to stay open.

So I saw Mirela first, before the other two.

She had got down the stairs in the same manner I had, by leaning and crawling. But now she was in the doorway, looking around. I wondered if she was looking about for a weapon. She knew very well where the knife block was kept. She came across the kitchen like a toddler on their first legs. It was only a matter of time before she crashed and burnt. I tried, with my last creeping thoughts, to will her to reach the knives before she fell.

The two men must have heard, for they looked round. Stan marched over to her as her body folded and collapsed. He lifted her easily, with his body-builder's muscles.

"We could do her first," said Grace.

"That's stupid," said Stan. "That one is the trouble. Do her first."

Like a fireman he carried Mirela out of the kitchen. I saw her fine ankles knock against the door frame. I saw him half turn and wink at the doctor. Grace did not see this. But even processed through the sludge of the injection, I understood entirely. Mirela was Stan's now, and he would do what he liked with her. They disappeared from view, leaving me with Grace. To do what he liked with.

Grace went back to arranging my body on the surface. I made a final agonizing effort. I touched the doctor's bare arm. I laid my hand on his tattoo. The healing rod. The sharp-tongued snake.

I watched Anaconda ripple across the laboratory surface, past Bunsen burners, flasks, and tripods, moving ever closer to me.

Anaconda was neither moral nor immoral. He was above and beside all that. He was nature; cruel as needs be. I felt the snake creep around my waist, tightening like a belt, then over my chest and along my back. Even in this spirit place, the paralyzing drug seeped through my blood. I was unable to move. I could not open my otherworld mouth to speak. Anaconda was the drug, squeezing the life from me.

This was spirit power, upturned. The rod of healing, deranged.

Grace had been filled with pride once. Being a doctor meant hard years of study, a life of dedication to the well-being of others. He'd sat in the tattooist's chair, a young medical student, desperate to learn to heal, keen to do good. He'd undergone an afternoon of pricking pain to have the healing rod imprinted, with his oath written within it. But somewhere along the doctor's journey, after he left this medical lab, he'd lost his sense of honourable direction. He'd set his spirit snake free to roam, free to do its natural will. A snake must do what its nature dictates. I understood that. Anaconda will always look for something to crush. The snake had been loosed from the rod, and hell had descended on the little town of Bridgwater.

I could feel the damp warmth of Trendle's fur and the cold wet nudge of his nose. Like a friendly dog. I could smell his river smell and it gave me a boost of strength. I was sure that Grace's snake respected my otter. He had attacked Anaconda without fear in the ice temple

Trendle's short legs were splayed on the polished wood of the lab bench. In his jaw he was holding the stick the wolf had given me. It was sprouting strange little blossoms. It was as long as an arm.

"The stick, Sabbie. The rod. The healing rod of the caduceus."

This was why the wolf had dropped it at my feet. It wasn't for Mirela or any client. It was a gift for me, in my time of greatest need. Taming the snake was to be my job. But Anaconda had been free from the rod's healing power for so long. He'd tasted the other way. Instead of giving life, easing pain, offering hope, he'd allowed the doctor to misuse his skills. Victims had died in the process.

The full length of the snake was wound round my body now. His scaly head swayed in front of me. Our faces were so close I could see nothing but the glitter of his black eyes. I strained every muscle against the punishing tightness of Anaconda's pressure and sucked in a tiny morsel of oxygen.

"Sabbie. Here, here. Take it."

The pulp of my finger touched the surface of the rod. Trendle dropped it into my open palm.

I could feel its benevolence as soon as I touched it. It held the power of life, well-being, and good health.

I tried to direct my thoughts into the mind of the snake, to keep them away from the crushing of my breath. *Come home. Come home. To your duty. To where you are meant to be. To what you are meant to do. First do no harm.*

The snaked flickered its tongue at me. I felt his merciless embrace loosen one notch. Enough to take a gasping breath. Enough to free my arm. I held the wand tight and lifted it into his sights.

Here it is. Home. Duty. Purpose. Do no harm.

———

A moment of blessed blackness and I was back. My eyelids were filled with cement and my body with pain and paralysis. There was a chemical smell at the back of my throat. It seemed to take an hour to force the grit of my eyelids apart. The doctor moved about like an image on a TV with poor reception. Time had passed; he'd changed into green theatre togs, a short-sleeved loose top and baggy bottoms. There was a cloth cap on his head. He was pulling on surgical gloves, lifting them from an open paper packet and snapping them over his wrists. The muscles of his right arm rippled as he moved, the tattoo rippling in response. In my mind, I called to Anaconda. I was no longer with him in the spirit world, but I could see him; his image was clear on the tattoo.

Home. Duty. Purpose. Do no harm.

The doctor chose two slender silver instruments. Scalpel in one hand. Forceps in the other. With the forceps he gripped a blade. He fixed the blade to the scalpel handle and laid scalpel and forceps on a cardboard tray. He added a pile of square white swabs.

He came towards me. He carried the tray. The tang of antiseptic hit my nose. An iced chill ran over my skin. I was naked—he'd stripped me while I was out cold, being crushed by Anaconda—he had ripped off my jeans and rugby shirt. And when Grace had finished, he would make sure I was properly weighted before he let the waters of Somerset do their job, turning me into pale ribbons of dead flesh, ready for the fish.

He was close to me now. He held the forceps. They were dripping with a white swab that was so cold as it painted my skin, it made me shudder.

"Shit," said Grace. "She's not out."

Anaconda. It was a whisper in my mind. I tried harder. *ANACONDA! First do no harm!*

I'd felt momentary sorrow for Anaconda in the medical lab. Neither the man nor the snake had imagined that crime would be the outcome of their self-sacrifice. Grace had slid away from dedication and his pledge to heal, exchanging noble aims for financial gain. With that, his totem snake slid from the rod. The thought saddened me. I lay on the brutal surface, stripped and waiting to die, and felt a single, boiling tear ooze from the corner of my eye and drop onto the stainless steel.

"Poor Anaconda," I whispered.

I saw Grace's eyes open wide, above his mask. He'd heard my voice.

Even if it did nothing to help me survive, I wanted him to know that I watched him now, as he took my life to keep his enterprise going. I forced my hand up and gripped the doctor's right wrist. I felt the power of the caduceus, the final vestiges of its goodness.

"I'm scrubbed!" snarled the doctor. "Stan! Get over here! You're going to have to help me."

There was silence. Stan was not around. He was still upstairs with Mirela.

"D'you hear?" roared the surgeon. "Help me, please!"

He said the wrong thing. He used the wrong words. He called to his snake, his totem, even though he did not know it.

"Help him, Anaconda," I moaned. "Come home. First—do—no—harm."

Grace stared at me. He must have thought I was delirious. I could see the frustration in his face. The lack of his scrub nurse Stan, the way I kept fighting the drug... everything was messing up his nice, simple, gold-lined procedure.

"Anaconda! First do no harm!" The words were slurred, but stronger, louder. "He needs your help. Come home."

I had little time left to even think. Very soon I would be unconscious again. Very soon, I would be dead. I was no match for the doctor. My only weapons against him were spirit world creatures.

Anaconda … it's time to take up your old duties. Did you not hear the call? Can you not remember your oath?

"First do no harm."

For a moment, I thought I'd heard my own thoughts. But Grace looked up, startled, the forceps in his hand. He had heard it too.

"First do no harm."

With a sort of yelp, Dr. Grace clutched his tattoo, as if it stung him. The yellow glow of his aura blinded me as pain attacked him. He stumbled. He lifted his right arm out in front of him. His eyes were wild inside their sockets. Behind his green mask, he howled a cry.

He backed away, yelping with pain. Then the yelps turned to roars. I could imagine how much pain there was. Anaconda had made his decision. He was trying to get home, and he'd do it in the only way he could; by winding himself around the rod of healing, crushing the doctor's arm into a pulp … or rather, crushing the aural field that was the doctor's spirit arm. The pain would burn like crazy. A snake of that size could pulverize flesh. I already knew Grace was a coward with pain, but worse for the doctor would be that he had no idea what was happening. Nothing in a physician's training explains the symptoms we feel in our spirit bodies … phantom limb pain, unexplained sickness. He roared his fear and agony as he stumbled away.

I tried to get a focus on the tattoo. It looked as it always had—a faded old tattoo. For a moment I wanted to reassure him, tell him that the pain would stop and that there was nothing to fear. But why would I comfort this man? What I had to think about was getting out of this place of death.

I was on my side, so all I had to do was tip myself over the narrow edge of the worktop, but it was like moving through bog, through the wet mud of Hinkley Point. It was like drowning and trying to fight against the slow descent to get to the air. I pushed with the elbow I was lying on, forcing my shoulders to follow my knees. The green cloths and cardboard tray clattered onto the kitchen floor. I followed. For a second, I was trapped in the terror of falling. Then it was too late to pull back, even if I'd had the strength.

I smashed into the floor. The impact shuddered through my body, a physical blow. I lost the world as pain shot through my jaw, shoulder, knees. But at least the pain cleared my dulled senses. My body was less numb. The earlier scant dose was wearing off.

I raised my head. Grace was stretched on the floor. Pain had overwhelmed him. Shrill screams were weakening into grunts. He was not looking at me, or at anything. He was barely conscious. He'd reached the place where Anaconda dwelt. I shifted slowly until I was up on all fours, keeping my eyes on him. I began to crawl backwards. My palm struck something cold and pencil-shaped. I looked down for a second. Under my hand was the instrument that had been ready to take my organs. The scalpel that had been on the cardboard tray as it spun to the floor. I let my fingers curl round the handle.

I needed to get out of here. I had to get out of the kitchen and escape through the yard, but I didn't have the strength to stand and run. Grace might return from the spirit realm with a different view of the world, but I could not be sure, so I kept a firm grip on the scalpel as I began the slow struggle to my feet.

"What the fuck is going on?"

I'd been so busy keeping Grace in my sights that I failed to see Stan arrive. Of course he'd heard the screams. Perhaps he thought at first they were my screams. That had given me a little extra time, but not long enough.

"Stan." I wasn't sure he'd understand me. My voice was warped like heated plastic. "Stan ..."

"What the fuck is wrong with him?" Stan gave the doctor a useless kick with the point of his shoe. He looked at me and his face narrowed. His eyes were slits of yellow, and a thin fang showed as he snarled. It was the cocktail stick he was chewing.

I started to move; a hunched and hobbling sort of limp. I needed to keep the nimble Stan on the other side of the maze of kitchen units. I concentrated on putting each foot in front of the other, holding onto surfaces as I progressed towards the lobby door. My hand rested on green cotton and I pulled until the sterile instruments and containers crashed to the ground.

"You bitch!" Stan was in front of me. "What the fuck did you do to him? I've had it with you." He actually laughed. He shouldered me up against the fridge door and held me there with the bend of one arm. "You pissed me off from the get-go, *Sabbie Daar*." He put his free hand over my bare breast and squeezed until he saw me react from the pain. The hand slid down over the wetness of my stomach, where Grace had smeared the antiseptic. I could smell his breath, sour like he often forgot dental hygiene. He pulled back his lips, as if to prove the point. The cocktail stick was gripped between his front teeth, the point sticking out. He bobbed his head towards my cheek. This was Stan's sort of kiss. Tiny pricks of pain with each one.

He spoke through clenched teeth. "You need to be wasted. Fast. No more trouble from you. Fucked ... then wasted."

He brought his face down upon my neck. He thrust and ground his hips into me, pushing me hard into the door of the fridge. The point of the cocktail stick went into my skin. I gasped.

Or Stan did.

I thought I'd gasped from the mean little pain he inflicted. But it was Stan; a single gasp, like the hiss of a snake.

His grip loosened. He reeled backwards. His face was wide with surprise—eyes, mouth, everything forming circles of shock. He didn't speak. His hands were at his stomach. Around his fingers, redness welled. The bright colour ran over his hands but he didn't move them. They were holding something that protruded from above the waistband of his jeans. Something pencil-thin and silver.

I couldn't work it out. The sludge in my brain stopped me understanding.

The scalpel clattered onto the floor and instantly the wound began to gush. The blood was running through his fingers over his jeans and down his legs. Stan stumbled towards the sinks and grabbed at a clean tea towel, pressing it into the wound. I heard him suck in breath and whimper, just once.

I started to edge away. My legs gave way as I felt the touch of a hand on my bare skin of my back. I swung round, panting. It had to be Grace, awake and on his feet.

Mirela stood motionless behind me, her pupils liquid black. We gripped each other. Our bodies swayed. We were both drugged. She had lost most of her clothes. I had lost all of mine.

Stan roared with anger and we turned to face him, as though mesmerised. He put out his bloodied hand. I could read his mind.

Two birds, in his kitchen. Both for the pot. Our minds were too slow and our bodies too feeble to fight back or even attempt to run. But his legs were sodden with his own blood. His body doubled over, grabbing the sink for support with a hand slippery with blood.

Mirela squealed. "One! two!" When I looked at her, I saw her eyes had a bright sharp focus. Her breathing was steady. Her hand squeezed my arm. It was a signal.

"One! two!"

We moved in perfect synchronization. Stan saw us coming. "Bitches," he barked.

We reached him. I took a fist of that floppy hairdo. Mirela punched at his shoulder. Between us, we took him down to the floor. His head went back and I heard the crack as it hit the cold ceramic tiles.

Lying there, Stan turned into a waxen image of himself. I was torn between running for my life and staunching his bleeding. I reached for a fresh tea towel to lay over the wound; my compromise. But Mirela had yanked a frying pan from its hook, a big wok-like metal thing. The two of us looked ready to cook and wipe up. She glanced at me, scorn in her eyes. She said two words. "For Kizzy."

Stan hollered with fright and pain as she lifted the wok and brought it down on his face. He thrashed once, then lay still.

Mirela glimmered a smile. She had woken quite a bit since I last saw her. "Where is other? Put he out too."

I trod warily to the space where Dr. Grace had writhed and fallen. There was no one there. We both stared at the empty space for long seconds. It was easy to imagine, after meeting Anaconda, that he'd dissolved into nothingness and left this Earth for good.

A powered roar came from outside. The throttle of a big bike. We ran, swerving and going off our feet. Through the kitchen and the lobby. We burst into the yard, but the Yamaha had gone.

Grace had come round with the fight gone out of him, thanks to Anaconda. Or perhaps he realized his two presumed victims had progressed to warrior status, complete with surgical and culinary weapons. A coward to the last, he'd sneaked out into the yard and taken off on his fat and shiny bike.

We stood for a while, catching our breath.

It was time to phone for the cops.

THIRTY-FOUR
CHRISTMAS EVE

"They'll be opening the doors soon," Andy whispered.

"*Unlocking* the doors, you mean." I was whispering too. Charter Hall. CORE. Not the place of no escape, although there seemed to be a great many in this town.

Friday night, less than sixty hours since I lay under Dr. Grace's scalpel, and I was back on my feet. On my gumshoes, as Rey might have said, had he been here. It was Christmas Eve and midwinter stood motionless at its deepest moment—zero degrees outside and Andy's Punto was in darkness, although the engine was running because Andy insisted we kept the heating on.

I had felt permanently chilled since I'd narrowly avoided being cut to pieces. Right now I was wearing a long-sleeved top over a vest top with a baggy jumper and a man's padded gillet over that, all tucked under my loosest warm coat. I had long woolly socks on under my jeans and boots pulled over them. And, despite the efficient heating in the car, I was still cold.

The sensation returned all the time, like a bad acid flash. Me. Naked. On cold steel. And the swab, icy with antiseptic, stroking my skin.

———

Mirela and I had been shipped to Bridgwater Hospital and made to stay there from Tuesday night to Thursday afternoon. They analyzed our blood and ran saline through our veins.

Marianne had stayed beside us all that time, flitting from my bed to Mirela's. Heaven knows how she had convinced the staff she should be allowed to stay, but convincing is what she did for a living. She had helped us get discharged and bundled us both back to Harold Street. Mirela would sleep in my spare bedroom until arrangements could be made for her to go home. In fact, she slept most of the time, only waking when I encouraged her to eat. She told me in fits and starts how Stan had raped her up in the office while Dr. Grace prepped me in the kitchen. An attack with a wok was, in Romani eyes, only the start of retribution for taking Mirela's purity. But Stan's cruelty had served us well twice over; Mirela had been shaken out of her sedation by the act committed upon her, and it had given Anaconda precious moments to return to Dr. Grace's tattoo.

She also told me about the day she'd disappeared. Stan had asked her if she'd heard from Kizzy. She'd been happy to tell him about the letter, but she thought he'd seemed surprised at its contents. That suggested Kizzy had not written exactly what Grace had expected her to write.

"Him tell me he had letter too, saying where Kizzy lived now."

423

Stan had concocted a story about better accommodations and better working conditions in the Finchbury Branch. He'd let her go home early, saying he'd help her transport her luggage. He'd sworn her to secrecy, of course.

"Stan say everyone want this good jobs like for Kizzy and me," Mirela had said. He'd picked her up in the Land Cruiser outside the house on the day her sister's body had been discovered on the cooling towers. "Him all smiles, driving big car. He take me to house in country."

"Pink," I had added.

"Yes. They put me in room. They lock door. They make sleep with drink." She had smiled. "When I dream, I am with Kizzy, so ... not mind, much." Mirela had become wretched, waiting for Kizzy to come back. I imagined her thinking *better dead and with Kizzy than endlessly searching for her.*

She was an easy victim.

But they had forgotten about me.

———

Thursday evening, Rey had called on me. He'd brought flowers, yellow roses. He could not have known I was off yellow at the moment. Like Juke's lilies, which were still going strong (probably thanks to genetic modification), they were gentled into a jug and a place on the breakfast bar, where they looked quite handsome.

Rey had taken me gingerly into his arms and kissed me. Perhaps he was getting confused and thought I really had an incision around my ribs. We sat on the sofa, wrapped in each other while he brought me up-to-date.

"We've arrested the elder Mr. Papazov," Rey had said. "But we'll need to release him soon."

"What?"

"On bail. He's not off the hook. But naturally, he's saying he knew nothing about any of this. And Stanislaus is backing him up."

The way Stan always looked nervous when his father was around suggested Papazov was telling the truth. Maybe this was Stan's solo venture, planning to get a financial head start on his father.

"Has Stan confessed?"

"That wasn't an issue. He knew you'd testify."

"Too bloody right."

"He's given us the name of the first dead girl," Rey had continued. "They'd brought her over last spring, but she never went missing, officially." He smiled. "They reused the same few passports, time and again. Young Romani are apparently interchangeable, even for the immigration authorities."

"Stan told you all that?"

"Yep, he's singing like Maria Callas."

"Has he given you other names in the chain?"

"We're getting there. Improbably, Stan is claiming he and Grace managed the work between them. According to Stan, they never used anaesthetic equipment. Mostly, I think, to keep the number of people involved down to a minimum. They used heavy injections of curare and hypnotics, and that can be dangerous; it's possibly why the young girl died last summer. Most of the victims did get paid, like Kate, for their one kidney, but with that first death, they hit on the idea of doing clean sweeps."

I had grimaced at that thought. "Any sightings of Grace?"

"Not yet, but info is dripping from our diva Stan, so it won't be long. Turns out Grace had been a plastic surgeon by trade, with practices in several European countries. He became involved with the *Mutri* when he was offered a lot of money to change some faces."

"So how did he end up doing what he did?"

"Something went wrong. Maybe a death; maybe a man was scarred. Whatever happened, he'd become friends with Stanislaus Papazov and found sanctuary back here in a tidy little business. He used his own equipment to set up at Papa Bulgaria."

"No wonder they kept everything so clean."

"They probably made more between midnight and four in the morning than all day delivering takeaway."

"Who would have believed it?"

"Looks like you did, Sabbie. If Mirela hadn't come to see you after Kizzy disappeared, we might still be searching for an answer."

Rey had to struggle hard to admit this. I had already caused Bridgwater CID massive embarrassment. The papers had not yet got the entire story … they were never going to get it from me … but headlines screamed the bits they'd gleaned. The broadsheets went for alliteration (as Lettice might have it): SHAMAN SOLVES SURGICAL SA-DISM. The tabloids had fun with puns. My favourite so far was PSYCH-DICK! LOCAL FORTUNETELLER NABS ORGAN SNATCHER!

"We'd have got there eventually. We just didn't get there quickly enough." Rey had stopped to check the chunk of watch clipped to his wrist. "Gary Abbott could blend into the seediest environment, but he was terrible at telling us things. Actually, he'd told us nothing, and now we'll never know just how close he'd got. We were focused on surgeons and hospitals. Papa Bulgaria was part of an entirely different equation."

"Until you arrested their chef."

"Yeah. See, we knew Jimmy was lying to us. But we couldn't work out in what way."

"He wasn't lying, Rey. He was confused. How is he now, by the way?"

"I don't know. Why should I know that?"

"Haven't you even made a courtesy call? To apologize?"

Rey had looked at me as if I'd asked him to babysit a kitten. He couldn't even apologize to me. His treatment of Jimmy Browne was seen to be procedural necessity.

"I'll do it," I'd told Rey. "I'll go and see him." My heart feared for Jimmy. It would be hard for him to get another job. Bridgwater had a long memory.

Something pulled at the skin on Rey's face. It was grinding him down that he had not protected me, but I'd never wanted that sort of relationship with the man I loved. I had taken the job at Papa Bulgaria with my eyes wide open. I had known from the get-go that they were bad people.

I'd walked with Rey to my door.

"What will happen to the scooter?"

When I'd returned home from the hospital, the scooter was parked outside my house, and my coat, keys, shoes, and both mobiles were placed tidily in my porch. It struck me that this approach to planning murder was at the same level as using Blu-Tack to hide iPhones. Everything had been bundled away by the Bridgwater police.

Rey frowned. "I have no idea. I'll have to look into it."

"No hurry. I never want to straddle that bike again."

"Ah! That reminds me. In an outhouse we searched behind the restaurant we found a yellow bicycle. I thought I'd seen you riding around on something similar."

This had felt like the last straw. I was never going to be paid by Papa, and it looked like I would soon be back on Hermes's saddle. I'd let out a long groan of despair.

"You did do so well," Rey had said, his hands smoothing the outsides of my arms. "Went through so much. I was hoping I could take you out. Friday, perhaps? A meal?"

"Really? Because I have the perfect idea in mind. A night of sleuthing, Rey, in memory of fellow maverick Gary Abbott."

That had caught him off-guard. His eyes had fired up. But he'd had to pretend, at least, that he disapproved. "What it is with you? Can't you learn to crochet or something?"

———

A telly-sofa-and-duvet day had made me feel a lot better, if no warmer. Christmas Eve morning I rose at seven, fed the hens, made porridge for Mirela, and gave a new client the first of their "two-for-one" aromatherapy sessions. I braved the shops in town and finally got round to my Christmas shopping.

After that, I'd taken a rest, to make sure I would be ready for that night.

I'd seen the poster outside the hall. Friday the 24th of December, CORE was holding a "Jesus is Born" special at Charter Hall. Mince pies and mulled fruit juice. Andy had sworn to face Eric and persuade Drea to come home. I really wanted to be part of it; I felt responsible for what had happened to Andy and Drea, and I cared about what would happen if Andy was allowed to confront Eric on his own. And now we had the force of the law on our side. Or at least, I was hoping we did.

The clock on the dashboard in Andy's Punto ticked on. No one—not even an out-of-hours traffic warden—asked us to move. The street was busy with Christmas party-goers, but there was no sign of a police car, marked or unmarked. There was no sign of Avon and Somerset's constabulary at all.

"I thought they'd roar up and go for it," said Andy.

"No. Rey was adamant about that. They won't storm in and terrorize a hall full of innocent people. They'll come softy, softly."

"They might not come at all."

"I think they'll come."

Andy leaned his head against the car window and all I could imagine was how the chill would seep into his brain. "I rang Drea's parents last night. To let them know."

"I don't suppose she's allowed to contact them."

"They're taking it badly. When she disappeared the first time, they fought to get her away from CORE. So this time . . . it took me a while to tell them the news. I knew it was going to devastate them."

I squeezed Andy's hand, where it covered the gearstick even though the handbrake was on. He flashed me a smile.

"You never let the feeling go," I agreed. "The lingering fear that the worse thing could happen again. Lightning could strike twice."

I knew that "lingering fear" was one of the reasons I had never traced my roots. I'd lost my mother—she'd faded away before my eyes, dying in a sordid bed, alone except for a six-year-old girl who couldn't help but keep a vigil for her because she had nowhere to go, no one to call upon.

In my logical mind, I knew that you can only lose your mother once, but my heart constantly reminded me that you can lose others—the replacements, the alternatives. It was bad enough knowing that Gloria and Philip were getting older, but at least they were solid parts of my world; they weren't going to disappear. It was the natural relatives that worried me. They're a bad risk. Best to never contact them, never link up. *They don't know you,* I told myself, *and they won't want to. Especially if you start off being the coloured girl who delivers their takeaway.*

I hadn't heard again from Lettice Mitchell. I felt bad for rejecting her, but I was sure she was fine, enjoying Christmas Eve canapés with Grandma Dare, no doubt. She would forget me as time went on. She would forget she ever had a cousin.

So it was ironic that I would never forget her.

Andy checked his watch against the dashboard clock. "Eric should be out any minute now." He was staring down the street, mute and alert as a stag on a hill.

I was terrified that Andy was going to challenge them. Not like before, when he'd only called Drea's name. This would be a confrontation between him and Eric; he was longing to lock antlers. I wondered who would come off best in a fight. Andy was young and in love, but Eric Atkinson had powerful shoulders and the belief that he was right about everything.

"Please don't try anything. Leave it to the police."

"What police?" muttered Andy.

Even I was getting jittery. Where was Rey and the backup he'd promised me?

He'd asked me out. In my hallway, hopping from foot to foot like a teenager. A proper date. That brought a candle-glow of warmth to my heart. He wanted to woo me. It was the missing brick from our courtship—in fact our courtship didn't have a single brick, as it had never taken place. Rey wanted to change that, start again. That added a candle-glow of light to my head. Heck, I was glowing with candles.

Except I'd been stupid enough to get him off the hook. Instead of simpering, and saying, *Oh, Rey, dinner would be lovely*, I'd told him about tonight. Me and Andy. I thought I'd seen his eyes fire up, but in the end, he wasn't here. It didn't look as if I'd ever get my proper date now.

I gasped and pointed. "The doors are opening."

Punters streamed into the chill of the night, their breath chuffing out as they laughed and chattered. They were like a stream of minor dragons.

"Smallish turnout," I remarked.

"Not surprising. It's no one's idea of a fun party."

"Yeah. And a bitter night. They're saying it might snow for Santa."

Minutes later, the Atkinson harem came through the big doors. Eric locked them while the women and children went ahead, shrouded in hoods and scarves against the weather. But I could spot Drea's outline among the pack, and so could Andy, his forehead was almost touching the windscreen.

Eric pocketed the key and strode after them, towards the car park. There was no sign of Rey.

I had been so sure when I'd swapped a proper date for a night of sleuthing. Rey had seemed keen, ready to take the risk. He hadn't contacted me to say otherwise. Naturally, he'd told me not to be anywhere in sight for this raid. He'd made it clear I should stay away, tuck myself up in bed, which was why I'd been unable to get any details.

I checked the replacement mobile Marianne had got for me. It was brand-new and I wasn't competent with it yet. But no, he hadn't called. I rang him. Mobile switched off. He was probably at home watching the news and drinking a whisky.

He'd promised. He'd *promised*.

"Right." Andy put his hand on the door. "That is it."

Some little cord twanged in my head. *Softly, softly . . .*

"Stop!" I hissed. "Don't get out! Drive!"

"What?"

"I know what's wrong. The police aren't here!"

"Yeah," said Andy. "That's the problem."

"No! They're not here because that's not where things will happen!" My heart yapped with my stupidity. "They'll be waiting in the car park."

Andy fumbled with the key, forgetting the car was still running for the heat, turning so hard so the engine ground. His feet jerked on the pedals. The car stalled and bumped.

"Come on!" I hissed, gripping the dashboard.

The wheels screeched as they finally found their grip. We sprang forward. Bony Elbows turned her head, a casual glance towards a noise.

"We shouldn't pass them. Keep the lights off and reverse. Go the long way!"

"What? You nuts?"

"It's too risky. Eric's got more eyes and ears than Brahma. And we can still be there before them."

Andy did a long, whining reverse and pulled out into a slow stream of traffic that steadily took us to the car park. There was no sign of the harem, but Andy pointed a finger from the steering wheel at a dark-blue Discovery standing alone close to the exit. "That's Eric's." He drove past it to the opposite end of the car park and tucked the Punto in behind a white van. "Where's your boy-friend's car?"

Rey drove a sporty Nissan, but I couldn't see anything so low-slung from my position.

Atkinson was leading the women and the children through the car park entrance when a jocund tune staccatoed into silence of the car. I'd yet to find out how to put the new mobile on silent.

"A text. It might be Rey," I whispered.

I worked my way through to my messages.

WISH ME LUCK. ABOUT TO GO OUT WITH BANG!

"Sabbie?" hissed Andy. "What does he say?"

I stuffed the phone into my pocket. "It wasn't Rey."

———

I'd had another visitor, after Rey had left on Thursday. Fergus had called bringing flowers of his own—gas station chrysanthemums dyed in garish colours.

I'd felt guilty about Fergus. Since I'd got out of the hospital, he'd been on my mind. I had imagined things about him that one should not imagine about any innocent man. "Is it my fault, Sabbie?" he'd asked as we sat down on the sofa. "Did you find yourself in such trouble because of anything I said about Papa Bulgaria?"

I had shaken my head. "I stepped into danger with my eyes wide shut. I knew the Papazovs were nasty. You told me that. I knew they were suspicious of me and that I'd outstayed my welcome. But I would never have guessed the truth if I hadn't seen it for myself." I kept going over and over things like that; thinking about them, talk-ing about them. It wasn't doing me any good. "Tell me about your plans, Fergus. Are you going back to Belfast?"

"I've got a string of interviews lined up, so I'll be fine. And the folk music scene is even bigger over there." He'd given me a sideways look. "I was going to go out with a bang, d'you remember?"

"Yeah." I had needed to suppress a shudder. "I do remember."

"But I guess you won't be at the Curate's Egg for a while."

"What's that got to do with it?"

"Kev has offered me a late-night spot. Tomorrow night, Christmas Eve, he thought he might throw a party, put out some free food, have some extra turns. My own songs I'm singing. I'll be last on."

I had beamed at him. "That's such good news!"

"I practice my songs in the flat, but no one has ever given me the chance to sing in public before."

"You'll be wonderful. They'll love you. But I can't promise I'll get there."

"You said you were doing something Friday. But I can imagine that now you're planning to stay in."

"Oh, I'm always up for adventure, Fergus, surely you know that by now?"

———

Andy gestured across the nighttime space of the car park, to where Atkinson's harem had reached their vehicle.

I could hear Eric's voice carry on the night air, and Bony Elbows's reply. Simple stuff … *put the buggy in the boot … get the babies strapped in*. Silently, Andy opened his door and stepped out, while they were busy.

The doors of the Discovery slammed. They were all in the four-by-four. The engine was starting up. The Discovery's lights went on, aggressive bulbs front and back that would blind adjacent drivers.

I slid out of my door, too, and tucked myself in next to Andy, who was kneeling behind a blue Fiesta. We watched the action by peering over the Fiesta's bonnet, like a couple of gangsters in a Hollywood movie.

"The police are a washout," said Andy.

Andy was right. Rey hadn't come. He wasn't a maverick after all. He *was* a washout.

Andy stood head and shoulders clear of our hiding place, staring over the bonnet of the white van.

"Please, Andy. Not this night. There'll be others."

Then the door of an unmarked car opened, and a uniformed cop strode over to Atkinson, just as the Discovery's wheels eased out of the parking place. The cop rapped on the driver's window.

Atkinson got out of the car and followed the policeman to the rear of his vehicle. I could almost hear the words ... *if you could follow me to the rear of your vehicle, please sir.*

I blinked, trying to focus. Someone had smashed the glass and the bulbs of Eric's rear lights.

"Officer." Atkinson's voice floated on the night air. "This is vandalism. It must have occurred since I left the car."

"Even so, sir, I'm afraid you won't be able to drive the vehicle with the back lights missing."

"That's outrageous," Atkinson exploded. "We've only got a few miles to go."

"Could I take a look at your driving licence sir?"

Atkinson raised both arms. "I don't carry it, I'm afraid."

Andy turned to me. "They can't take him on a dodgy light."

"Who smashed it, d'you think?"

We watched the copper go back to his car. I heard the radio fizz. Something moved on the periphery of my vision. A figure strode across the car park, his heels hitting the tarmac and bouncing to the balls of his feet, fast and sure. I loved the rhythm of his gait, the way the silhouette of his thin-soled shoes rocked with each step. I grinned. Rey had not lost all his sneaky sergeant ways.

"Sir," said Rey, his voice raised, long before he reached Atkinson, "can you ask your passengers to step out of the vehicle, please?"

"What's this about?" said Atkinson. I thought he was cottoning on. He gazed around and I yanked Andy to the ground.

"I'm going to get her," he hissed at me.

"Not yet." I hung onto his coat. "Not yet!"

The three women oozed out. Drea's thin legs slid down onto the tarmac.

Rey took in the women, gesturing to them. "Can I ask you sir, your relationship to these ladies?"

"We're his wives," said Bony Elbows, her bosom rising. "And proud of it."

"Wives? You must understand, sir that bigamy is an offence in this country," said Rey. "If you are a bigamist, I am in my right to arrest you here and now. You'd be in the cells overnight."

"You wouldn't do that," said Bony. Even her mouth was boned now, her whole body had become hard and dangerous.

"Wouldn't I? I think that depends on whether this is, in fact, your husband."

"Of course he's our husband!" That was Naomi, the youngest wife, who was standing with her baby tight in her arms. "We are married in the eyes of God."

In a blink, Rey responded. "And each of the ladies in question? Did they enter this… union with their eyes open? With their full consent?" He turned slightly, so that he was addressing the two younger wives. "Did you give your full and free consent?"

The officer, who had been leaning into his car, working the radio, stood up, one hand raised, as if he had the answer to the teacher's question. "This vehicle is registered to an Exeter address, sir," he said, as he marched back to the Discovery. "Were you planning to travel back to Exeter?"

"It's—ah—well." Atkinson seemed to be spitting nut shells from his mouth. He swung round to the bony bitch of a first wife.

"We're going no farther than Taunton," she said. "And if you would be so kind, officers, we'll be on our way."

"Perhaps you could inform us of the address you'll be staying at tonight," said Rey.

A descending cascade of sobs rose into the air. Drea dipped into the car and lifted her little boy out, chuntering to him in toddler language. Andy's face puckered in pain. "Zac picks up on atmospheres so quickly. He knows something's wrong." He stood and began his journey across the car park. I let him go. It seemed my part in this was almost over.

"Zac!" cried Andy. "Ziggidy Zac!

"Andy Pandy!" came a piping voice. Andy stopped in his tracks. Something slipped past Drea, something red and fast, making a beeline for Andy. Drea's little boy hurtled into Andy's arms. He was scooped up and held tight. Over Andy's shoulder, I could see his round face, eyes closed and lips pressed onto Andy's neck.

"Drea!" Andy called. "You have to believe the police. Eric is not your legal husband!"

"What is this?" asked Rey. He swung back to Atkinson, who'd become very quiet. "*Are* you married to these ladies?" He spoke as if such an accusation occurred in the line of police duty ever few days.

437

Atkinson knew how to bat awkward questions. "That is my child. That man is stealing my child." He pointed a finger, as I'd seen him do on the stage of the hall.

Rey didn't respond, but Andy did. "This is Drea's child," he said. "No man can be sure of paternity."

Drea didn't say anything. Her mouth was working, as if trying to hold onto a scream. Under the car park lighting her face was sickly, eyes glittering wet. Her body leaned towards Andy, like they were joined by a thread.

In long strides, Atkinson was around the big-boy bonnet of his car and facing Andy. He put grey hands over the shoulders of the little boy, as if offering benediction. I saw his steel eyes bore into Andy's face. I could not see Andy's expression, but I hoped he was curbing the urge to stick a fist into Eric's face.

Then I saw something that neither of the men did. Drea was taking wobbly steps towards her child. She walked as if still recovering from a debilitating illness. Andy looked up, and he must have smiled, because Drea attempted to return it, her wet lips straining into a thin line.

"Hand me my child," said Atkinson.

"Drea's child," said Andy, his voice carrying across the car park.

"My wife," said Atkinson.

"No. The woman I will marry."

Atkinson's voice quavered upwards. "The Lord hath joined us, only the Lord can put us asunder. You are but a quivering mass of sin cowering under the serpent's tail!"

I gripped the bonnet of the Fiesta as my stomach knotted. Andy was able to ward off Eric's brainwashing techniques, but Drea slowed at his words—quivered and cowered as if the devil was upon her. The uniformed cop started off towards the group, but Rey put a hand on his upper arm as if to say, *let's see how this plays out.*

"I want to marry you, Drea," Andy called. He was ignoring Eric. Even the child in his arms seemed to be ignoring him. He was clinging to Andy's neck as if he didn't want to be passed like a parcel to the other man. "In a proper church. With a proper service; registrar, the lot. We know it's our right. Our path in Christ."

"The Lord hath joined us!" bellowed Atkinson.

"Codswallop," said Andy. "*Dangerous* codswallop. I am never letting evil back in our lives."

He turned, sharp as a drill sergeant, and walked away, Zac in his arms. Now I could see his face. It was an impassive mask of control. He had not let Atkinson threaten him. He'd been in CORE. He knew how Atkinson controlled people.

Eric turned his attentions to Drea, striding the few metres between them, his hand ready to grab and keep her. I saw her gasp. She had to make the choice on her own. Her path. I could not help at all and Andy could only help by combating Eric's will.

Eric was almost upon her when she swerved haphazardly and broke into a sort of skittering run.

Andy heard her heels on the tarmac. I saw his head rise, as if he might stop now, and wait, or turn and call to her.

But he didn't. He took his time, heading towards his car with purpose.

It was a masterly stroke. Over his shoulder, the child was the one looking at Drea. I saw his little hand stretch out to her, imploring.

Behind them, Eric was on his toes, arms raised, fists tight, shoulders heaving. I was willing Andy to stay strong, to keep walking, to keep his head turned away from Atkinson's intimidating stance, to keep his temper cool.

"You're nearly there," I whispered. "Let the child do the calling for you."

Something flashed across my mind. A dark cave, glowing lights. My dream, the night Mirela had come to my house. The woman following the man from darkness into light. Orpheus, defying the god of the underworld, Hades, to reclaim his dead wife, Eurydice. But he had erred. He'd looked back at her as they escaped into the world of the living, and lost her forever.

Don't look back!

As Andy reached the Punto, Drea caught him up. She stood alongside him, one hand ruffling her son's hair, as they strapped him into the toddler seat Andy had kept at the ready. They looked at each other but did not touch. They climbed into the front of the car. The engine fired into life.

Rey didn't speak again until Drea and Andy were out of sight. "Well, sir, I'll allow you to proceed, so long as you take care, on the understanding that you leave your temporary address with us now and present your driving licence and insurance at Bridgwater Police Station within forty-eight hours."

There was a long pause. In silence, Eric took the notebook the constable offered him and scribbled his address. With a cautious action, Rey helped the young wife clip the baby into the harness, and closed the door on Bony Elbows.

"Is it understood, sir? Licence and insurance?"

"Yes, officer, that's understood." Atkinson's voice was low and dangerous.

"I wouldn't call a detective an officer," I whispered under my breath. "Not if I was you."

The Discovery drove away with ponderous care. The first officer got into the unmarked car and turned in the opposite direction as the vehicles hit the road.

I was still crouching behind a car. I stood, properly, and stepped out into the open. I looked at Rey.

He was standing so solitary, but his shoulders were not hunched or bowed. His stance told the world he was ready for the next case Somerset might throw at him.

"Fancy some music?" I called across the cars between us.

"Sorry?"

"A Christmas drink at the Egg, Rey? Fergus is doing a gig. Going out with a bang."

"Now I've heard it all."

He held out his hand to me.

I walked across and took it.

THE END

© Andy Chittock

ABOUT THE AUTHOR

Nina Milton holds an MA in creative writing, works as a tutor and writer for the Open College of the Arts, is a prize-winning short story writer, and has authored several children's books, including *Sweet'n'Sour, Tough Luck,* and *Intergalactic Holiday. Unraveled Visions* is her second novel with Midnight Ink.

www.MidnightInkBooks.com

From the gritty streets of New York City to sacred tombs in the Middle East, it's always midnight somewhere. Join us online at any hour for fresh new voices in mystery fiction.

At midnightinkbooks.com you'll also find our author blog, new and upcoming books, events, book club questions, excerpts, mystery resources, and more.

Midnight Ink Ordering Information

Order Online:

• Visit our website www.midnightinkbooks.com, select your books, and order them on our secure server.

Order by Phone:

• Call toll-free within the U.S. and Canada at 1-888-NITE-INK (1-888-648-3465)
• We accept VISA, MasterCard, and American Express

Order by Mail:

Send the full price of your order (MN residents add 6.875% sales tax) in U.S. funds, plus postage & handling to:

Midnight Ink
2143 Wooddale Drive
Woodbury, MN 55125-2989

Postage & Handling:

Standard (U.S. & Canada). If your order is:
$25.00 and under, add $4.00
$25.01 and over, FREE STANDARD SHIPPING

AK, HI, PR: $16.00 for one book plus $2.00 for each additional book.

International Orders (airmail only):
$16.00 for one book plus $3.00 for each additional book

Orders are processed within 12 business days. Please allow for normal shipping time.
Postage and handling rates subject to change.